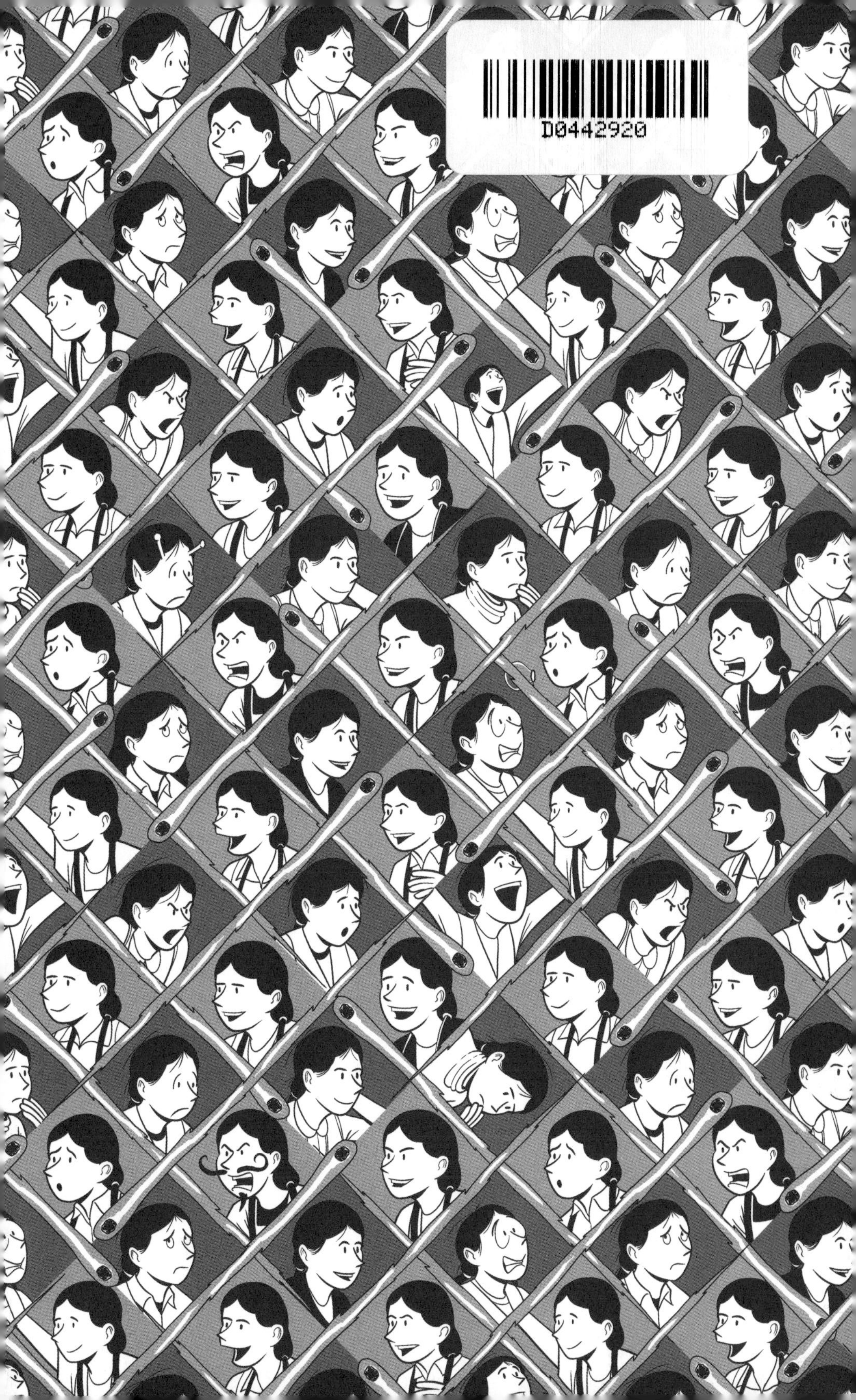

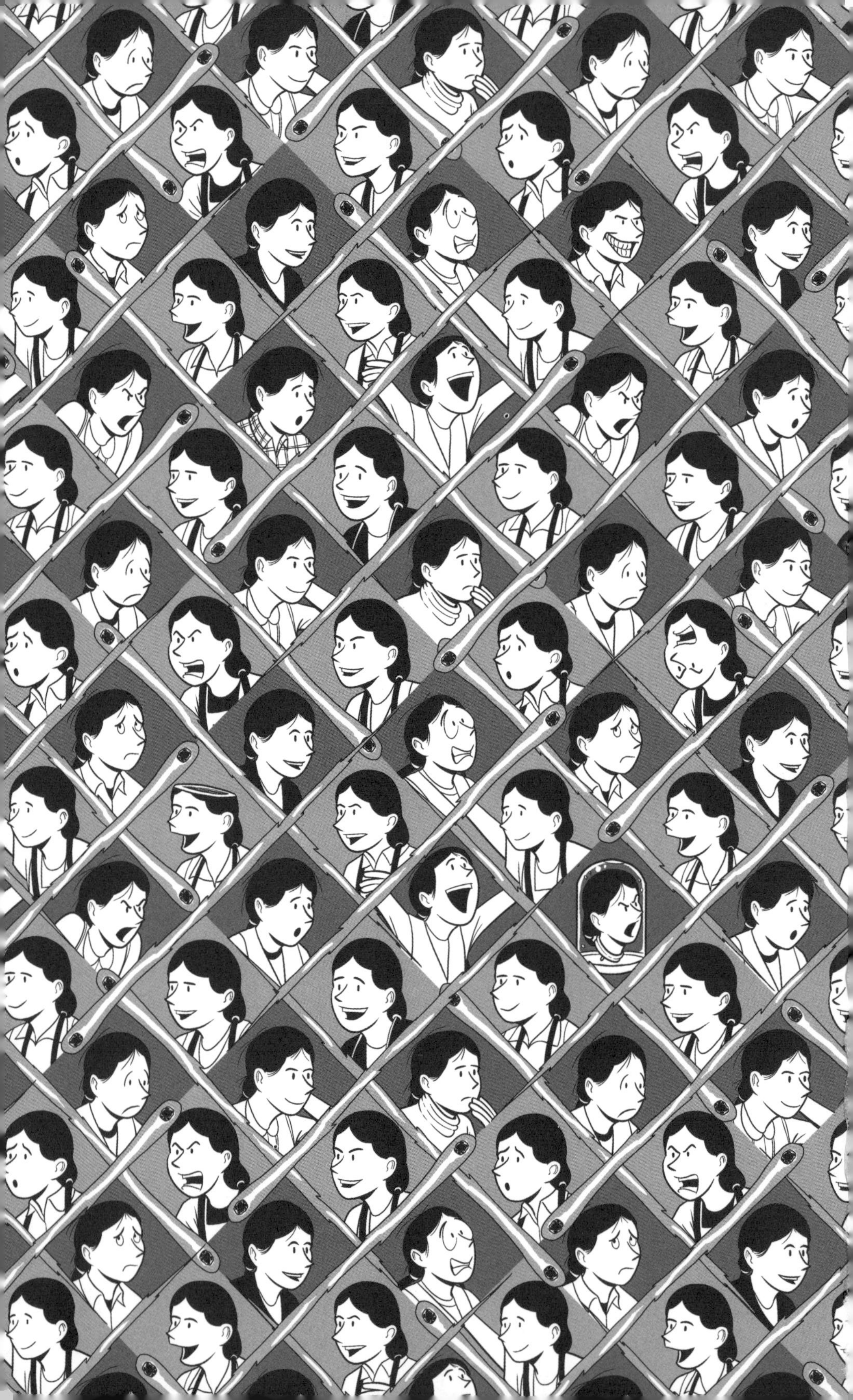

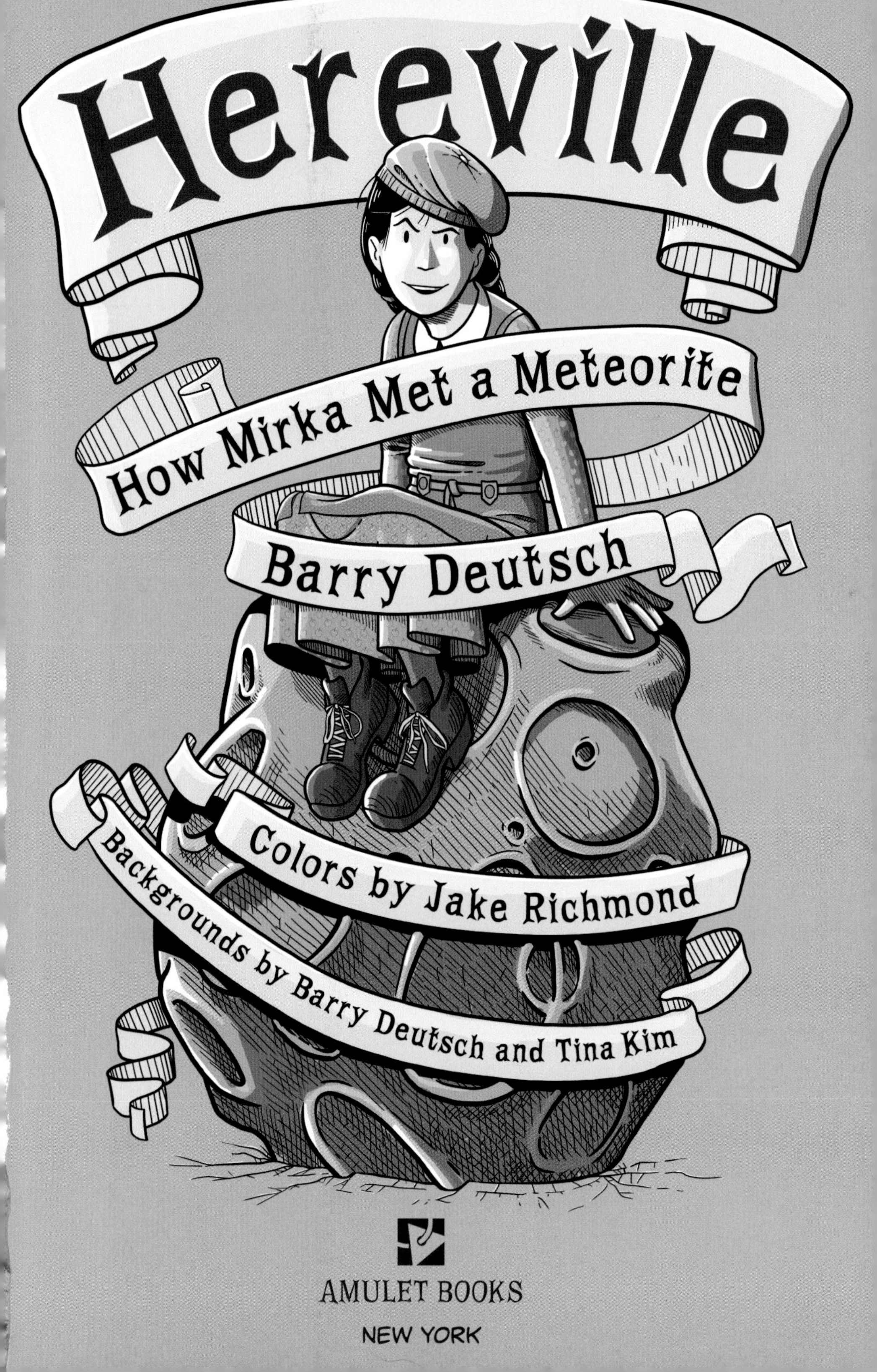
Hereville
How Mirka Met a Meteorite
Barry Deutsch
Colors by Jake Richmond
Backgrounds by Barry Deutsch and Tina Kim

AMULET BOOKS
NEW YORK

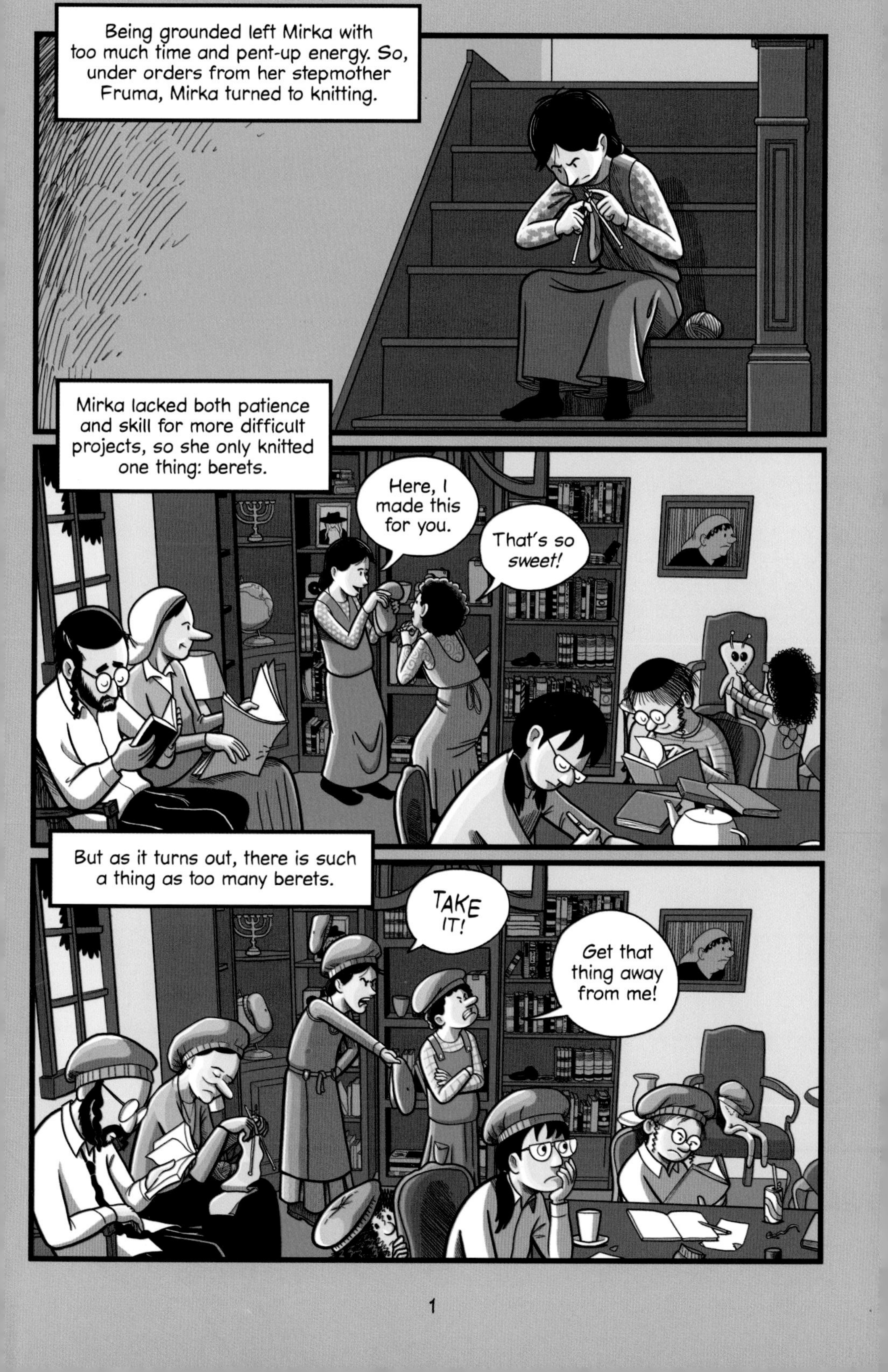
Being grounded left Mirka with too much time and pent-up energy. So, under orders from her stepmother Fruma, Mirka turned to knitting.
Mirka lacked both patience and skill for more difficult projects, so she only knitted one thing: berets.
Here, I made this for you.
That's so *sweet!*
But as it turns out, there is such a thing as too many berets.
TAKE IT!
Get that thing away from me!

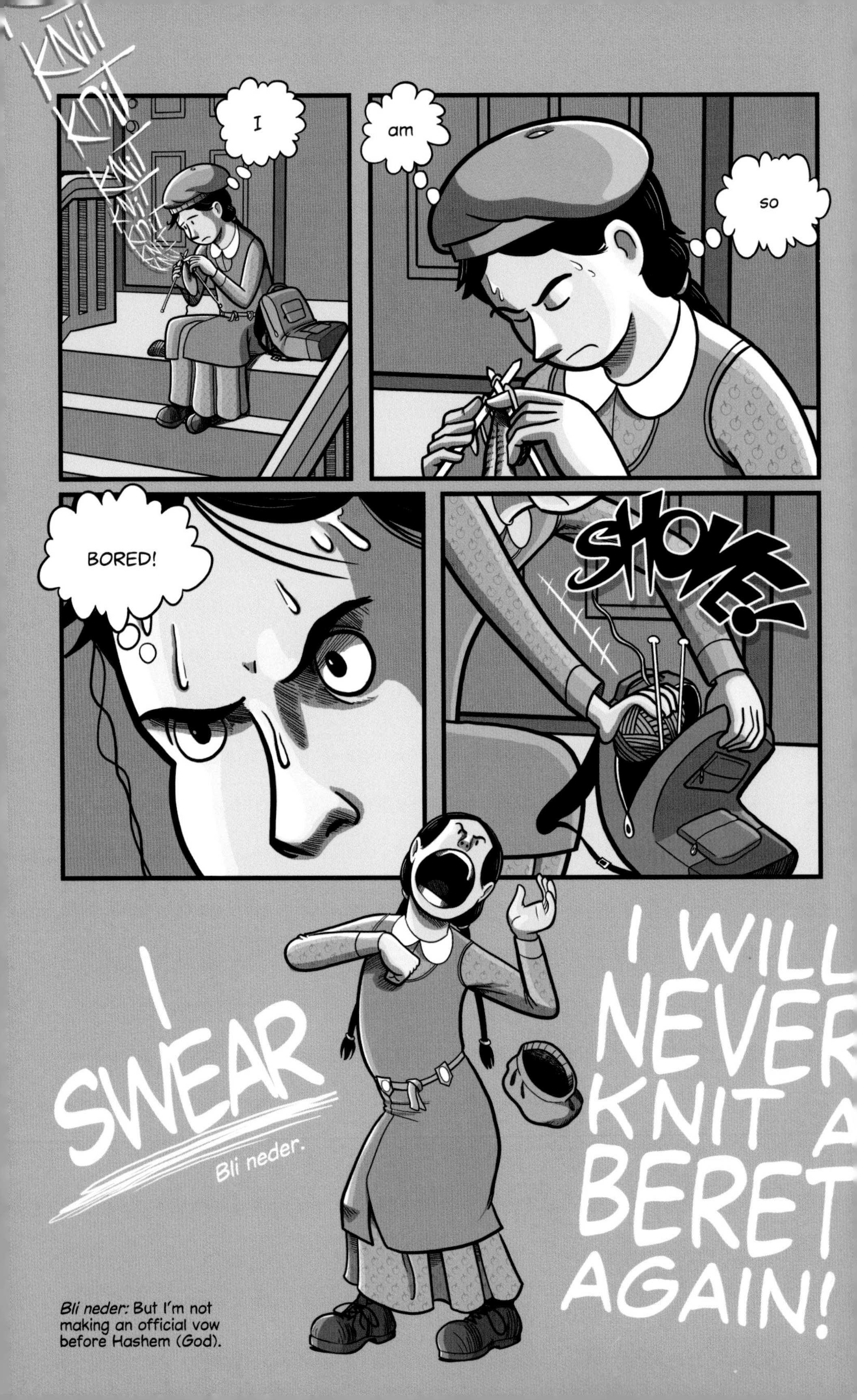

Knit
Knit
Knit
Knit
Knit
I
am
so
BORED!
SHOVE!
I SWEAR
Bli neder.
I WILL NEVER KNIT A BERET AGAIN!
Bli neder: But I'm not making an official vow before Hashem (God).

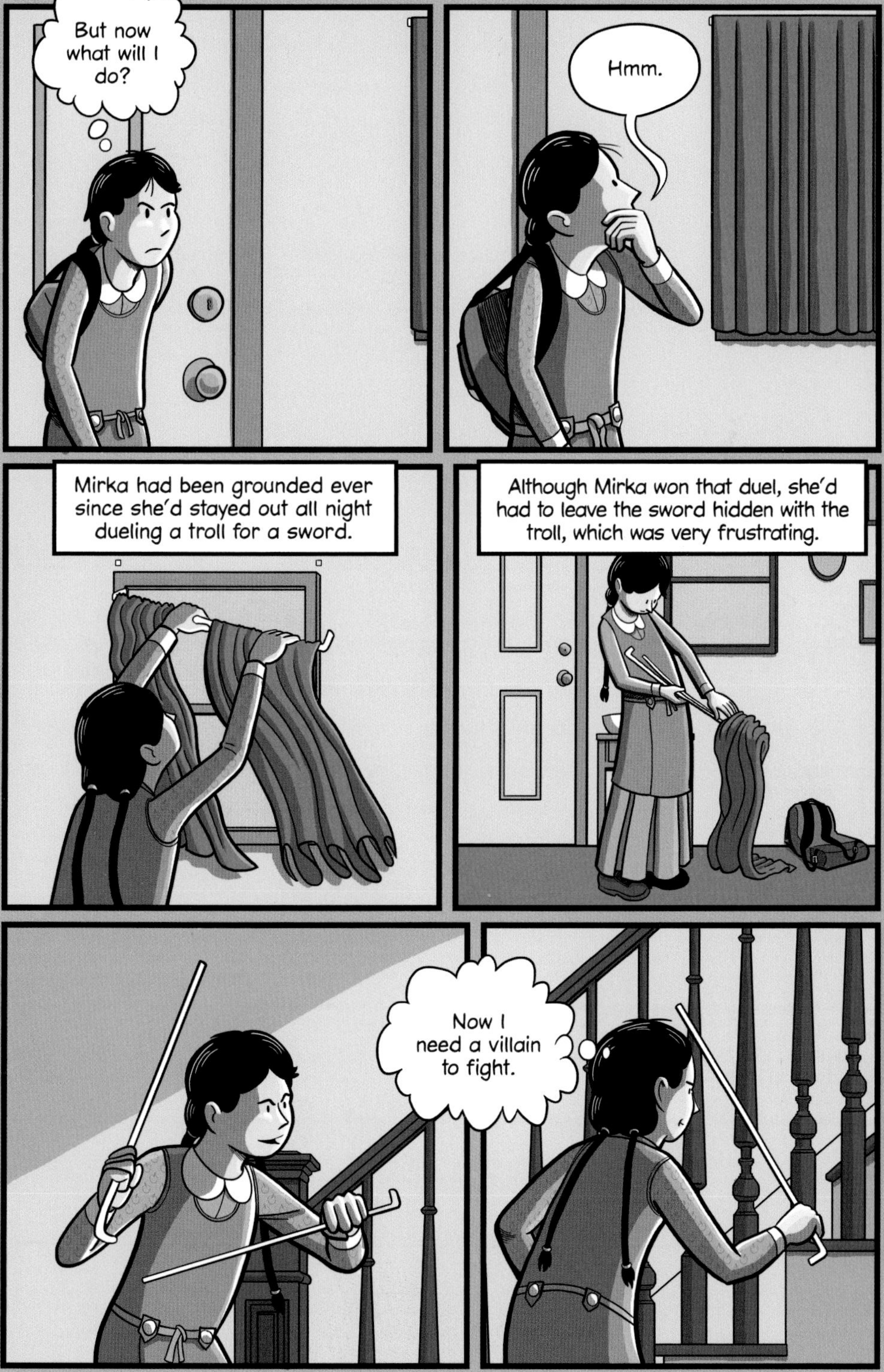
But now what will I do?
Hmm.
Mirka had been grounded ever since she'd stayed out all night dueling a troll for a sword.
Although Mirka won that duel, she'd had to leave the sword hidden with the troll, which was very frustrating.
Now I need a villain to fight.

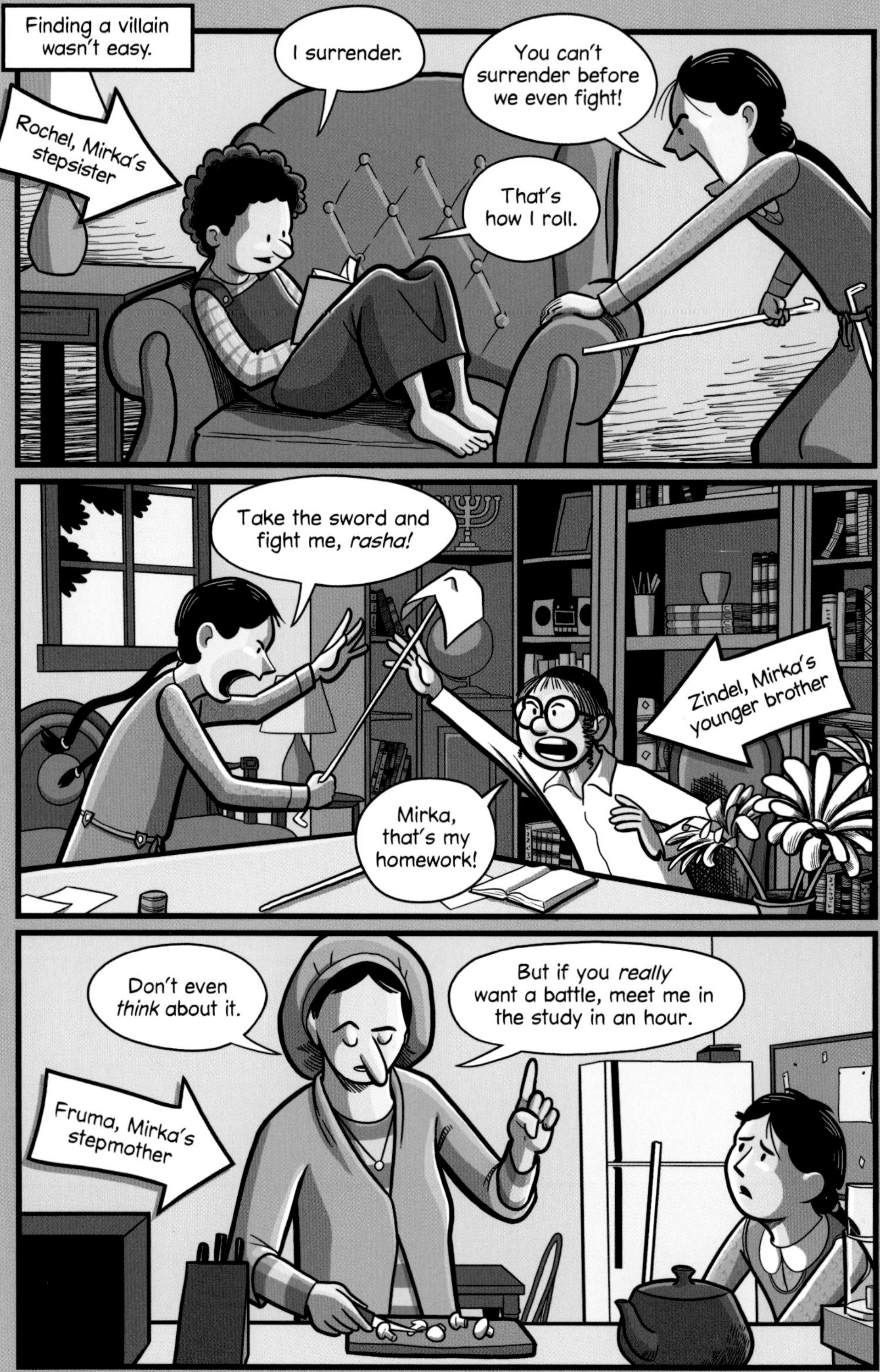

Finding a villain wasn't easy.
Rochel, Mirka's stepsister
I surrender.
You *can't* surrender before we even fight!
That's how I roll.
Take the sword and fight me, *rasha!*
Zindel, Mirka's younger brother
Mirka, that's my homework!
Fruma, Mirka's stepmother
Don't even *think* about it.
But if you *really* want a battle, meet me in the study in an hour.

Rasha: Evildoer

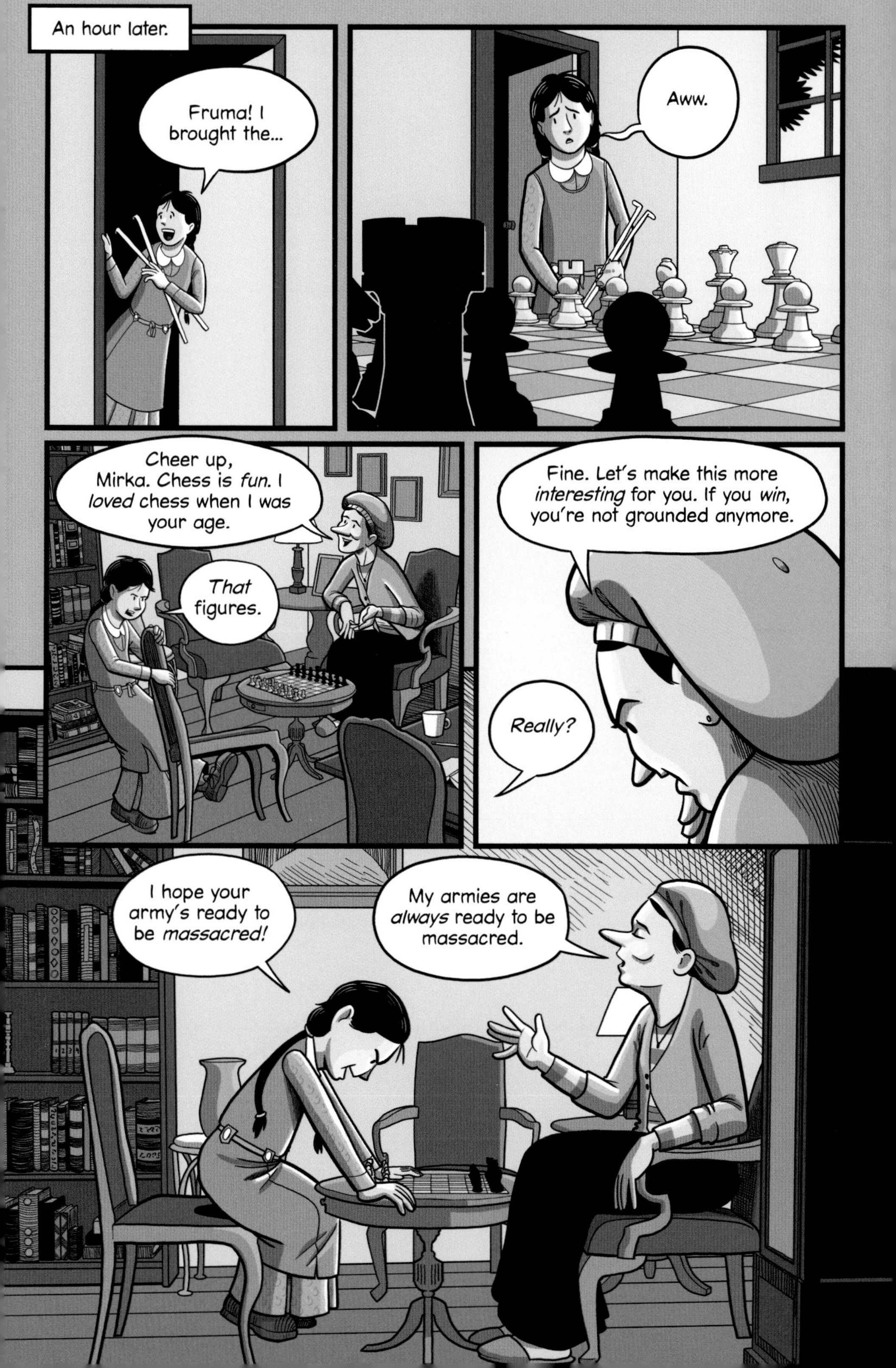
An hour later.
Fruma! I brought the...
Aww.
Cheer up, Mirka. Chess is *fun.* I *loved* chess when I was your age.
That figures.
Fine. Let's make this more *interesting* for you. If you *win,* you're not grounded anymore.
Really?
I hope your army's ready to be *massacred!*
My armies are *always* ready to be massacred.

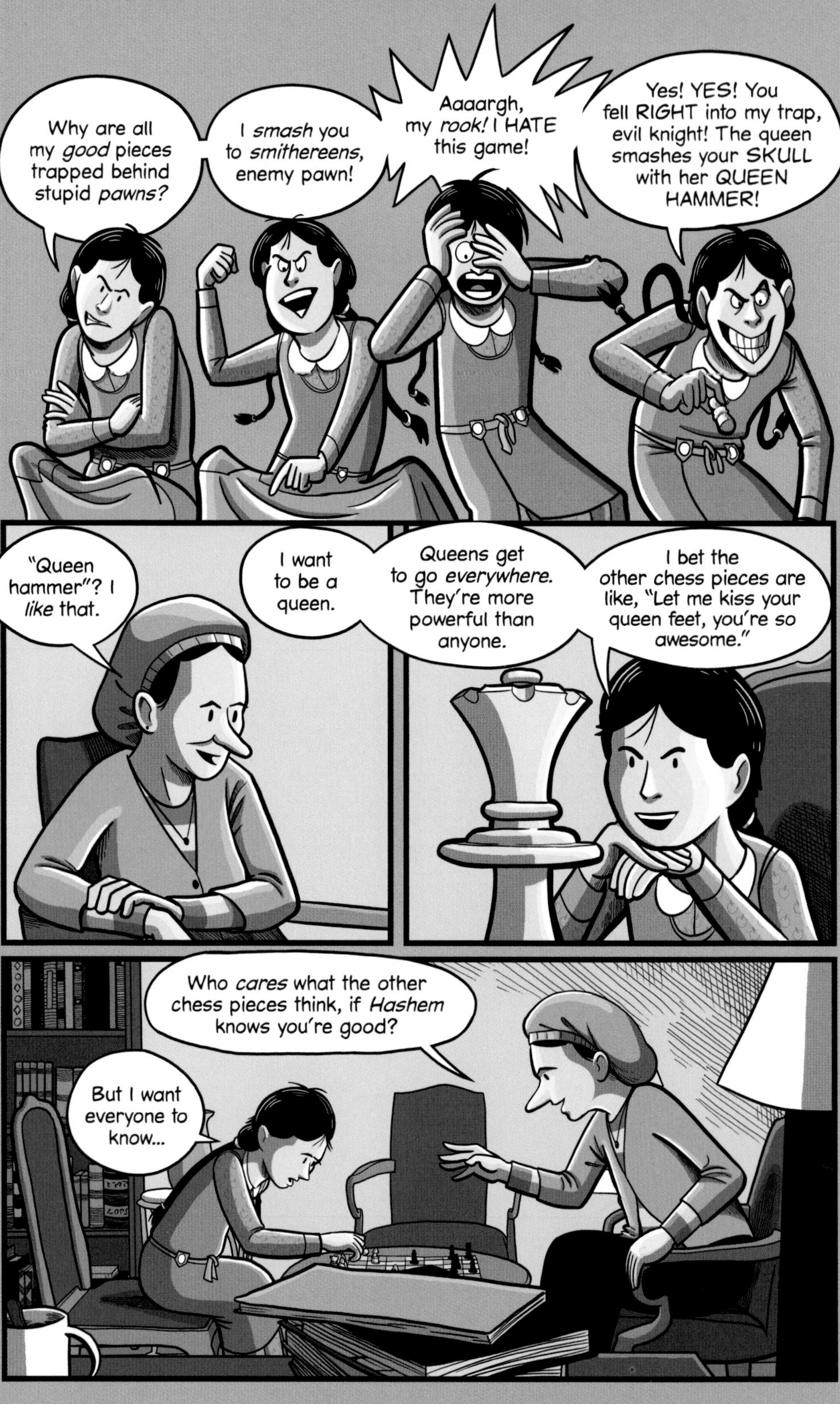
Why are all my *good* pieces trapped behind stupid *pawns?*
I *smash* you to *smithereens,* enemy pawn!
Aaaargh, my *rook!* I HATE this game!
Yes! YES! You fell RIGHT into my trap, evil knight! The queen smashes your SKULL with her QUEEN HAMMER!
"Queen hammer"? I *like* that.
I want to be a queen.
Queens get to go *everywhere.* They're more powerful than anyone.
I bet the other chess pieces are like, "Let me kiss your queen feet, you're so awesome."
Who *cares* what the other chess pieces think, if *Hashem* knows you're good?
But I want everyone to know...

Hashem: God

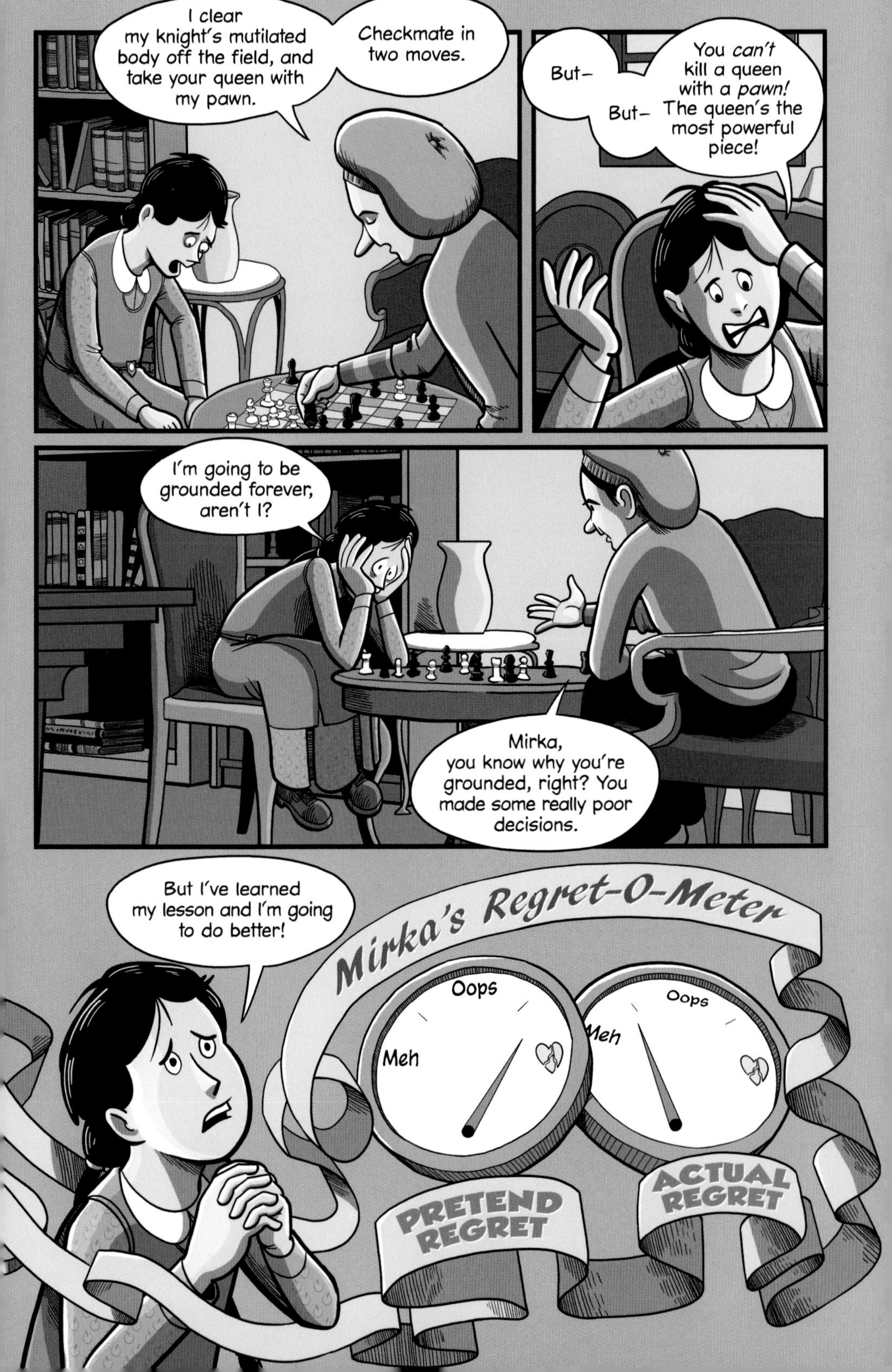
I clear my knight's mutilated body off the field, and take your queen with my pawn.
Checkmate in two moves.
But–
But–
You *can't* kill a queen with a *pawn!* The queen's the most powerful piece!
I'm going to be grounded forever, aren't I?
Mirka, you know why you're grounded, right? You made some really poor decisions.
But I've learned my lesson and I'm going to do better!
Mirka's Regret-O-Meter
Oops
Meh
Oops
Meh
PRETEND REGRET
ACTUAL REGRET

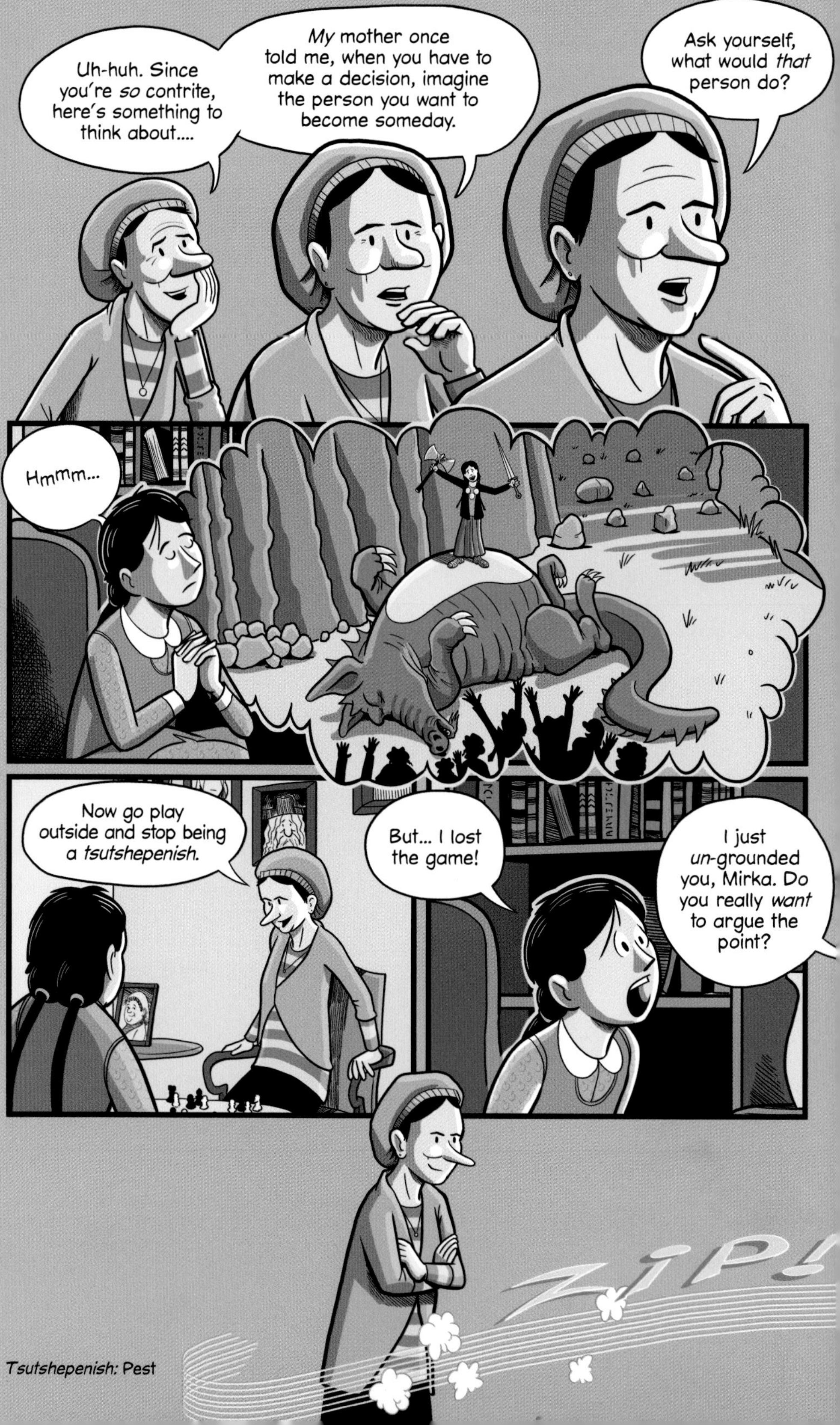
Uh-huh. Since you're *so* contrite, here's something to think about....
My mother once told me, when you have to make a decision, imagine the person you want to become someday.
Ask yourself, what would *that* person do?
Hmmm...
Now go play outside and stop being a *tsutshepenish.*
But... I lost the game!
I just *un*-grounded you, Mirka. Do you really *want* to argue the point?
ZIP!

Tsutshepenish: Pest

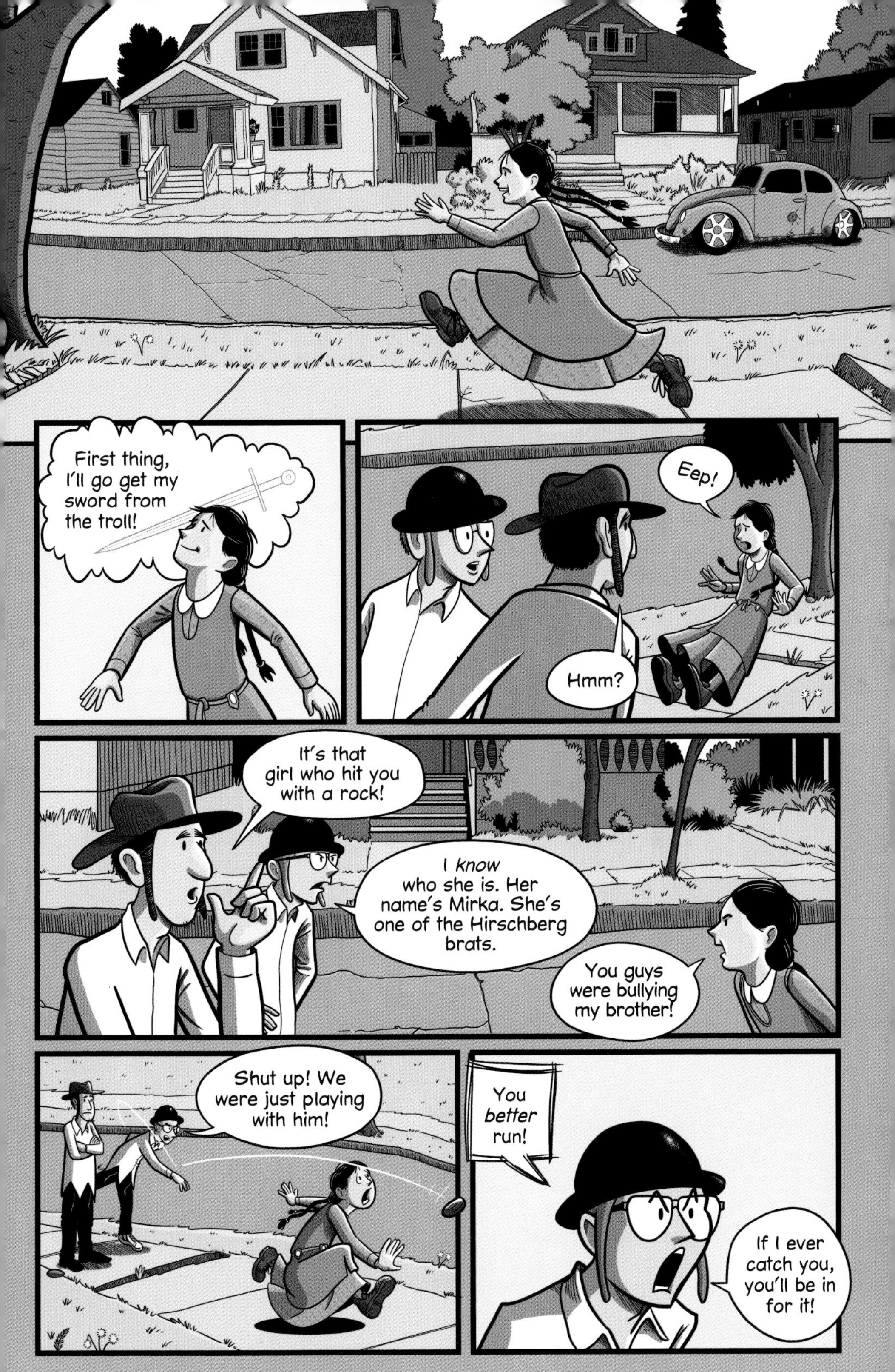
First thing, I'll go get my sword from the troll!
Eep!
Hmm?
It's that girl who hit you with a rock!
I *know* who she is. Her name's Mirka. She's one of the Hirschberg brats.
You guys were bullying my brother!
Shut up! We were just playing with him!
You *better* run!
If I ever catch you, you'll be in for it!

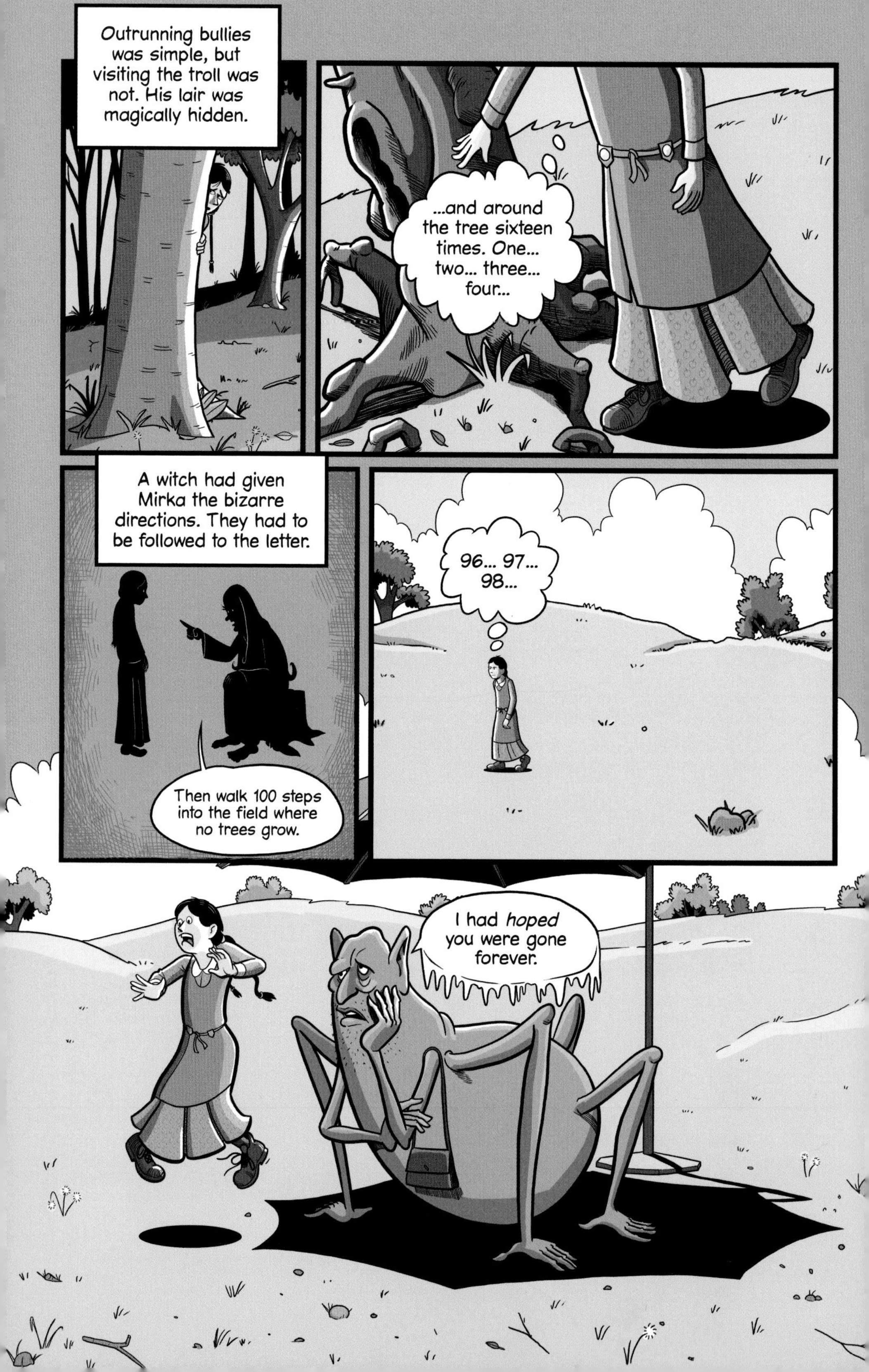
Outrunning bullies was simple, but visiting the troll was not. His lair was magically hidden.
...and around the tree sixteen times. One... two... three... four...
A witch had given Mirka the bizarre directions. They had to be followed to the letter.
Then walk 100 steps into the field where no trees grow.
96... 97... 98...
I had *hoped* you were gone forever.

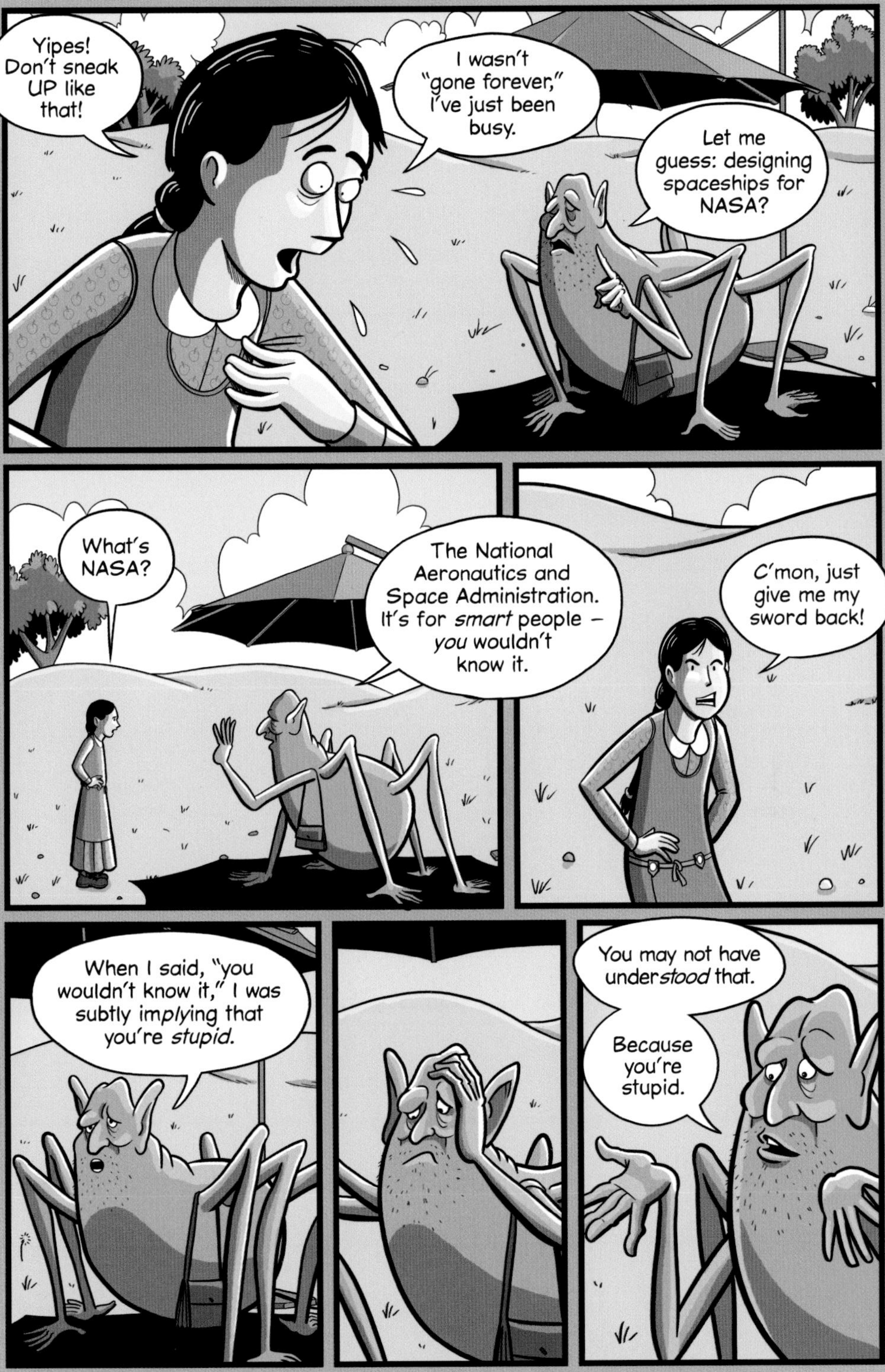
Yipes! Don't sneak UP like that!
I wasn't "gone forever," I've just been busy.
Let me guess: designing spaceships for NASA?
What's NASA?
The National Aeronautics and Space Administration. It's for *smart* people – *you* wouldn't know it.
C'mon, just give me my sword back!
When I said, "you wouldn't know it," I was subtly im*plying* that you're *stupid.*
You may not have under*stood* that.
Because you're stupid.

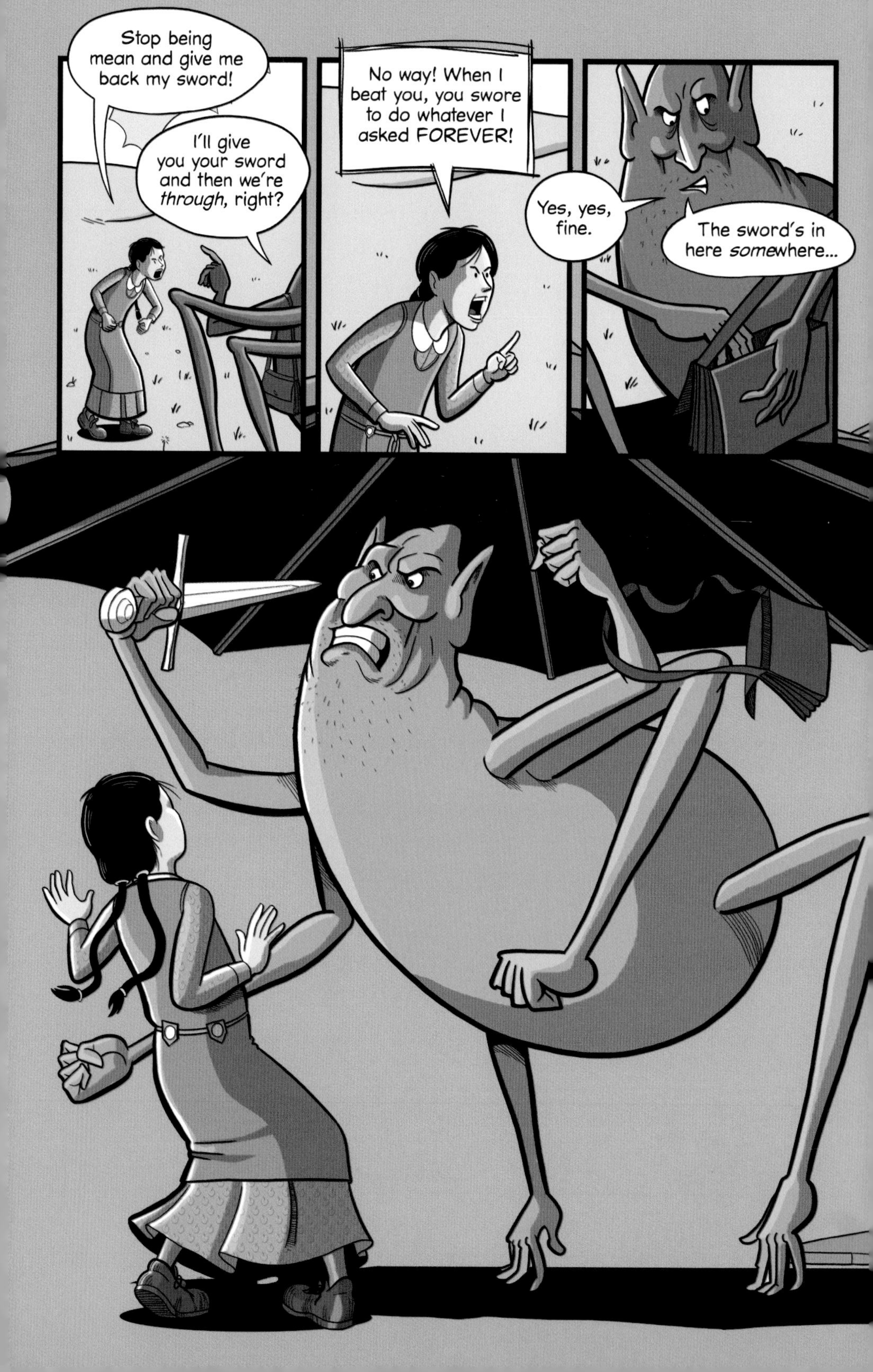
Stop being mean and give me back my sword!
I'll give you your sword and then we're *through*, right?
No way! When I beat you, you swore to do whatever I asked FOREVER!
Yes, yes, fine.
The sword's in here *some*where...

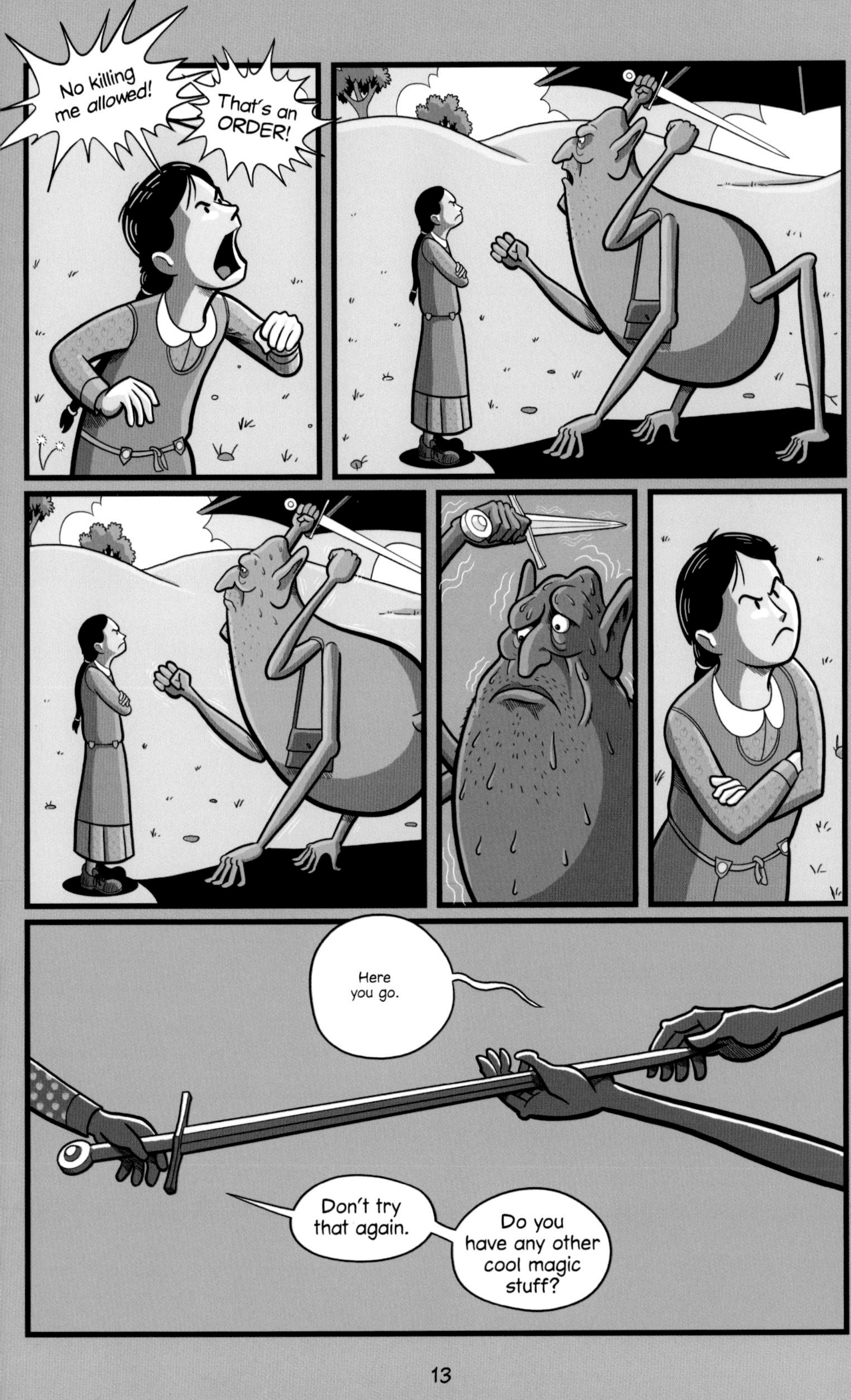
No killing me allowed!
That's an ORDER!
Here you go.
Don't try that again.
Do you have any other cool magic stuff?

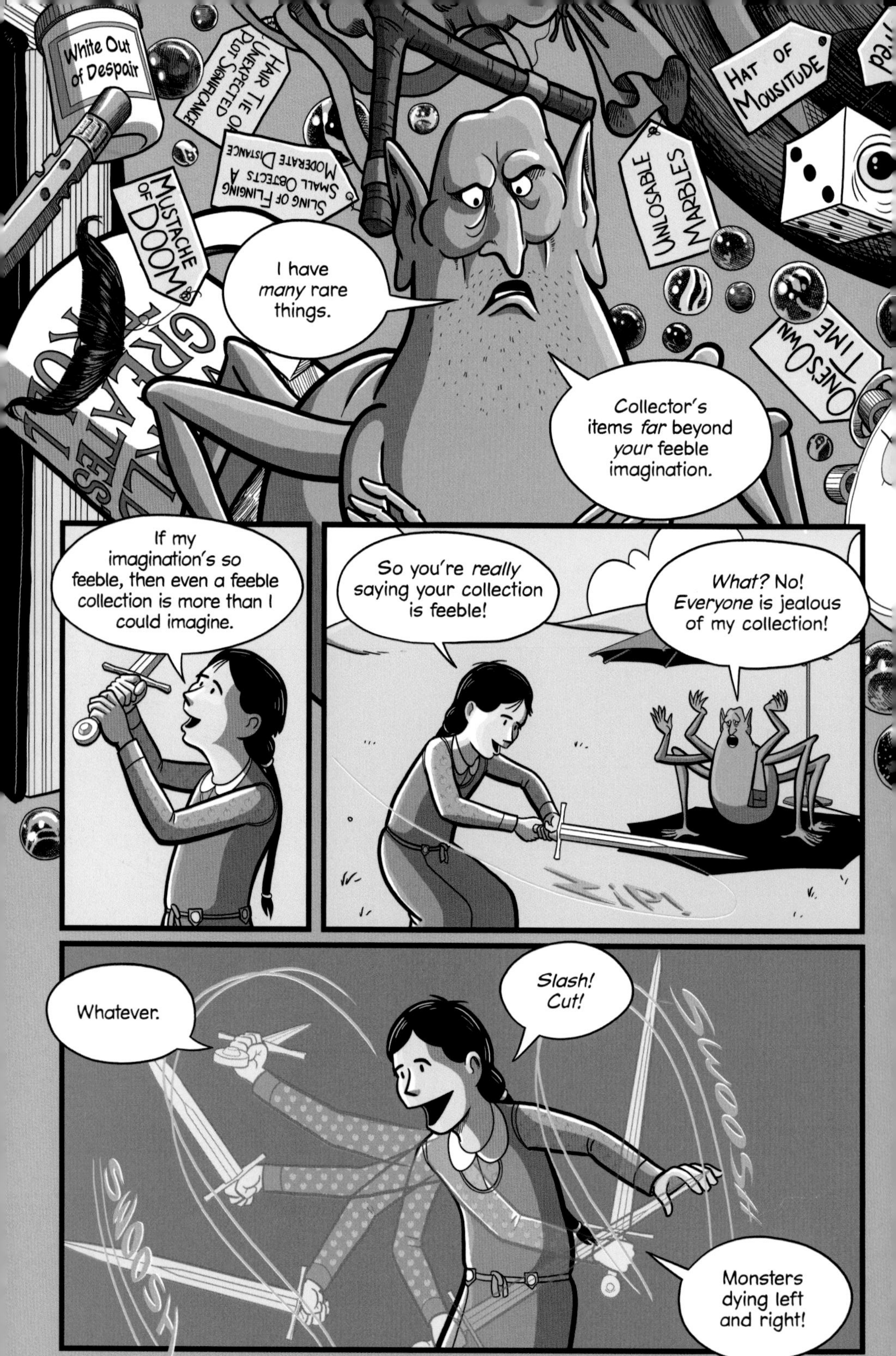
White Out of Despair
Hair Tie of Unexpected Plot Significance
Sling of Flinging Small Objects a Moderate Distance
Mustache of Doom
Hat of Mousitude
Unlosable Marbles
One's Own Time
I have *many* rare things.
Collector's items *far* beyond *your* feeble imagination.
If my imagination's so feeble, then even a feeble collection is more than I could imagine.
So you're *really* saying your collection is feeble!
What? No! *Everyone* is jealous of my collection!
ZIP!
Whatever.
Slash! Cut!
SWOOSH
SWOOSH
SWOOSH
Monsters dying left and right!

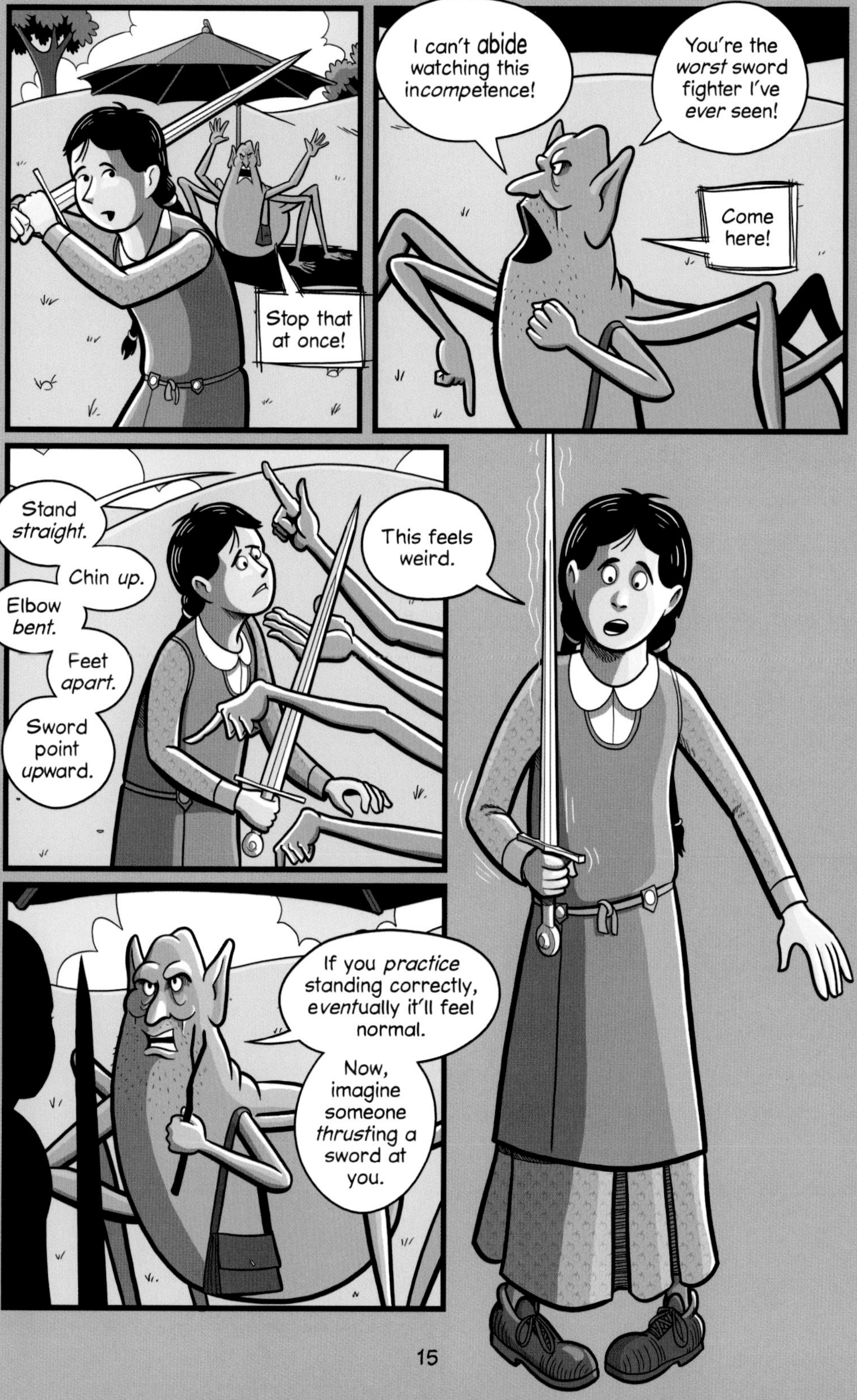
Stop that at once!
I can't abide watching this incompetence!
You're the *worst* sword fighter I've *ever* seen!
Come here!
Stand *straight.*
Chin up.
Elbow *bent.*
Feet *apart.*
Sword point *upward.*
This feels weird.
If you *practice* standing correctly, *eventually* it'll feel normal.
Now, imagine someone *thrusting* a sword at you.

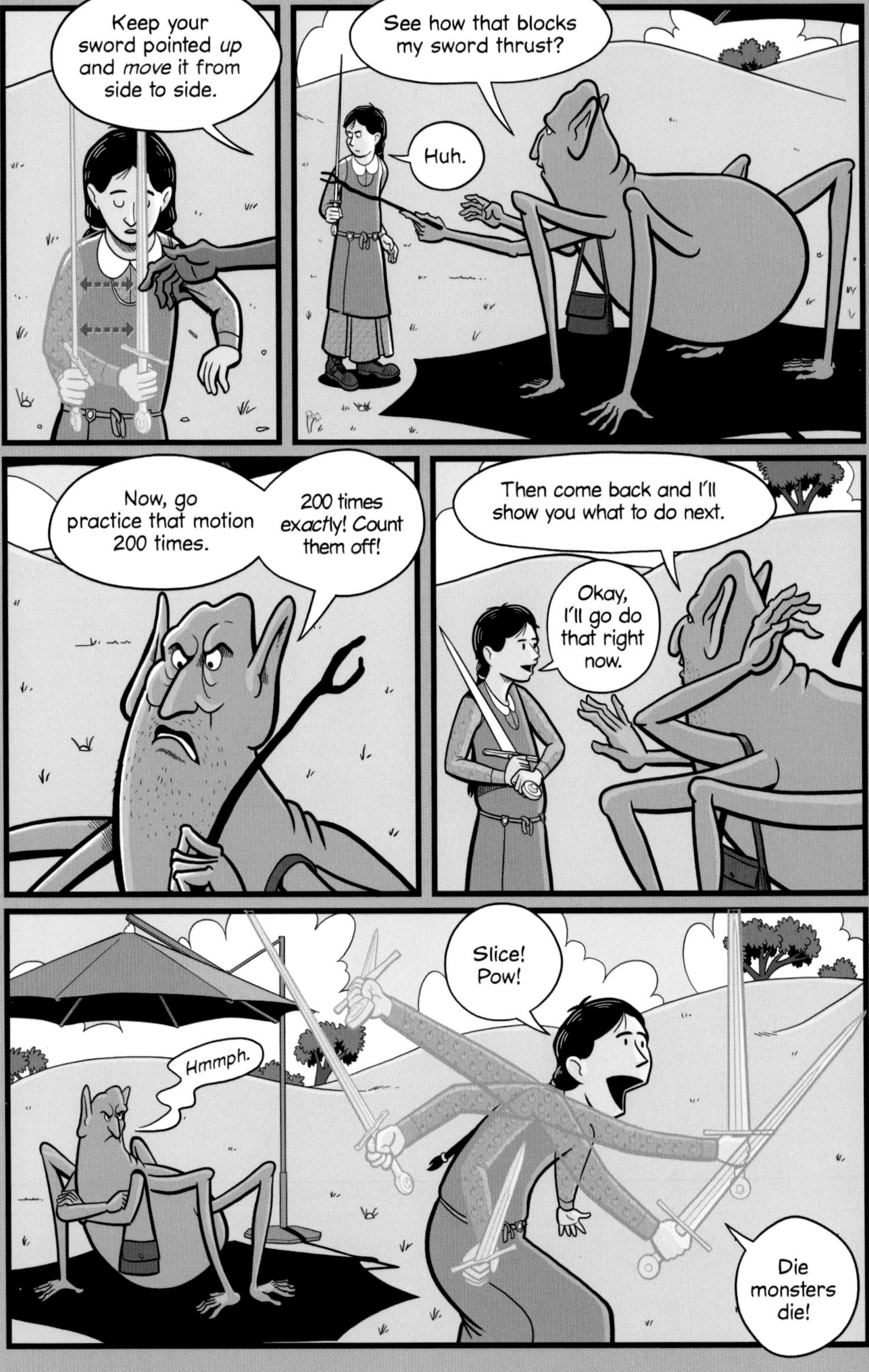

Keep your sword pointed *up* and *move* it from side to side.
See how that blocks my sword thrust?
Huh.
Now, go practice that motion 200 times.
200 times *exactly*! Count them off!
Then come back and I'll show you what to do next.
Okay, I'll go do that right now.
Hmmph.
Slice! Pow!
Die monsters die!

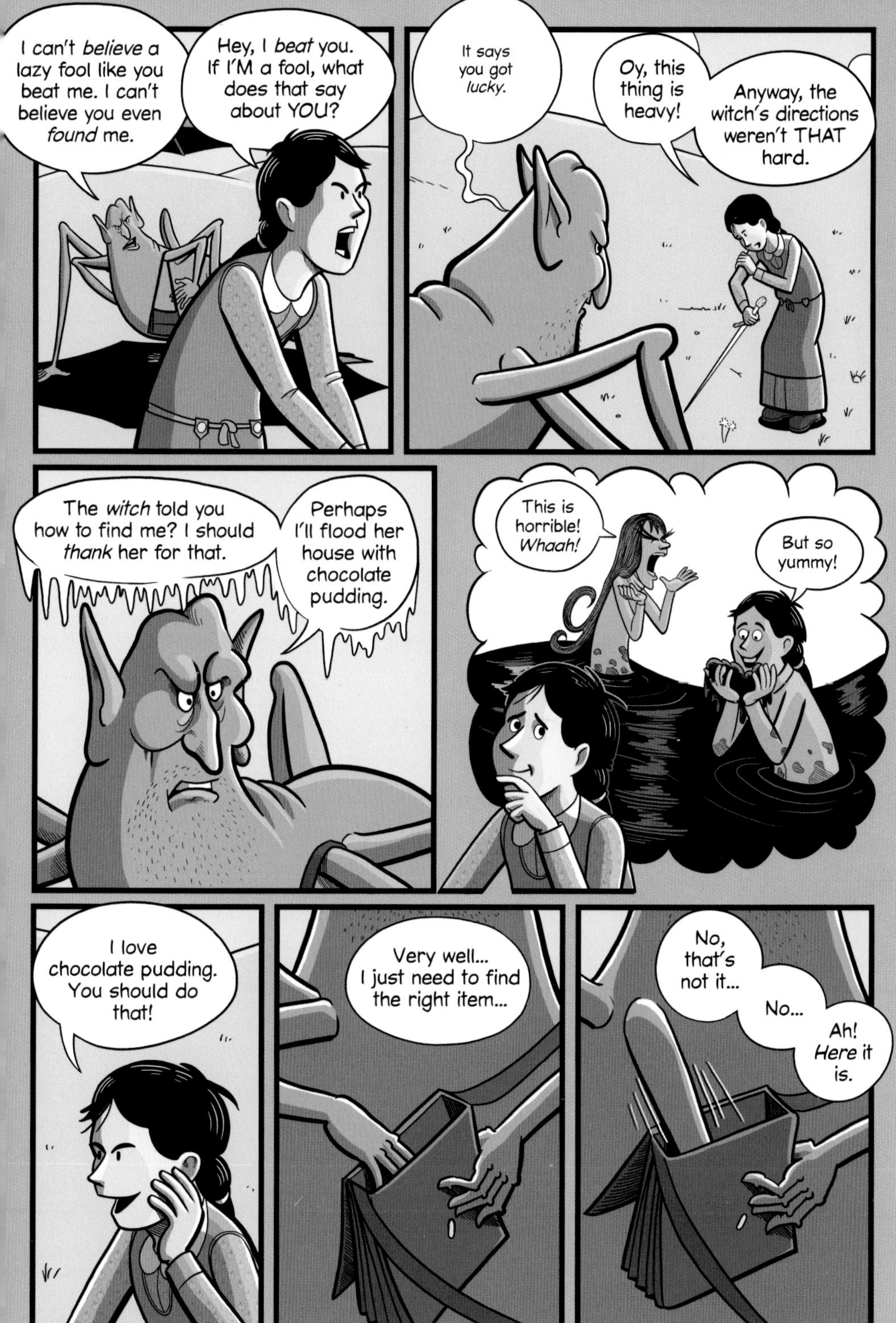
I can't *believe* a lazy fool like you beat me. I can't believe you even *found* me.
Hey, I *beat* you. If I'M a fool, what does that say about YOU?
It says you got *lucky*.
Oy, this thing is heavy!
Anyway, the witch's directions weren't THAT hard.
The *witch* told you how to find me? I should *thank* her for that.
Perhaps I'll flood her house with chocolate pudding.
This is horrible! *Whaah!*
But so yummy!
I love chocolate pudding. You should do that!
Very well... I just need to find the right item...
No, that's not it...
No...
Ah! *Here* it is.

Oy: Golly

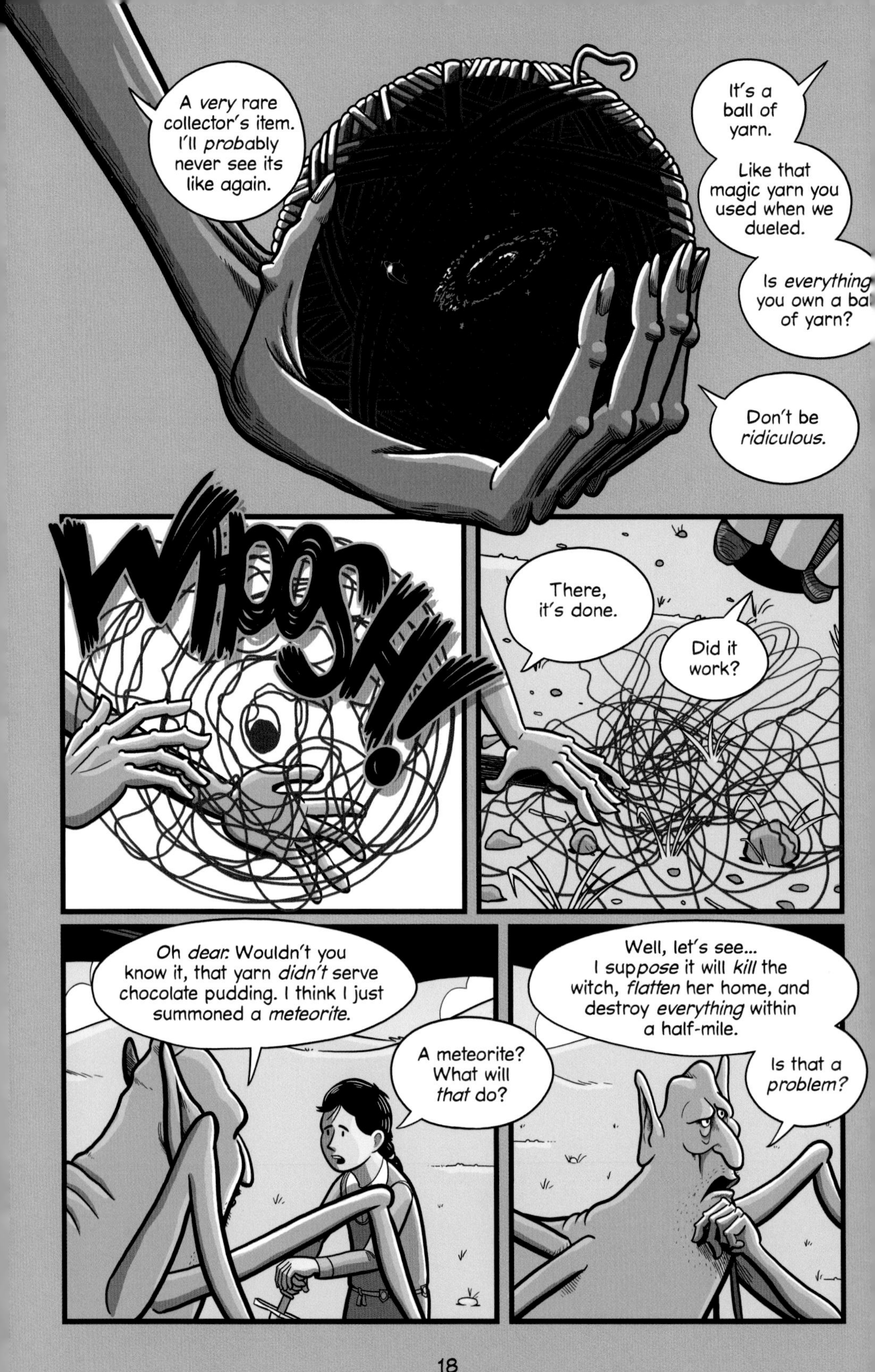
A *very* rare collector's item. I'll *probably* never see its like again.
It's a ball of yarn.
Like that magic yarn you used when we dueled.
Is *everything* you own a ball of yarn?
Don't be *ridiculous.*
WHOOSH!
There, it's done.
Did it work?
Oh *dear.* Wouldn't you know it, that yarn *didn't* serve chocolate pudding. I think I just summoned a *meteorite.*
A meteorite? What will *that* do?
Well, let's see... I sup*pose* it will *kill* the witch, *flatten* her home, and destroy *everything* within a half-mile.
Is that a *problem?*

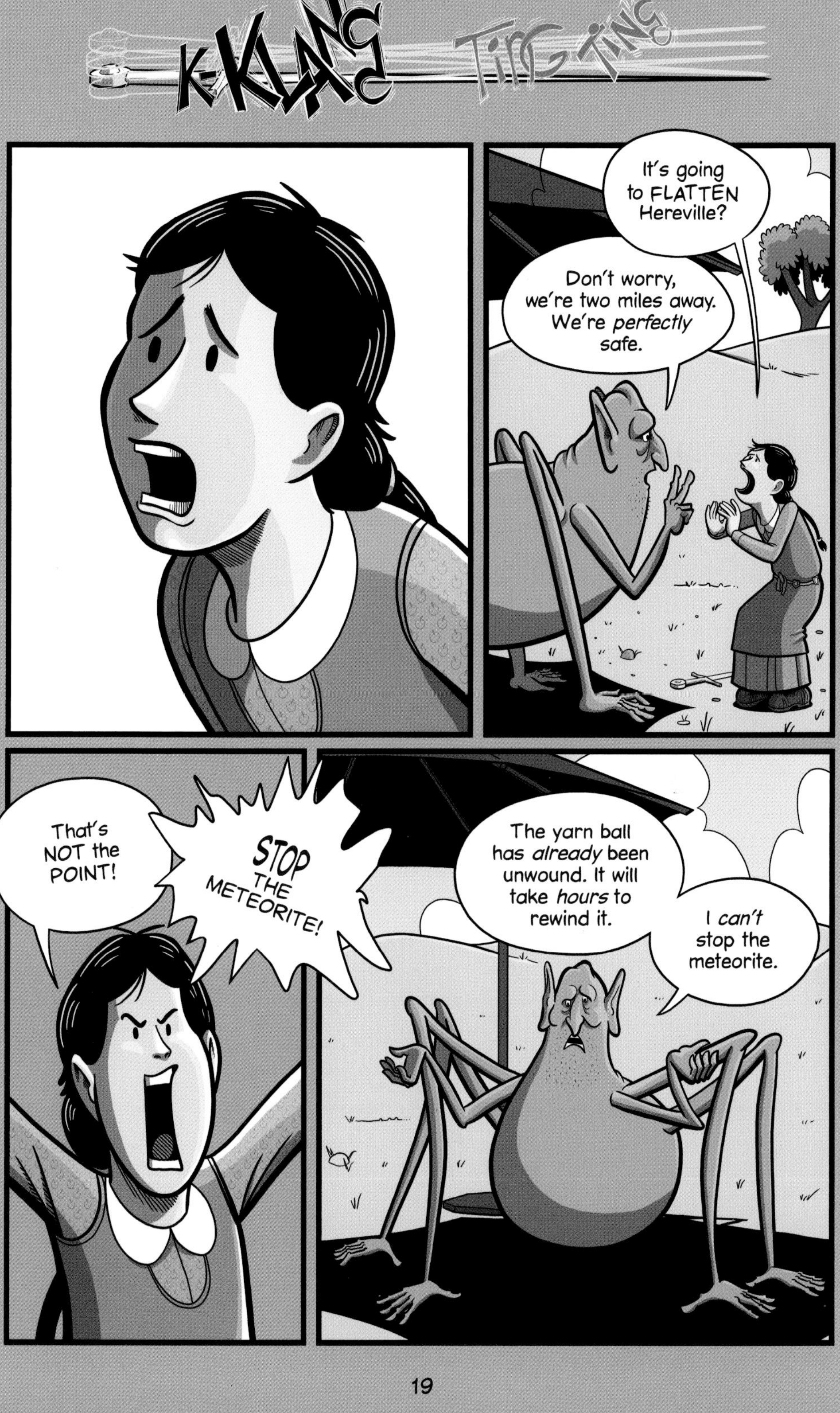
K-KLANG
TING TING
It's going to FLATTEN Hereville?
Don't worry, we're two miles away. We're *perfectly* safe.
That's NOT the POINT!
STOP THE METEORITE!
The yarn ball has *already* been unwound. It will take *hours* to rewind it.
I *can't* stop the meteorite.

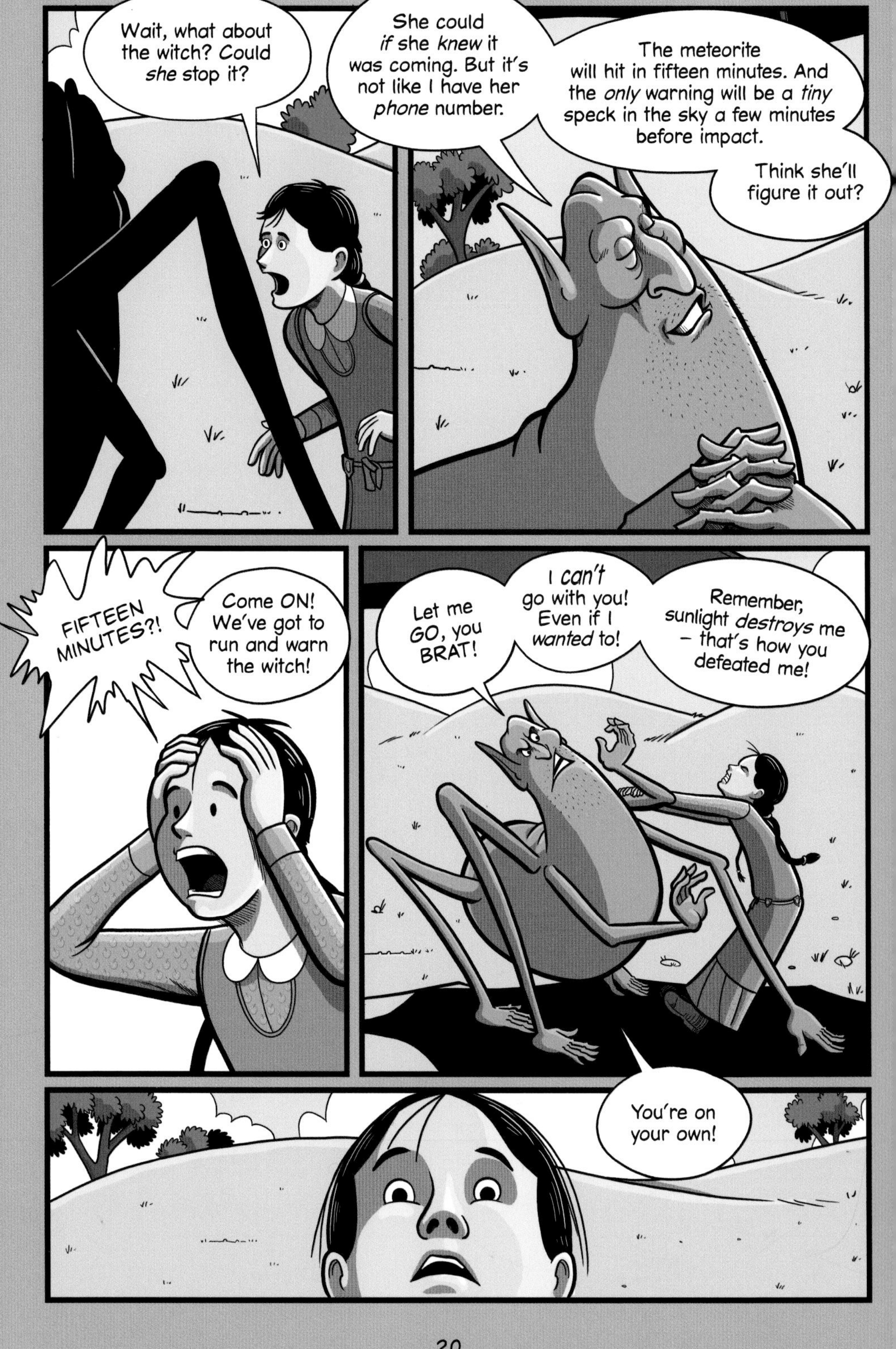
Wait, what about the witch? Could she stop it?
She could if she knew it was coming. But it's not like I have her phone number.
The meteorite will hit in fifteen minutes. And the only warning will be a tiny speck in the sky a few minutes before impact.
Think she'll figure it out?
FIFTEEN MINUTES?!
Come ON! We've got to run and warn the witch!
Let me GO, you BRAT!
I can't go with you! Even if I wanted to!
Remember, sunlight destroys me – that's how you defeated me!
You're on your own!

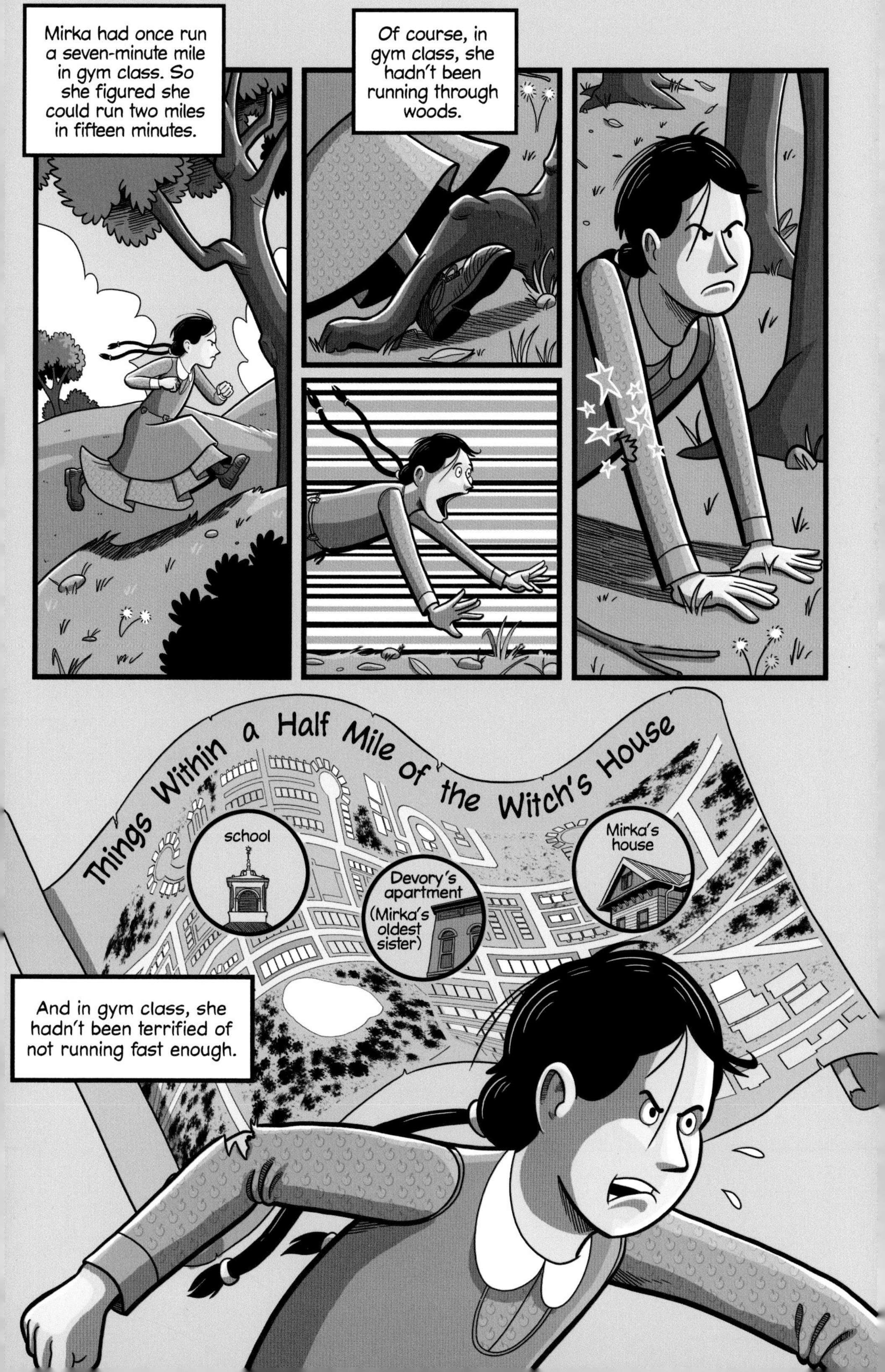
Mirka had once run a seven-minute mile in gym class. So she figured she could run two miles in fifteen minutes.
Of course, in gym class, she hadn't been running through woods.
Things Within a Half Mile of the Witch's House
school
Devory's apartment
(Mirka's oldest sister)
Mirka's house
And in gym class, she hadn't been terrified of not running fast enough.

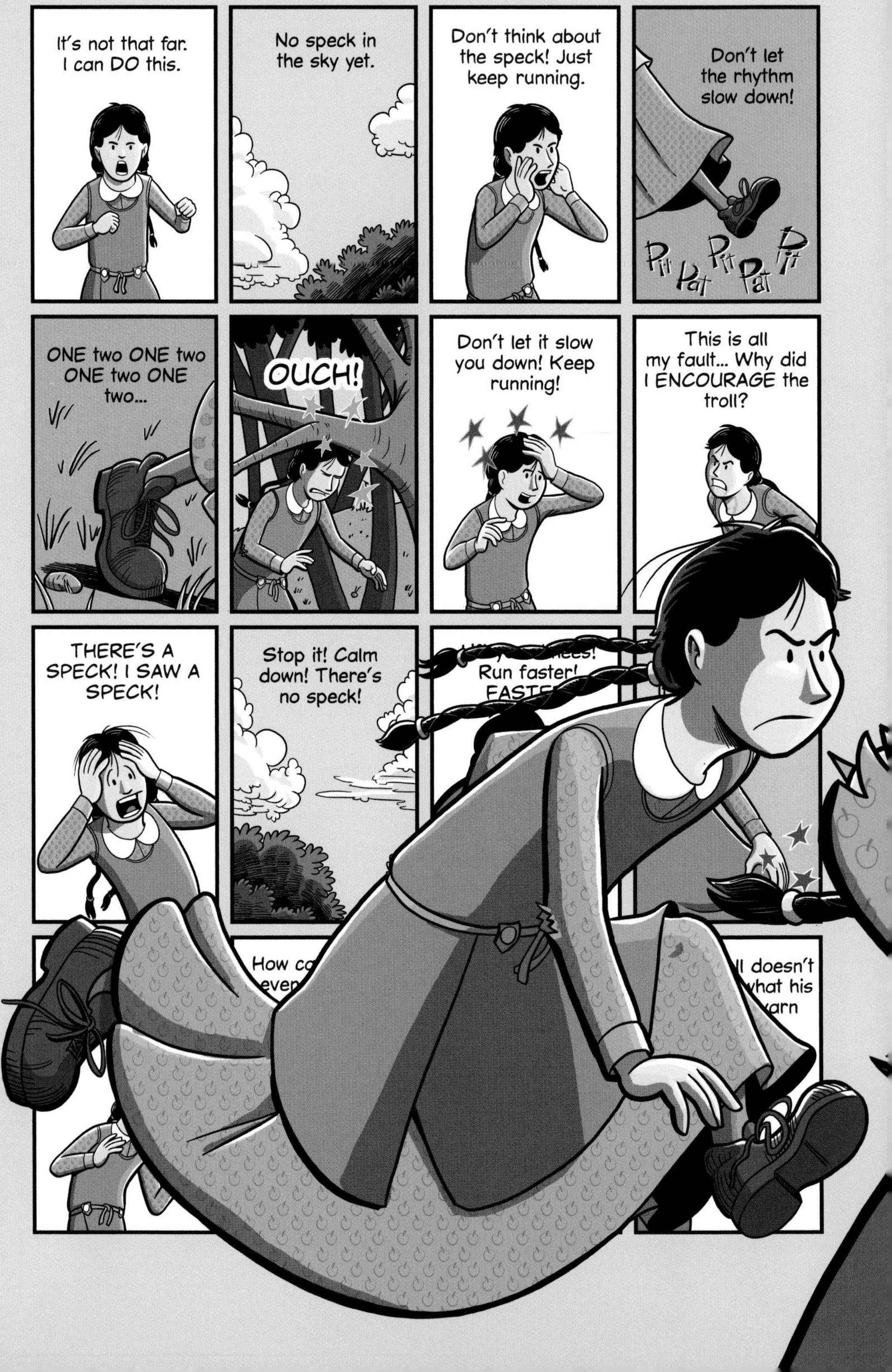
It's not that far. I can DO this.
No speck in the sky yet.
Don't think about the speck! Just keep running.
Don't let the rhythm slow down!
Pit Pat Pit Pat Pit
ONE two ONE two ONE two ONE two...
OUCH!
Don't let it slow you down! Keep running!
This is all my fault... Why did I ENCOURAGE the troll?
THERE'S A SPECK! I SAW A SPECK!
Stop it! Calm down! There's no speck!
Run faster!

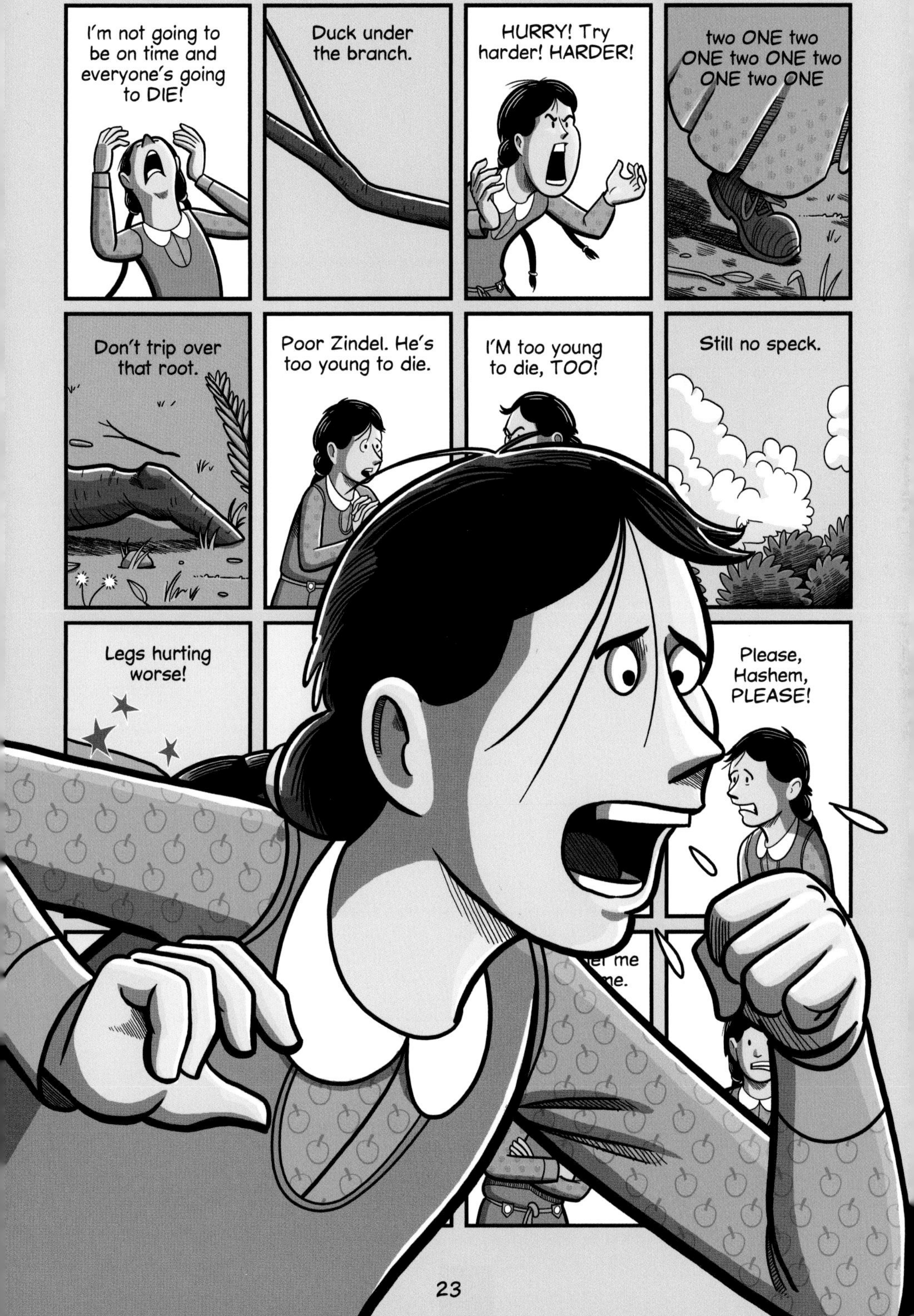
I'm not going to be on time and everyone's going to DIE!
Duck under the branch.
HURRY! Try harder! HARDER!
two ONE two ONE two ONE two ONE two ONE
Don't trip over that root.
Poor Zindel. He's too young to die.
I'M too young to die, TOO!
Still no speck.
Legs hurting worse!
Please, Hashem, PLEASE!

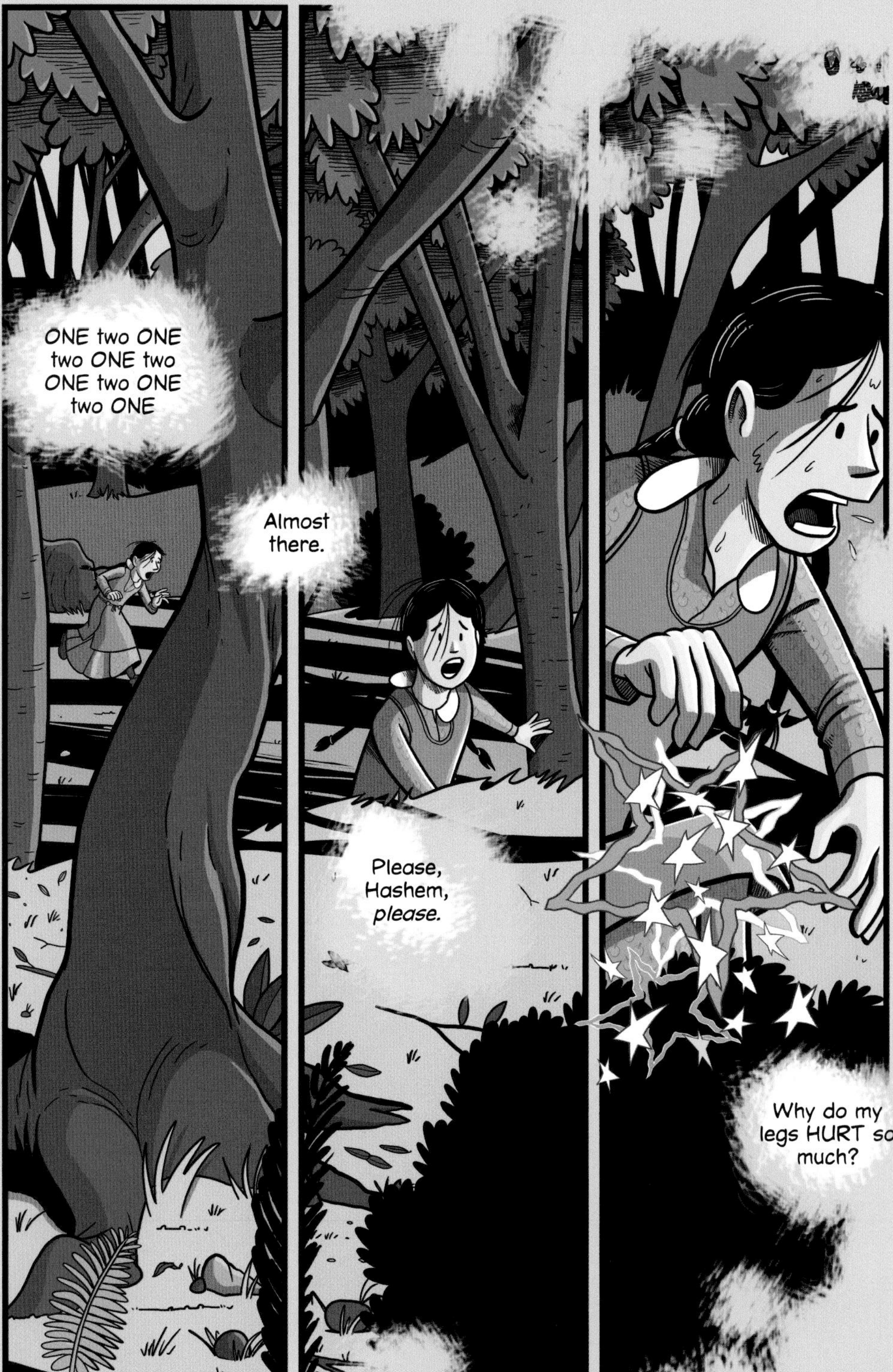
ONE two ONE two ONE two ONE two ONE two ONE
Almost there.
Please, Hashem, *please.*
Why do my legs HURT so much?

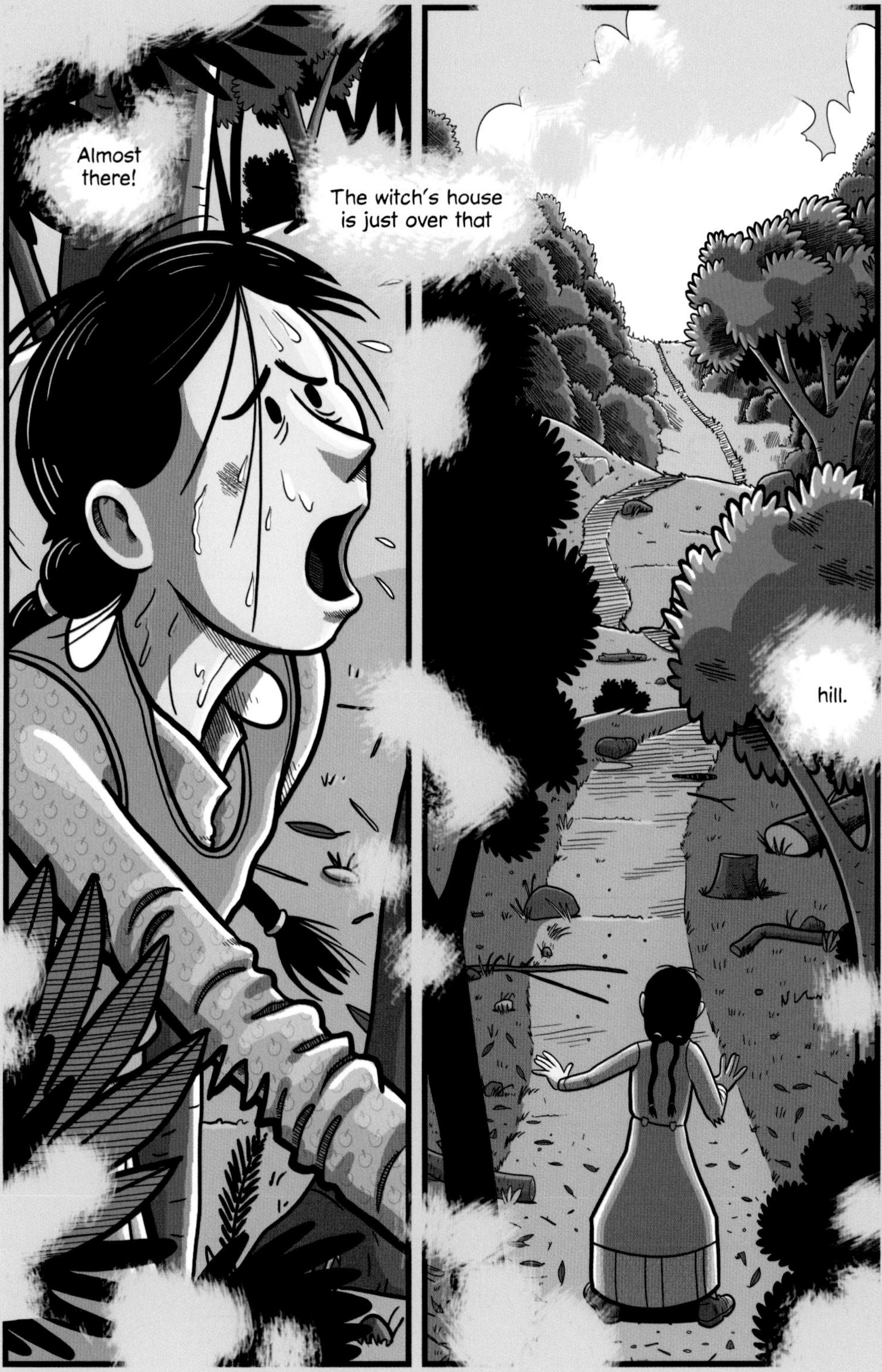
Almost there!
The witch's house is just over that
hill.

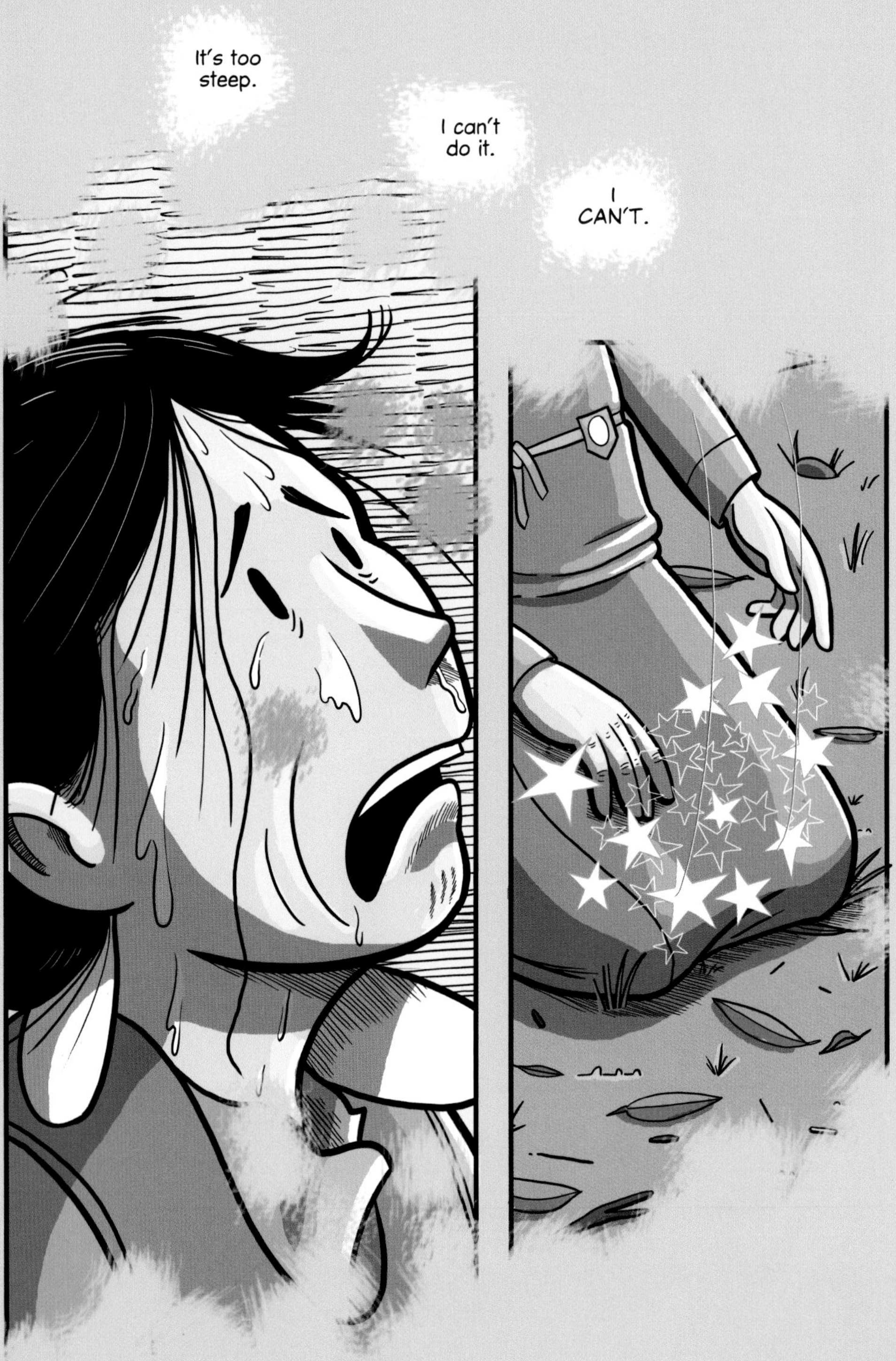
It's too steep.
I can't do it.
I CAN'T.

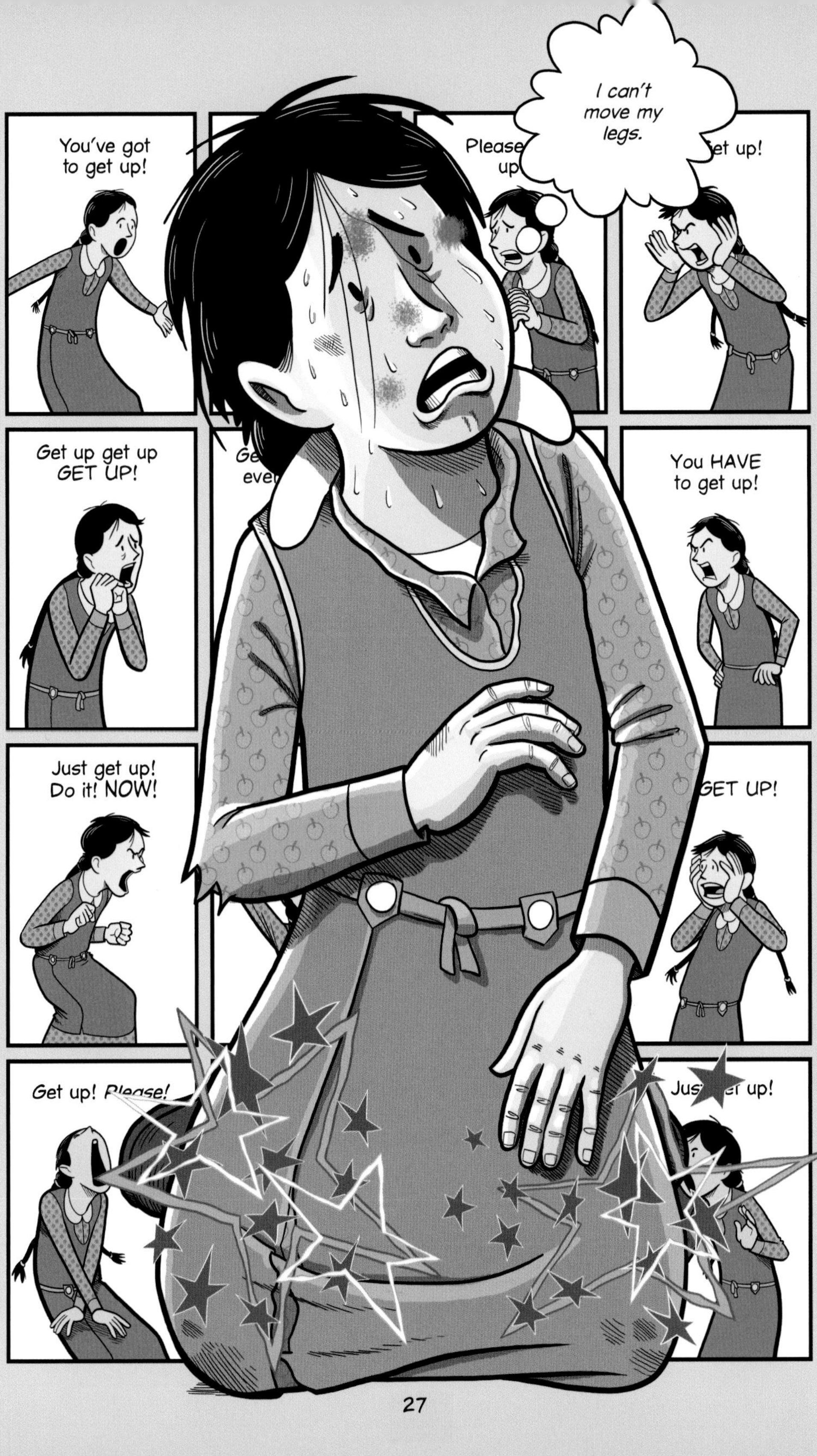
You've got to get up!
Please
up
I can't move my legs.
et up!
Get up get up GET UP!
You HAVE to get up!
Just get up! Do it! NOW!
GET UP!
Get up! Please!
up!

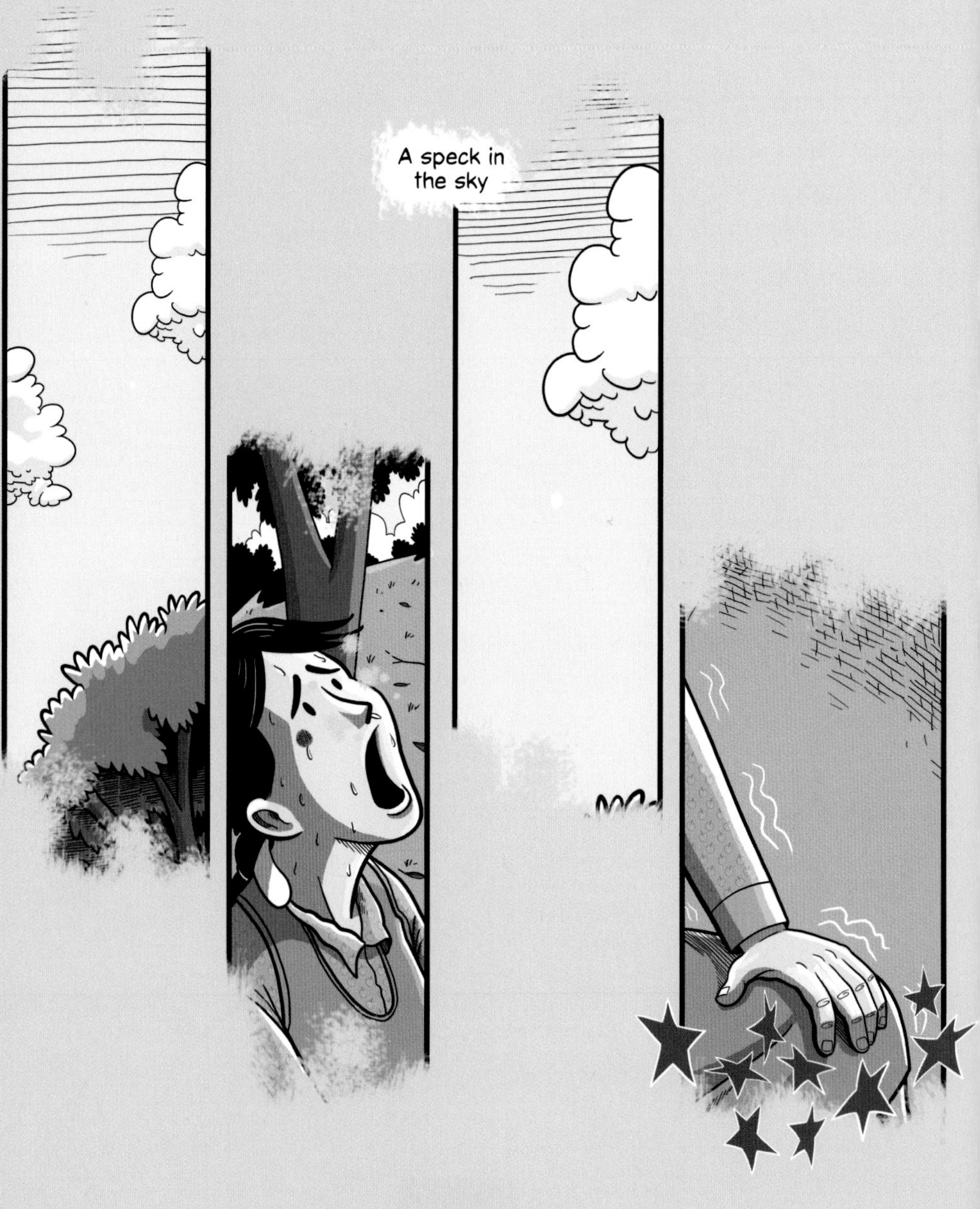
A speck in the sky

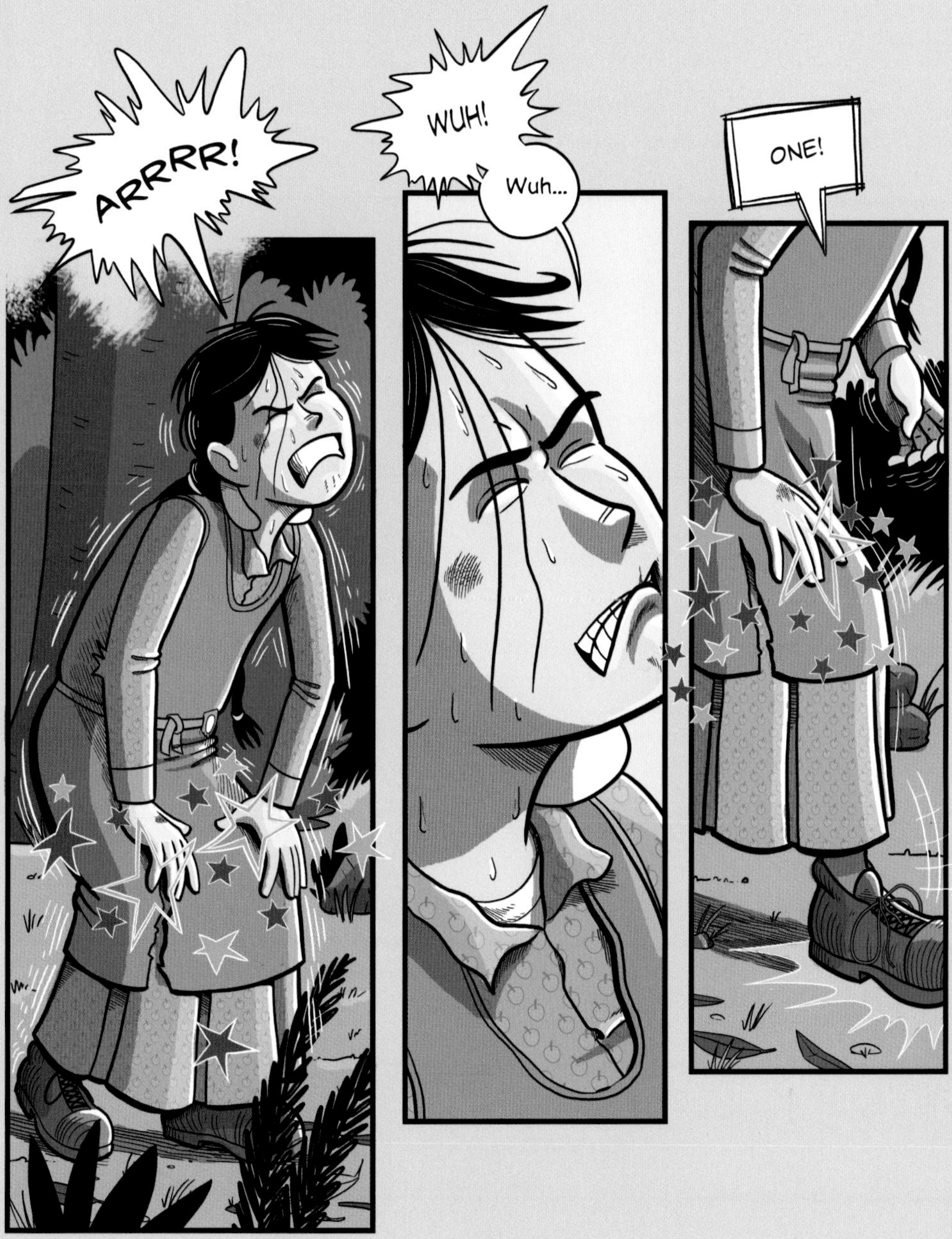
ARRRR!
WUH!
Wuh...
ONE!

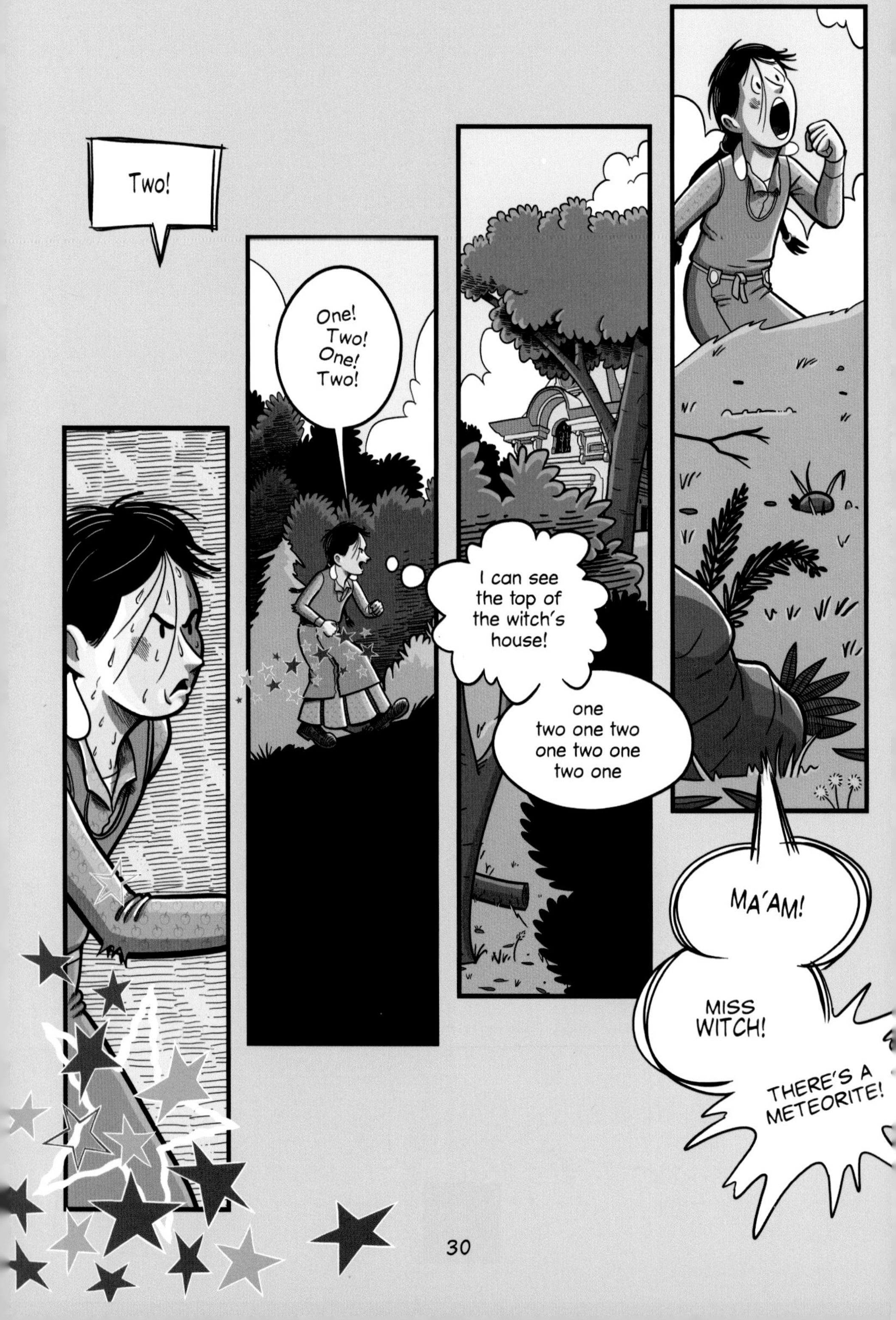

Two!
One!
Two!
One!
Two!
I can see the top of the witch's house!
one two one two one two one two one
MA'AM!
MISS WITCH!
THERE'S A METEORITE!

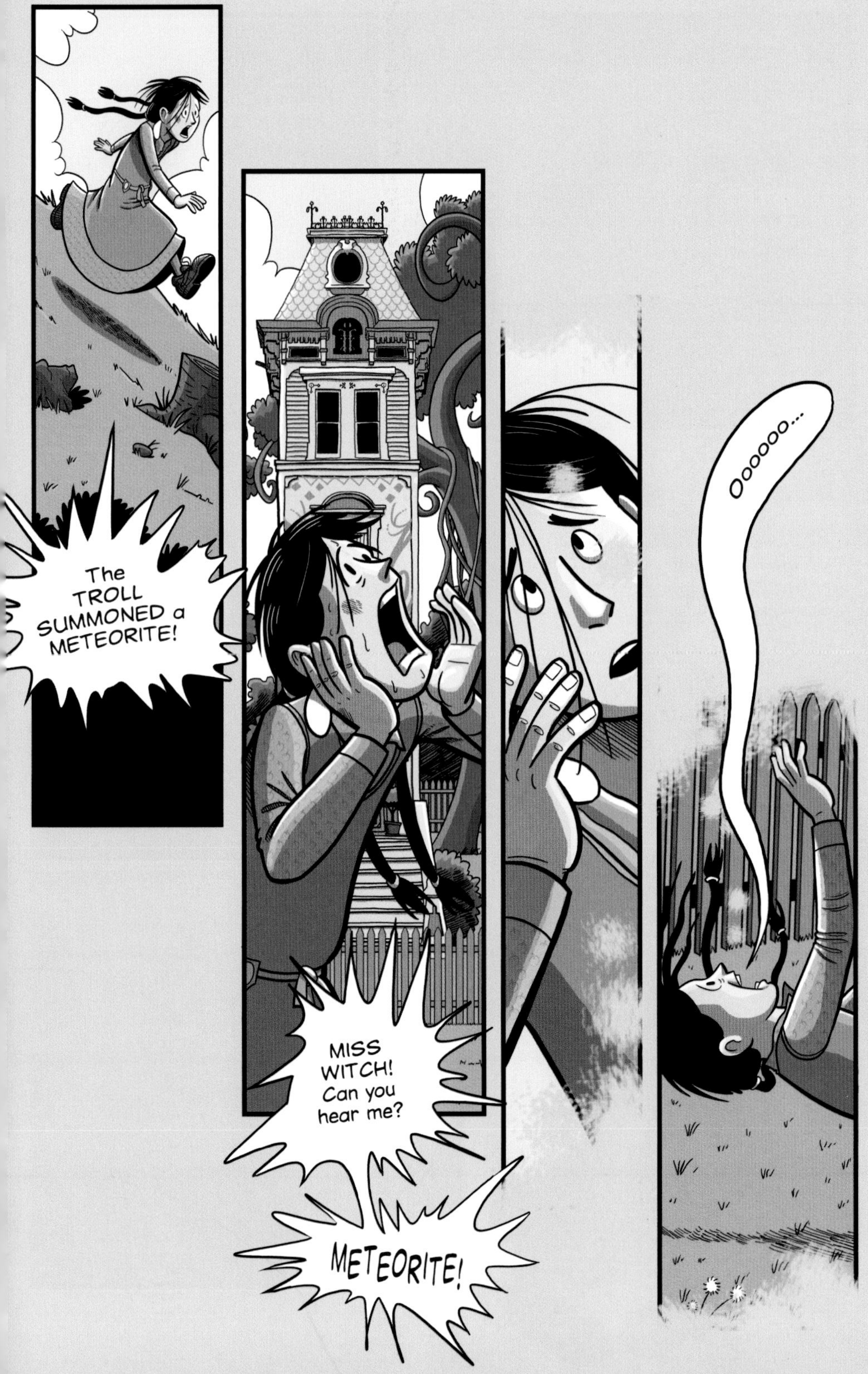
The TROLL SUMMONED a METEORITE!
MISS WITCH! Can you hear me?
METEORITE!
Oooooo...

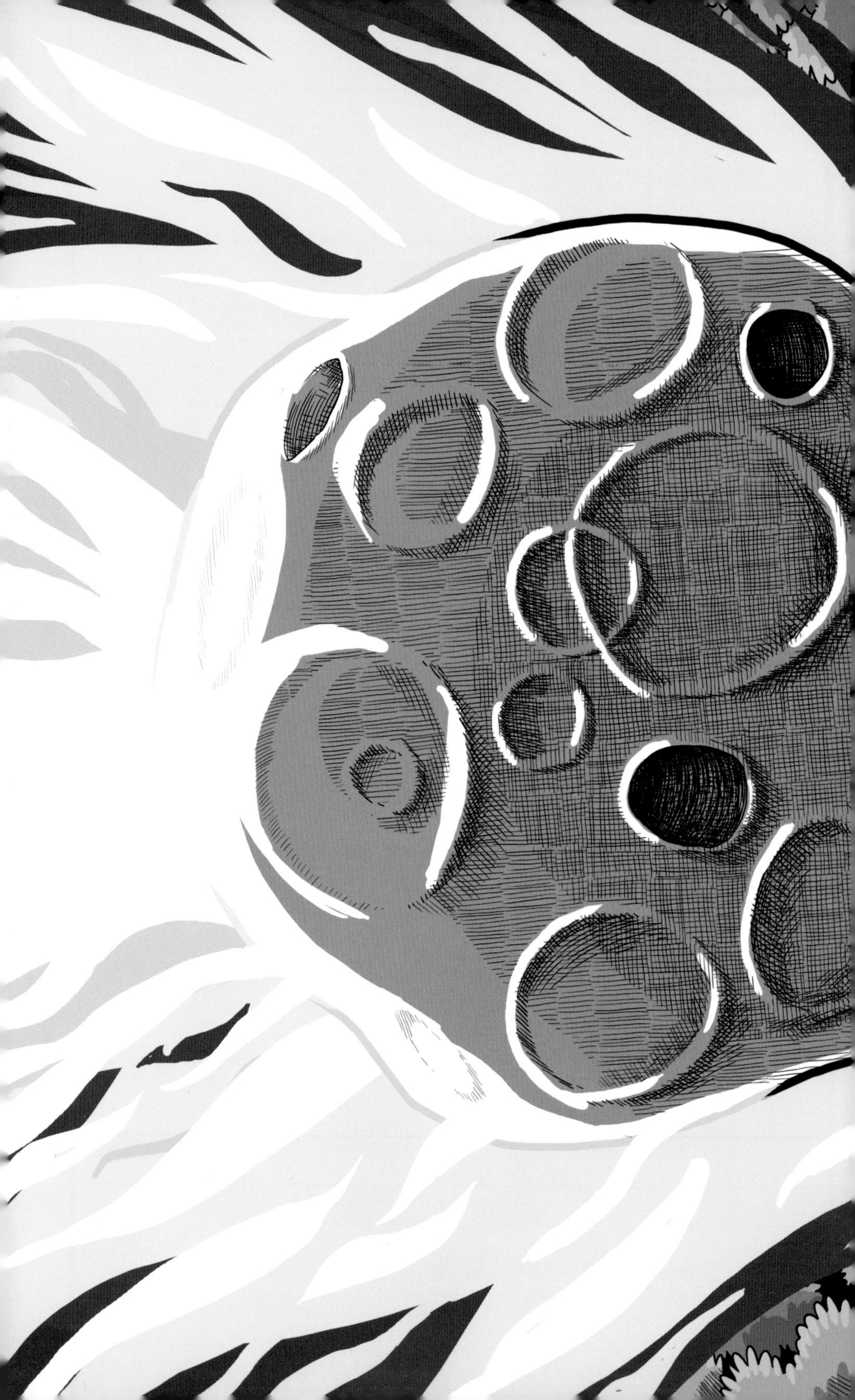

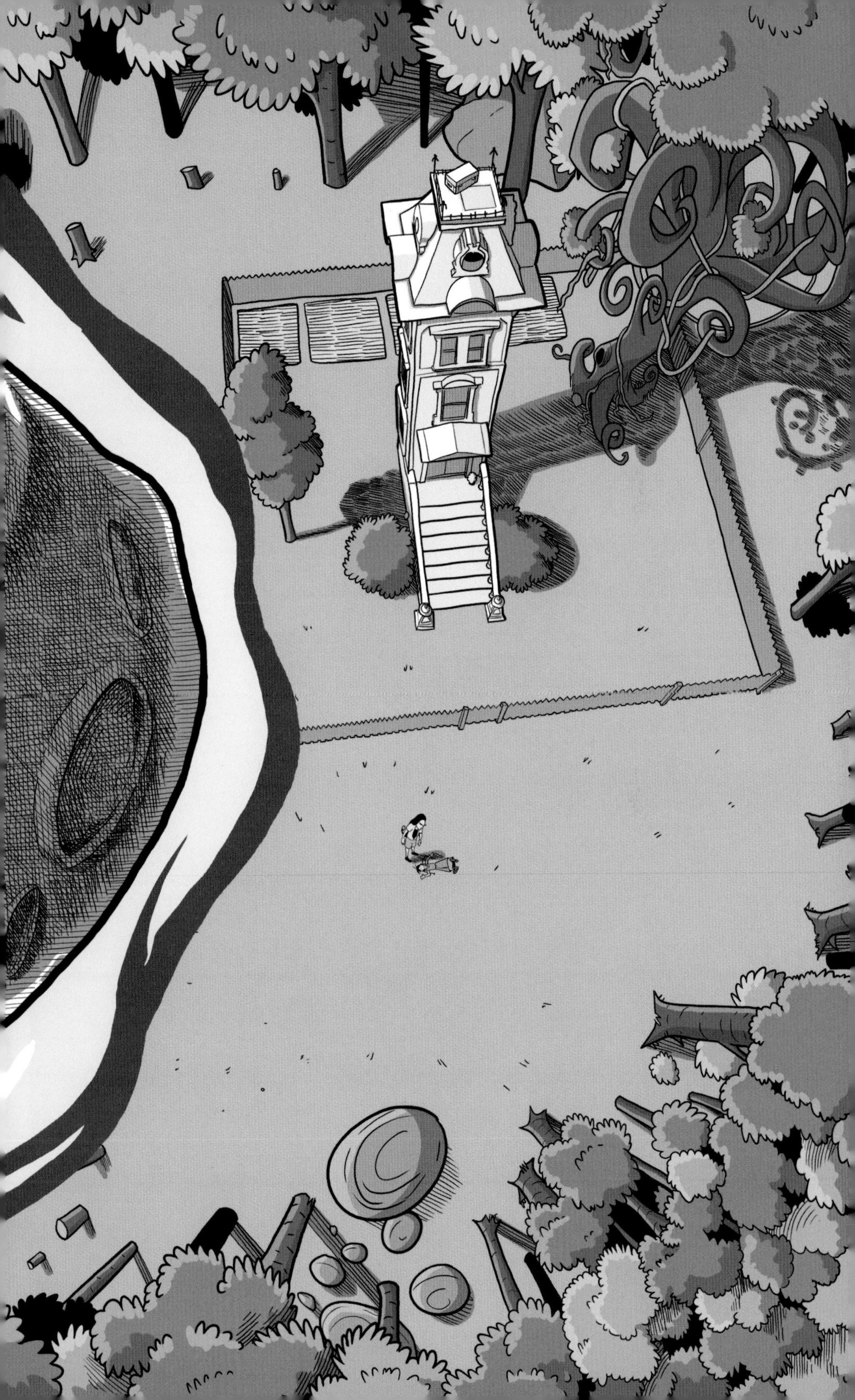

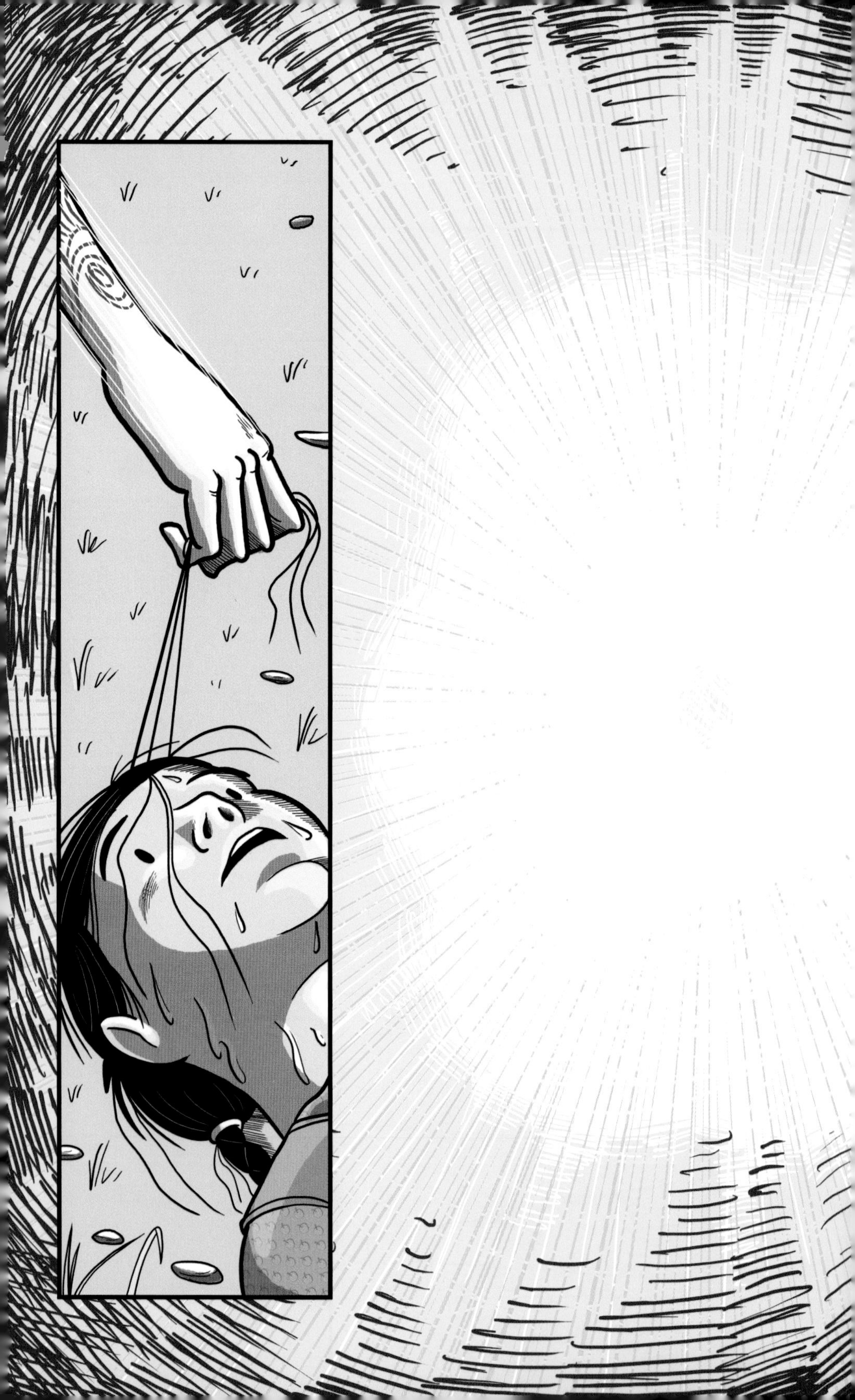

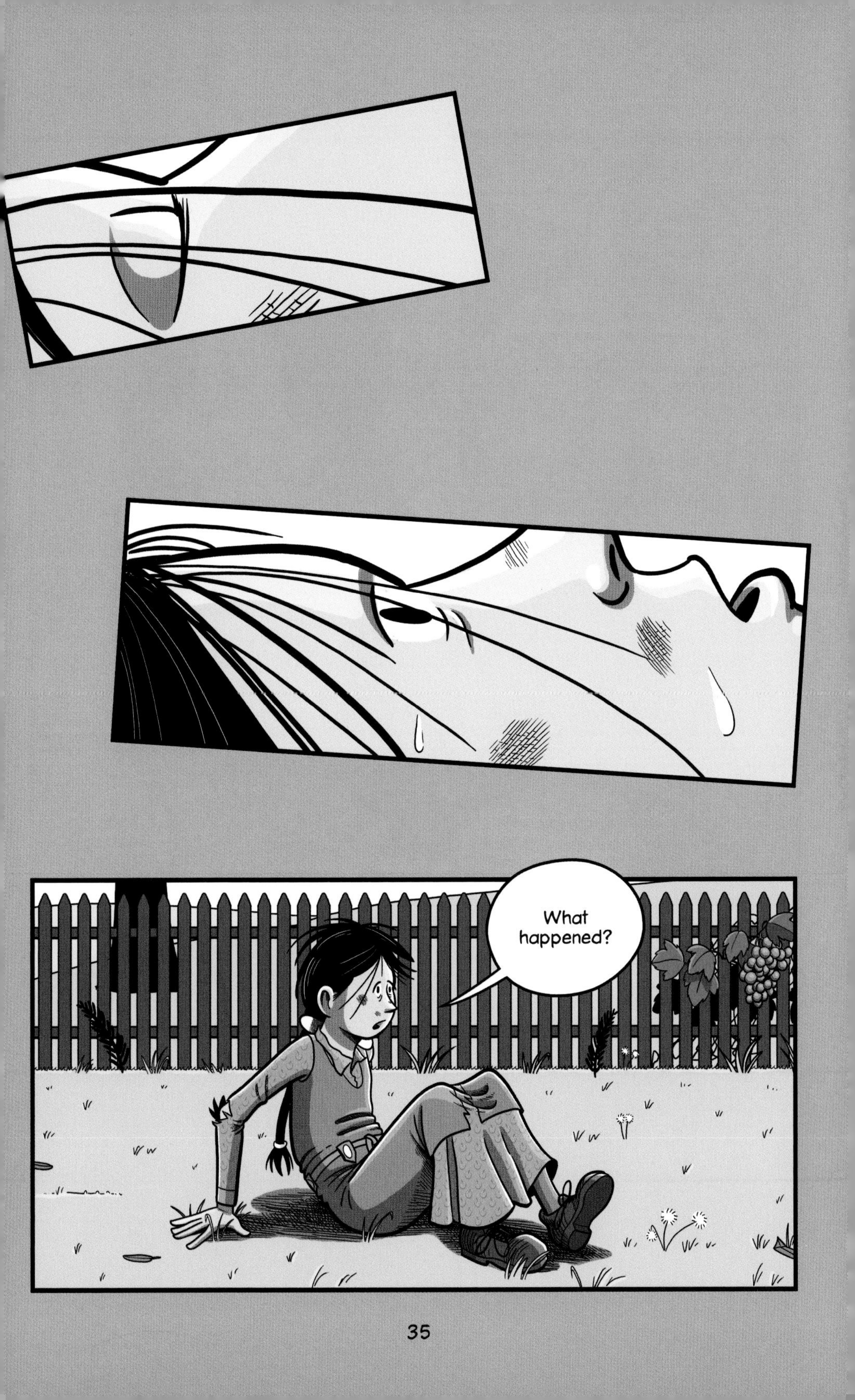
What happened?

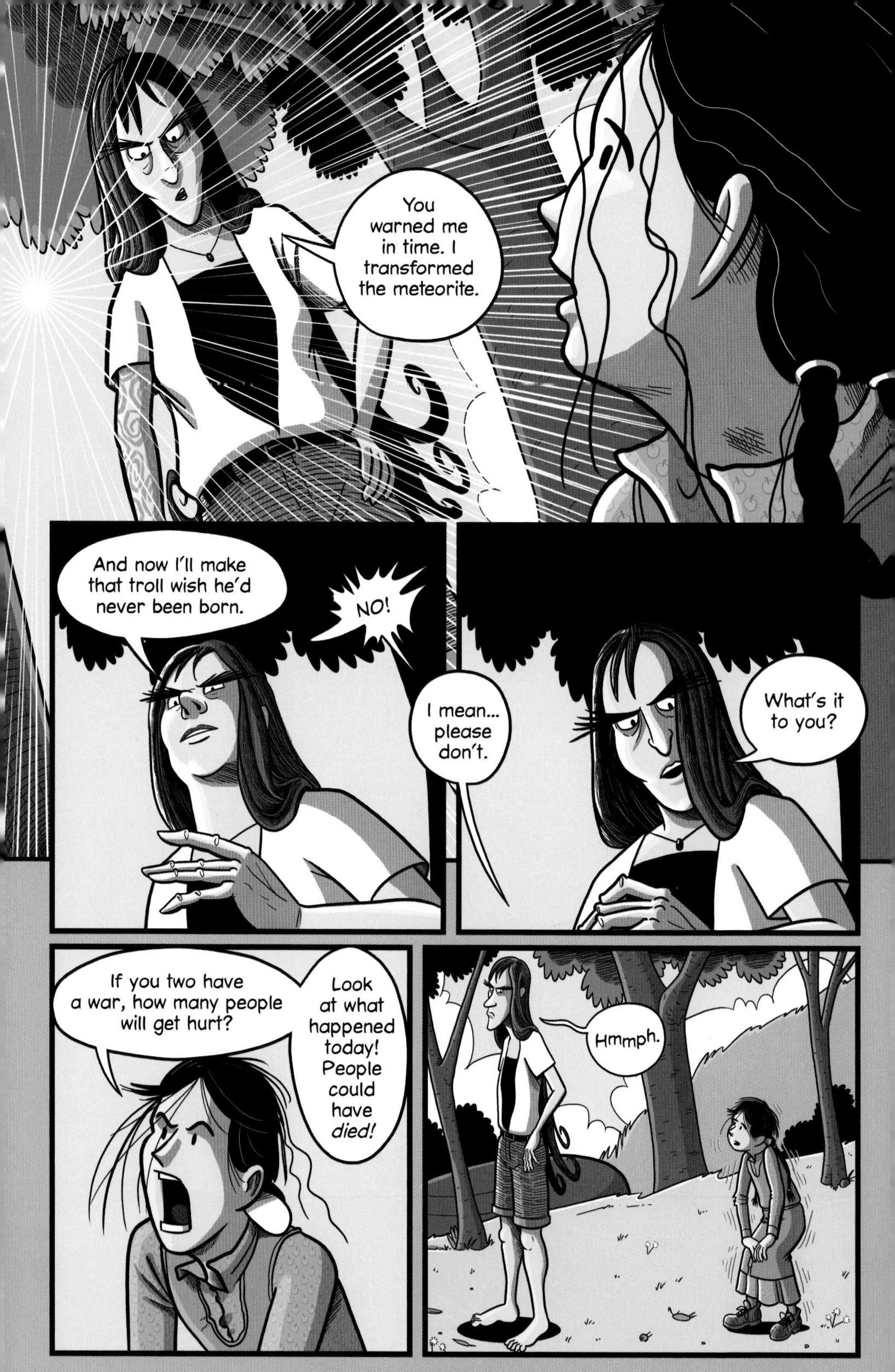
You warned me in time. I transformed the meteorite.
And now I'll make that troll wish he'd never been born.
NO!
I mean... please don't.
What's it to you?
If you two have a war, how many people will get hurt?
Look at what happened today! People could have *died!*
Hmmph.

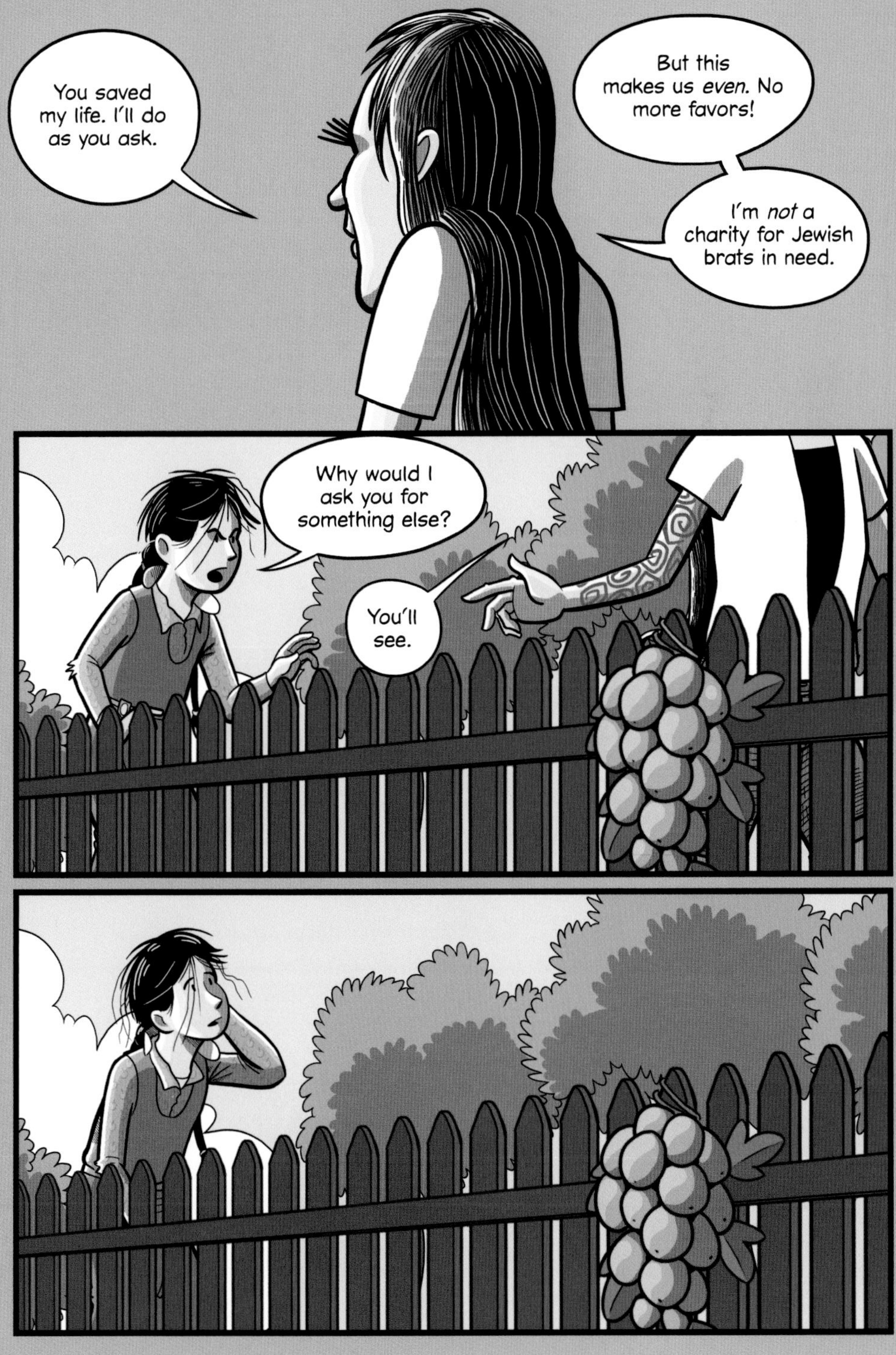
You saved my life. I'll do as you ask.
But this makes us *even*. No more favors!
I'm *not* a charity for Jewish brats in need.
Why would I ask you for something else?
You'll see.

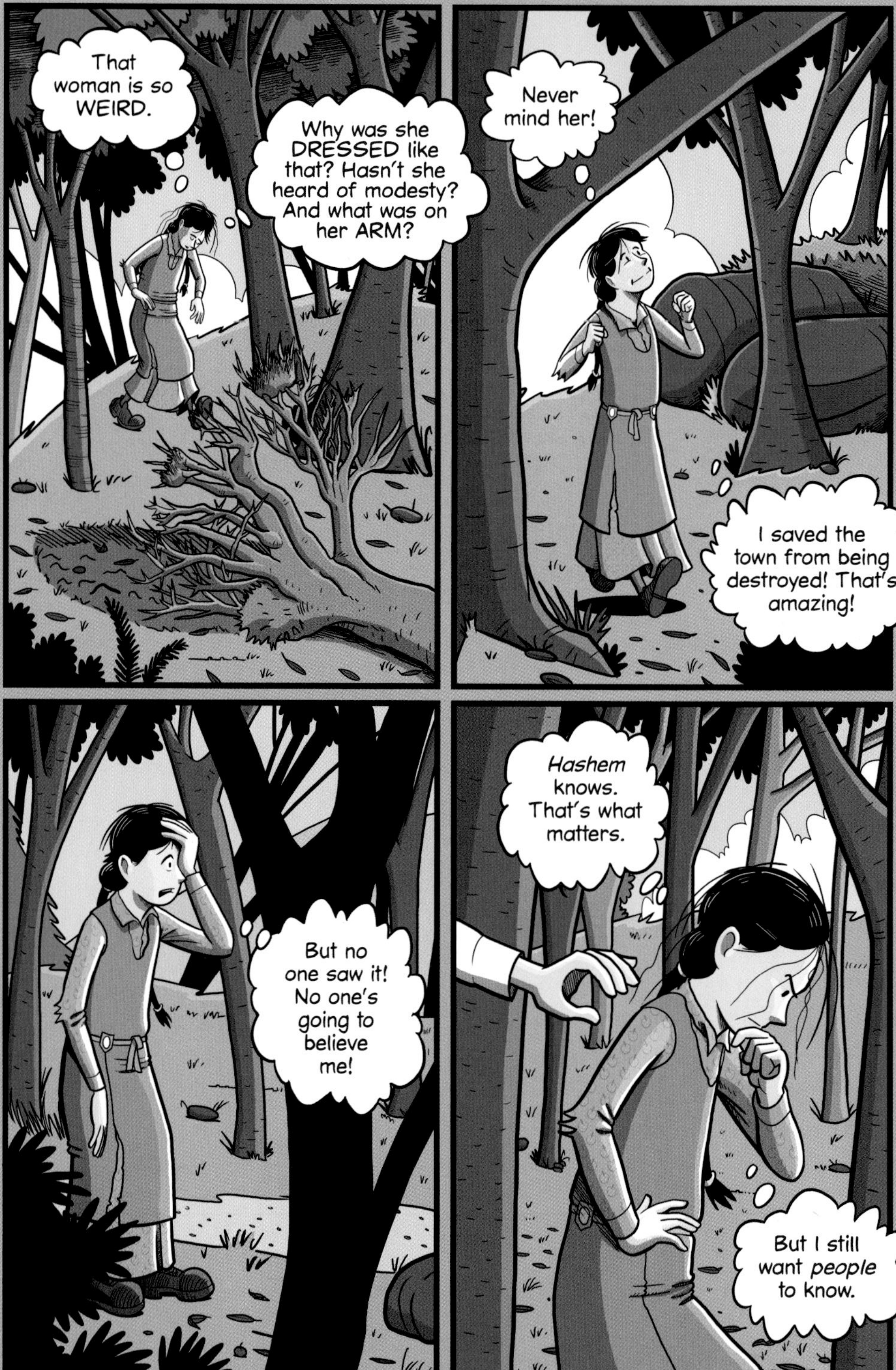
That woman is so WEIRD.
Why was she DRESSED like that? Hasn't she heard of modesty? And what was on her ARM?
Never mind her!
I saved the town from being destroyed! That's amazing!
But no one saw it! No one's going to believe me!
Hashem knows. That's what matters.
But I still want *people* to know.

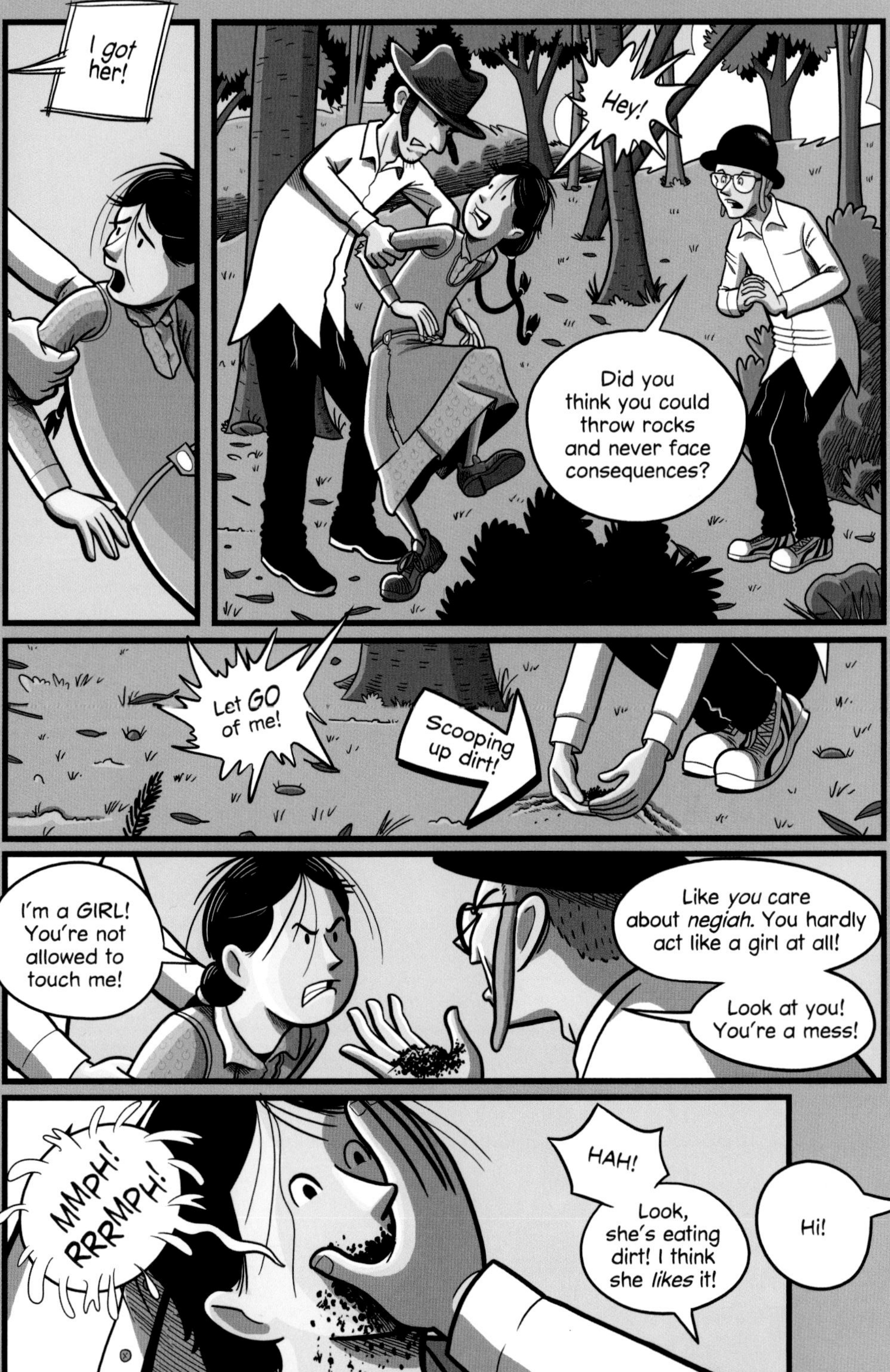
I got her!
Hey!
Did you think you could throw rocks and never face consequences?
Let GO of me!
Scooping up dirt!
I'm a GIRL! You're not allowed to touch me!
Like *you* care about *negiah*. You hardly act like a girl at all!
Look at you! You're a mess!
MMPH! RRRMPH!
HAH!
Look, she's eating dirt! I think she *likes* it!
Hi!

Negiah: The rule against unrelated people of the opposite sex touching.

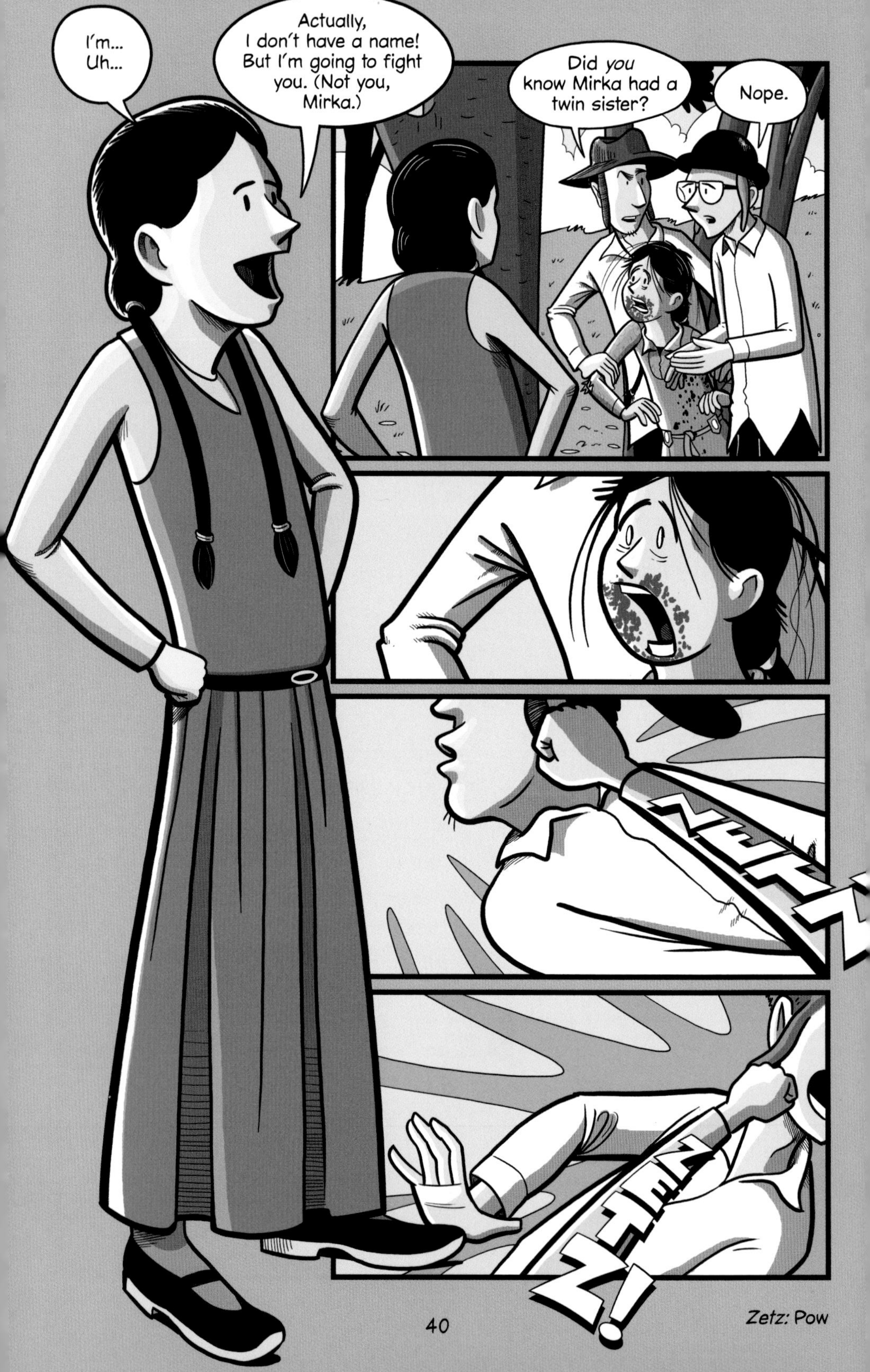
I'm...
Uh...
Actually, I don't have a name! But I'm going to fight you. (Not you, Mirka.)
Did *you* know Mirka had a twin sister?
Nope.
ZETZ!
ZETZ!

Zetz: Pow

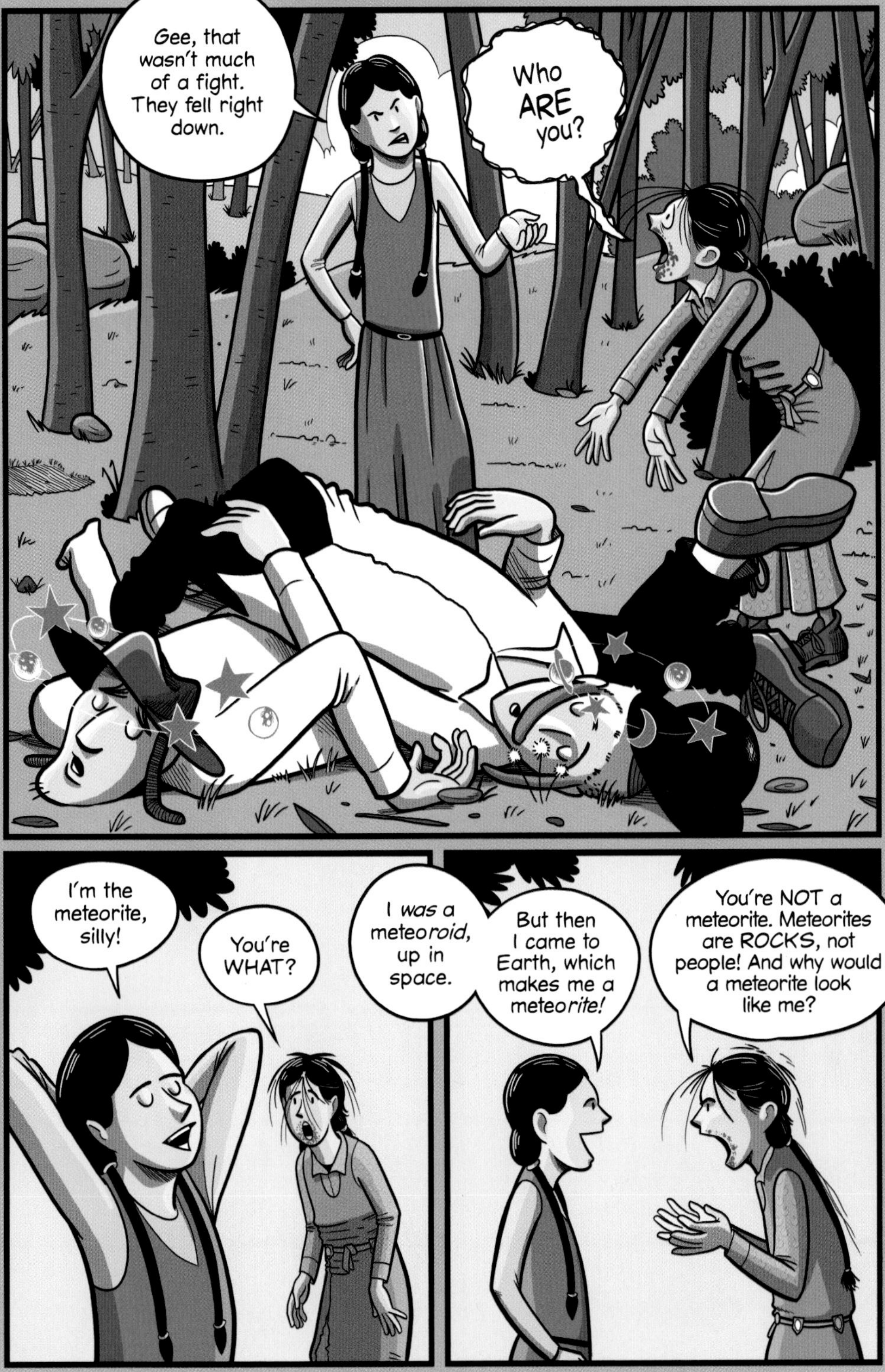
Gee, that wasn't much of a fight. They fell right down.
Who ARE you?
I'm the meteorite, silly!
You're WHAT?
I *was* a meteo*roid*, up in space.
But then I came to Earth, which makes me a meteo*rite!*
You're NOT a meteorite. Meteorites are ROCKS, not people! And why would a meteorite look like me?

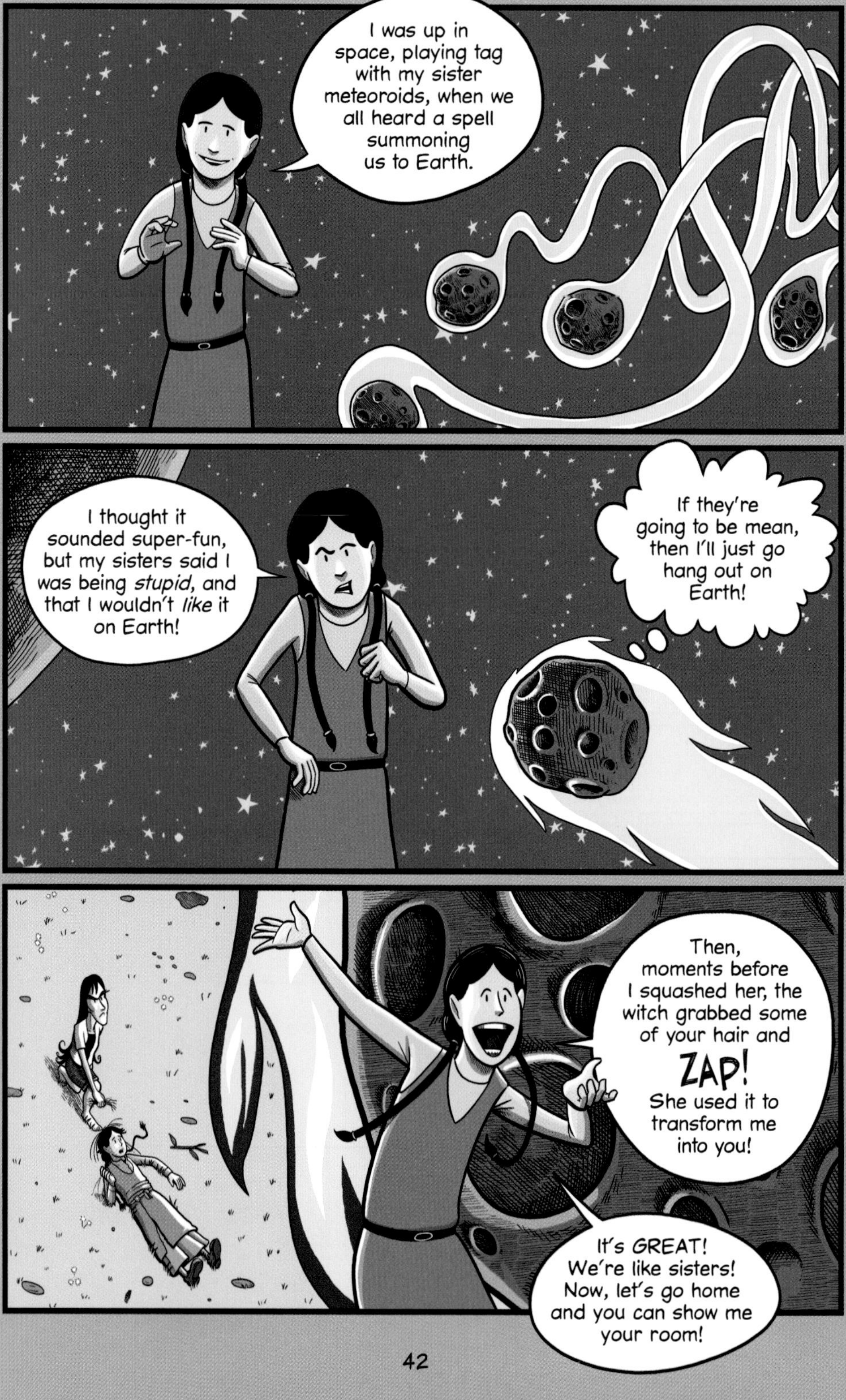
I was up in space, playing tag with my sister meteoroids, when we all heard a spell summoning us to Earth.
I thought it sounded super-fun, but my sisters said I was being *stupid*, and that I wouldn't *like* it on Earth!
If they're going to be mean, then I'll just go hang out on Earth!
Then, moments before I squashed her, the witch grabbed some of your hair and
ZAP!
She used it to transform me into you!
It's GREAT! We're like sisters! Now, let's go home and you can show me your room!

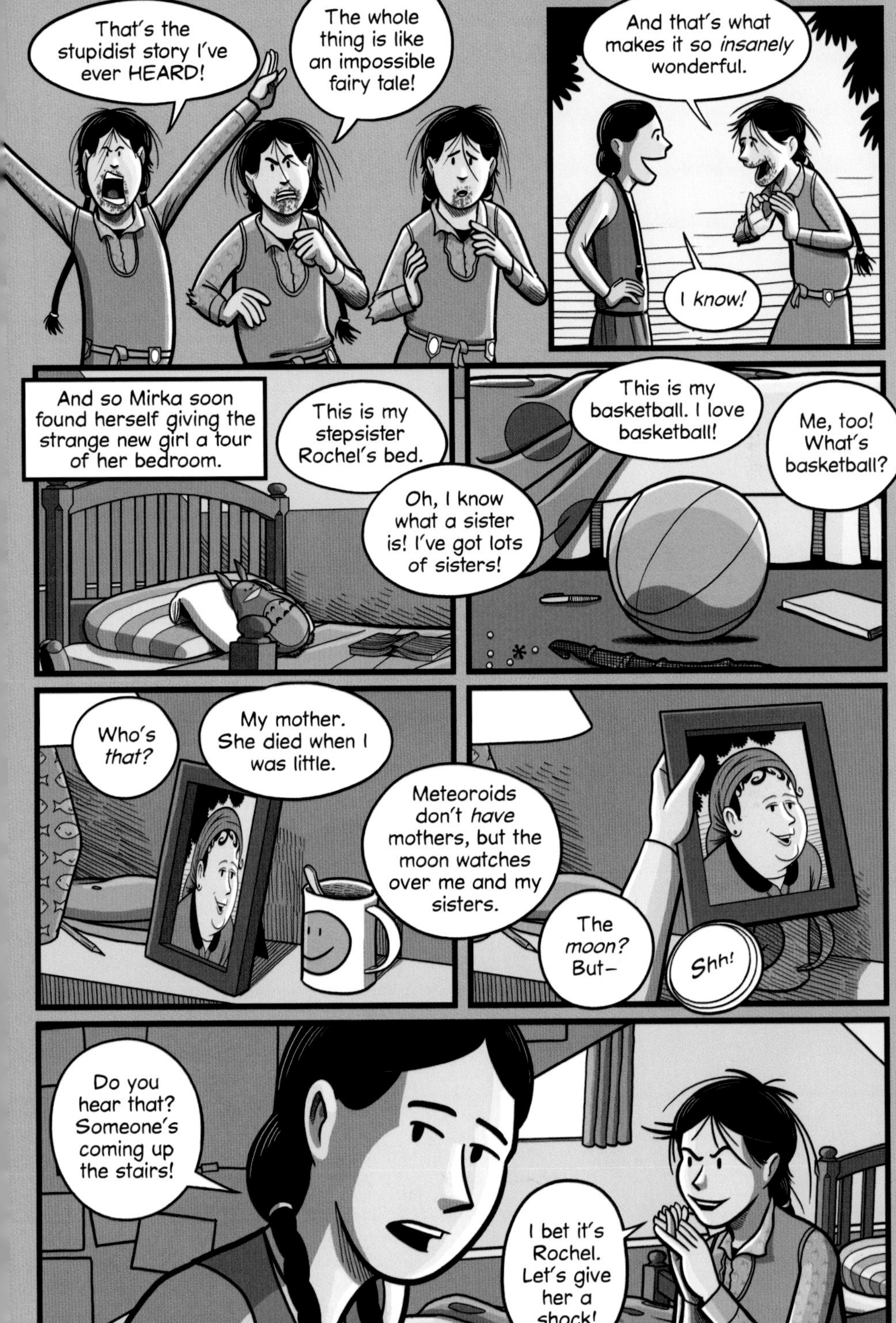

That's the stupidist story I've ever HEARD!
The whole thing is like an impossible fairy tale!
And that's what makes it so *insanely* wonderful.
I know!
And so Mirka soon found herself giving the strange new girl a tour of her bedroom.
This is my stepsister Rochel's bed.
Oh, I know what a sister is! I've got lots of sisters!
This is my basketball. I love basketball!
Me, too! What's basketball?
Who's *that?*
My mother. She died when I was little.
Meteoroids don't *have* mothers, but the moon watches over me and my sisters.
The *moon?* But–
Shh!
Do you hear that? Someone's coming up the stairs!
I bet it's Rochel. Let's give her a shock!

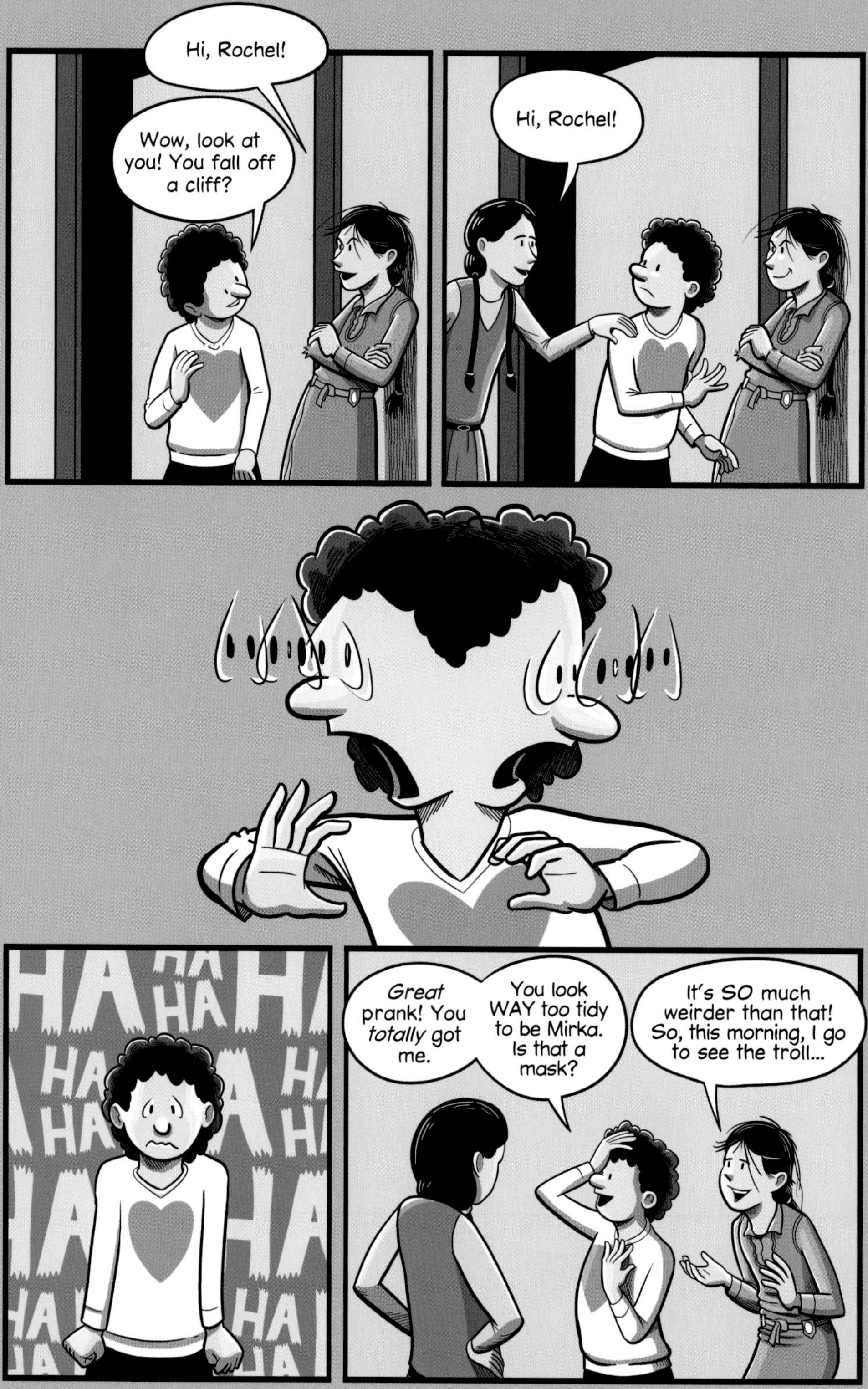
Hi, Rochel!
Wow, look at you! You fall off a cliff?
Hi, Rochel!
HA HA HA HA HA HA HA HA HA HA HA HA HA HA
Great prank! You *totally* got me.
You look WAY too tidy to be Mirka. Is that a mask?
It's SO much weirder than that! So, this morning, I go to see the troll...

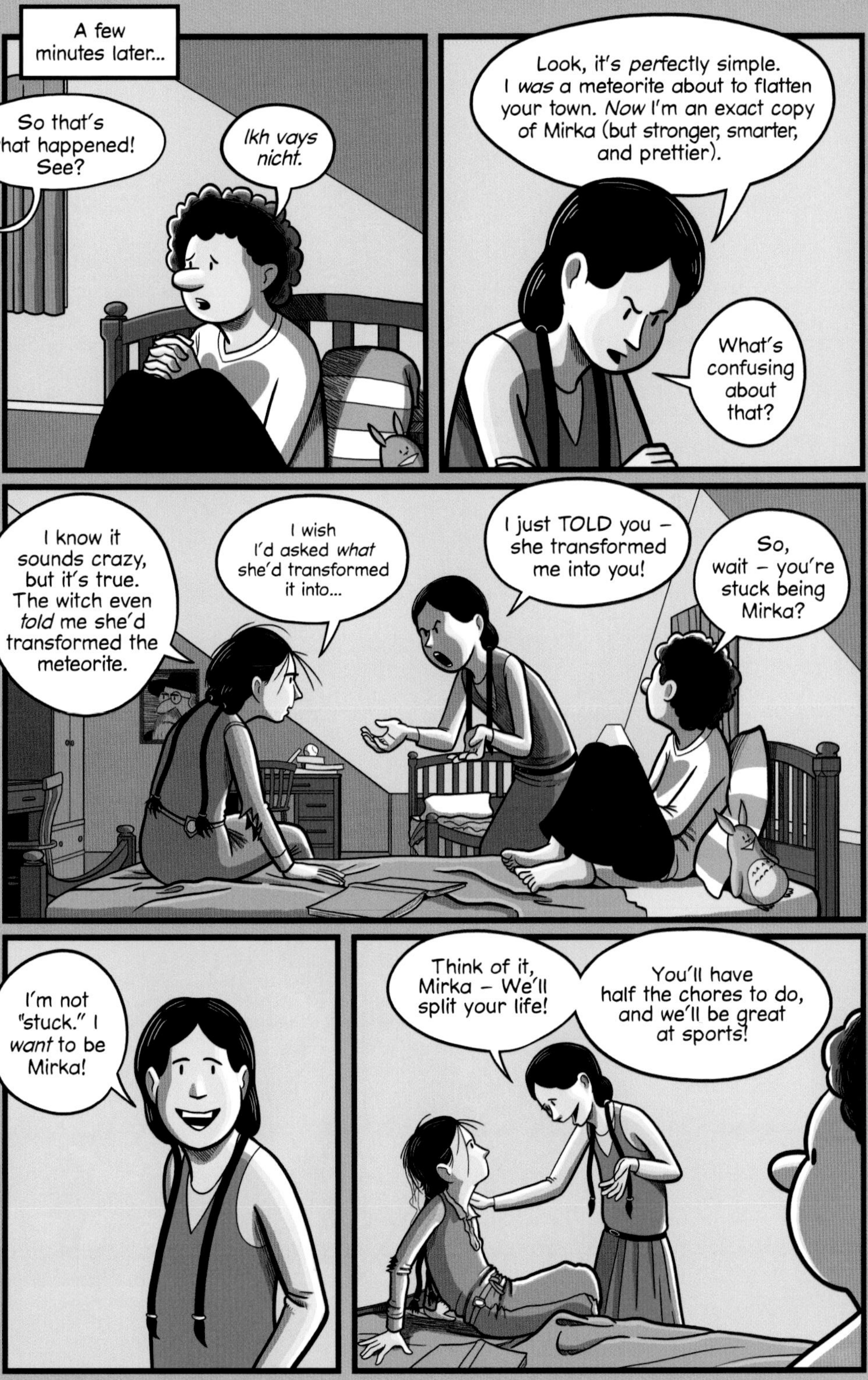
A few minutes later...
So that's what happened! See?
Ikh vays nicht.
Look, it's perfectly simple. I was a meteorite about to flatten your town. Now I'm an exact copy of Mirka (but stronger, smarter, and prettier).
What's confusing about that?
I know it sounds crazy, but it's true. The witch even told me she'd transformed the meteorite.
I wish I'd asked what she'd transformed it into...
I just TOLD you – she transformed me into you!
So, wait – you're stuck being Mirka?
I'm not "stuck." I want to be Mirka!
Think of it, Mirka – We'll split your life!
You'll have half the chores to do, and we'll be great at sports!

Ikh vays nicht: I don't know.

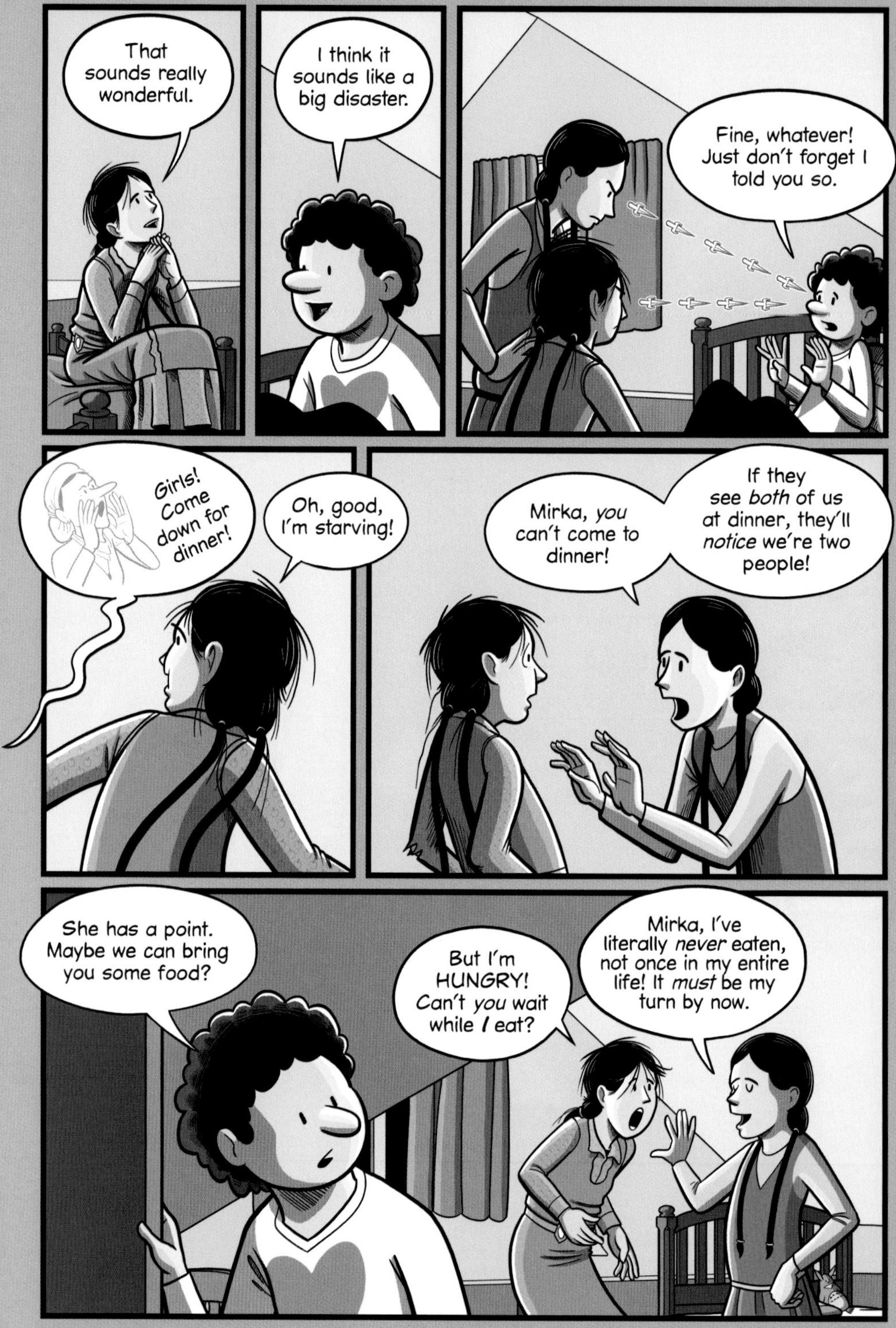
That sounds really wonderful.
I think it sounds like a big disaster.
Fine, whatever! Just don't forget I told you so.
Girls! Come down for dinner!
Oh, good, I'm starving!
Mirka, *you* can't come to dinner!
If they see *both* of us at dinner, they'll *notice* we're two people!
She has a point. Maybe we can bring you some food?
But I'm HUNGRY! Can't *you* wait while *I* eat?
Mirka, I've literally *never* eaten, not once in my entire life! It *must* be my turn by now.

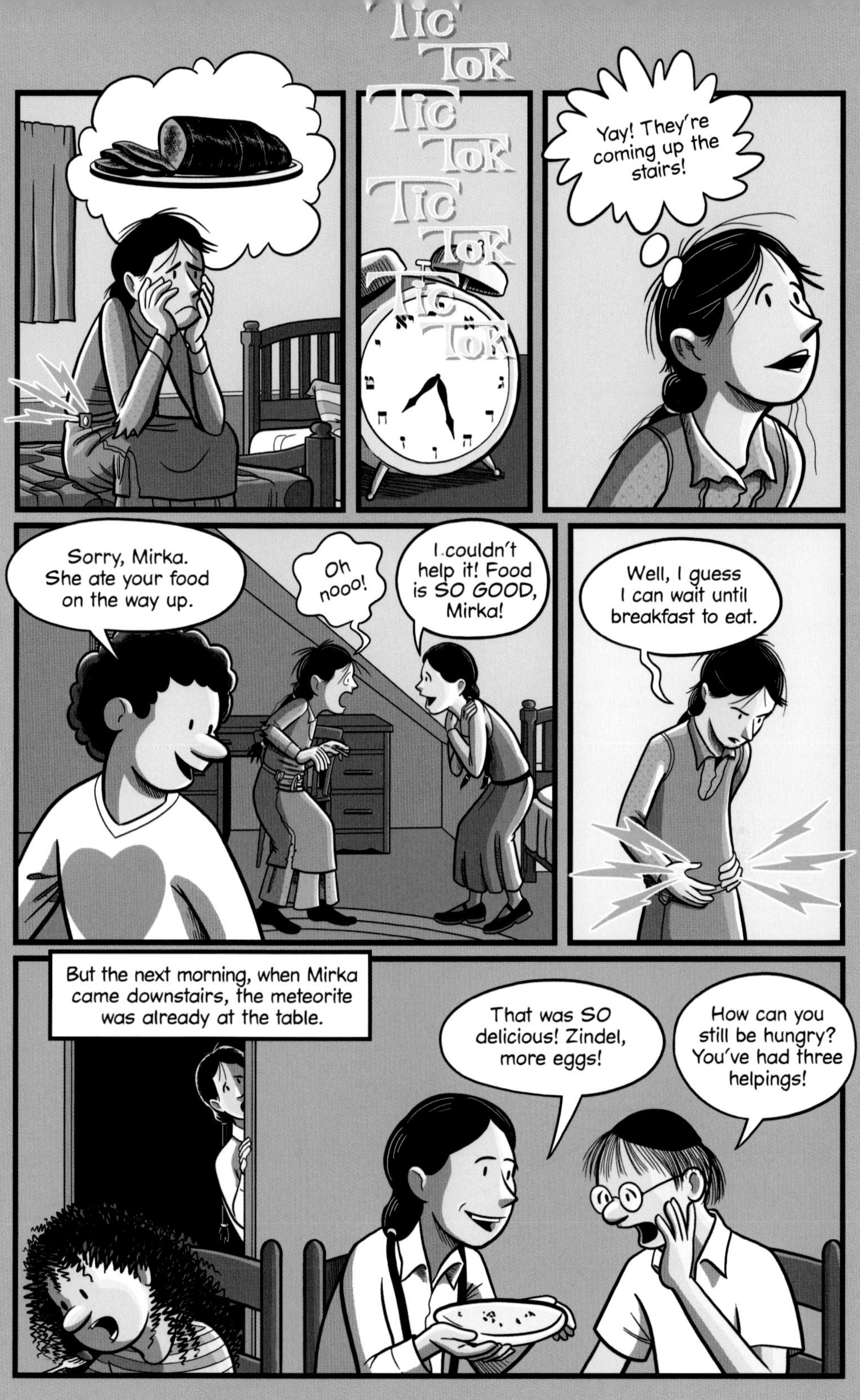
Tic
Tok
Tic
Tok
Tic
Tok
Tic
Tok
Yay! They're coming up the stairs!
Sorry, Mirka. She ate your food on the way up.
Oh nooo!
I couldn't help it! Food is SO GOOD, Mirka!
Well, I guess I can wait until breakfast to eat.
But the next morning, when Mirka came downstairs, the meteorite was already at the table.
That was SO delicious! Zindel, more eggs!
How can you still be hungry? You've had three helpings!

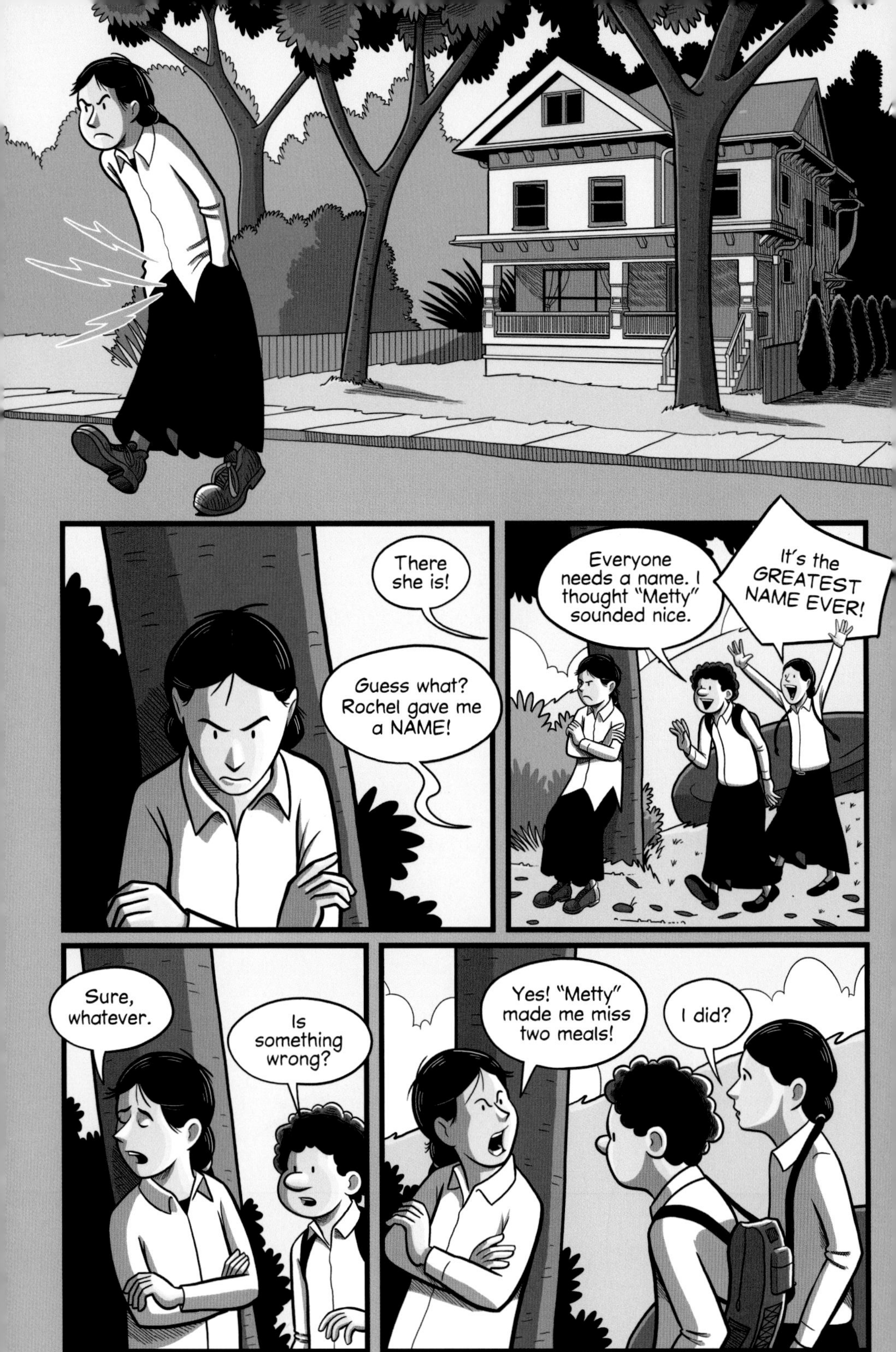
There she is!
Guess what? Rochel gave me a NAME!
Everyone needs a name. I thought "Metty" sounded nice.
It's the GREATEST NAME EVER!
Sure, whatever.
Is something wrong?
Yes! "Metty" made me miss two meals!
I did?

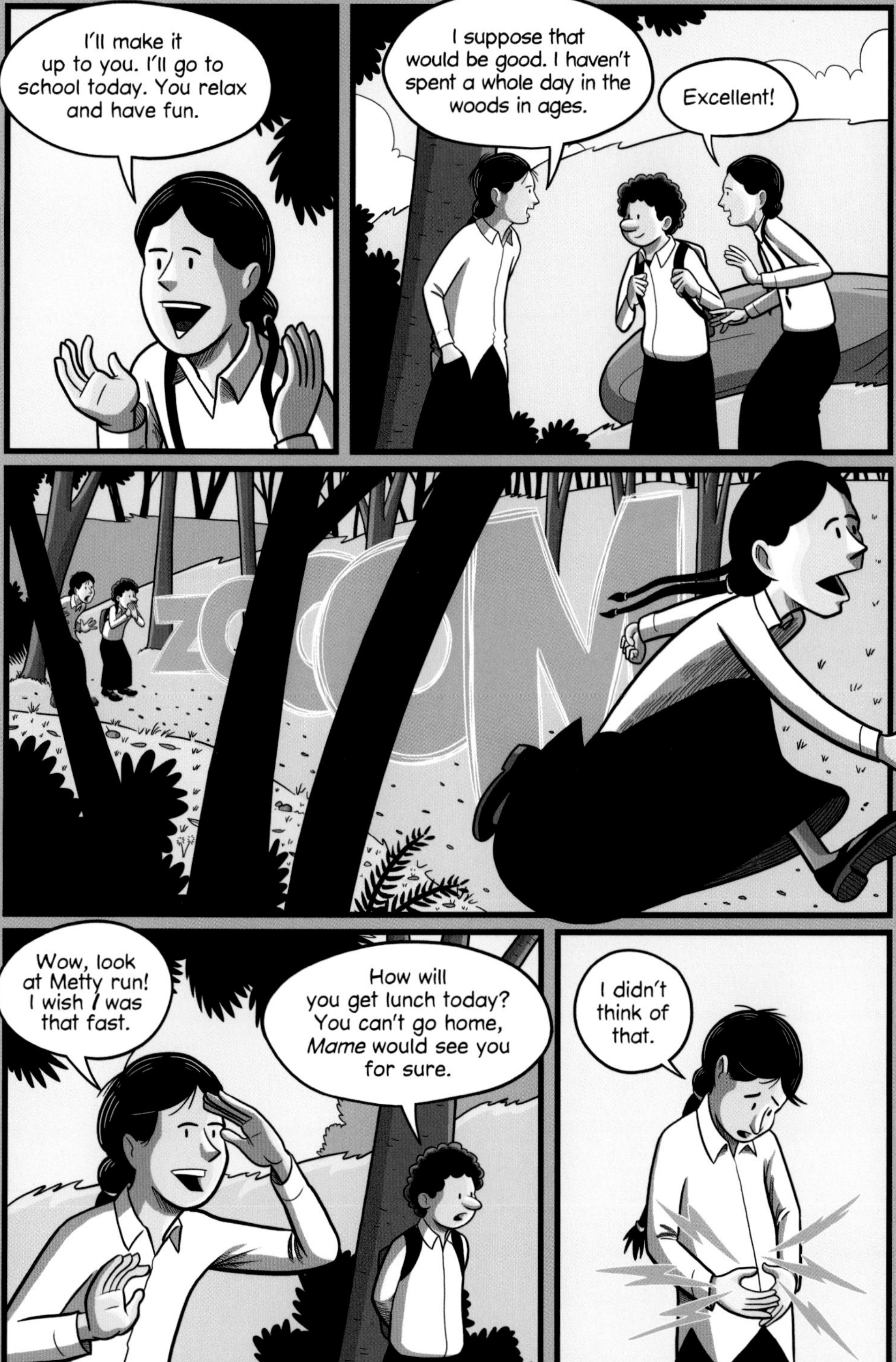
I'll make it up to you. I'll go to school today. You relax and have fun.
I suppose that would be good. I haven't spent a whole day in the woods in ages.
Excellent!
ZOOM
Wow, look at Metty run! I wish *I* was that fast.
How will you get lunch today? You can't go home, *Mame* would see you for sure.
I didn't think of that.

Mame: Mom

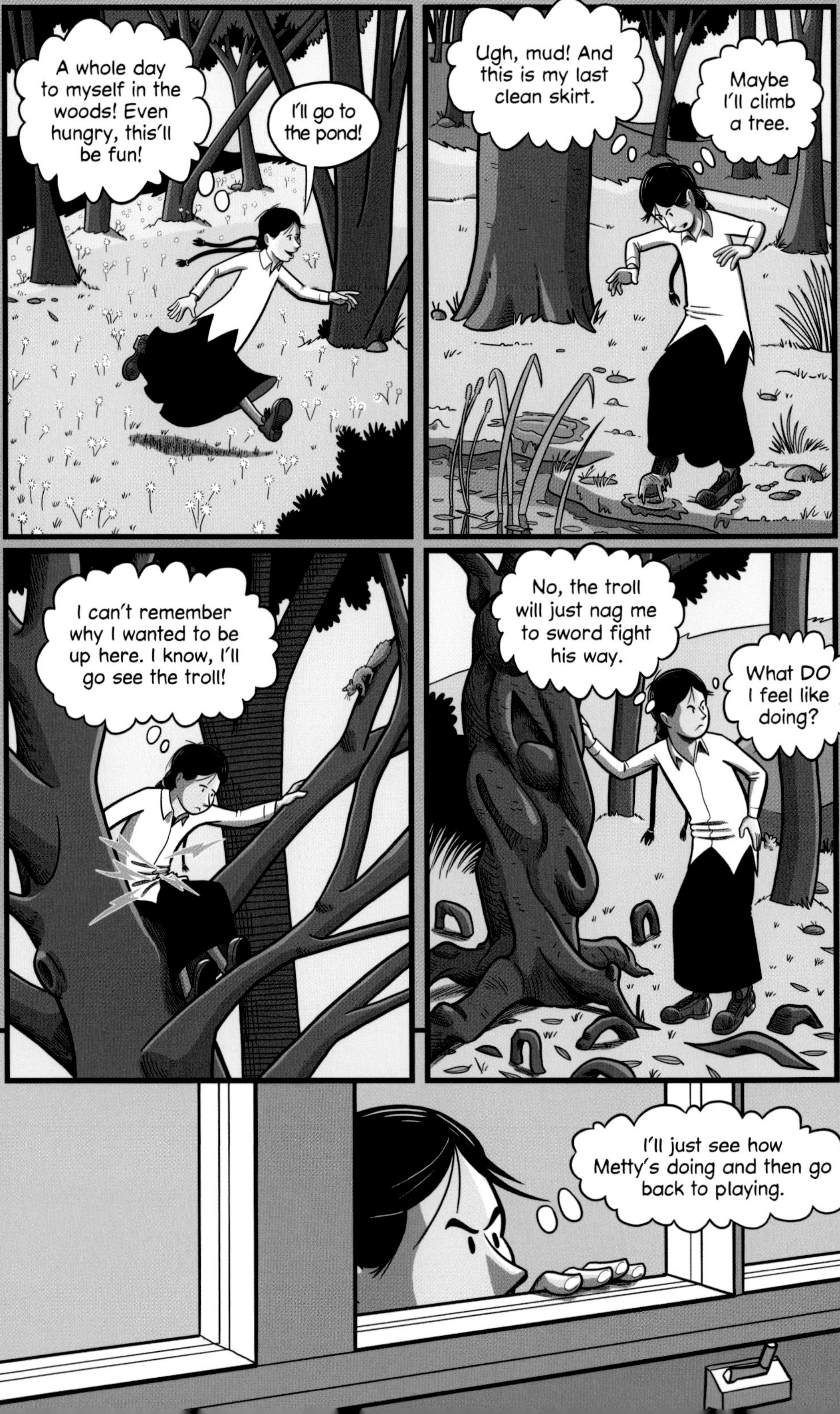

A whole day to myself in the woods! Even hungry, this'll be fun!
I'll go to the pond!
Ugh, mud! And this is my last clean skirt.
Maybe I'll climb a tree.
I can't remember why I wanted to be up here. I know, I'll go see the troll!
No, the troll will just nag me to sword fight his way.
What DO I feel like doing?
I'll just see how Metty's doing and then go back to playing.

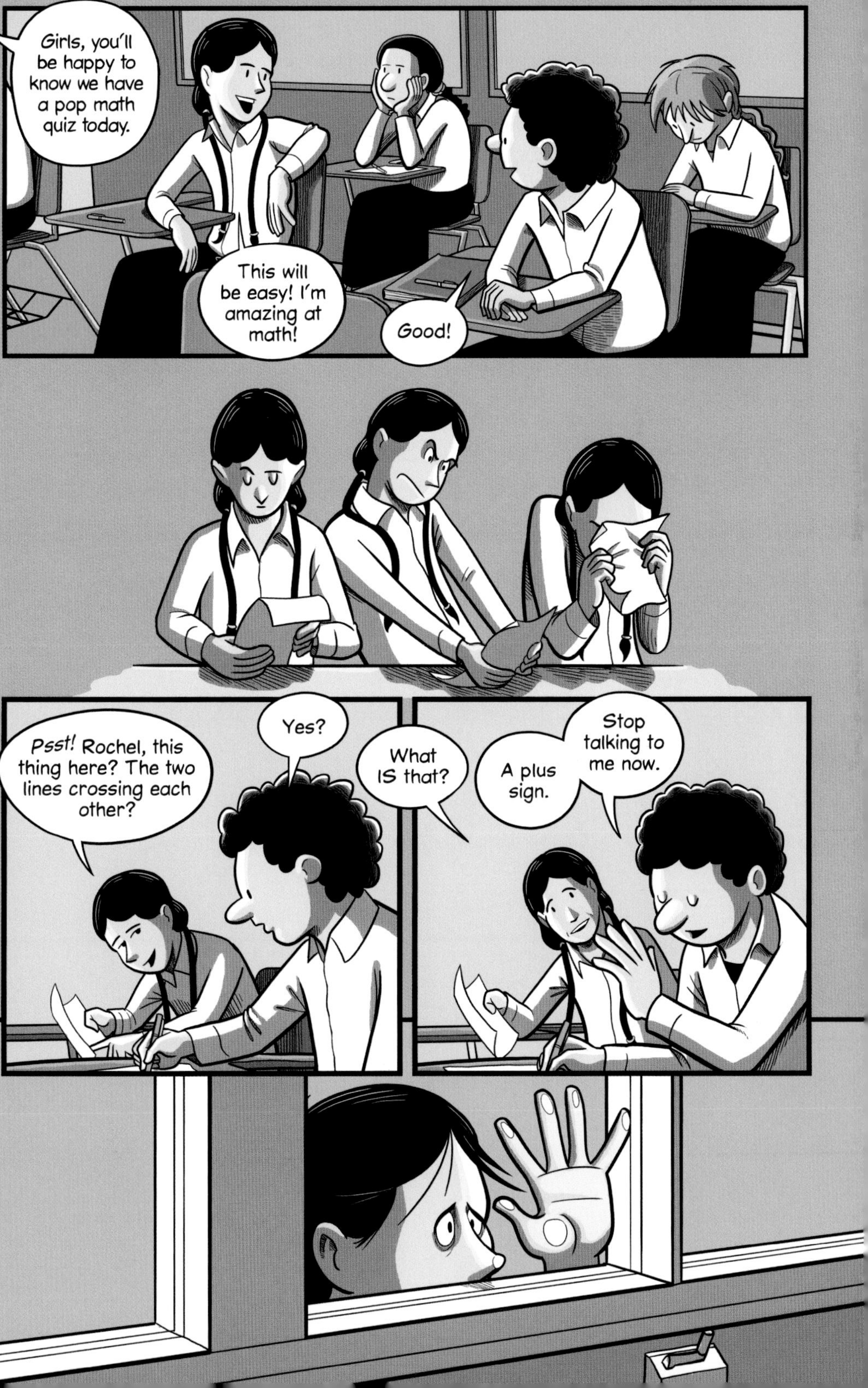
Girls, you'll be happy to know we have a pop math quiz today.
This will be easy! I'm amazing at math!
Good!
Psst! Rochel, this thing here? The two lines crossing each other?
Yes?
What IS that?
A plus sign.
Stop talking to me now.

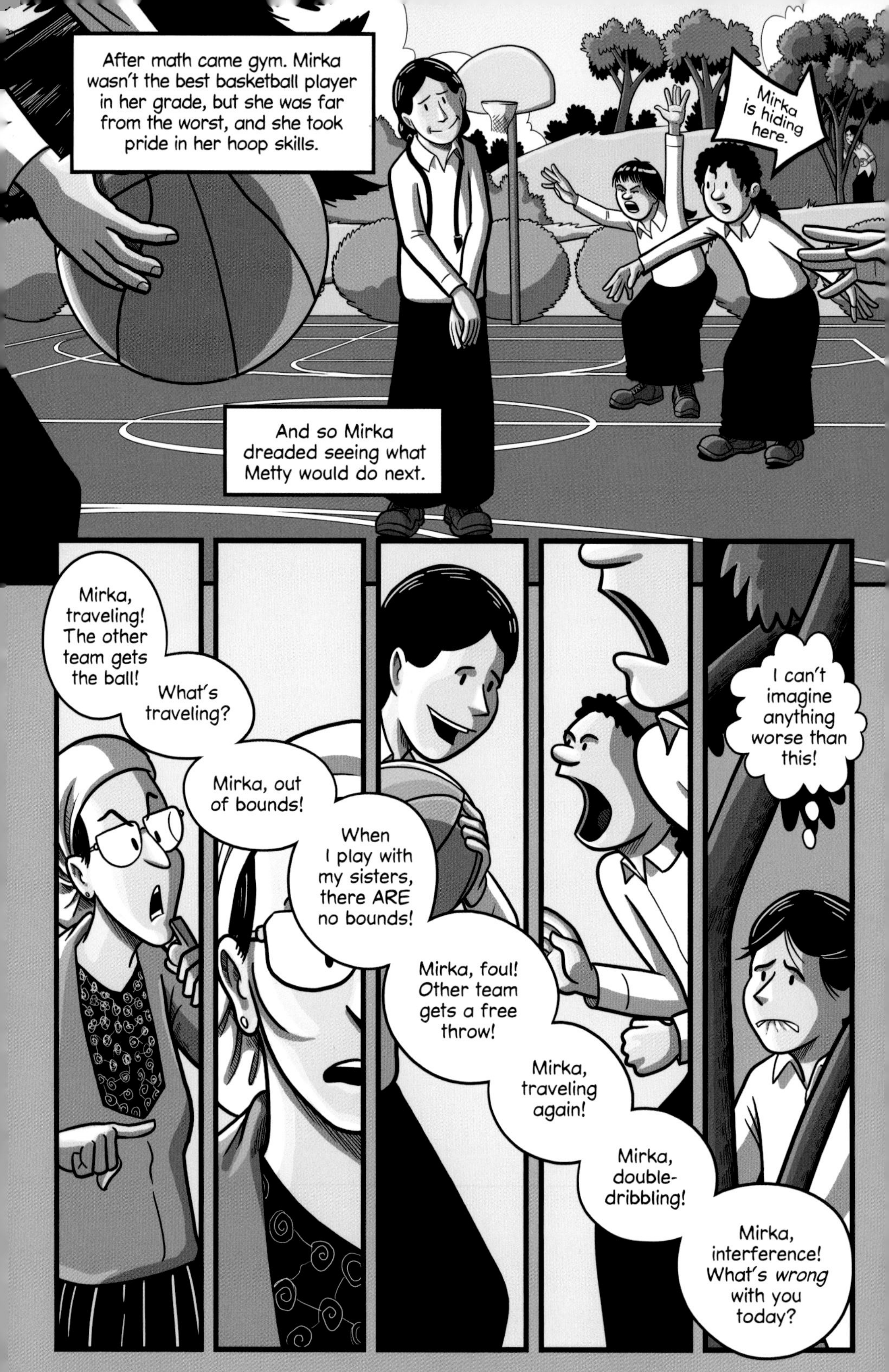
After math came gym. Mirka wasn't the best basketball player in her grade, but she was far from the worst, and she took pride in her hoop skills.
Mirka is hiding here.
And so Mirka dreaded seeing what Metty would do next.
Mirka, traveling! The other team gets the ball!
What's traveling?
Mirka, out of bounds!
When I play with my sisters, there ARE no bounds!
Mirka, foul! Other team gets a free throw!
Mirka, traveling again!
Mirka, double-dribbling!
I can't imagine anything worse than this!
Mirka, interference! What's *wrong* with you today?

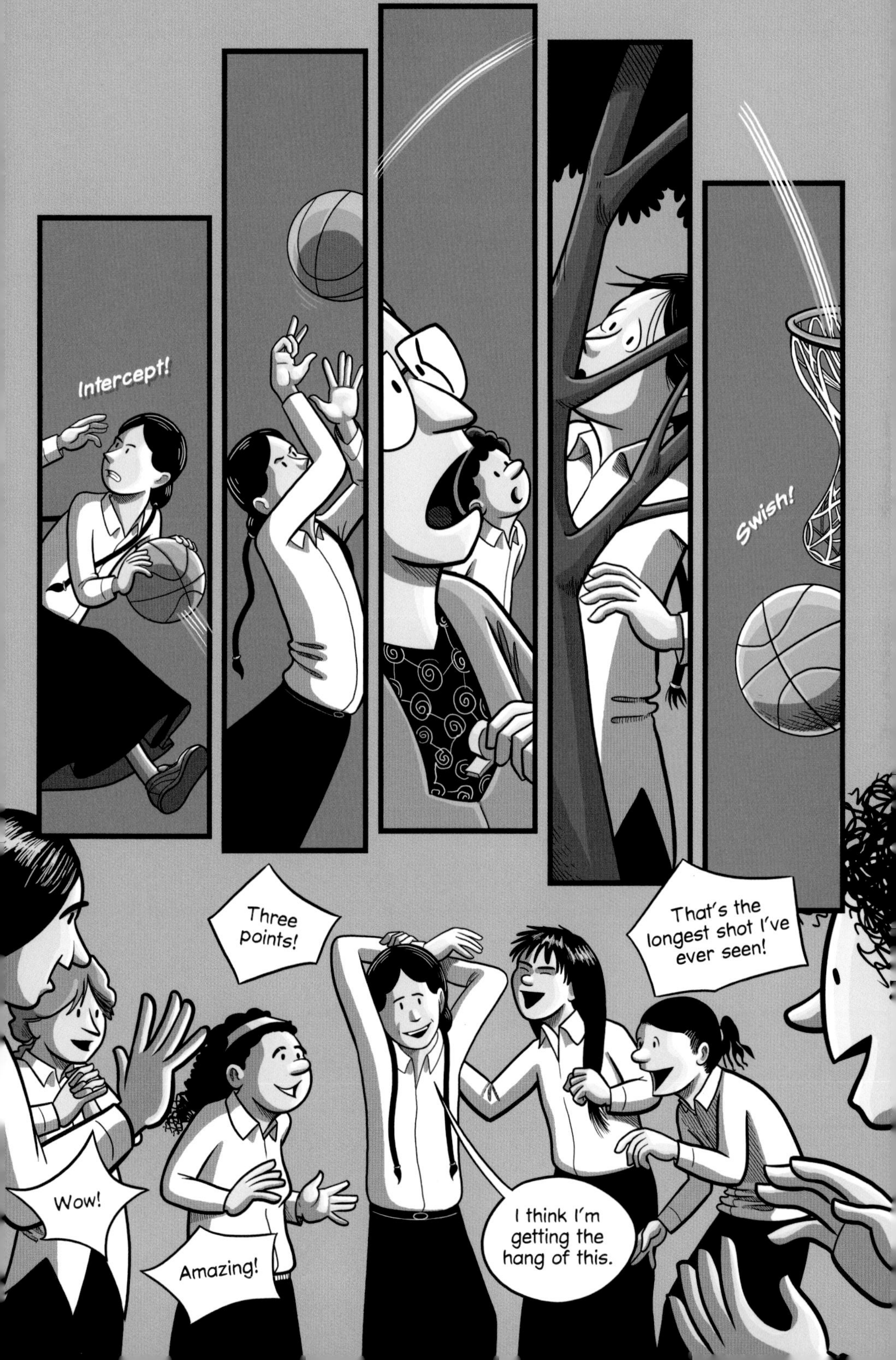
Intercept!
Swish!
Three points!
That's the longest shot I've ever seen!
Wow!
Amazing!
I think I'm getting the hang of this.

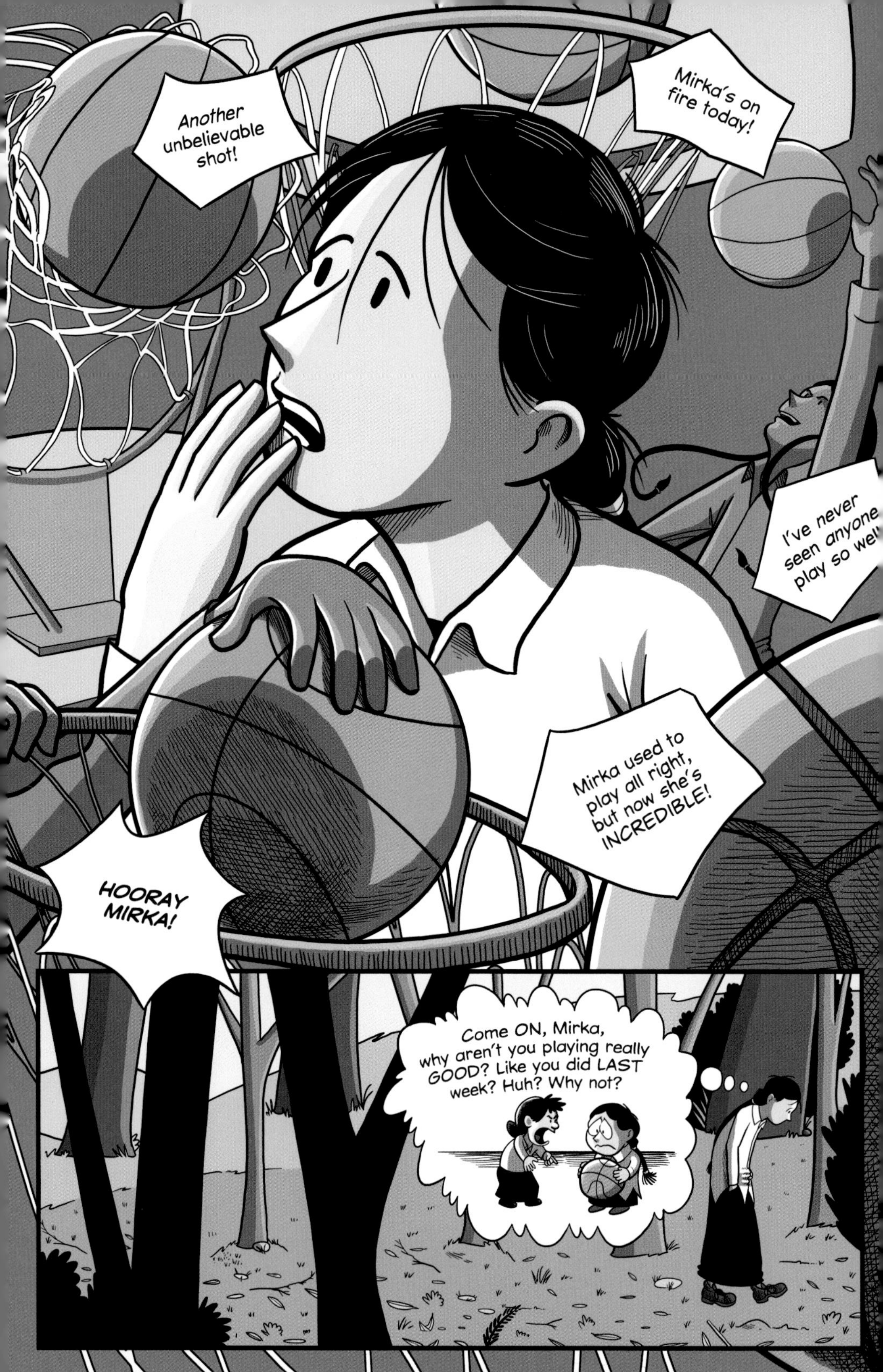

Another unbelievable shot!
Mirka's on fire today!
I've never seen anyone play so well
Mirka used to play all right, but now she's INCREDIBLE!
HOORAY MIRKA!
Come ON, Mirka, why aren't you playing really GOOD? Like you did LAST week? Huh? Why not?

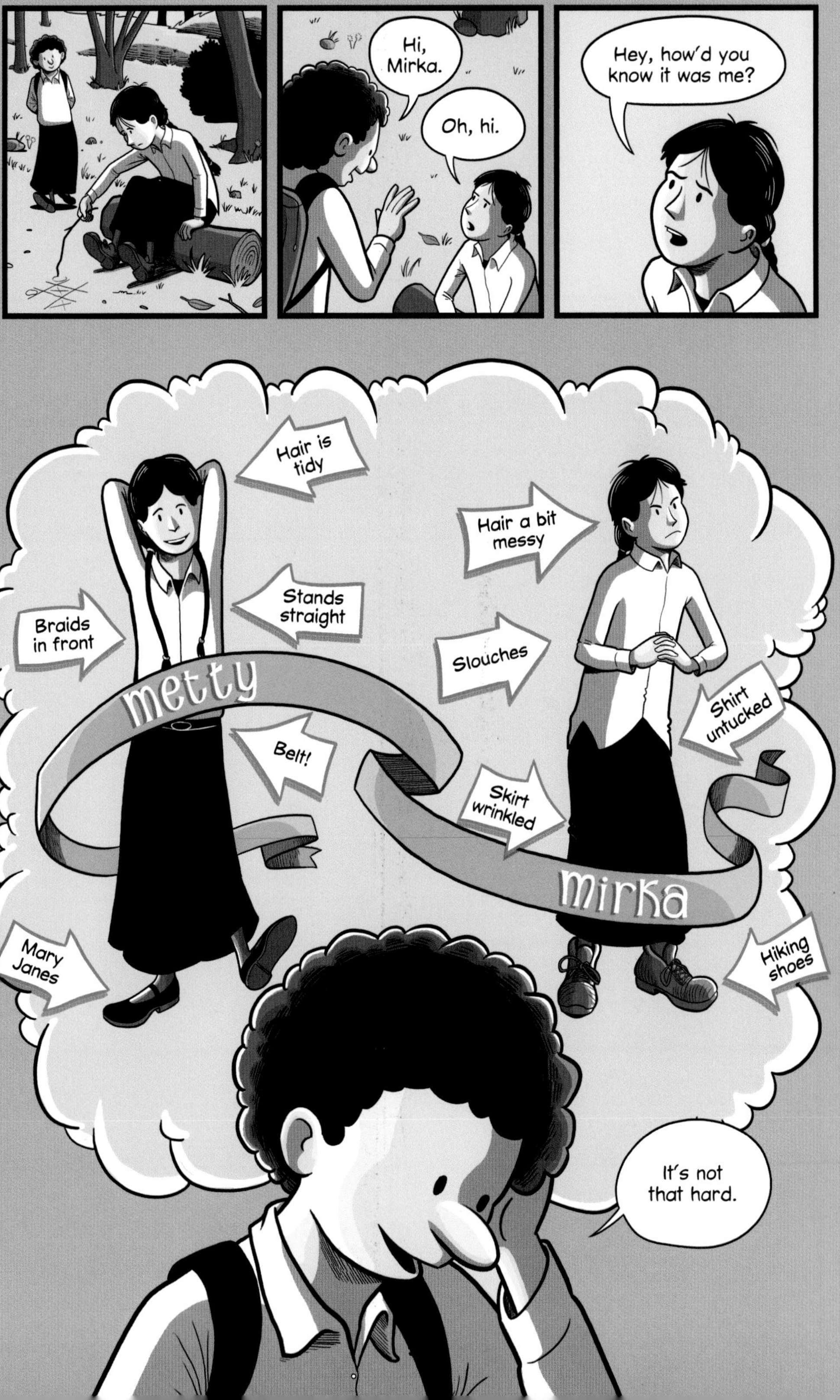
Hi, Mirka.
Oh, hi.
Hey, how'd you know it was me?
Hair is tidy
Stands straight
Braids in front
Belt!
Mary Janes
Hair a bit messy
Slouches
Shirt untucked
Skirt wrinkled
Hiking shoes
metty
mirka
It's not that hard.

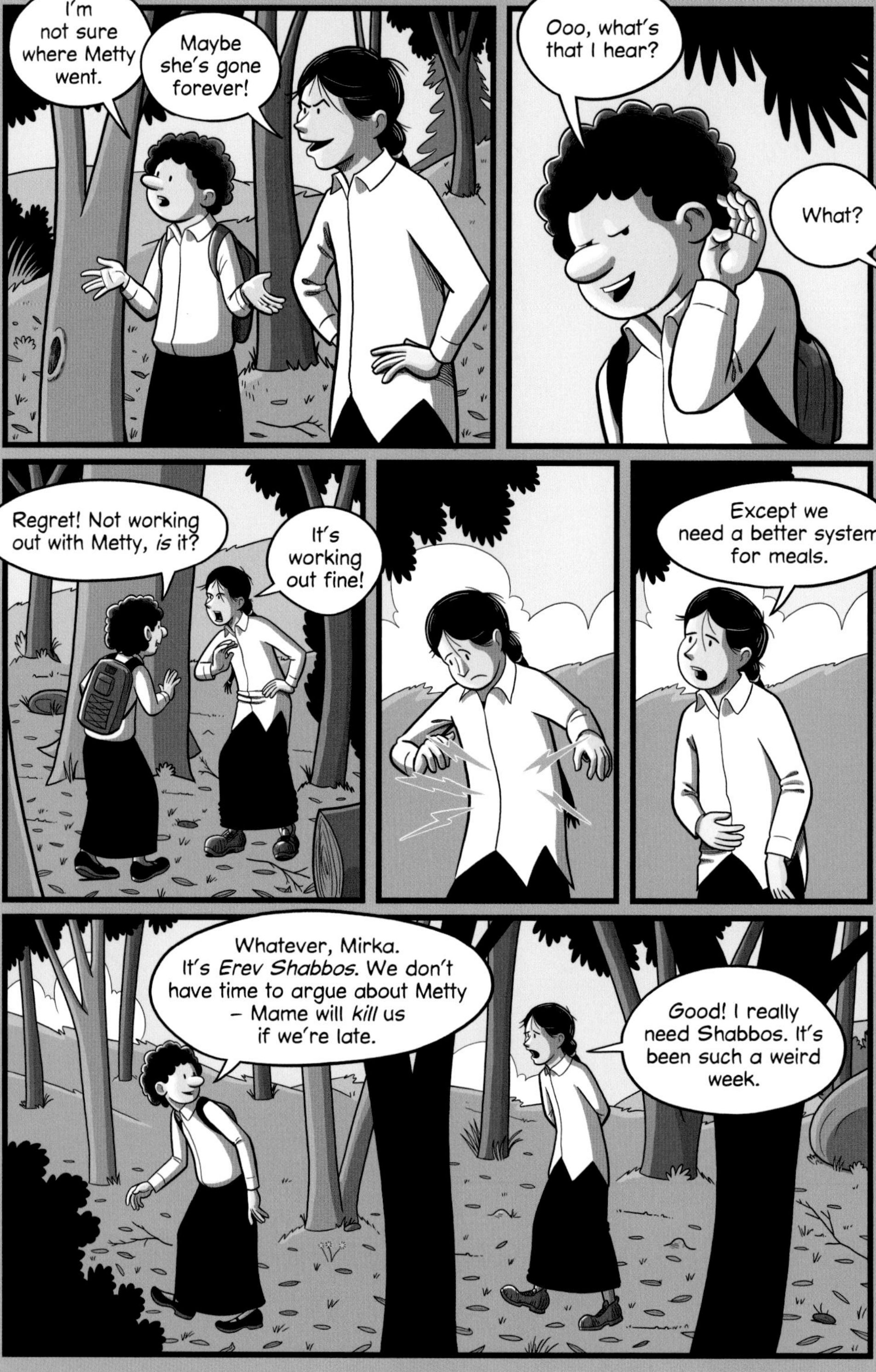
I'm not sure where Metty went.
Maybe she's gone forever!
Ooo, what's that I hear?
What?
Regret! Not working out with Metty, *is* it?
It's working out fine!
Except we need a better system for meals.
Whatever, Mirka. It's *Erev Shabbos*. We don't have time to argue about Metty – Mame will *kill* us if we're late.
Good! I really need Shabbos. It's been such a weird week.

Erev Shabbos: Friday

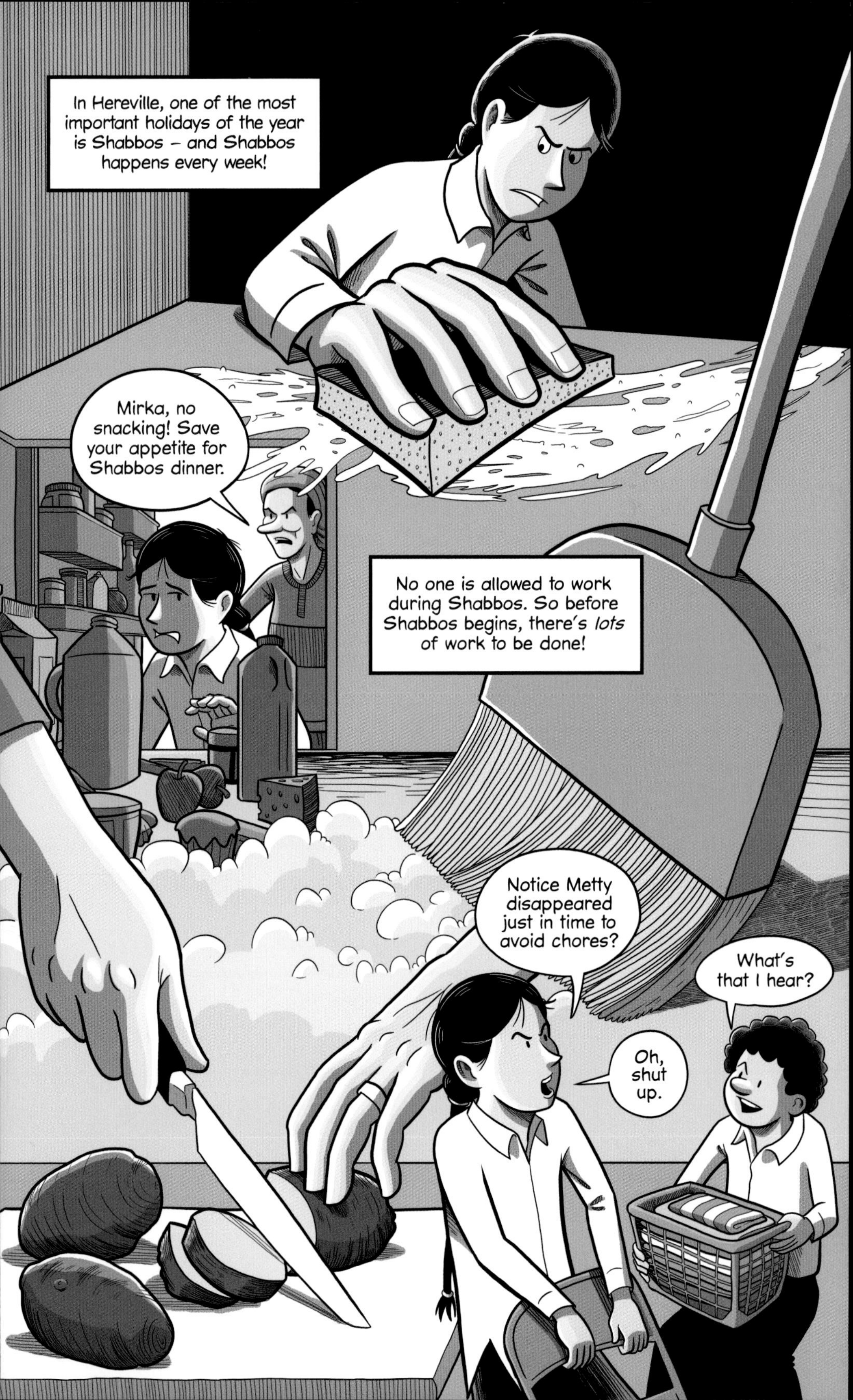
In Hereville, one of the most important holidays of the year is Shabbos – and Shabbos happens every week!
Mirka, no snacking! Save your appetite for Shabbos dinner.
No one is allowed to work during Shabbos. So before Shabbos begins, there's *lots* of work to be done!
Notice Metty disappeared just in time to avoid chores?
What's that I hear?
Oh, shut up.

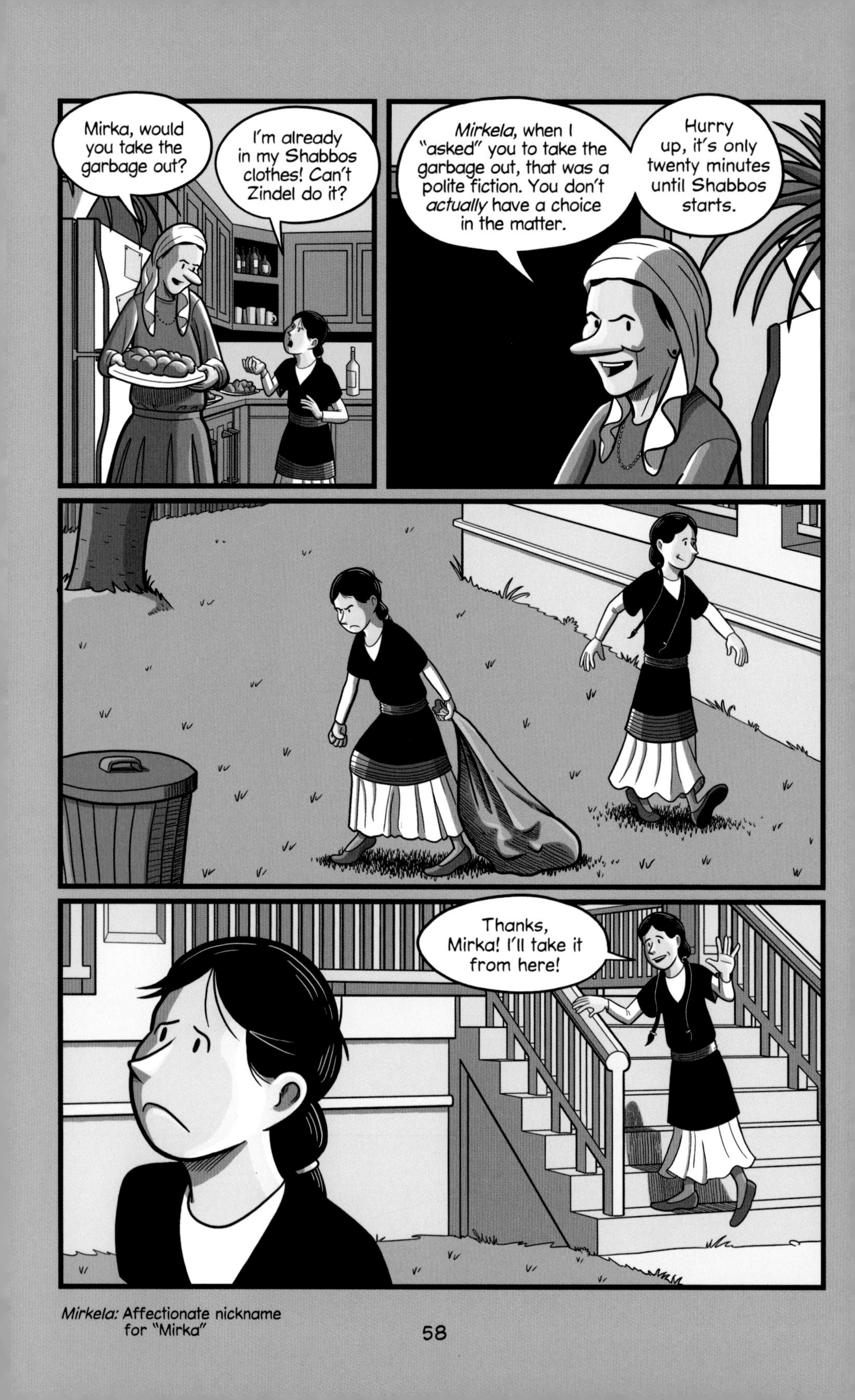
Mirka, would you take the garbage out?
I'm already in my Shabbos clothes! Can't Zindel do it?
Mirkela, when I "asked" you to take the garbage out, that was a polite fiction. You don't *actually* have a choice in the matter.
Hurry up, it's only twenty minutes until Shabbos starts.
Thanks, Mirka! I'll take it from here!

Mirkela: Affectionate nickname for "Mirka"

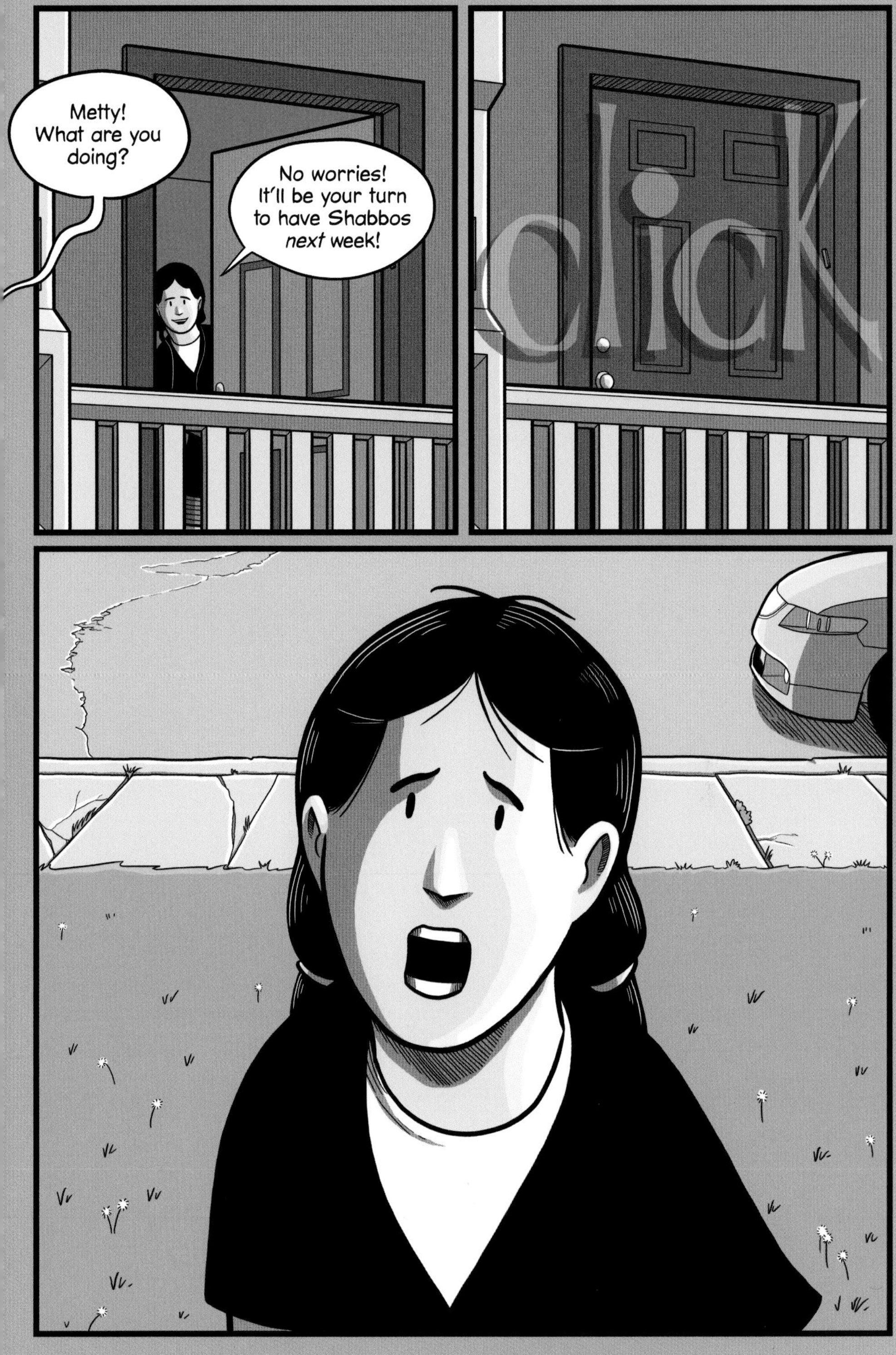
Metty! What are you doing?
No worries! It'll be your turn to have Shabbos *next* week!
click

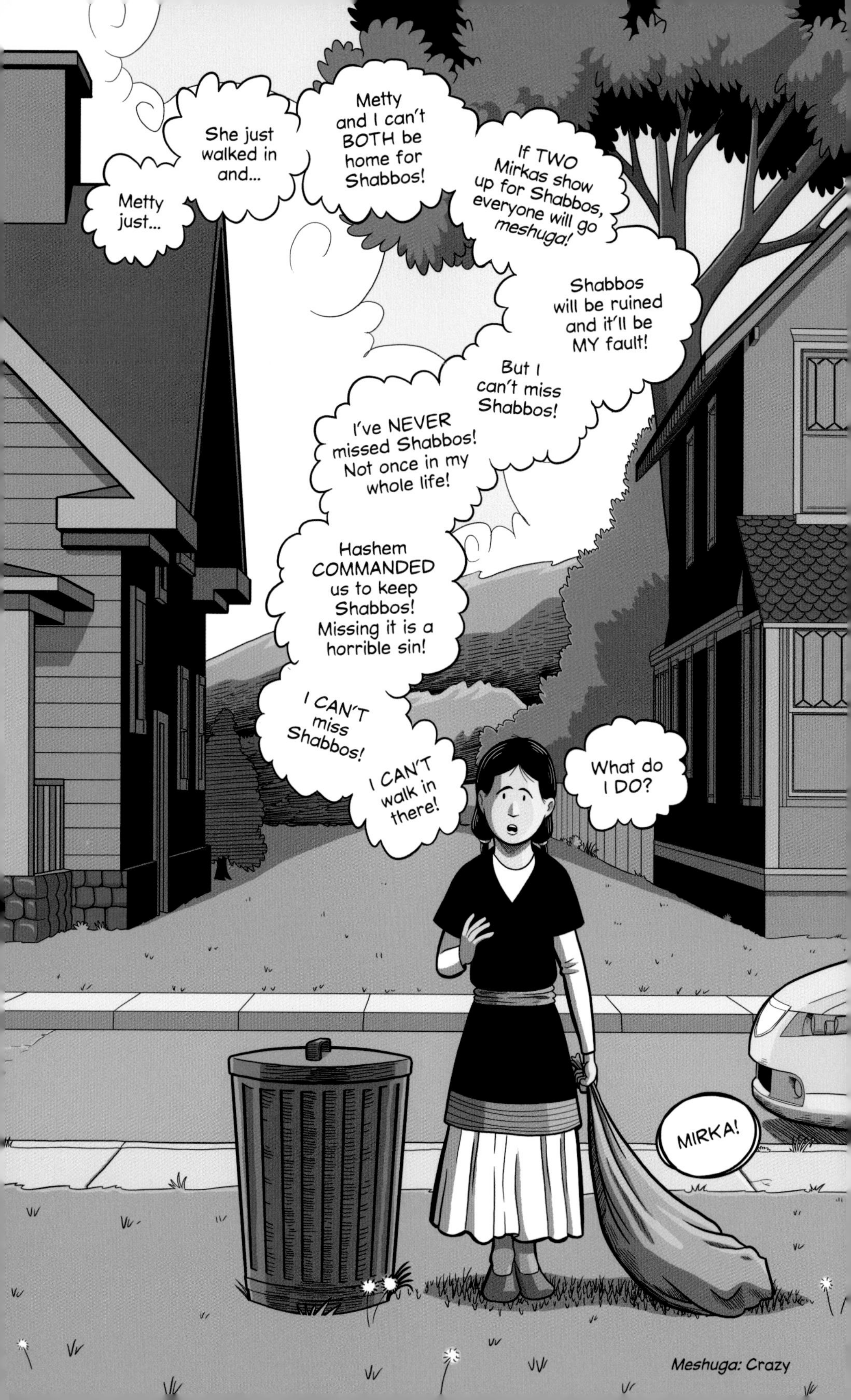
Metty just...
She just walked in and...
Metty and I can't BOTH be home for Shabbos!
If TWO Mirkas show up for Shabbos, everyone will go meshuga!
Shabbos will be ruined and it'll be MY fault!
But I can't miss Shabbos!
I've NEVER missed Shabbos! Not once in my whole life!
Hashem COMMANDED us to keep Shabbos! Missing it is a horrible sin!
I CAN'T miss Shabbos!
I CAN'T walk in there!
What do I DO?
MIRKA!

Meshuga: Crazy

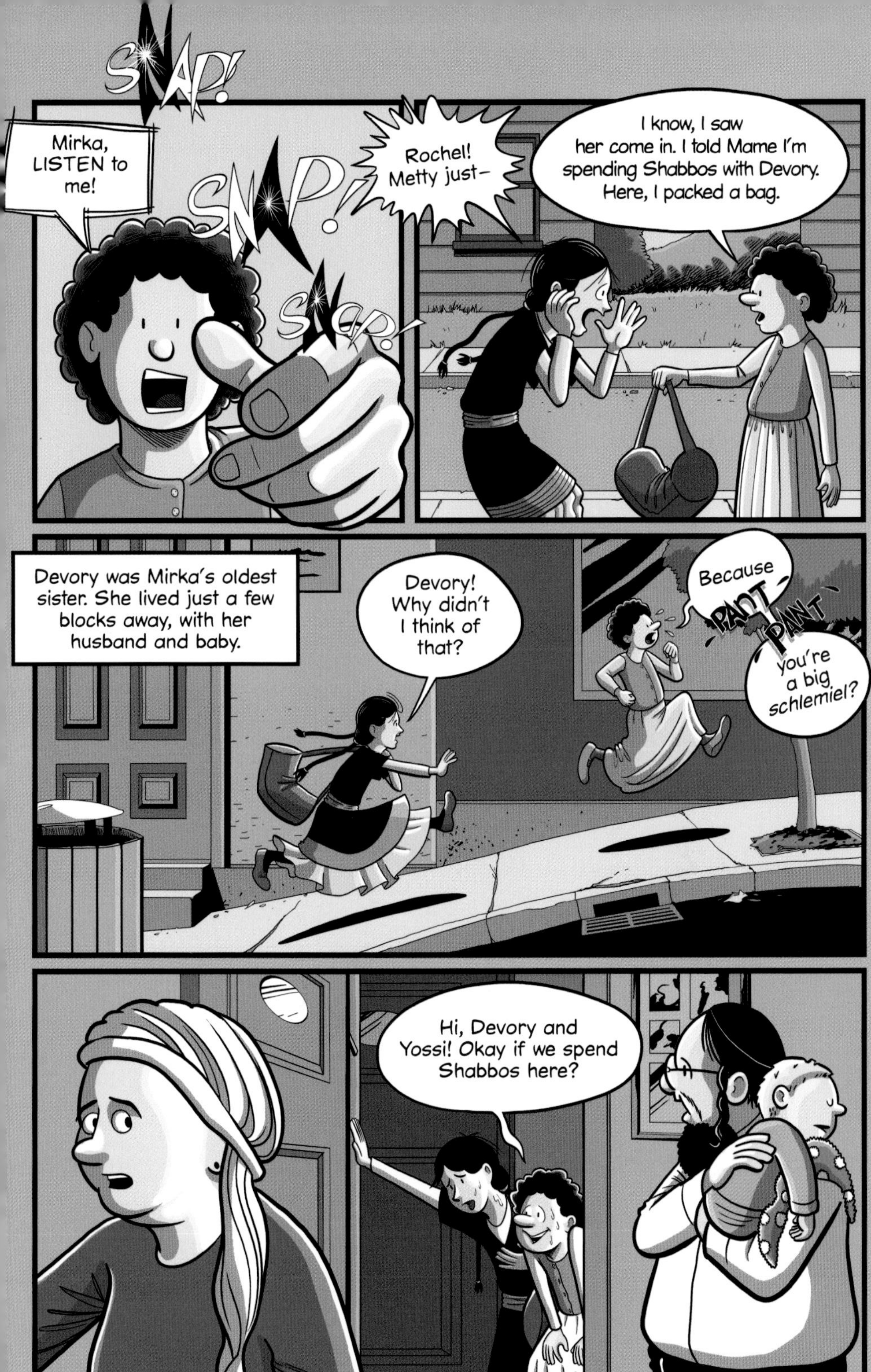
SNAP!
Mirka, LISTEN to me!
SNAP!
SNAP!
Rochel! Metty just–
I know, I saw her come in. I told Mame I'm spending Shabbos with Devory. Here, I packed a bag.
Devory was Mirka's oldest sister. She lived just a few blocks away, with her husband and baby.
Devory! Why didn't I think of that?
Because
PANT PANT
you're a big schlemiel?
Hi, Devory and Yossi! Okay if we spend Shabbos here?

Schlemiel: A stupid, awkward person

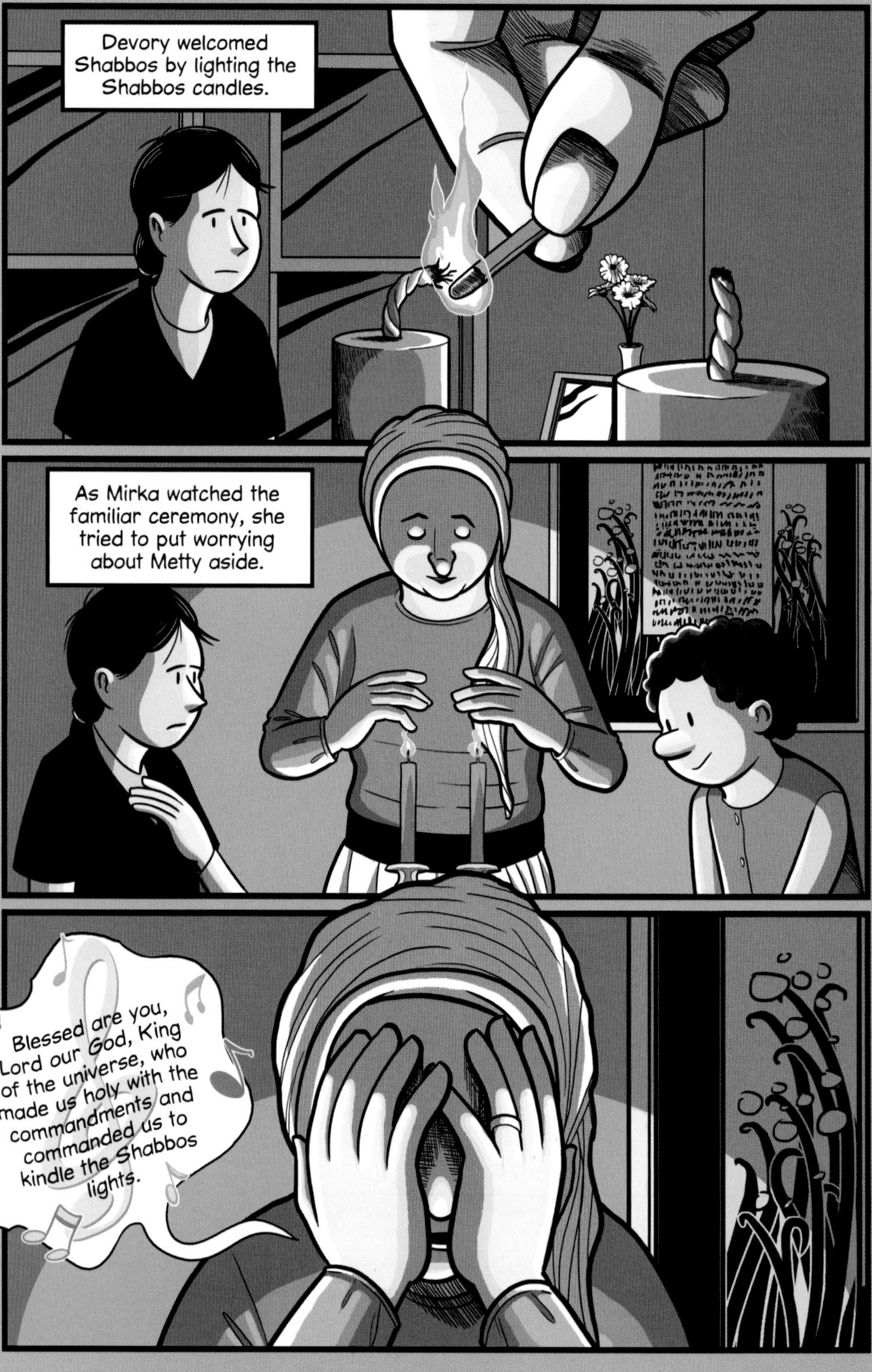
Devory welcomed Shabbos by lighting the Shabbos candles.
As Mirka watched the familiar ceremony, she tried to put worrying about Metty aside.
Blessed are you, Lord our God, King of the universe, who made us holy with the commandments and commanded us to kindle the Shabbos lights.

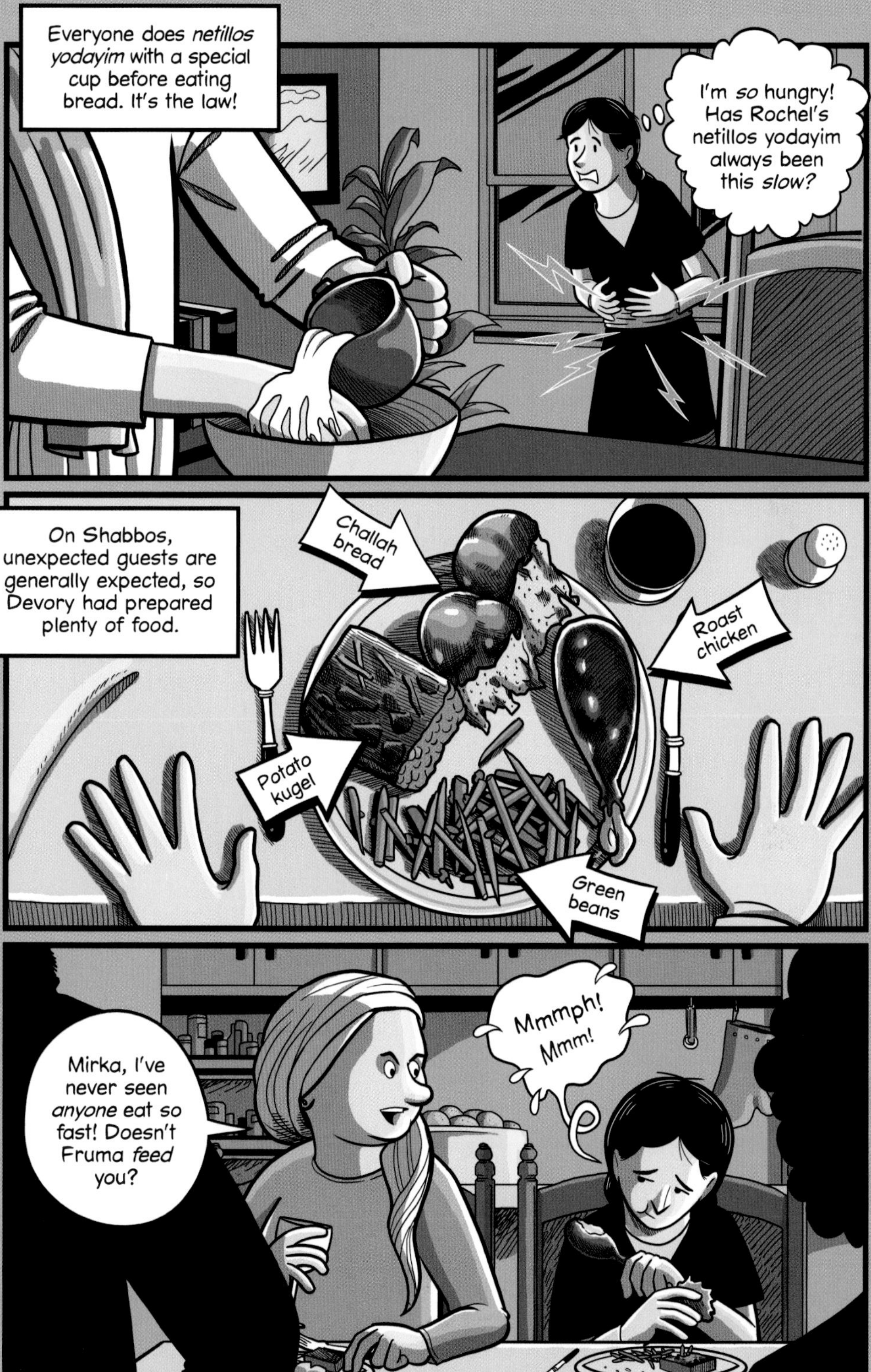
Everyone does *netillos yodayim* with a special cup before eating bread. It's the law!
I'm *so* hungry! Has Rochel's netillos yodayim always been this *slow?*
On Shabbos, unexpected guests are generally expected, so Devory had prepared plenty of food.
Challah bread
Roast chicken
Potato kugel
Green beans
Mirka, I've never seen *anyone* eat so fast! Doesn't Fruma *feed* you?
Mmmph! Mmm!

Netillos yodayim: Handwashing

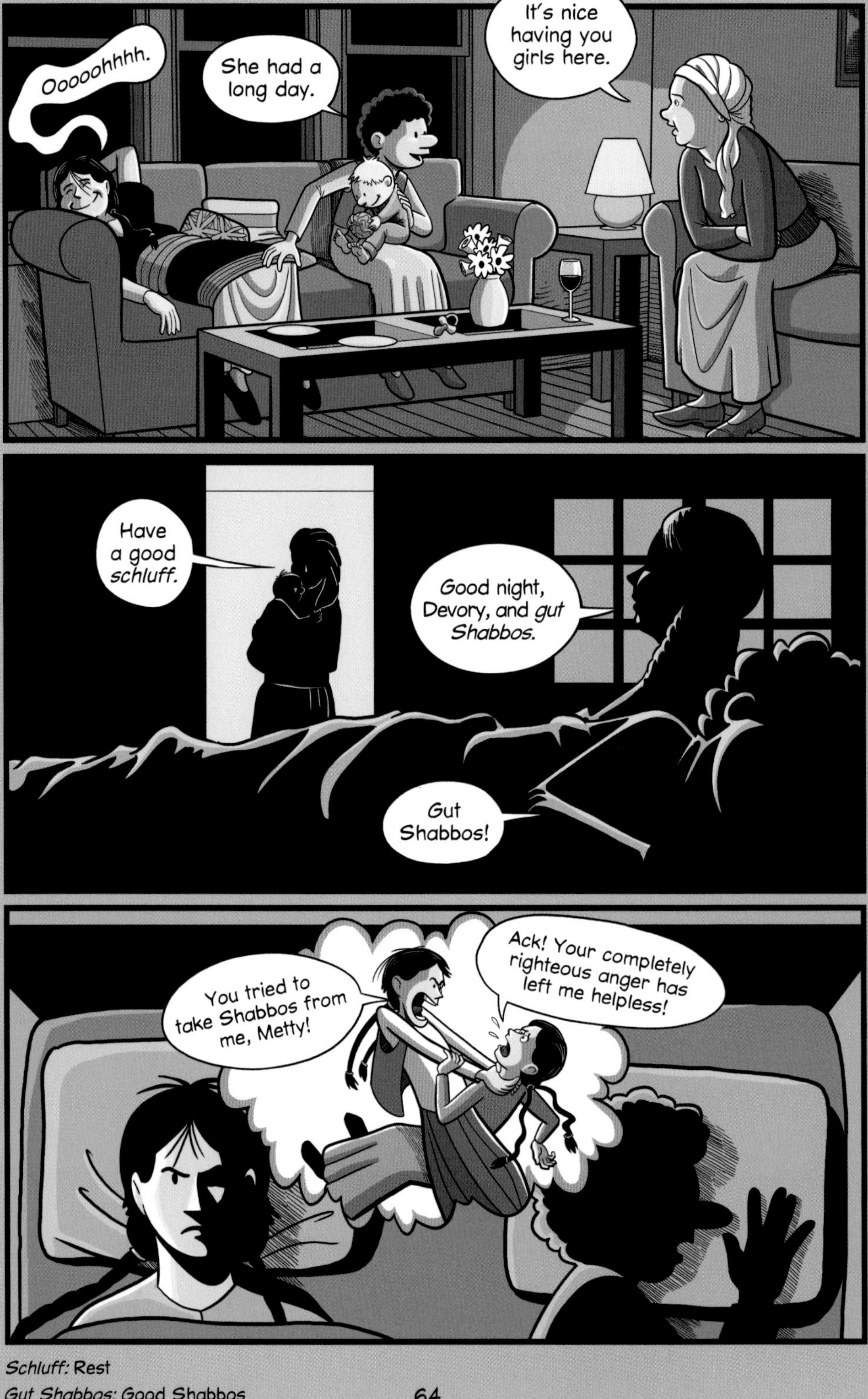
Ooooohhhh.
She had a long day.
It's nice having you girls here.
Have a good *schluff.*
Good night, Devory, and *gut Shabbos.*
Gut Shabbos!
You tried to take Shabbos from me, Metty!
Ack! Your completely righteous anger has left me helpless!

Schluff: Rest

Gut Shabbos: Good Shabbos

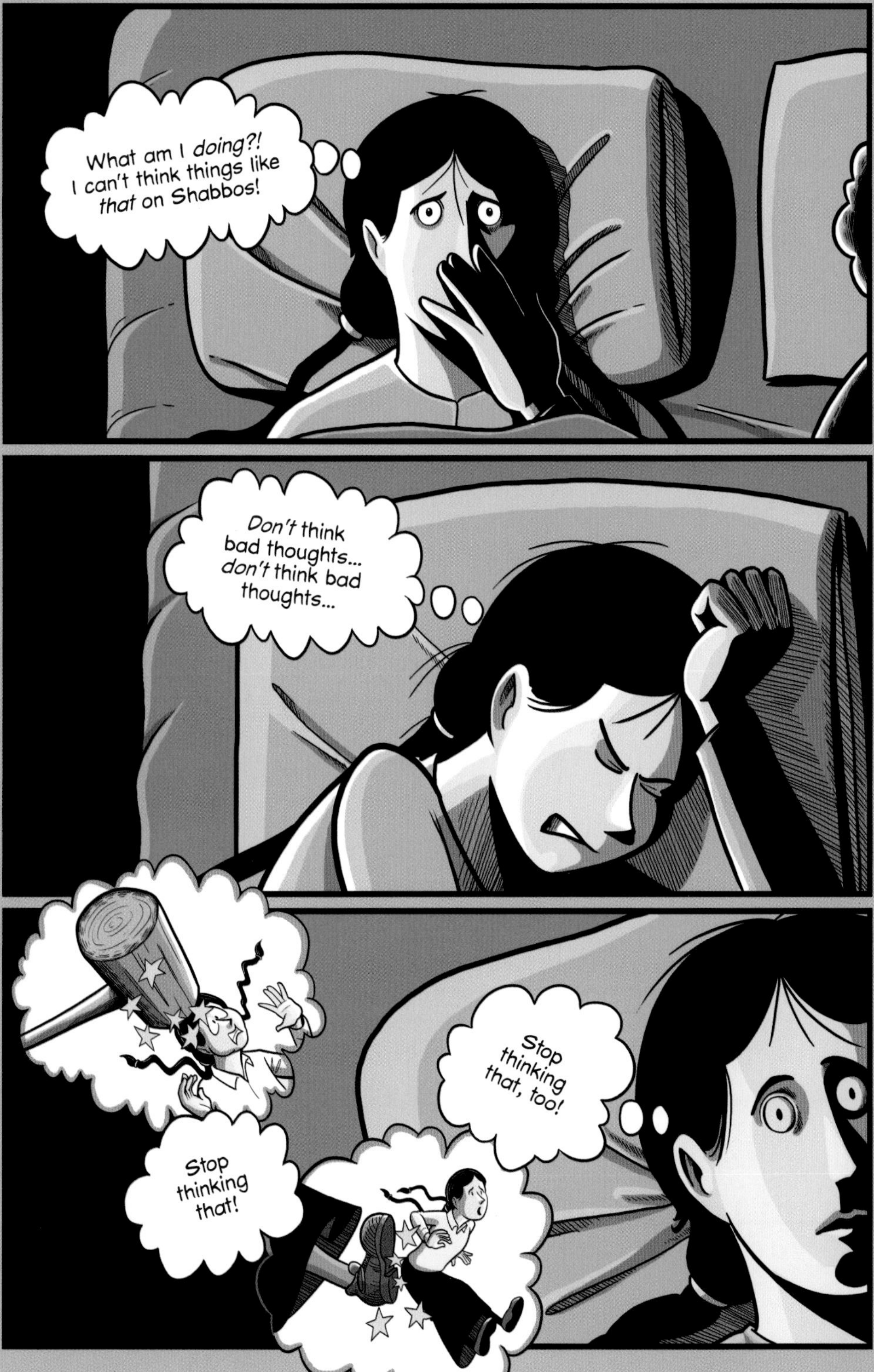

What am I *doing?!* I can't think things like *that* on Shabbos!
Don't think bad thoughts... *don't* think bad thoughts...
Stop thinking that!
Stop thinking that, too!

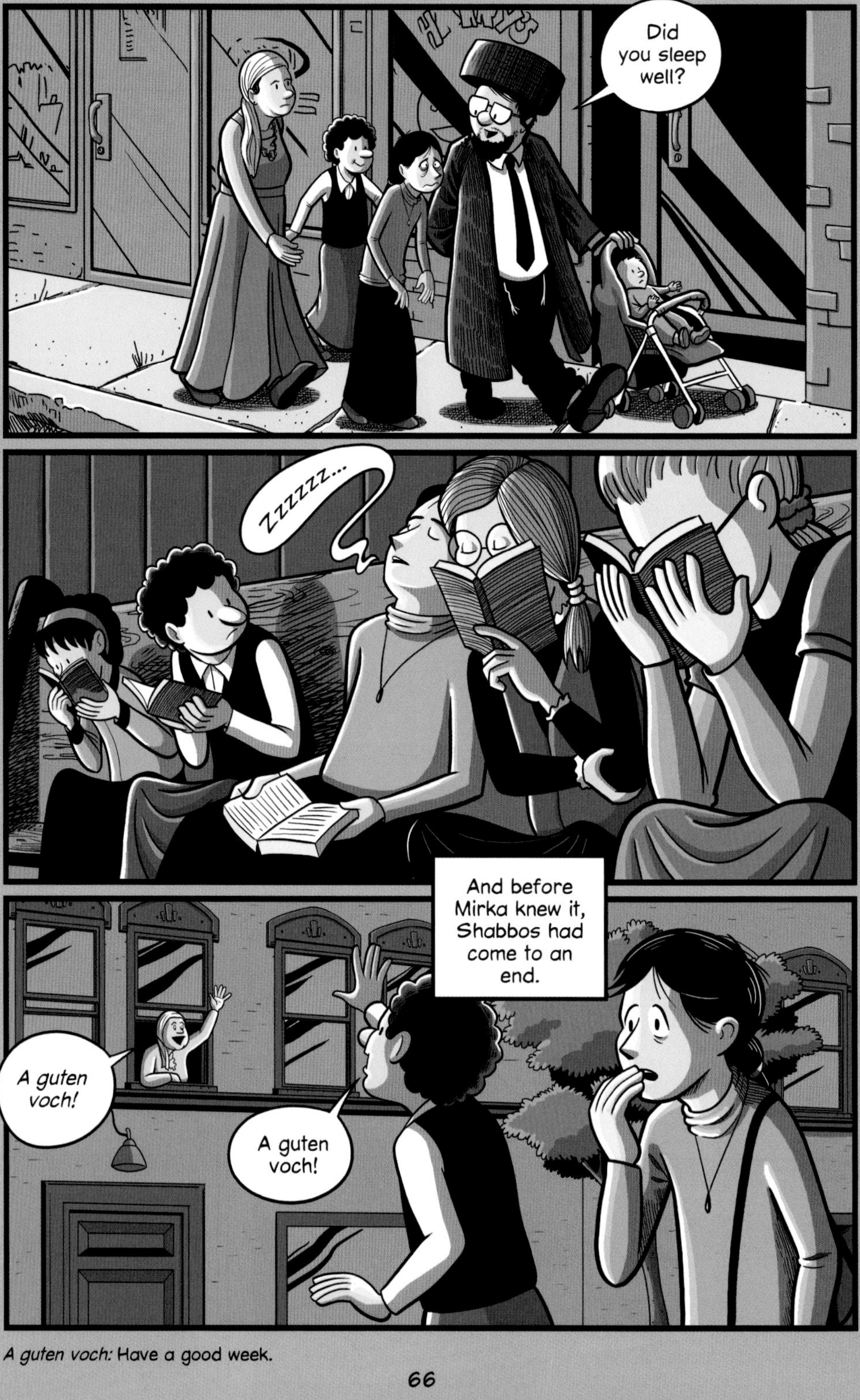
Did you sleep well?
Zzzzzz...
And before Mirka knew it, Shabbos had come to an end.
A guten voch!
A guten voch!

A guten voch: Have a good week.

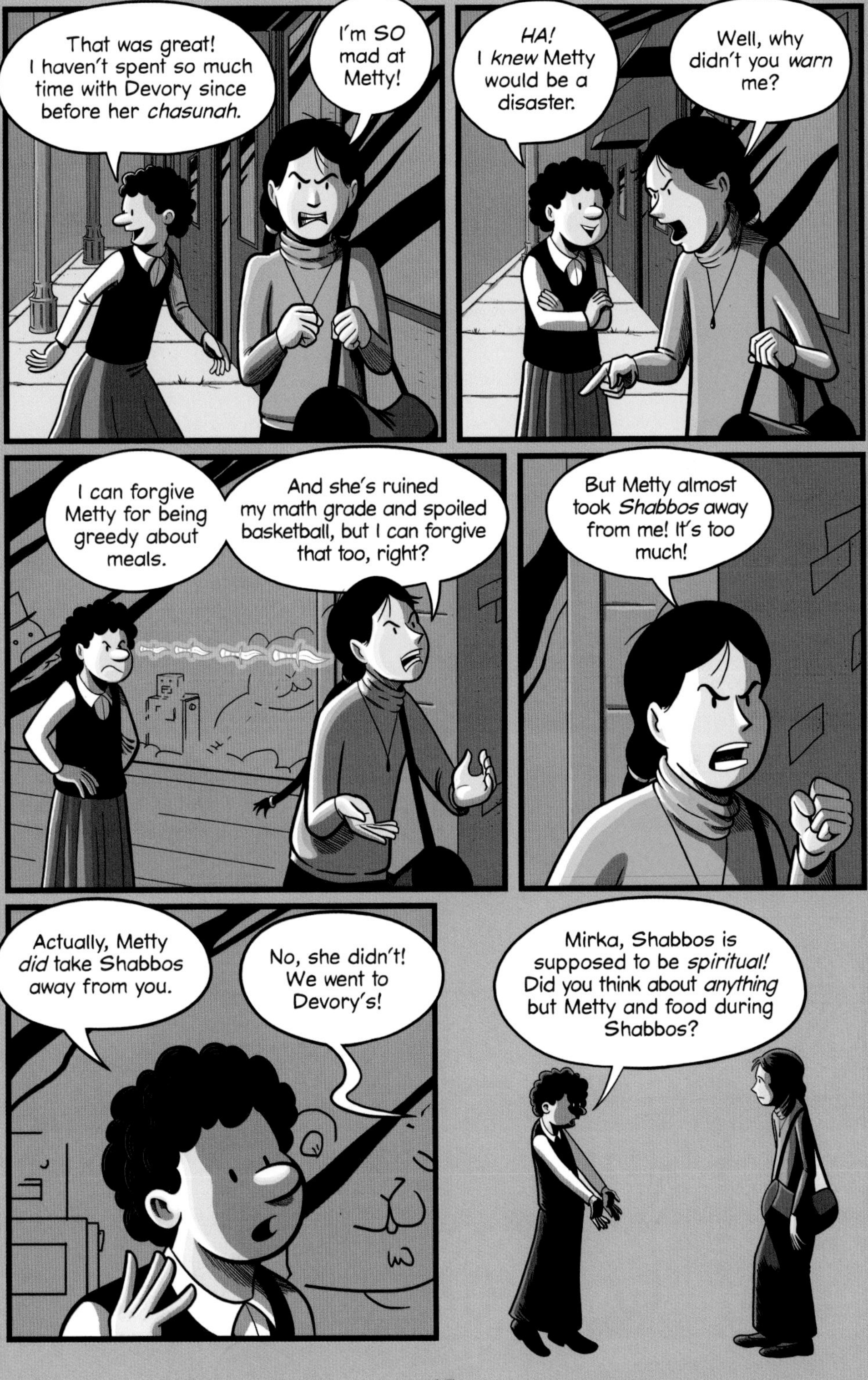
That was great! I haven't spent so much time with Devory since before her *chasunah.*
I'm SO mad at Metty!
HA! I *knew* Metty would be a disaster.
Well, why didn't you *warn* me?
I can forgive Metty for being greedy about meals.
And she's ruined my math grade and spoiled basketball, but I can forgive that too, right?
But Metty almost took *Shabbos* away from me! It's too much!
Actually, Metty *did* take Shabbos away from you.
No, she didn't! We went to Devory's!
Mirka, Shabbos is supposed to be *spiritual!* Did you think about *anything* but Metty and food during Shabbos?

Chasunah: Wedding

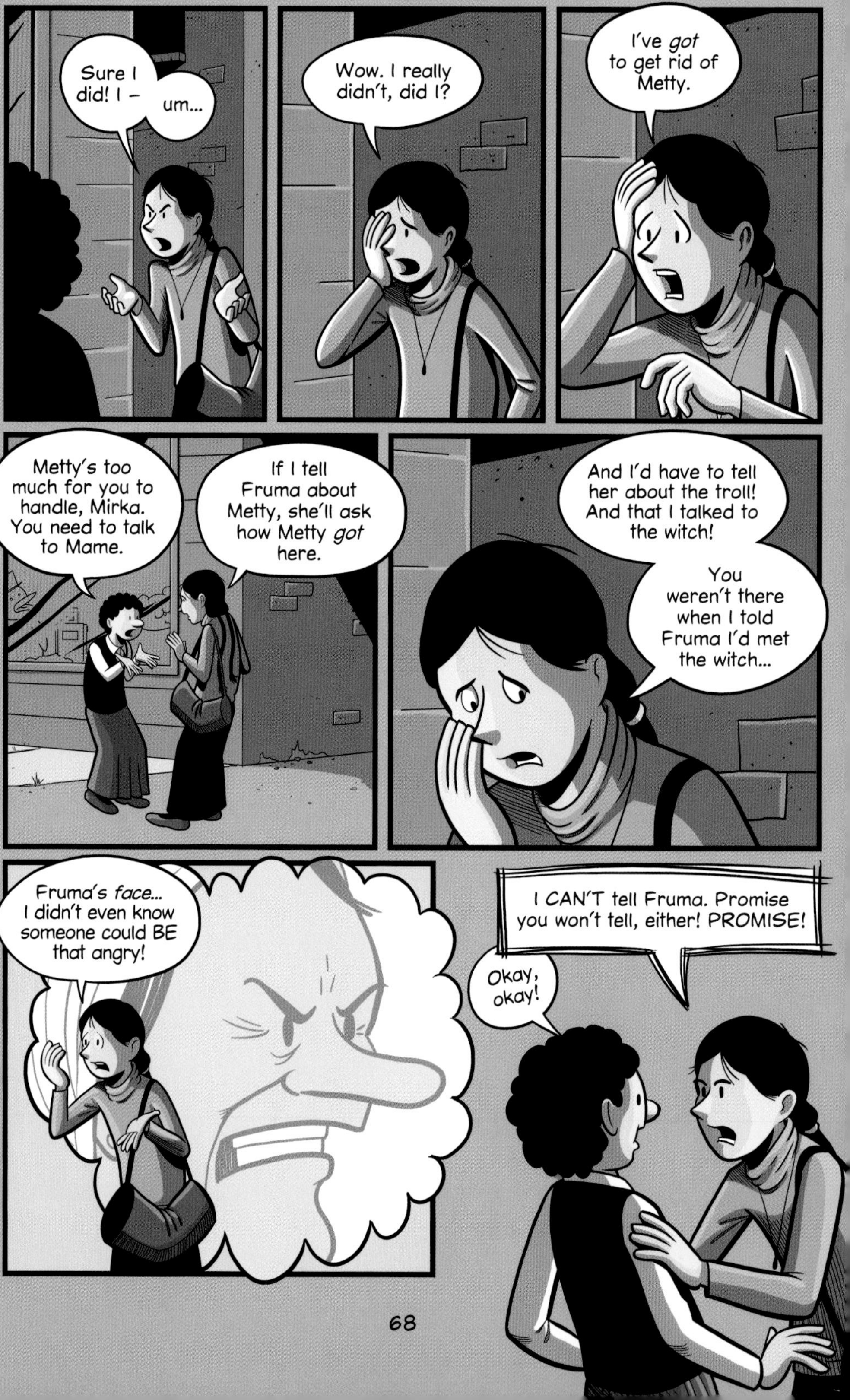
Sure I did! I –
um...
Wow. I really didn't, did I?
I've *got* to get rid of Metty.
Metty's too much for you to handle, Mirka. You need to talk to Mame.
If I tell Fruma about Metty, she'll ask how Metty *got* here.
And I'd have to tell her about the troll! And that I talked to the witch!
You weren't there when I told Fruma I'd met the witch...
Fruma's *face*... I didn't even know someone could BE that angry!
I CAN'T tell Fruma. Promise you won't tell, either! PROMISE!
Okay, okay!

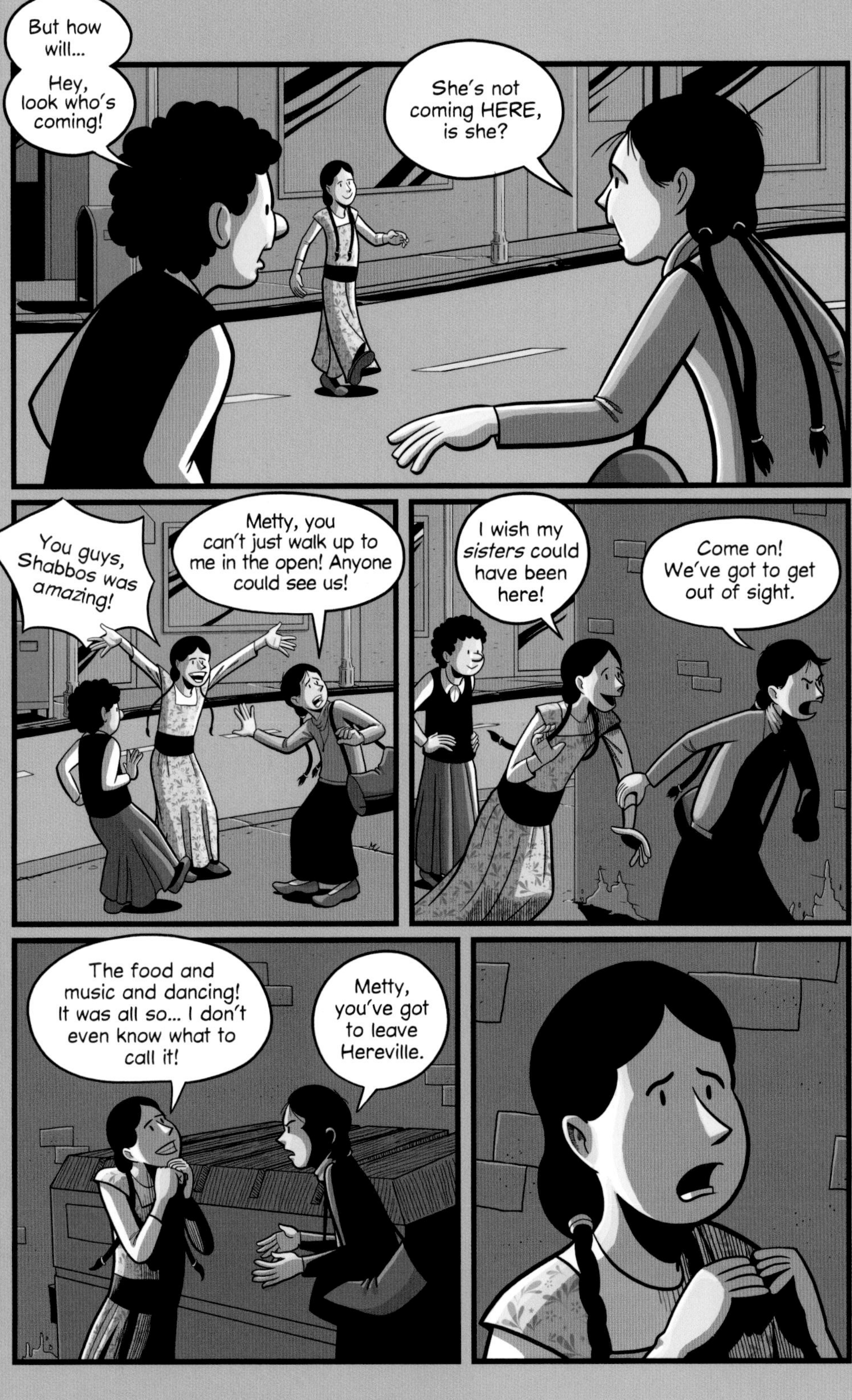
But how will...
Hey, look who's coming!
She's not coming HERE, is she?
You guys, Shabbos was amazing!
Metty, you can't just walk up to me in the open! Anyone could see us!
I wish my *sisters* could have been here!
Come on! We've got to get out of sight.
The food and music and dancing! It was all so... I don't even know what to call it!
Metty, you've got to leave Hereville.

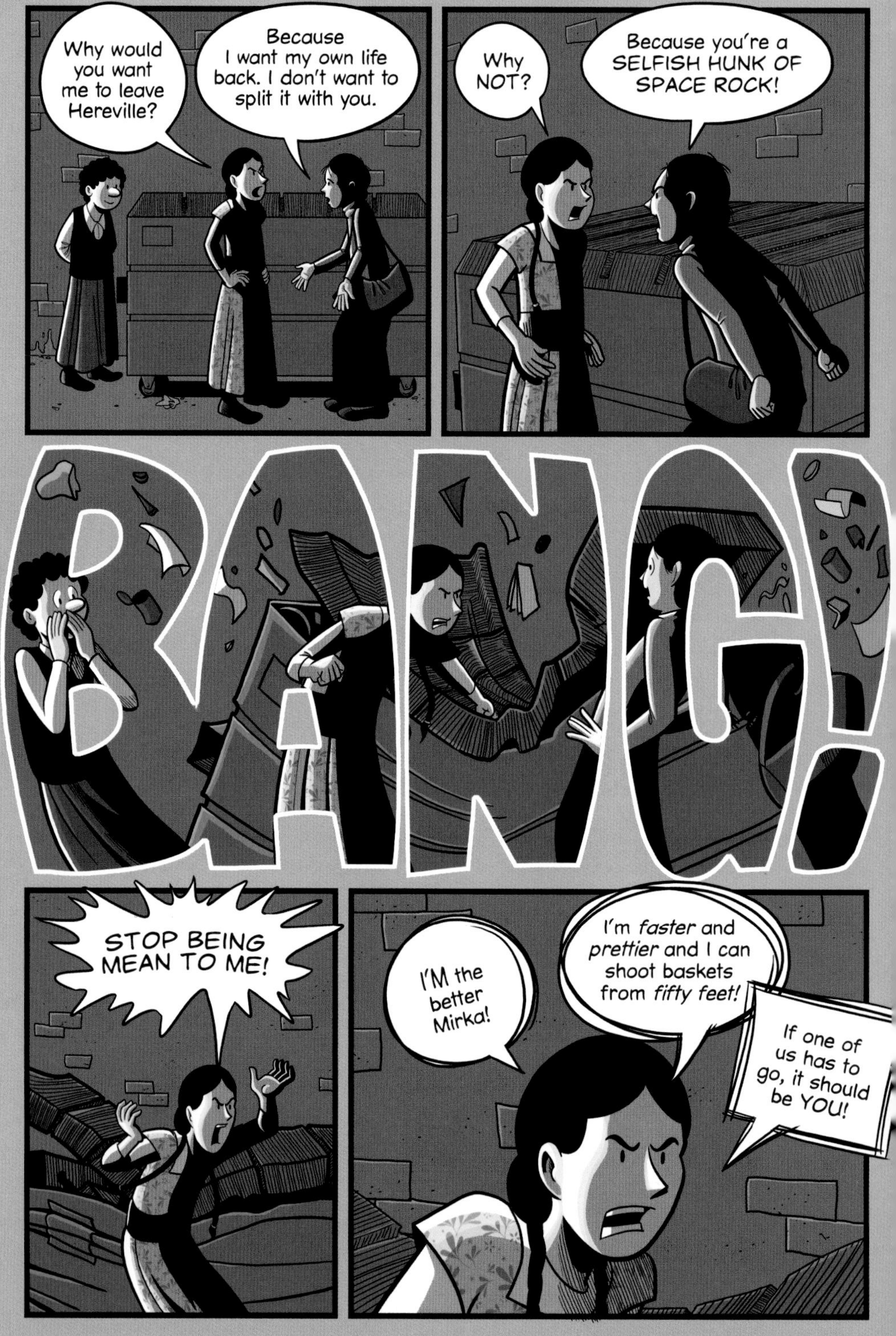
Why would you want me to leave Hereville?
Because I want my own life back. I don't want to split it with you.
Why NOT?
Because you're a SELFISH HUNK OF SPACE ROCK!
BANG!
STOP BEING MEAN TO ME!
I'M the better Mirka!
I'm *faster* and *prettier* and I can shoot baskets from *fifty feet!*
If one of us has to go, it should be YOU!

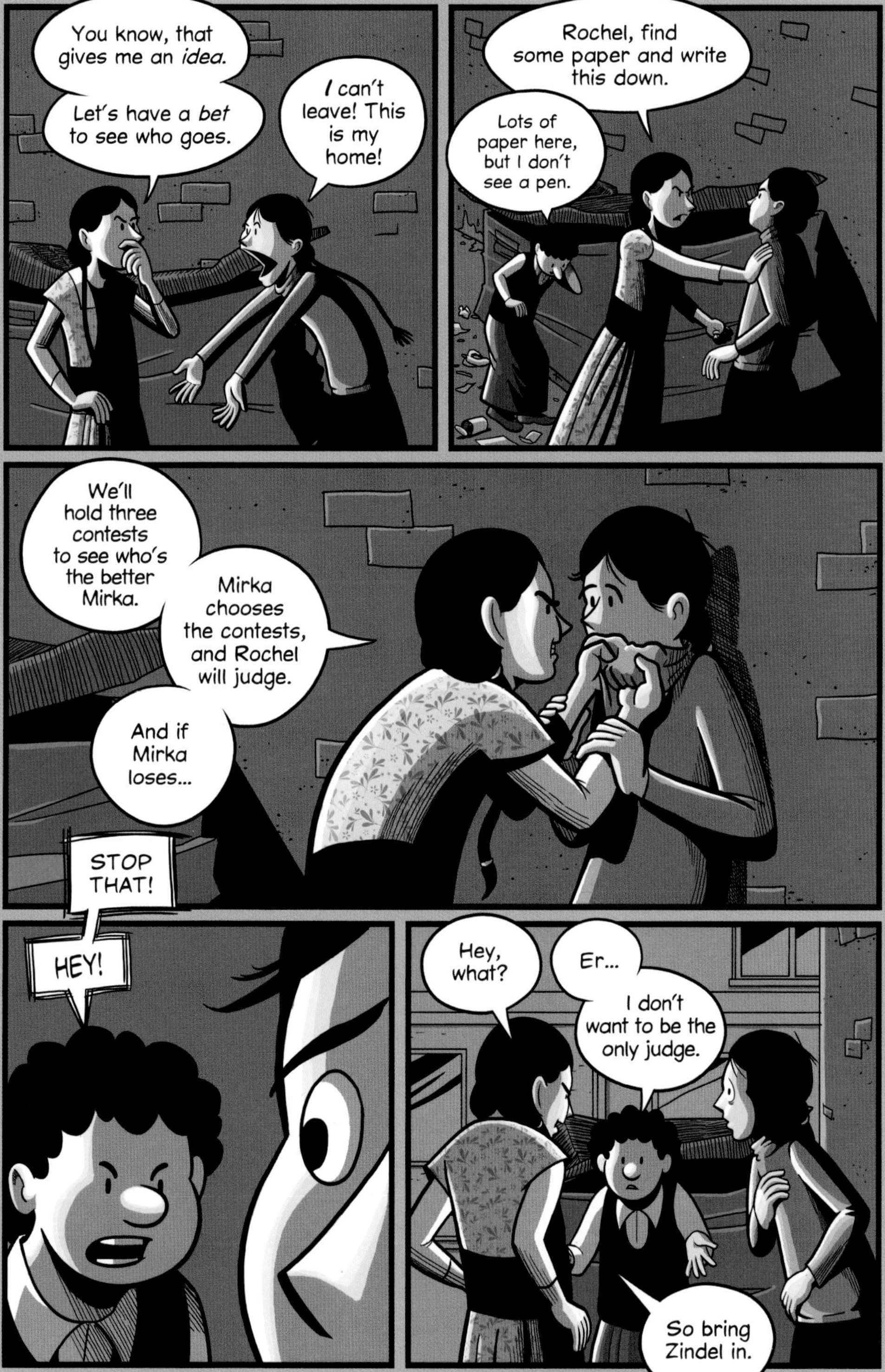
You know, that gives me an *idea*.
Let's have a *bet* to see who goes.
I can't leave! This is my home!
Rochel, find some paper and write this down.
Lots of paper here, but I don't see a pen.
We'll hold three contests to see who's the better Mirka.
Mirka chooses the contests, and Rochel will judge.
And if Mirka loses...
STOP THAT!
HEY!
Hey, what?
Er...
I don't want to be the only judge.
So bring Zindel in.

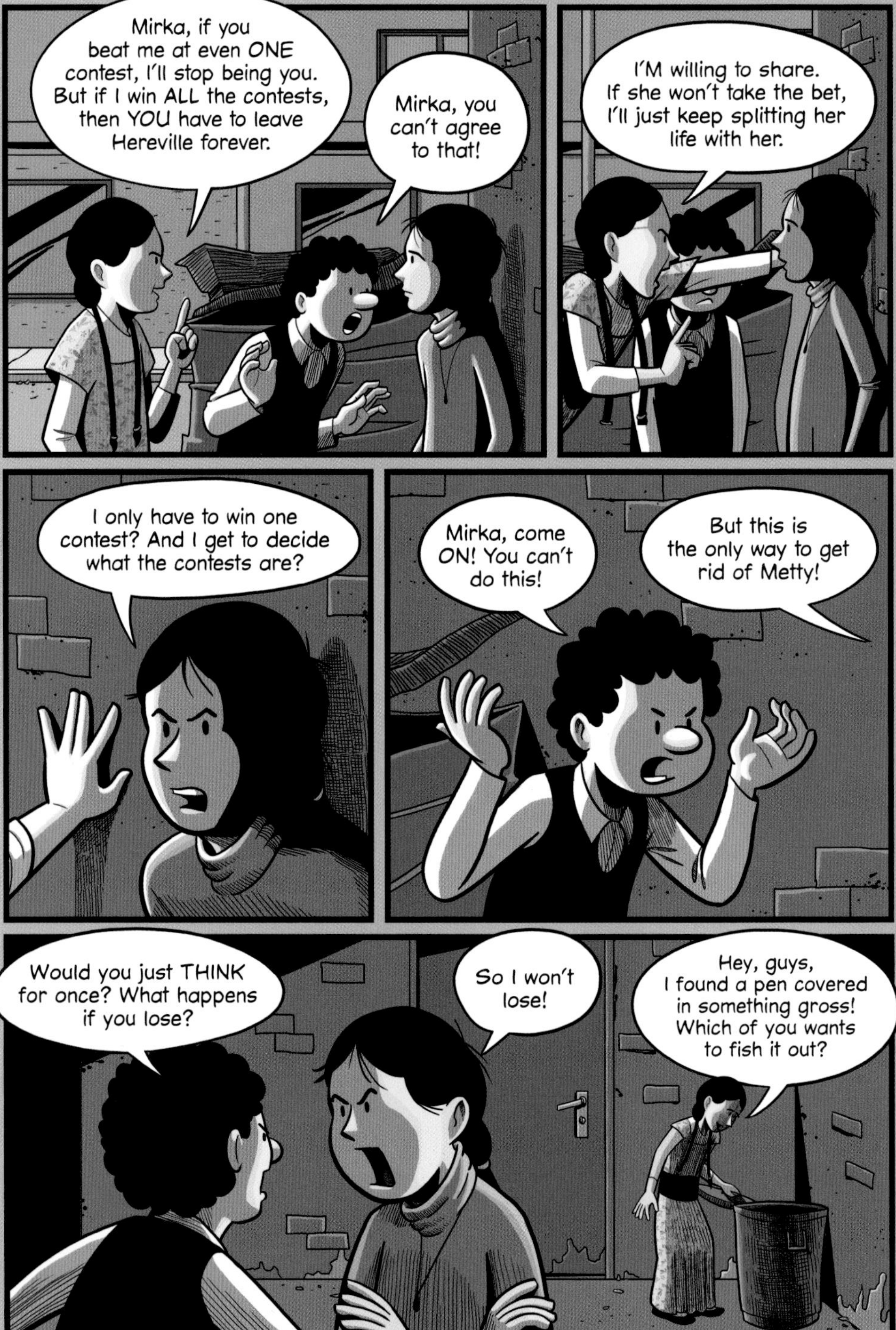
Mirka, if you beat me at even ONE contest, I'll stop being you. But if I win ALL the contests, then YOU have to leave Hereville forever.
Mirka, you can't agree to that!
I'M willing to share. If she won't take the bet, I'll just keep splitting her life with her.
I only have to win one contest? And I get to decide what the contests are?
Mirka, come ON! You can't do this!
But this is the only way to get rid of Metty!
Would you just THINK for once? What happens if you lose?
So I won't lose!
Hey, guys, I found a pen covered in something gross! Which of you wants to fish it out?

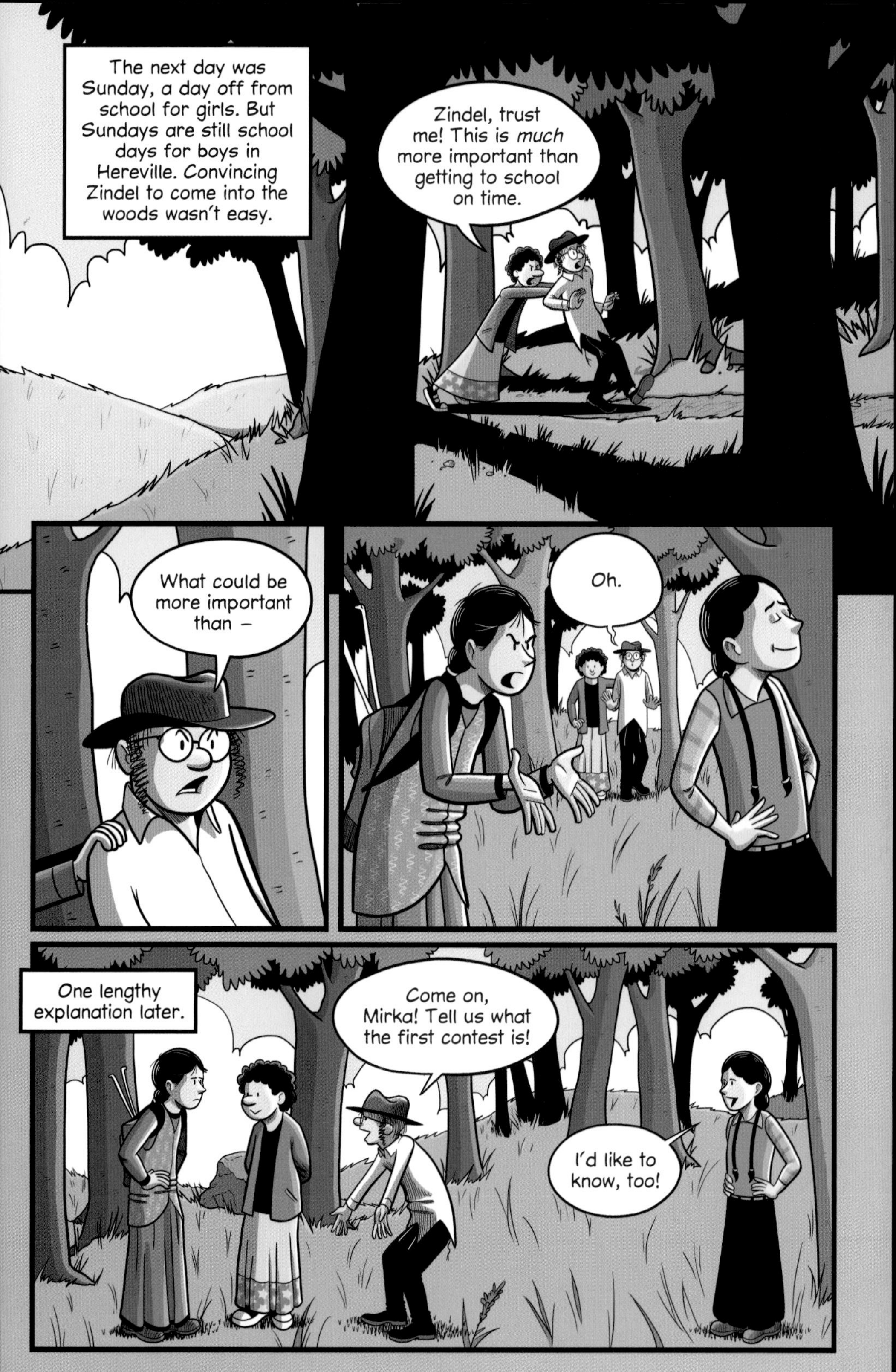
The next day was Sunday, a day off from school for girls. But Sundays are still school days for boys in Hereville. Convincing Zindel to come into the woods wasn't easy.
Zindel, trust me! This is *much* more important than getting to school on time.
What could be more important than –
Oh.
One lengthy explanation later.
Come on, Mirka! Tell us what the first contest is!
I'd like to know, too!

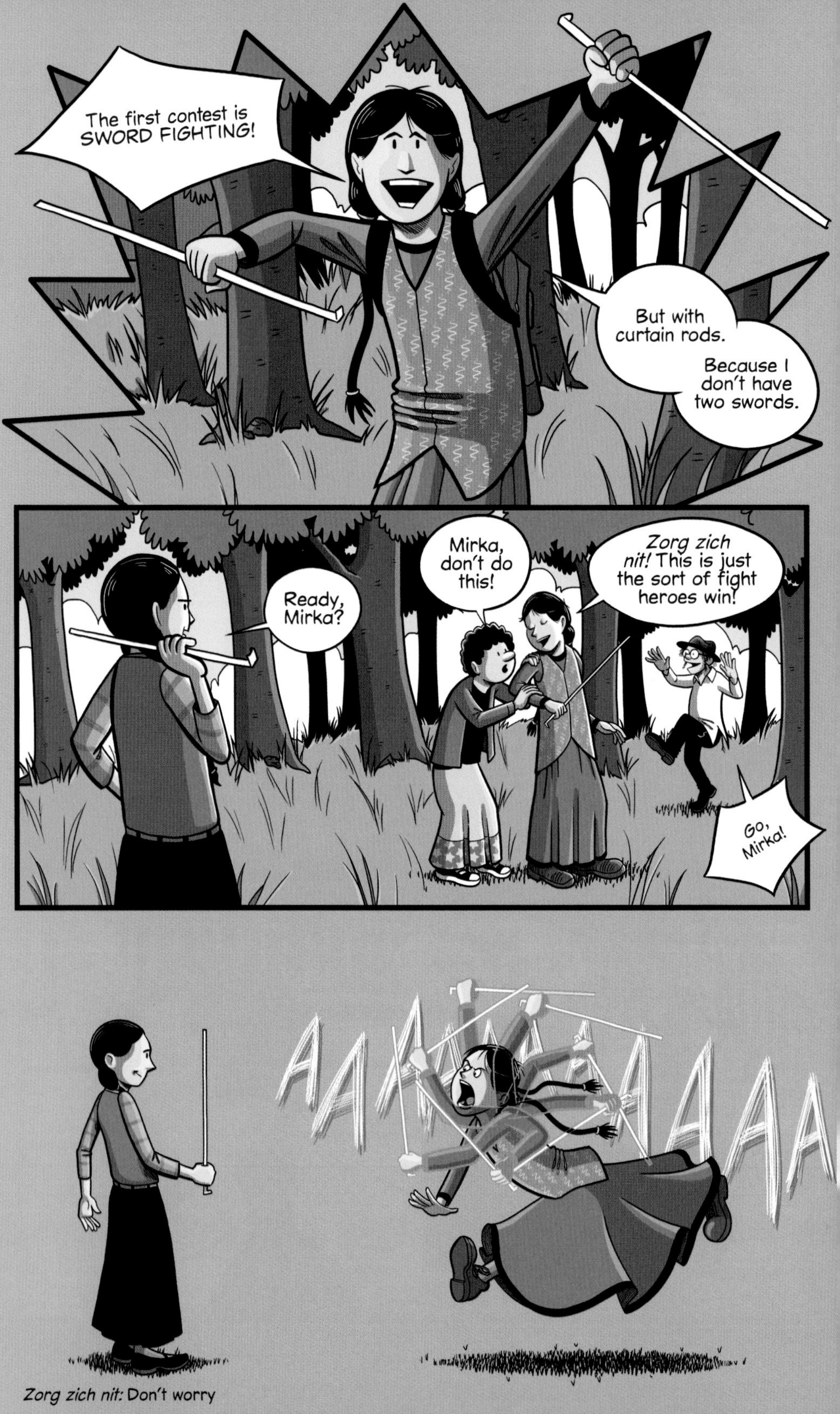
The first contest is SWORD FIGHTING!
But with curtain rods.
Because I don't have two swords.
Ready, Mirka?
Mirka, don't do this!
Zorg zich nit! This is just the sort of fight heroes win!
Go, Mirka!
AAAAAAAAAAAA

Zorg zich nit: Don't worry

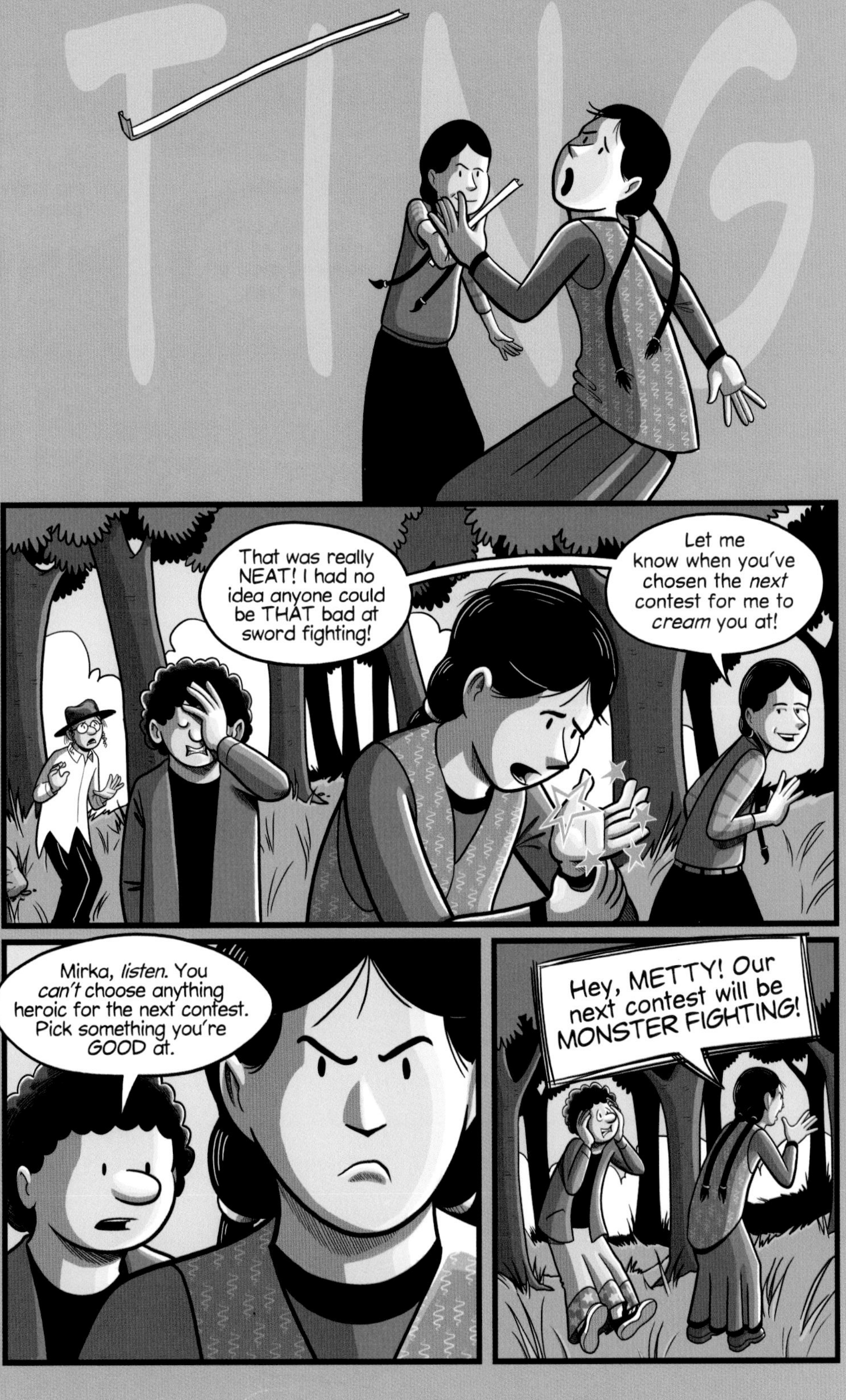
TING
That was really NEAT! I had no idea anyone could be THAT bad at sword fighting!
Let me know when you've chosen the *next* contest for me to *cream* you at!
Mirka, *listen.* You *can't* choose anything heroic for the next contest. Pick something you're GOOD at.
Hey, METTY! Our next contest will be MONSTER FIGHTING!

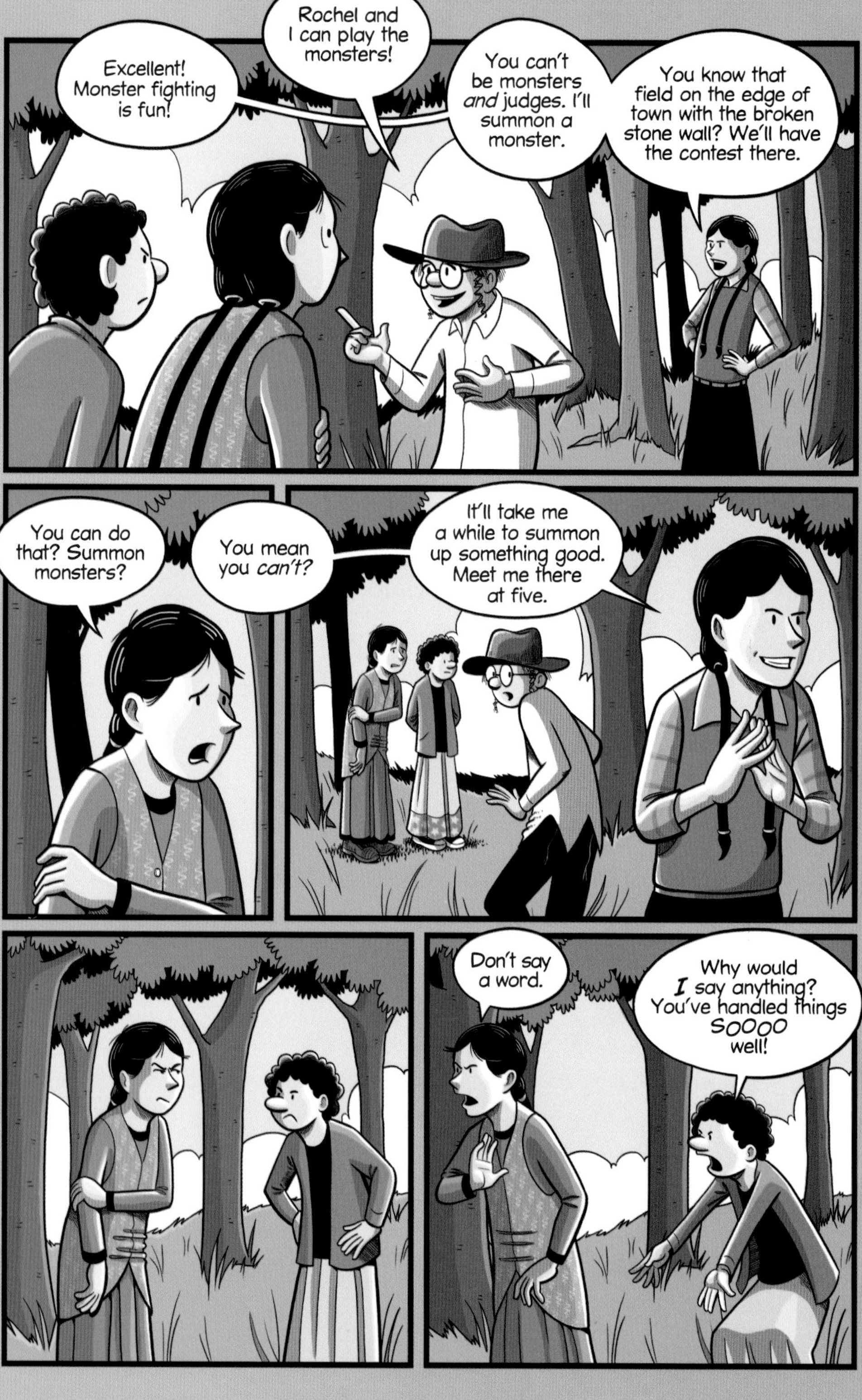
Excellent! Monster fighting is fun!
Rochel and I can play the monsters!
You can't be monsters *and* judges. I'll summon a monster.
You know that field on the edge of town with the broken stone wall? We'll have the contest there.
You can do that? Summon monsters?
You mean you *can't*?
It'll take me a while to summon up something good. Meet me there at five.
Don't say a word.
Why would *I* say anything? You've handled things SOOOO well!

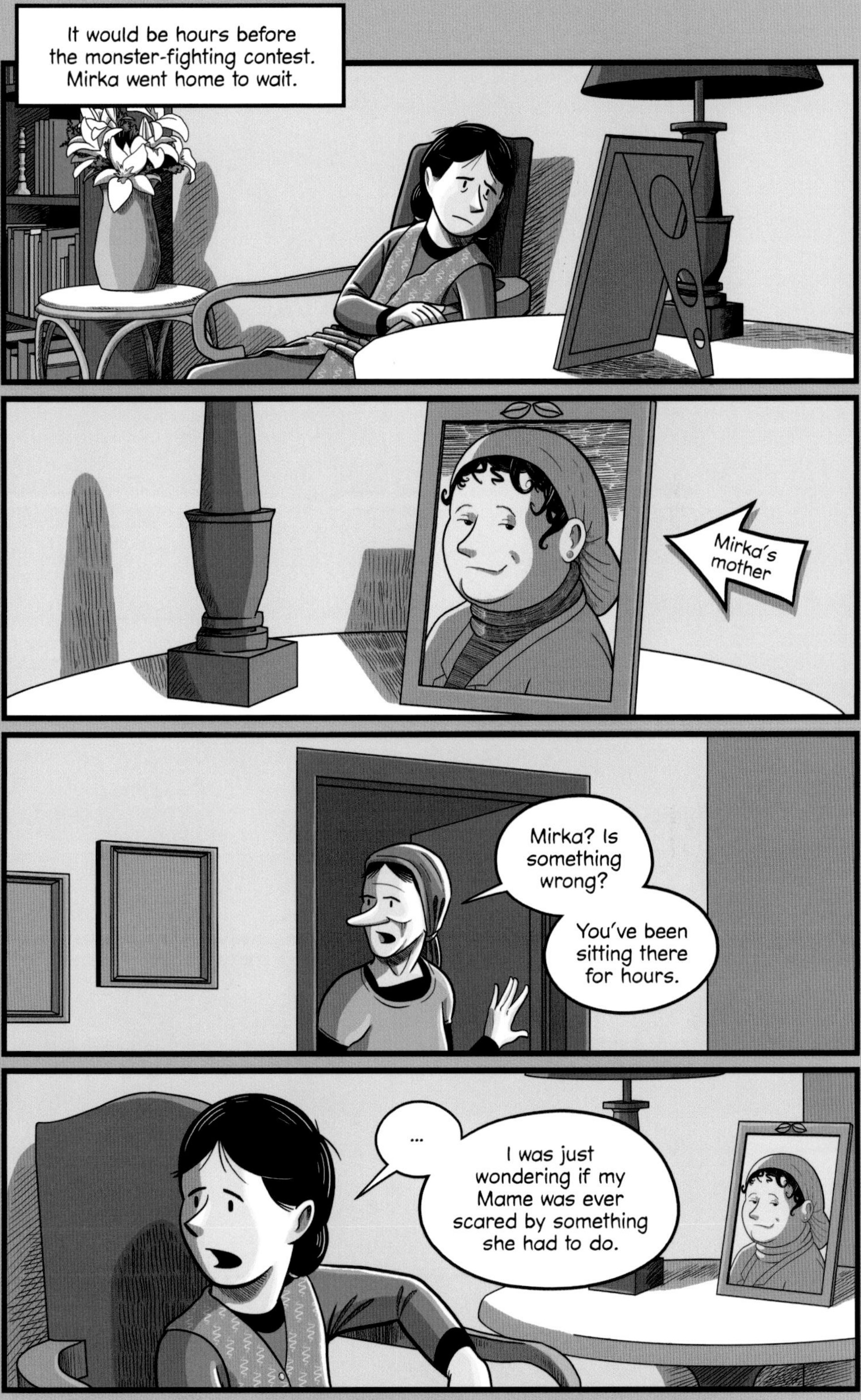
It would be hours before the monster-fighting contest. Mirka went home to wait.
Mirka's mother
Mirka? Is something wrong?
You've been sitting there for hours.
...
I was just wondering if my Mame was ever scared by something she had to do.

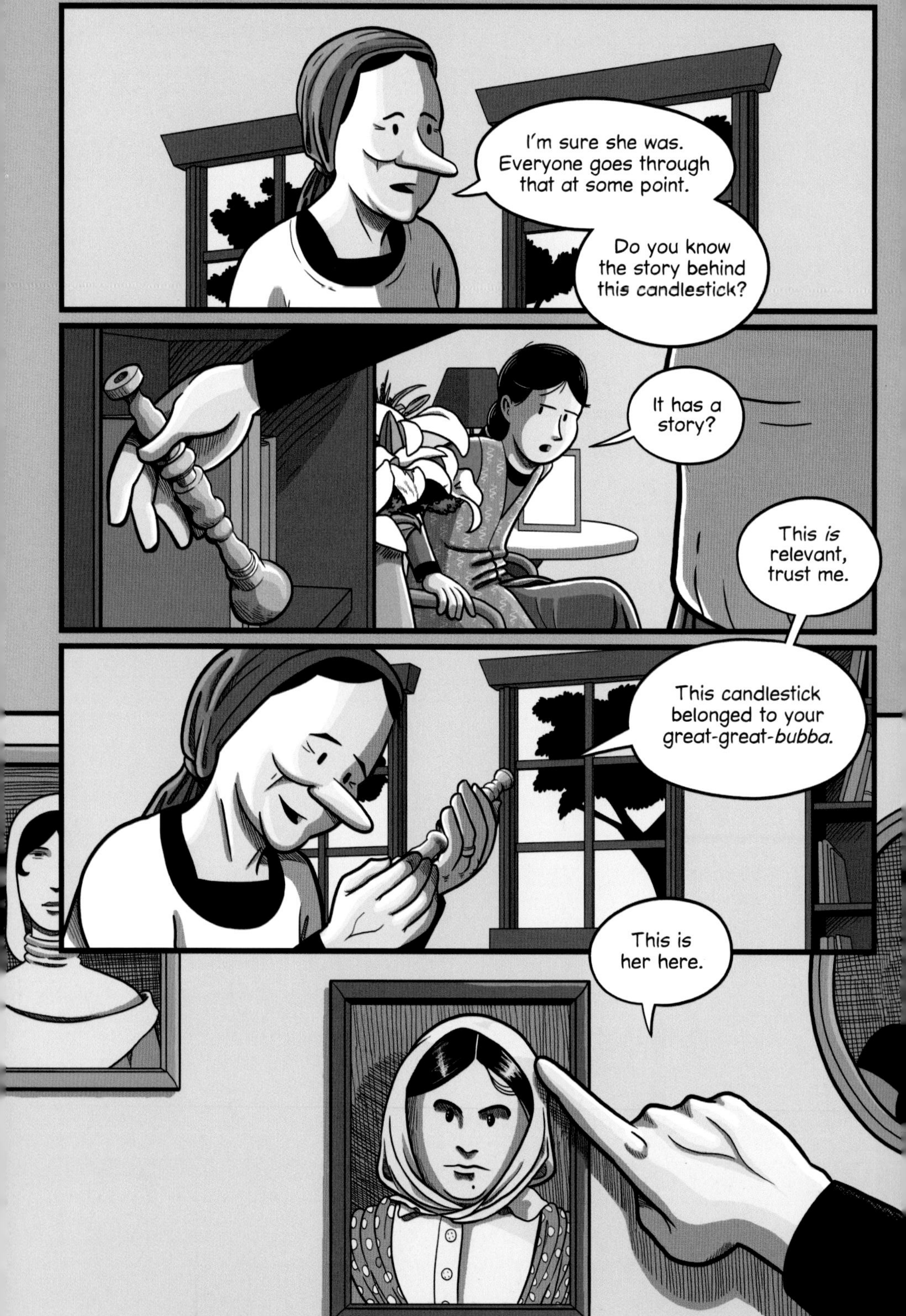
I'm sure she was. Everyone goes through that at some point.
Do you know the story behind this candlestick?
It has a story?
This *is* relevant, trust me.
This candlestick belonged to your great-great-*bubba.*
This is her here.

Bubba: grandmother

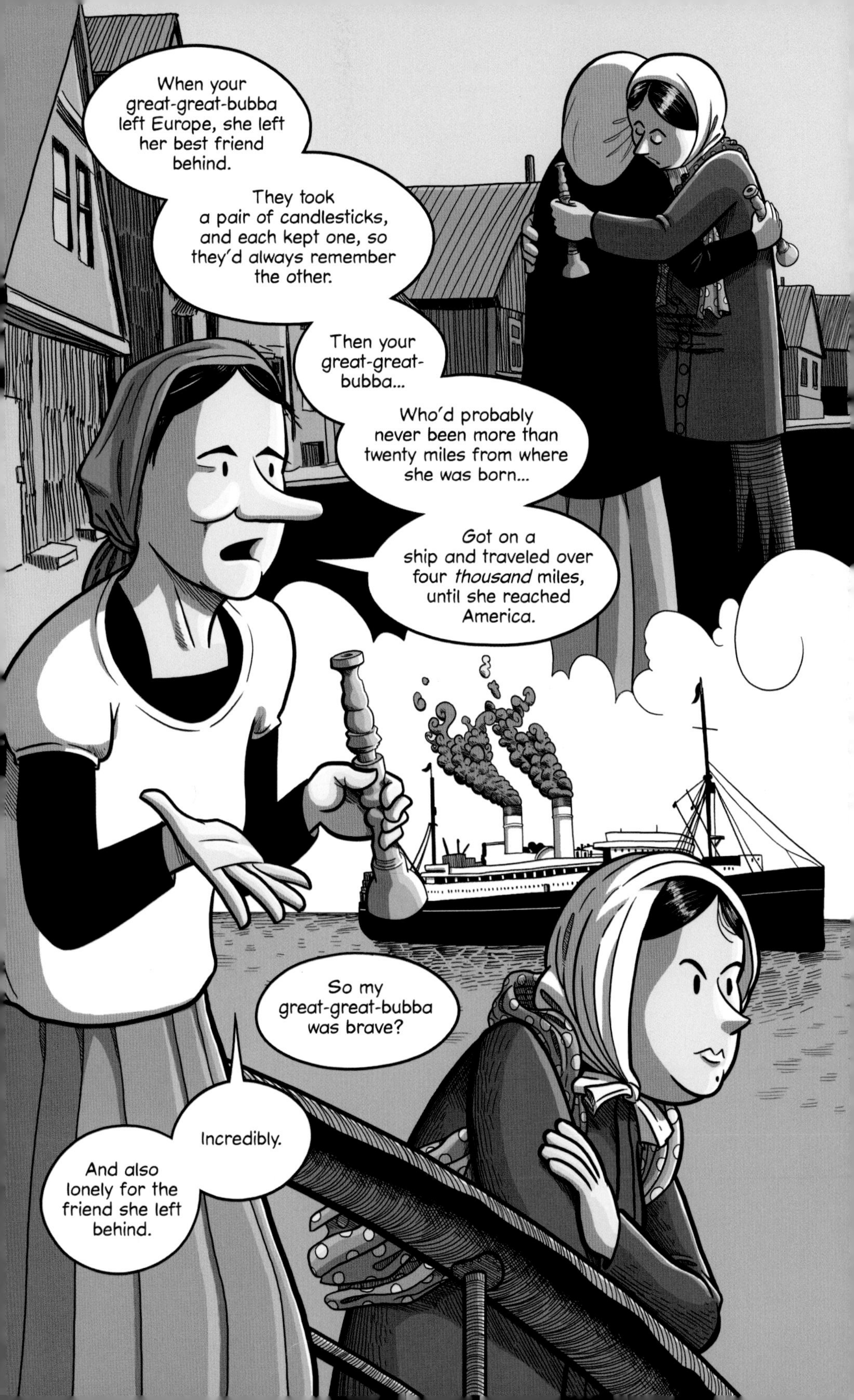
When your great-great-bubba left Europe, she left her best friend behind.
They took a pair of candlesticks, and each kept one, so they'd always remember the other.
Then your great-great-bubba...
Who'd probably never been more than twenty miles from where she was born...
Got on a ship and traveled over four *thousand* miles, until she reached America.
So my great-great-bubba was brave?
Incredibly.
And also lonely for the friend she left behind.

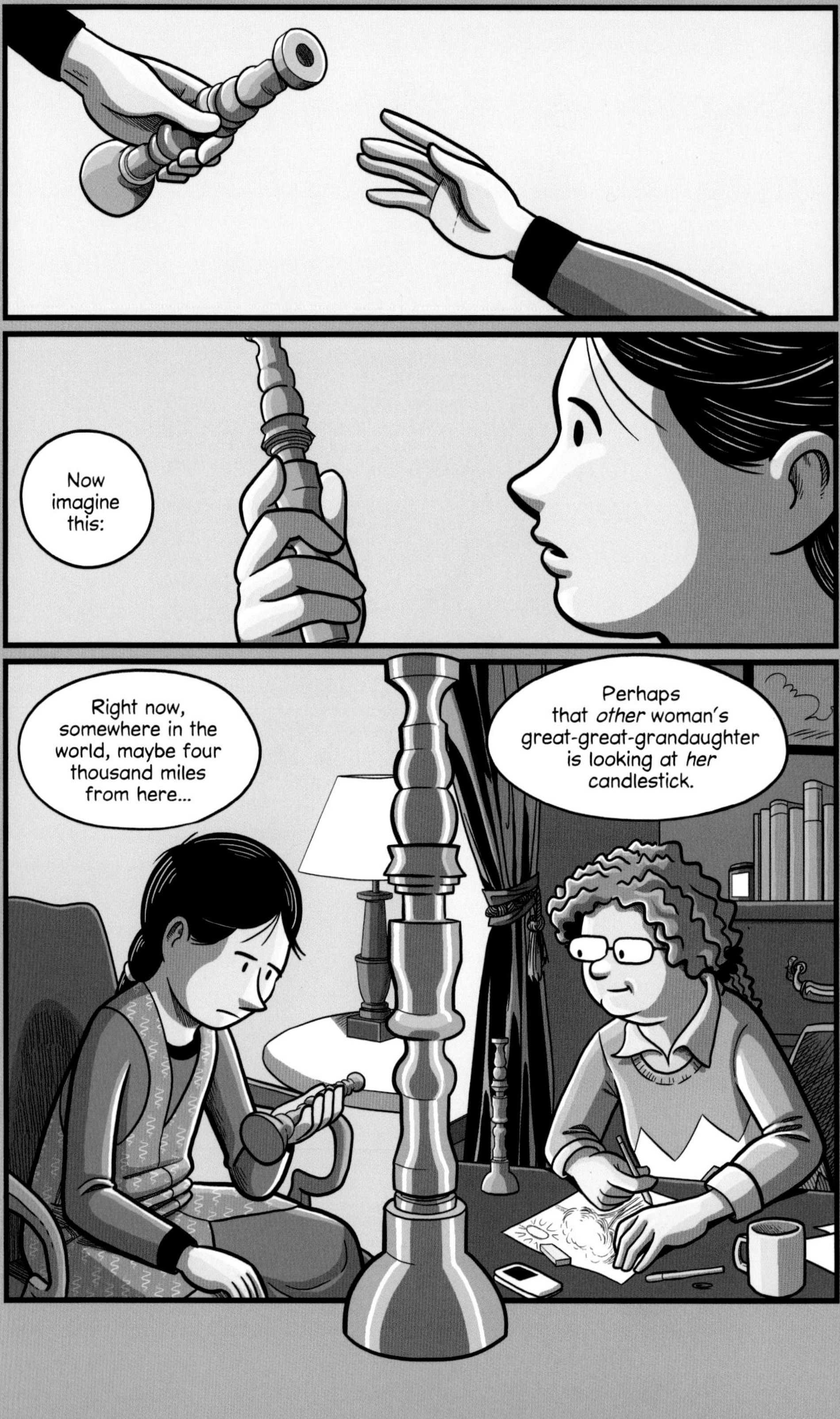
Now imagine this:
Right now, somewhere in the world, maybe four thousand miles from here...
Perhaps that *other* woman's great-great-grandaughter is looking at *her* candlestick.

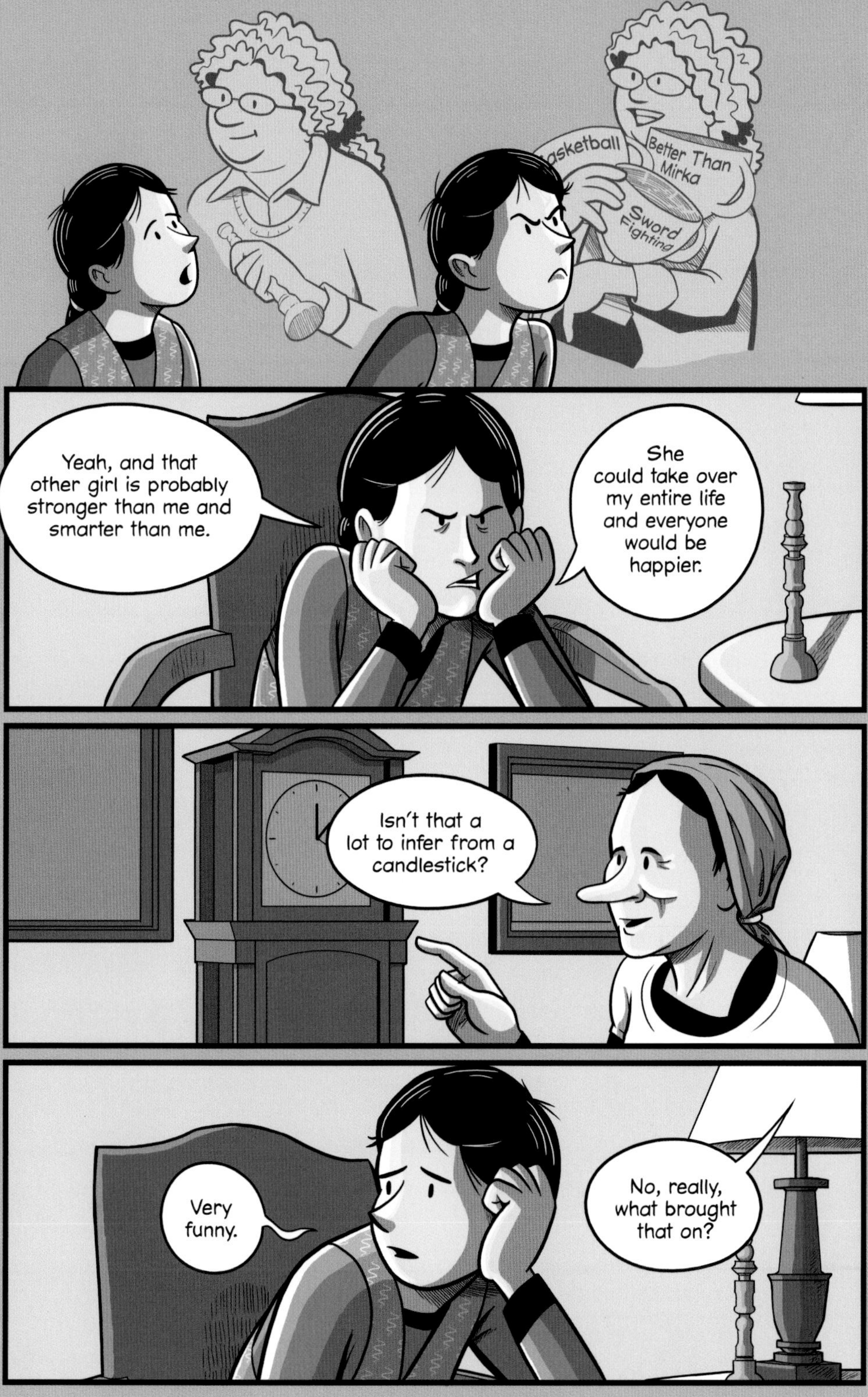
Basketball
Better Than Mirka
Sword Fighting
Yeah, and that other girl is probably stronger than me and smarter than me.
She could take over my entire life and everyone would be happier.
Isn't that a lot to infer from a candlestick?
Very funny.
No, really, what brought that on?

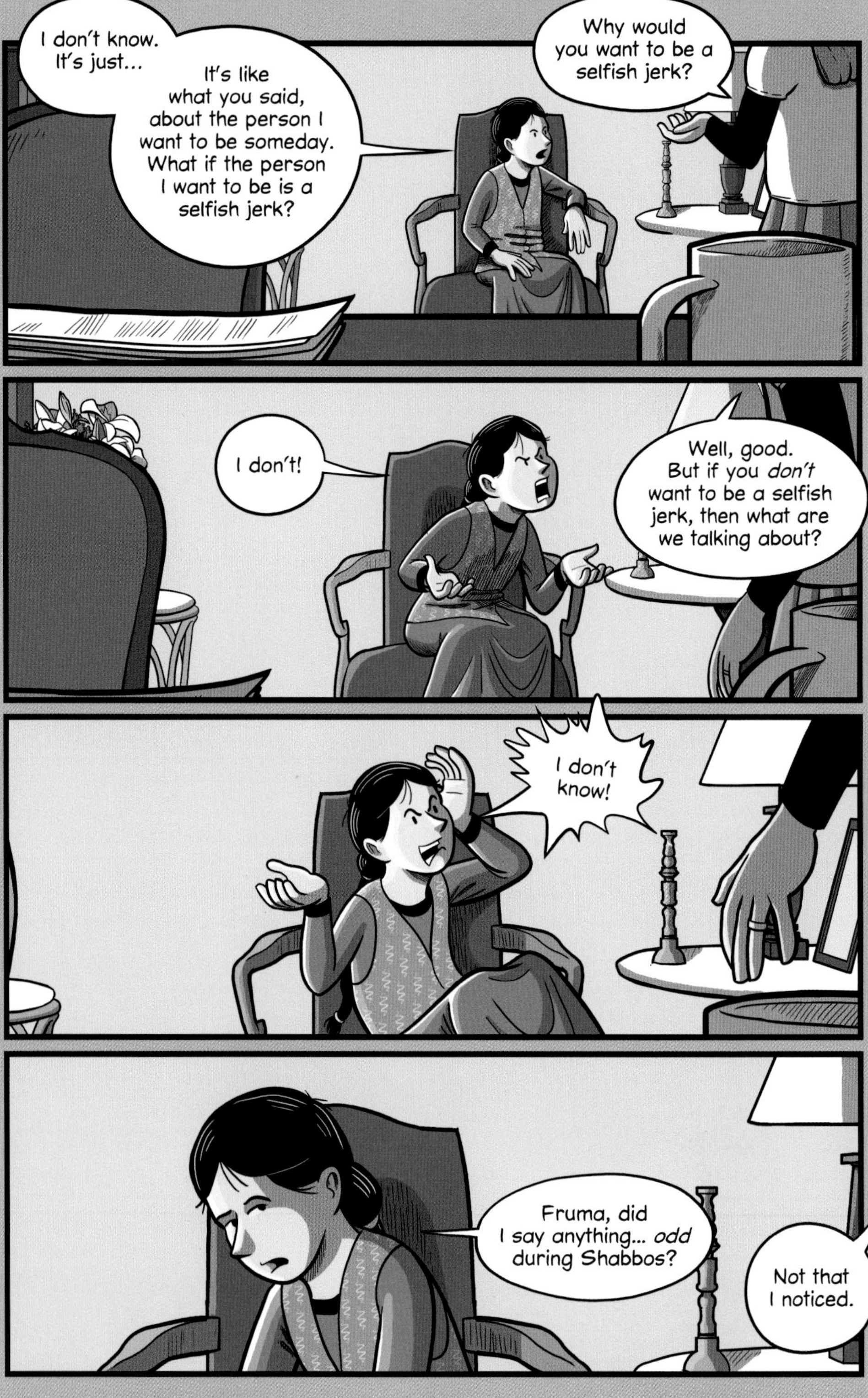
I don't know. It's just...
It's like what you said, about the person I want to be someday. What if the person I want to be is a selfish jerk?
Why would you want to be a selfish jerk?
I don't!
Well, good. But if you *don't* want to be a selfish jerk, then what are we talking about?
I don't know!
Fruma, did I say anything... *odd* during Shabbos?
Not that I noticed.

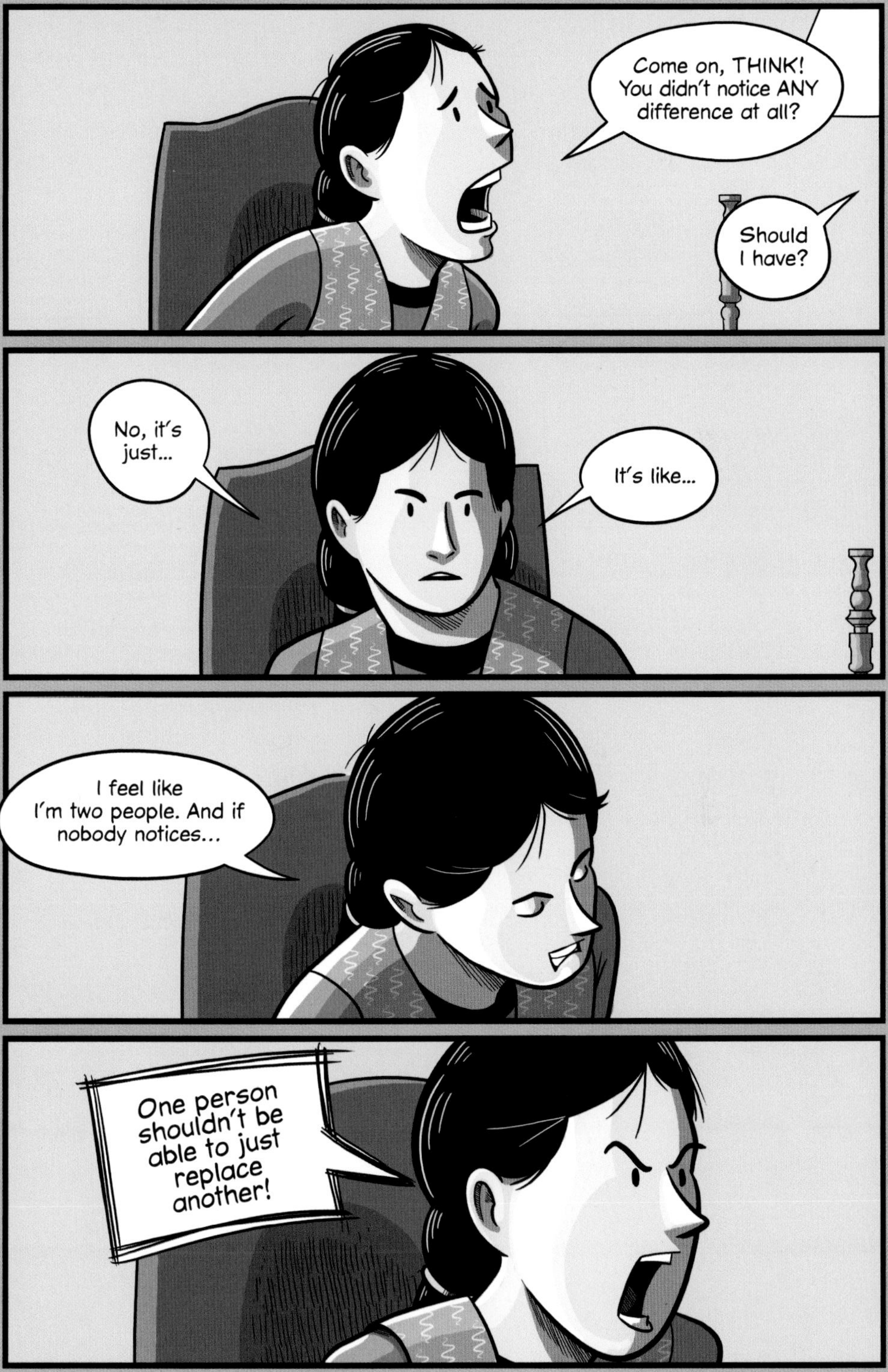
Come on, THINK! You didn't notice ANY difference at all?
Should I have?
No, it's just...
It's like...
I feel like I'm two people. And if nobody notices...
One person shouldn't be able to just replace another!

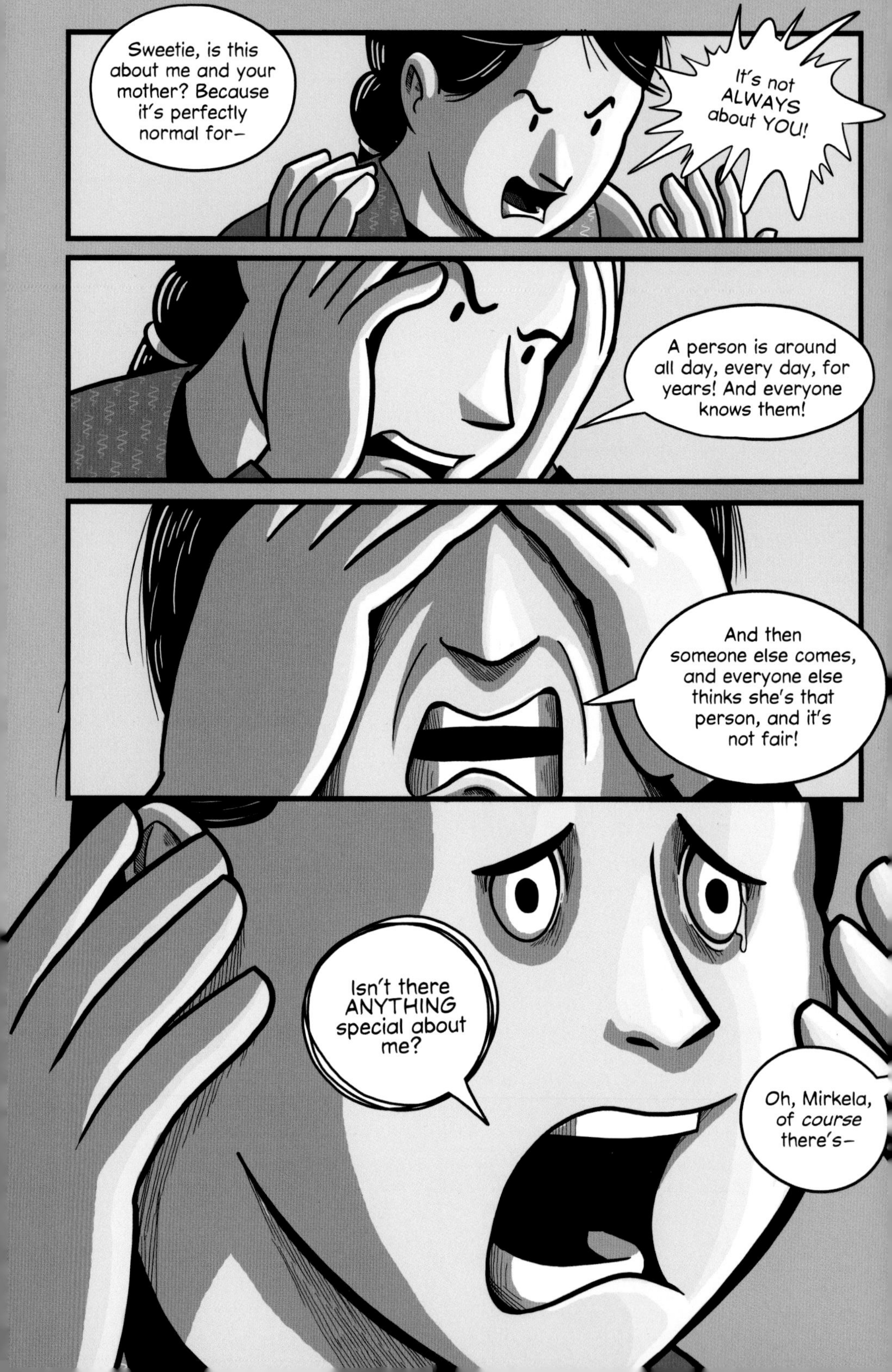
Sweetie, is this about me and your mother? Because it's perfectly normal for–
It's not ALWAYS about YOU!
A person is around all day, every day, for years! And everyone knows them!
And then someone else comes, and everyone else thinks she's that person, and it's not fair!
Isn't there ANYTHING special about me?
Oh, Mirkela, of *course* there's–

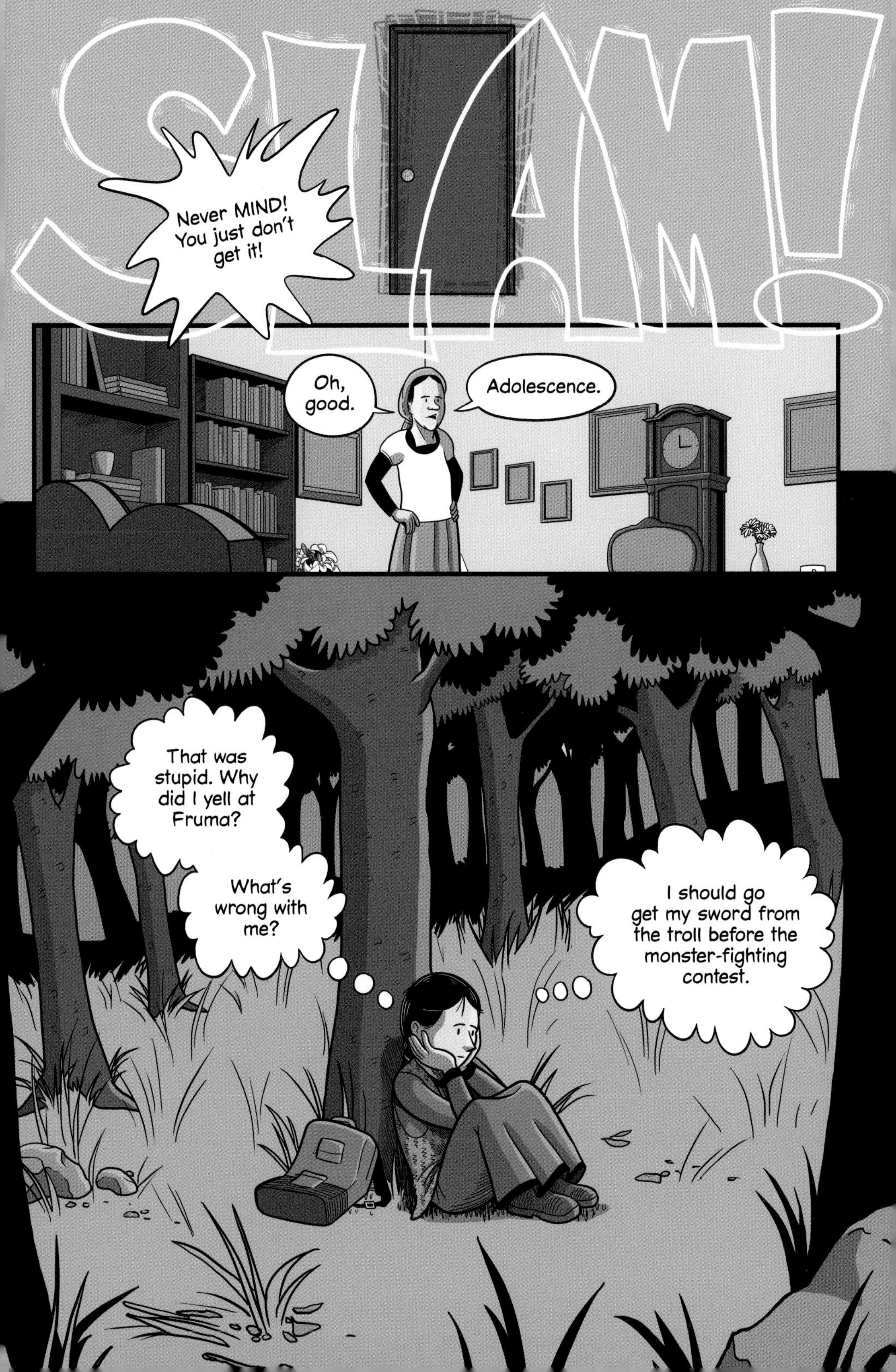
SLAM!
Never MIND! You just don't get it!
Oh, good.
Adolescence.
That was stupid. Why did I yell at Fruma?
What's wrong with me?
I should go get my sword from the troll before the monster-fighting contest.

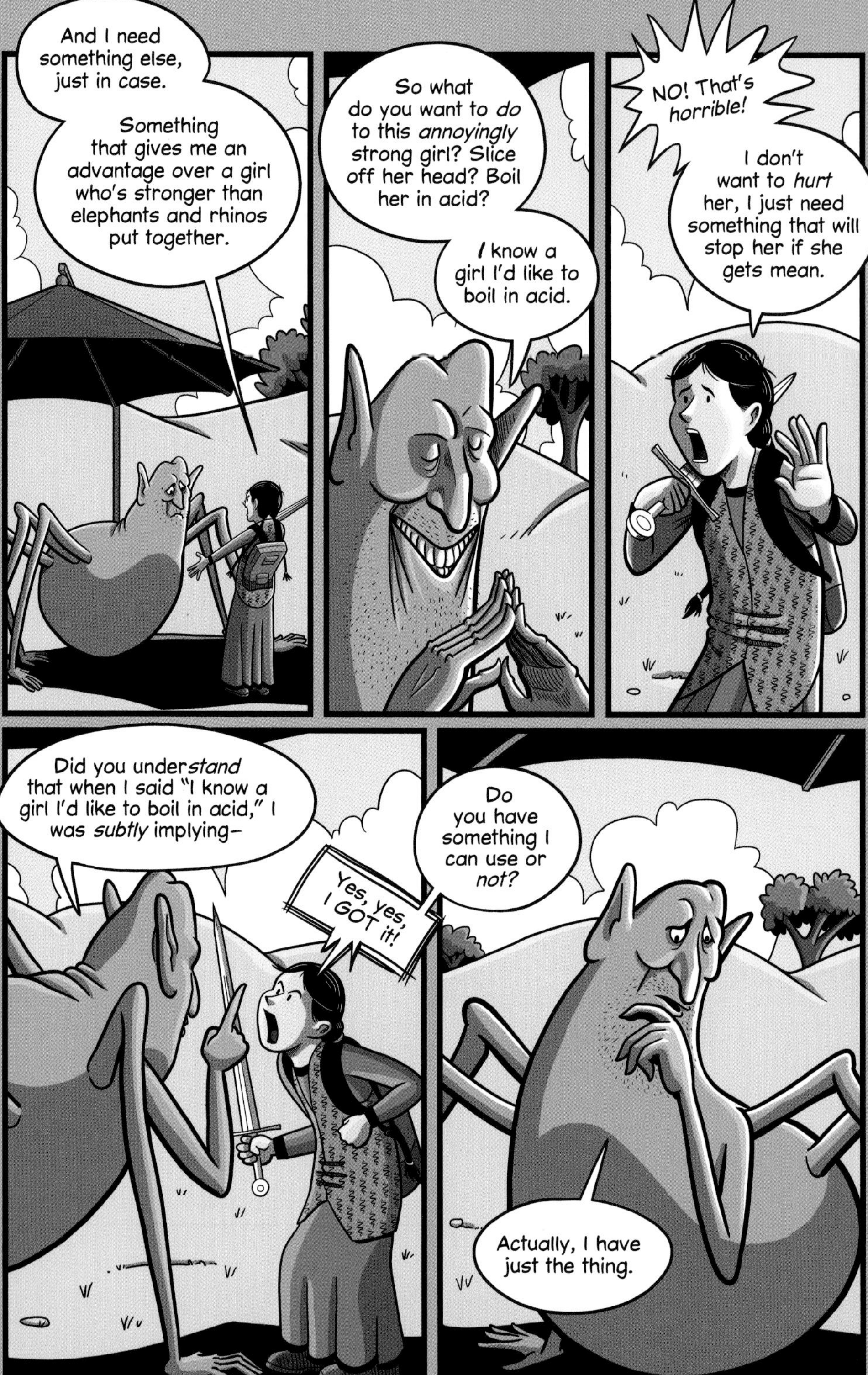
And I need something else, just in case.
Something that gives me an advantage over a girl who's stronger than elephants and rhinos put together.
So what do you want to *do* to this *annoyingly* strong girl? Slice off her head? Boil her in acid?
I know a girl I'd like to boil in acid.
NO! That's *horrible!*
I don't want to *hurt* her, I just need something that will stop her if she gets mean.
Did you under*stand* that when I said "I know a girl I'd like to boil in acid," I was *subtly* implying–
Yes, yes, I GOT it!
Do you have something I can use or *not?*
Actually, I have just the thing.

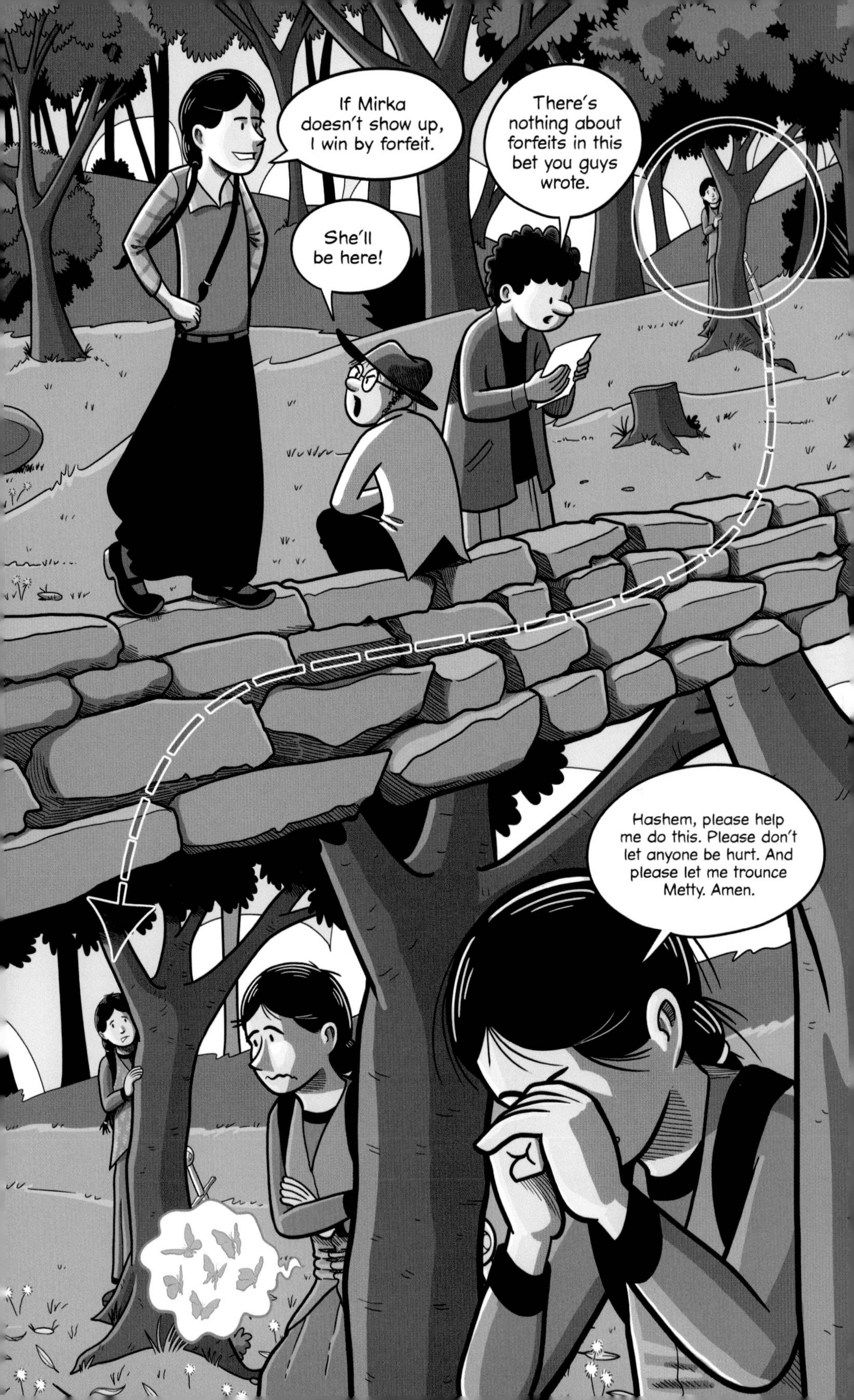
If Mirka doesn't show up, I win by forfeit.
There's nothing about forfeits in this bet you guys wrote.
She'll be here!
Hashem, please help me do this. Please don't let anyone be hurt. And please let me trounce Metty. Amen.

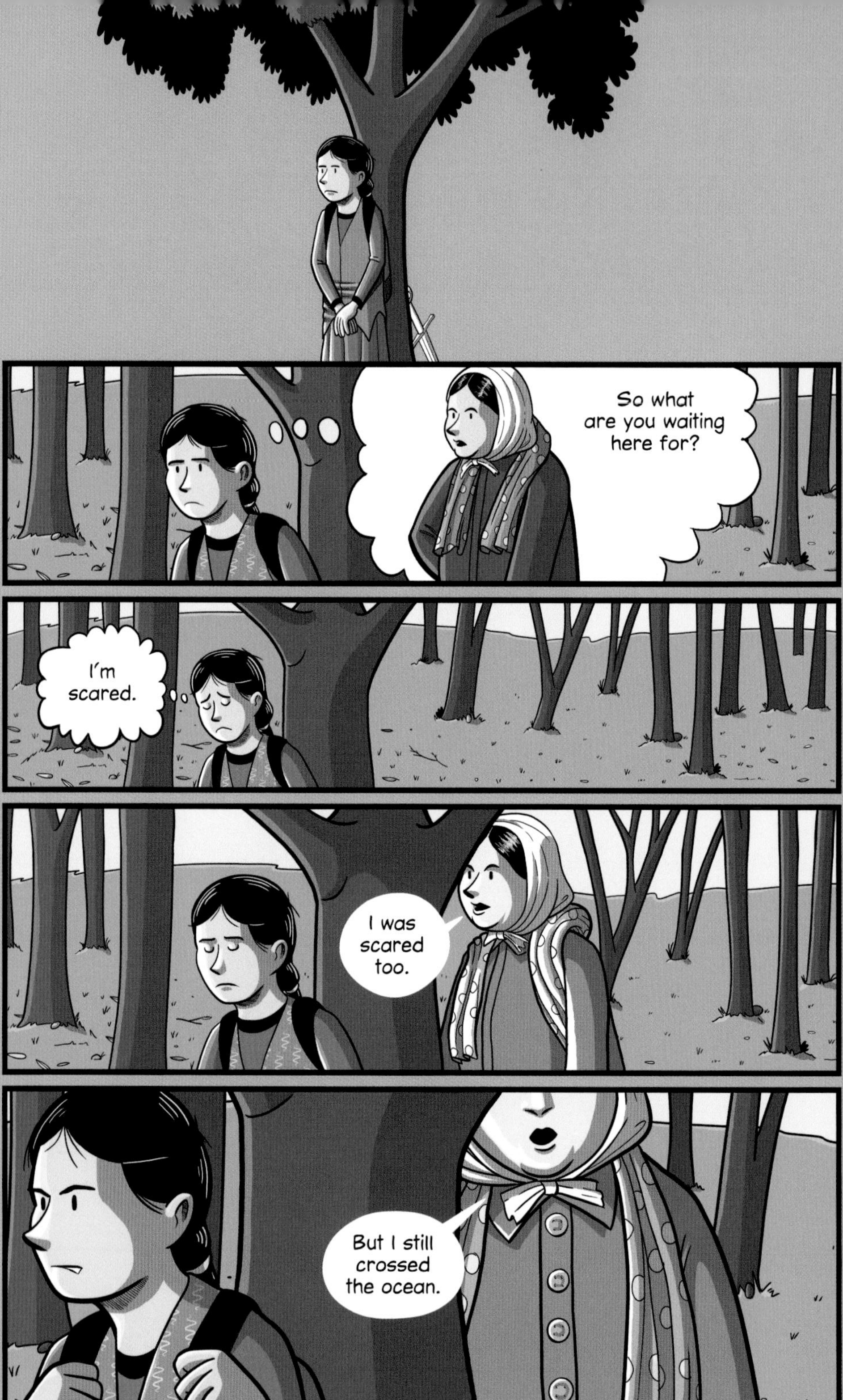
So what are you waiting here for?
I'm scared.
I was scared too.
But I still crossed the ocean.

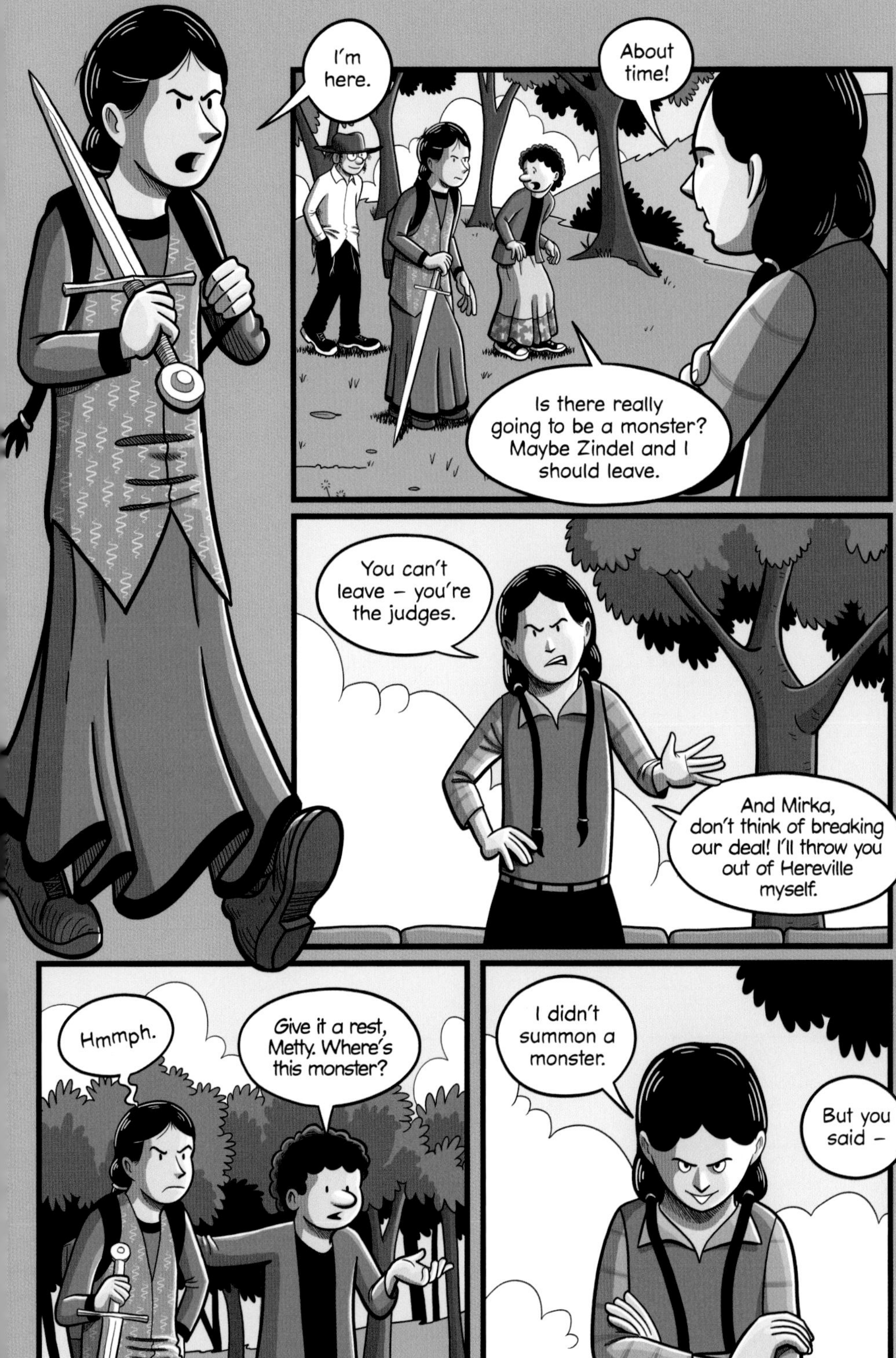
I'm here.
About time!
Is there really going to be a monster? Maybe Zindel and I should leave.
You can't leave – you're the judges.
And Mirka, don't think of breaking our deal! I'll throw you out of Hereville myself.
Hmmph.
Give it a rest, Metty. Where's this monster?
I didn't summon a monster.
But you said –

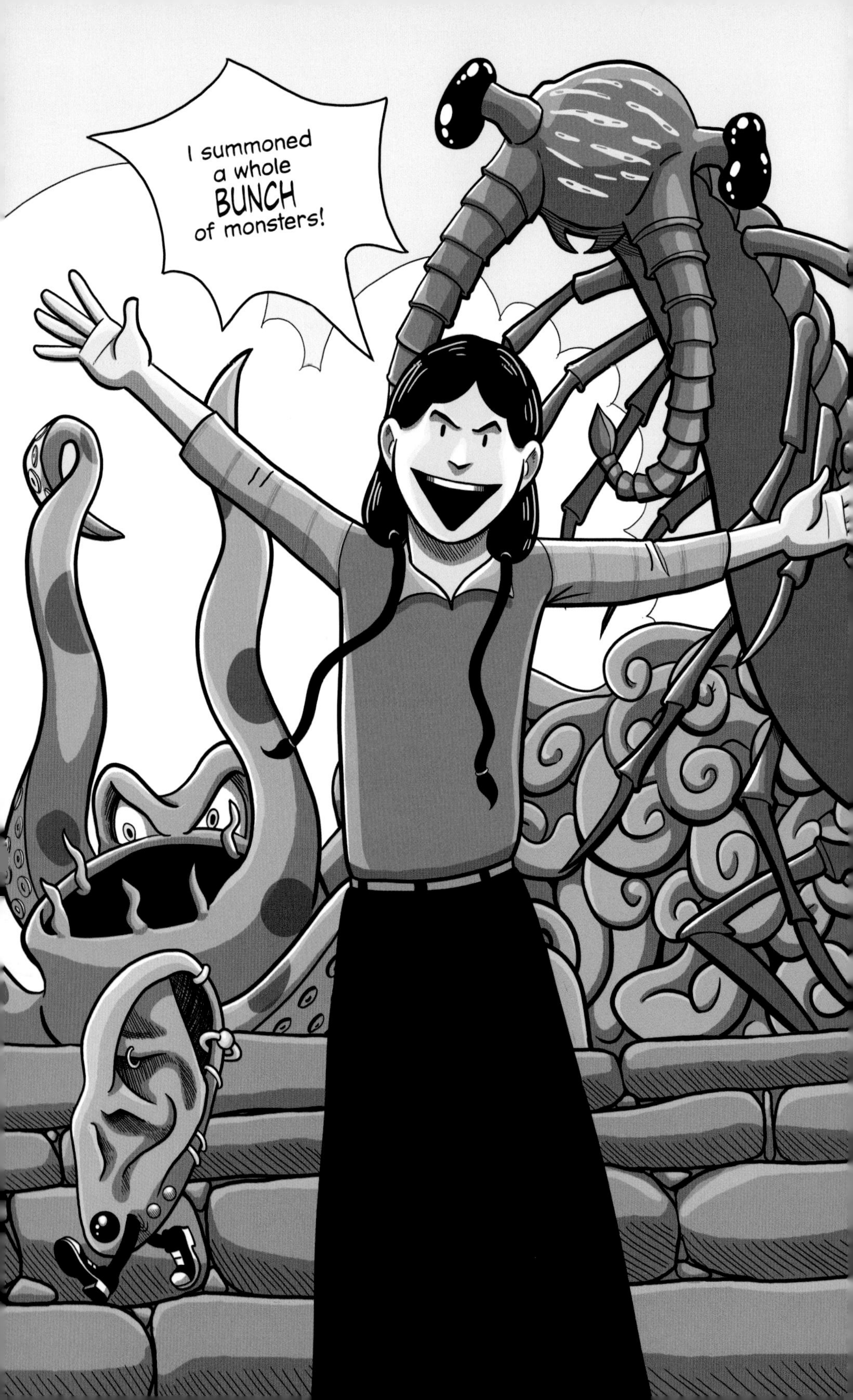
I summoned a whole BUNCH of monsters!

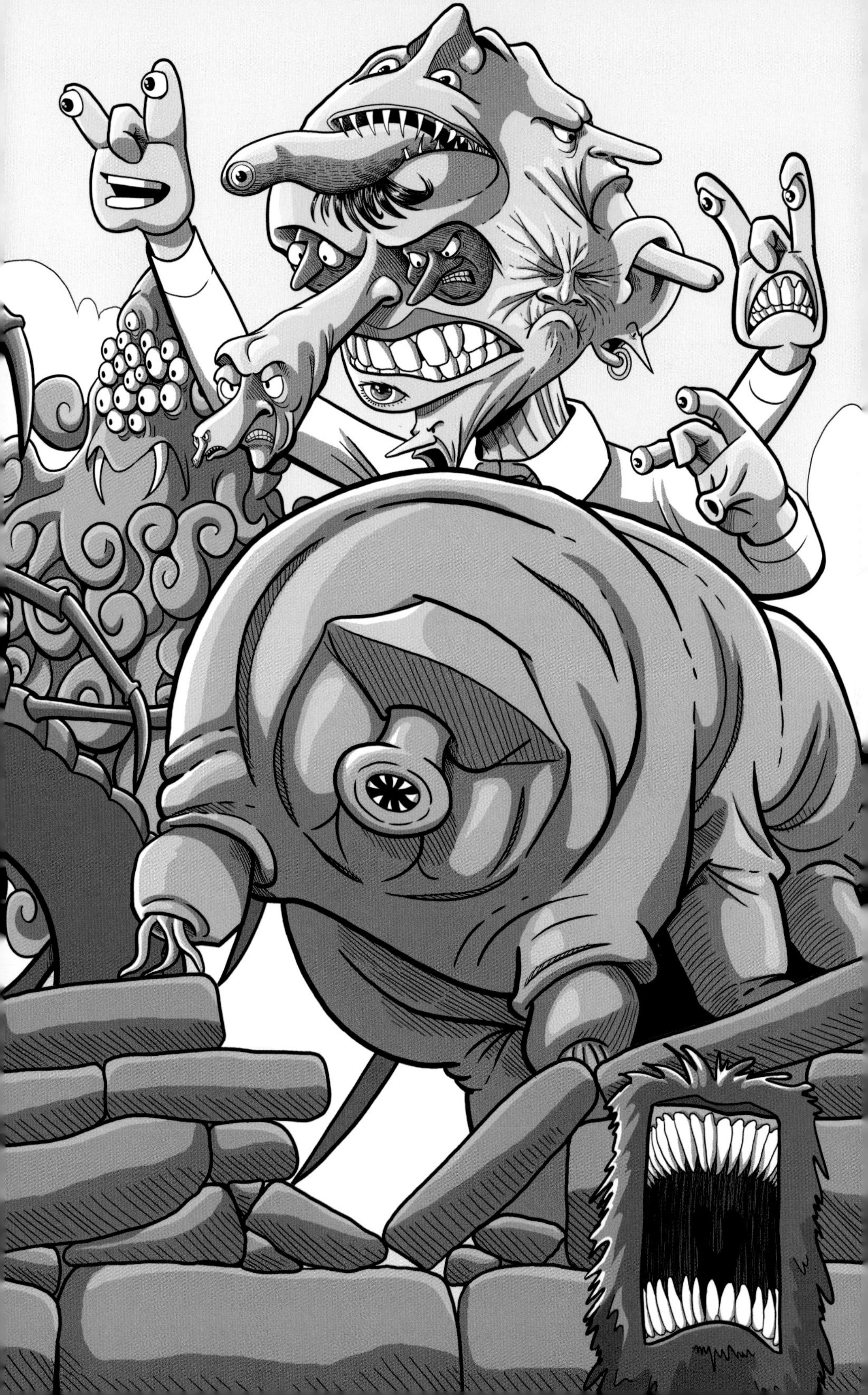

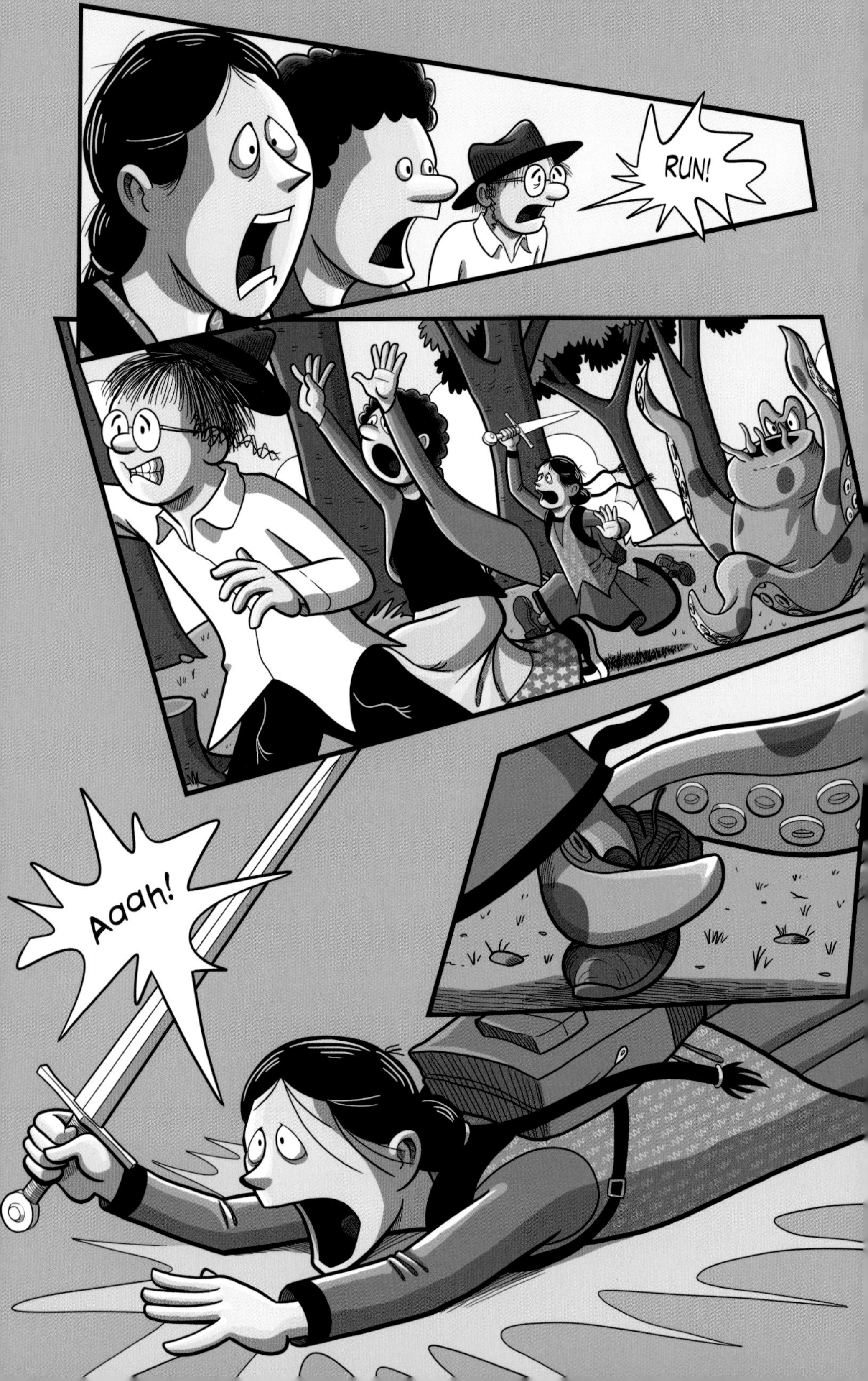
RUN!
Aaah!

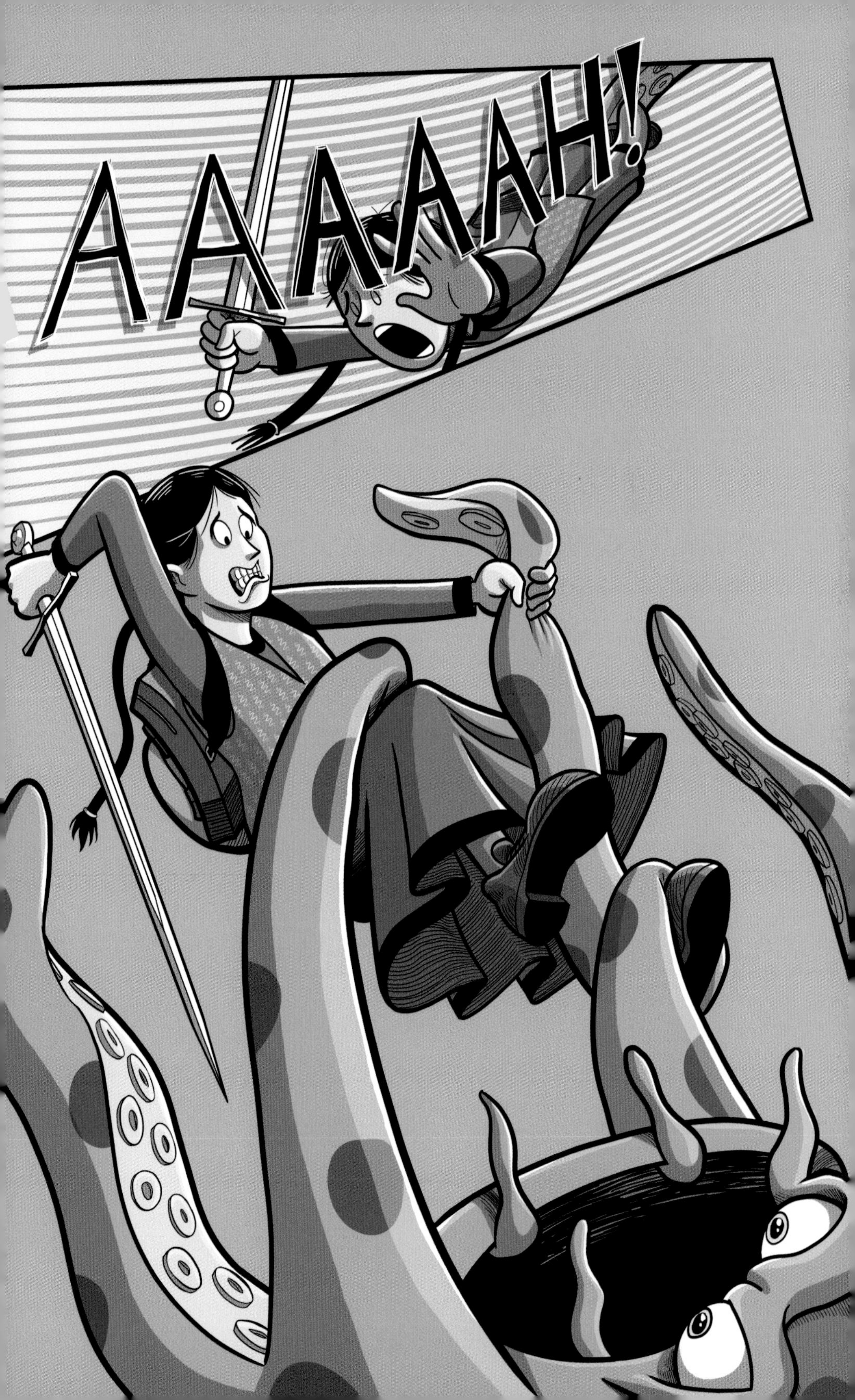
AAAAAH!

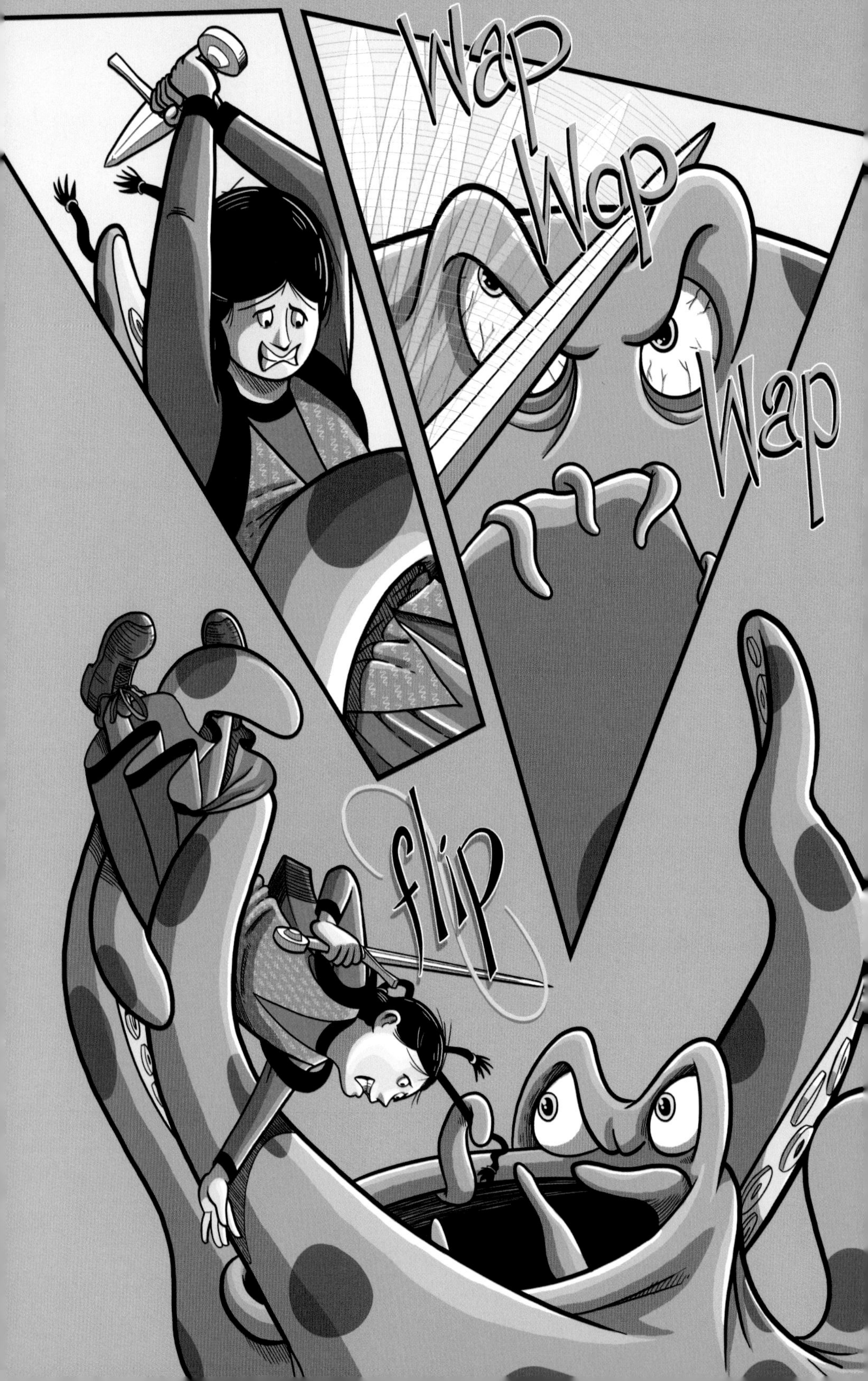
Wap
Wap
Wap
flip

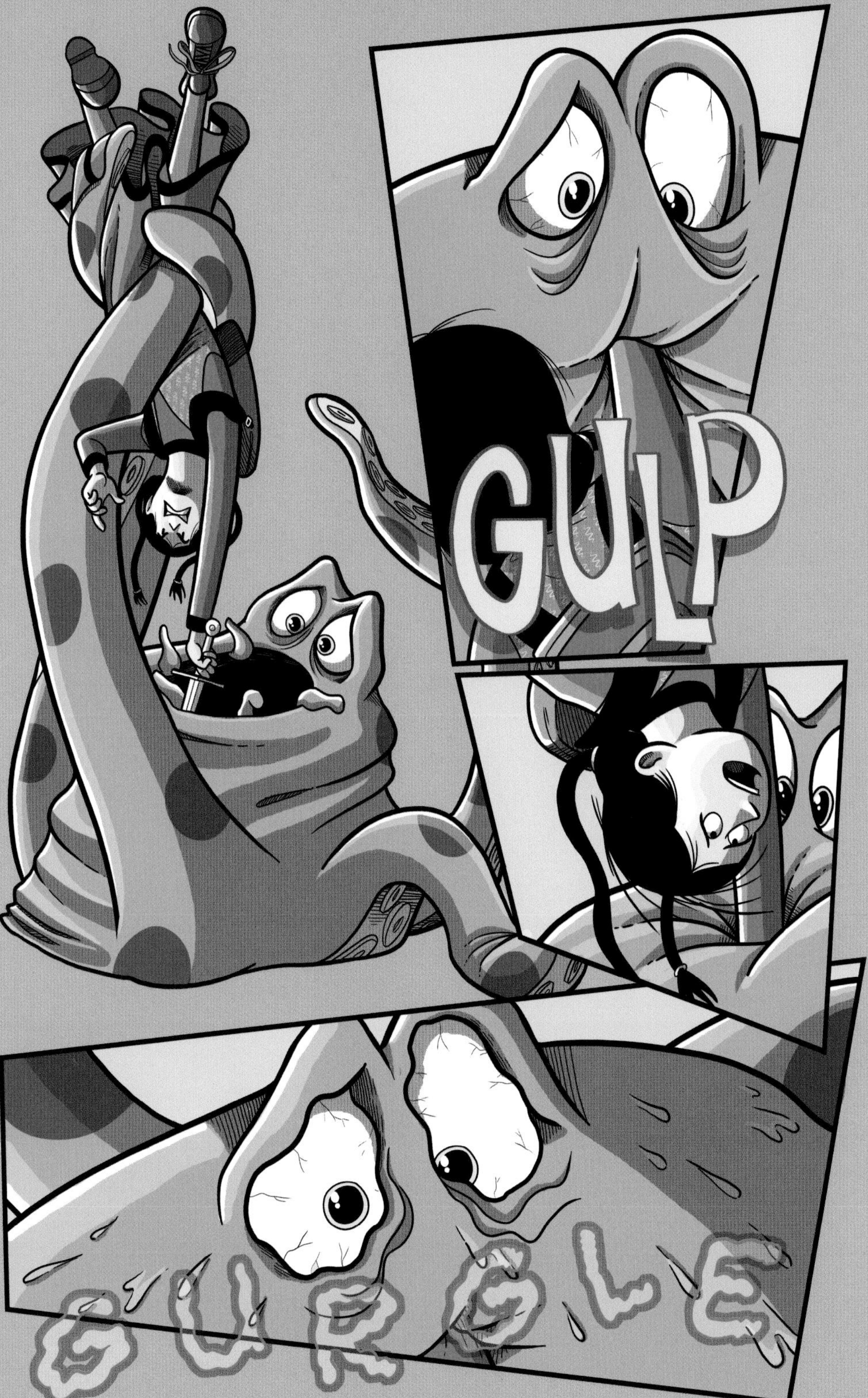
GULP
GURGLE

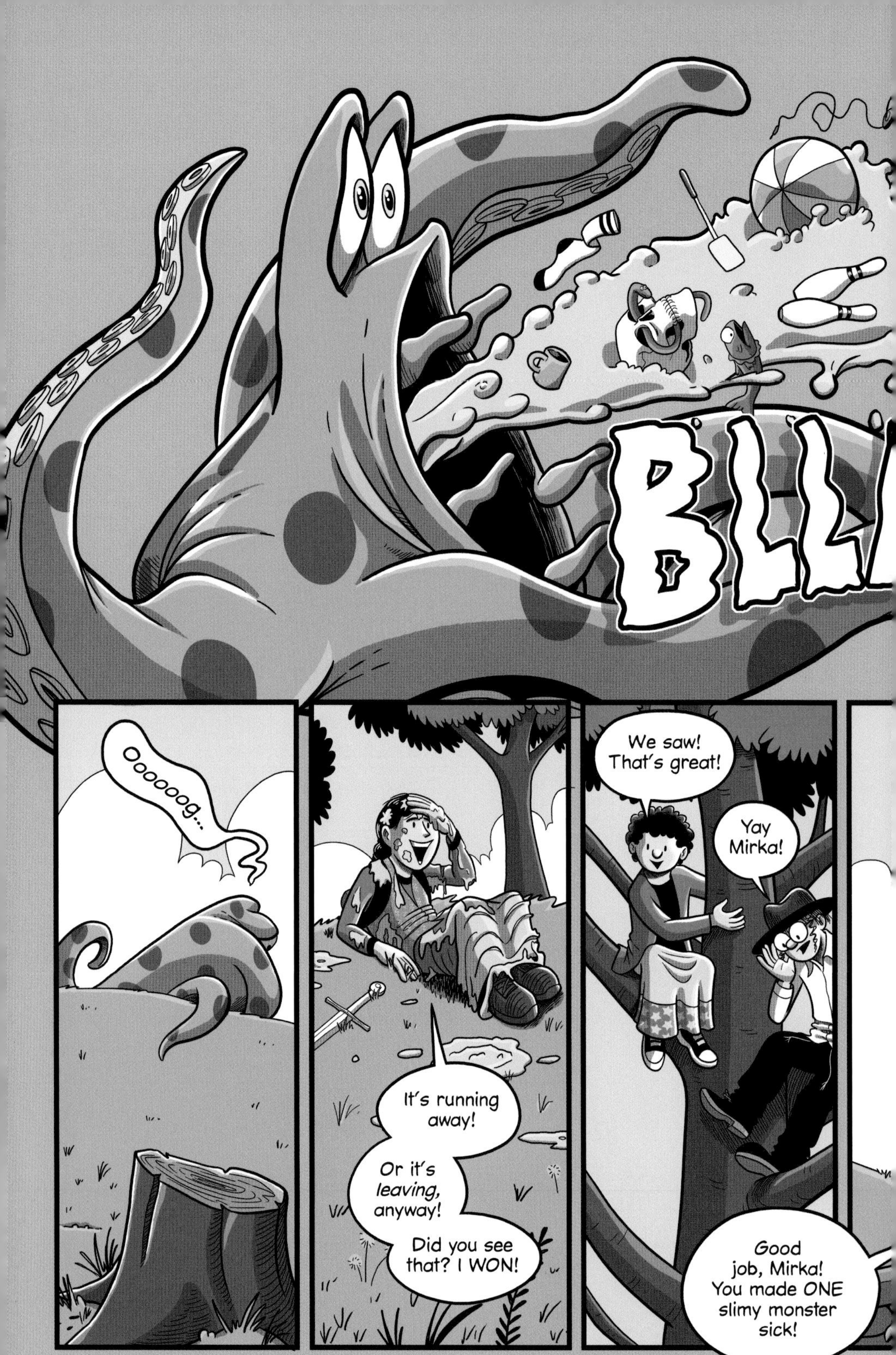
BLL
Oooooog...
It's running away!
Or it's *leaving*, anyway!
Did you see that? I WON!
We saw! That's great!
Yay Mirka!
Good job, Mirka! You made ONE slimy monster sick!

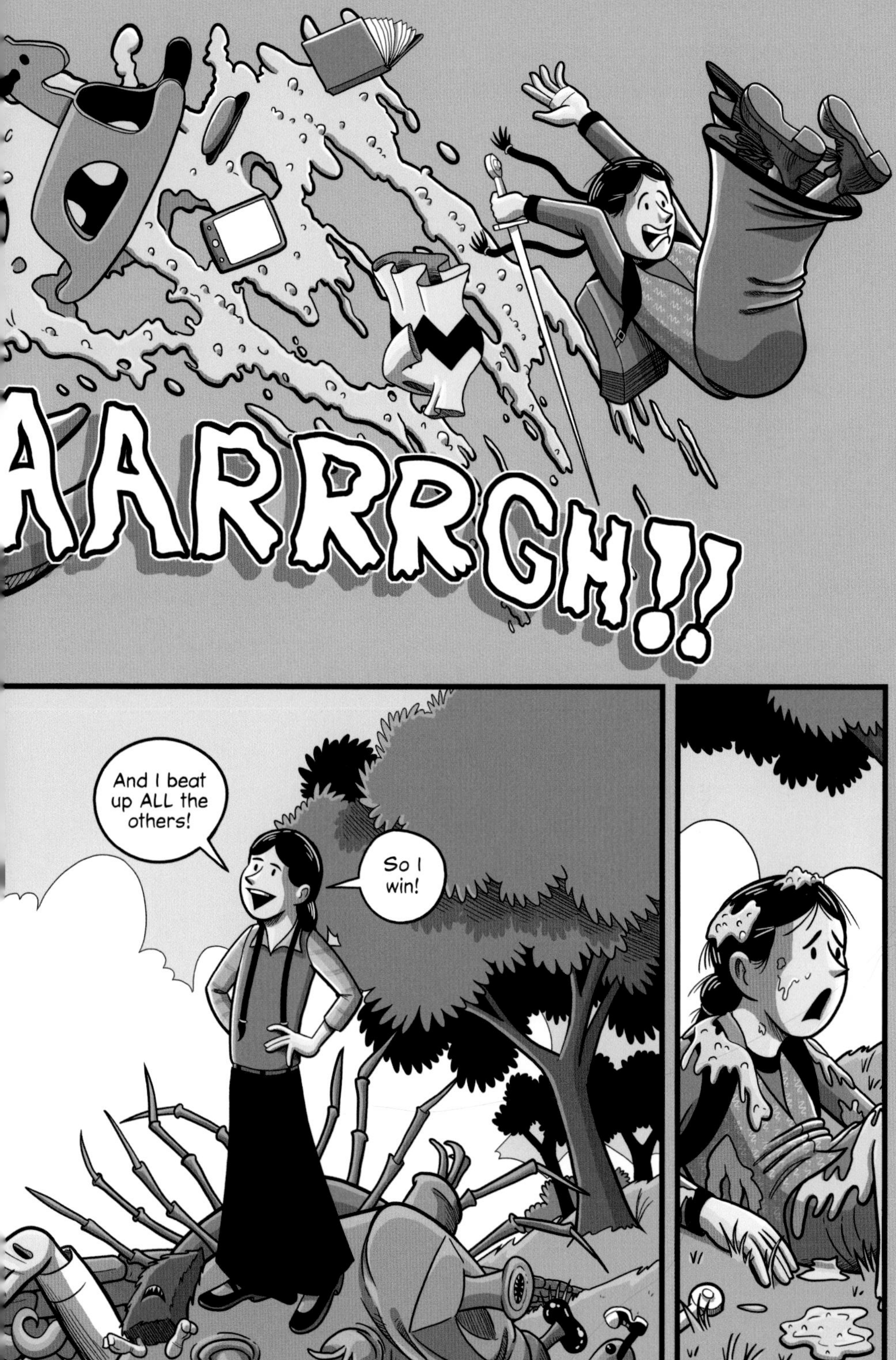
AARRRGH!!
And I beat up ALL the others!
So I win!

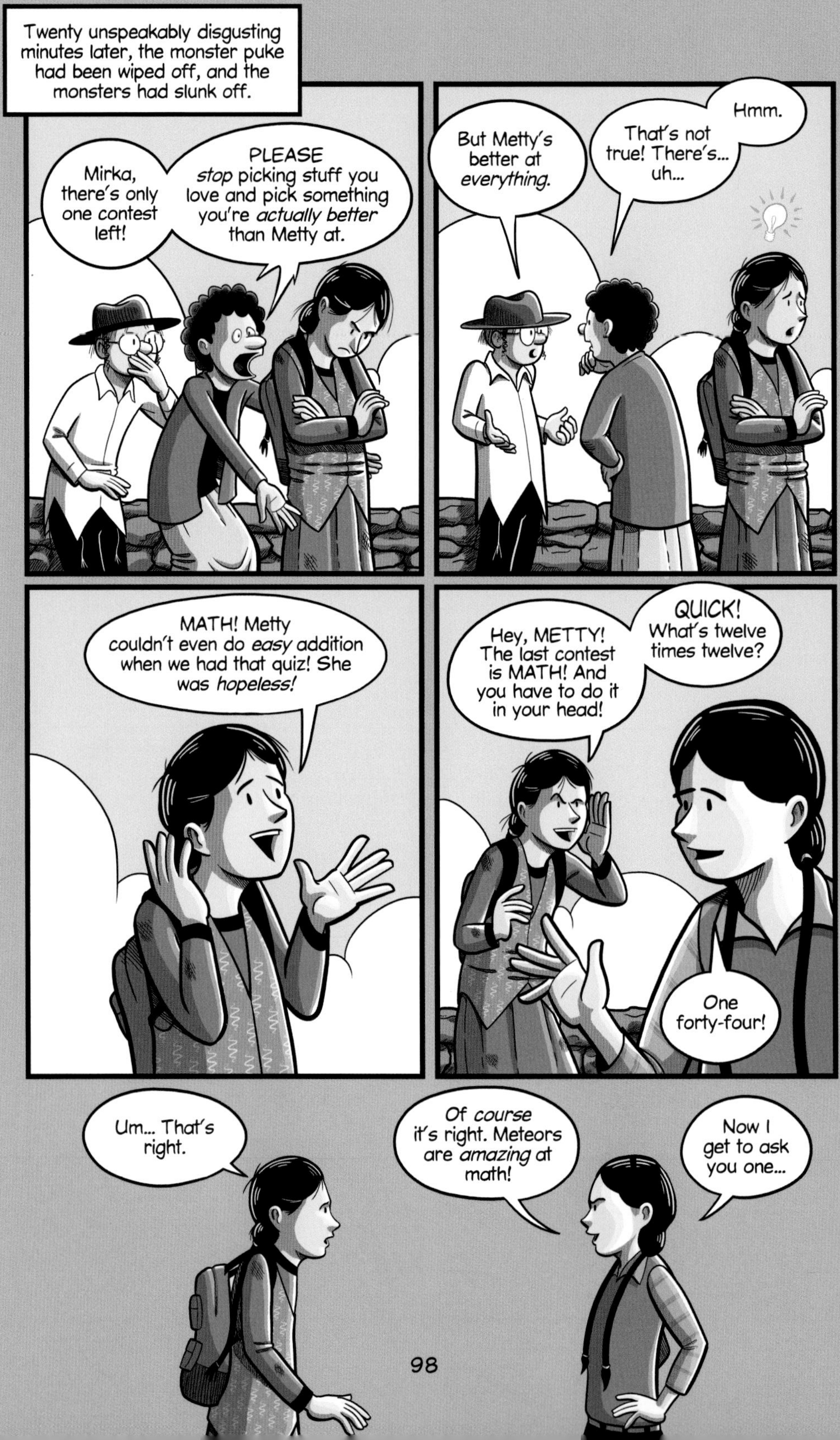
Twenty unspeakably disgusting minutes later, the monster puke had been wiped off, and the monsters had slunk off.
Mirka, there's only one contest left!
PLEASE *stop* picking stuff you love and pick something you're *actually better* than Metty at.
But Metty's better at *everything*.
That's not true! There's... uh...
Hmm.
MATH! Metty couldn't even do *easy* addition when we had that quiz! She was *hopeless!*
Hey, METTY! The last contest is MATH! And you have to do it in your head!
QUICK! What's twelve times twelve?
One forty-four!
Um... That's right.
Of *course* it's right. Meteors are *amazing* at math!
Now I get to ask you one...

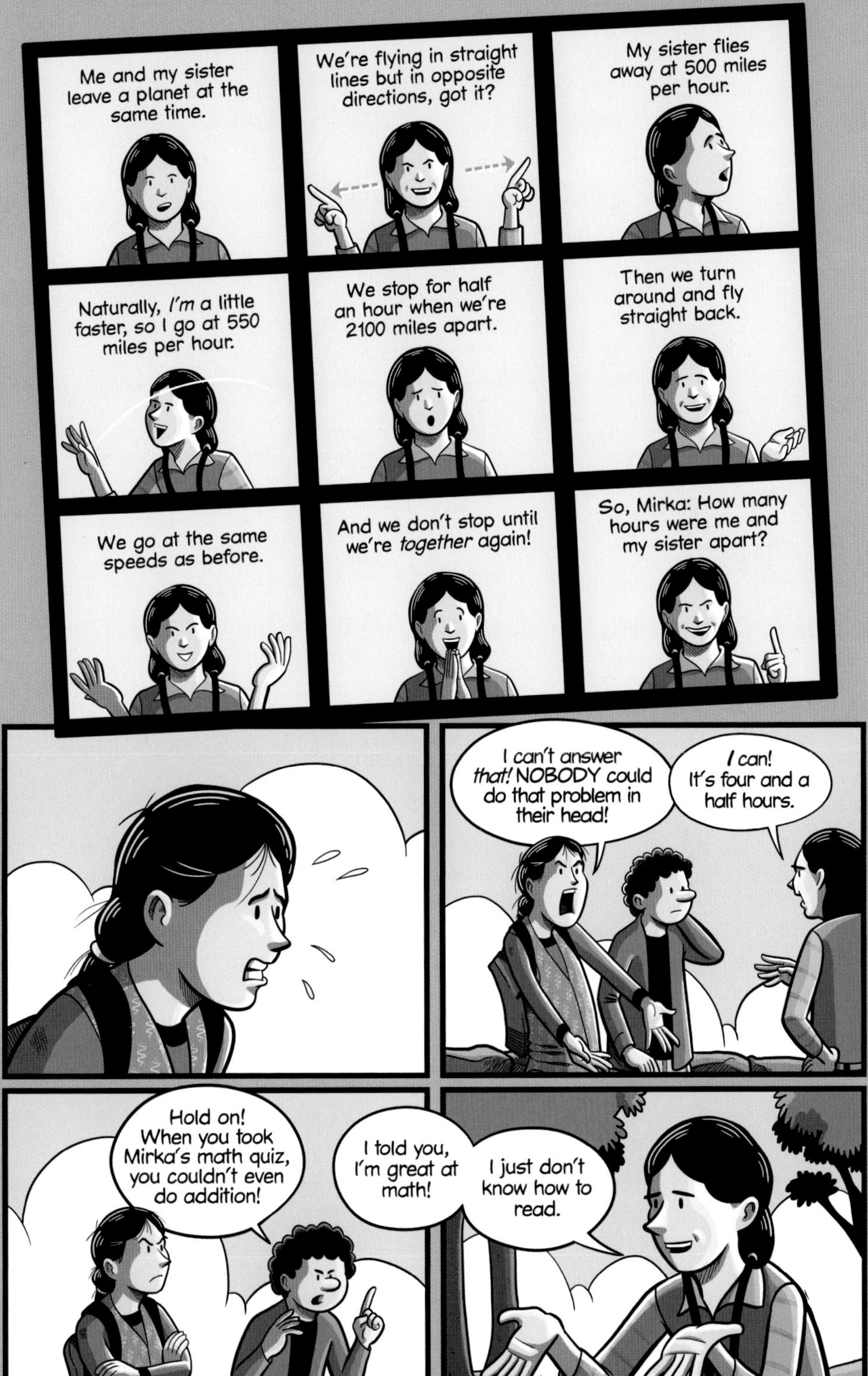
Me and my sister leave a planet at the same time.
We're flying in straight lines but in opposite directions, got it?
My sister flies away at 500 miles per hour.
Naturally, *I'm* a little faster, so I go at 550 miles per hour.
We stop for half an hour when we're 2100 miles apart.
Then we turn around and fly straight back.
We go at the same speeds as before.
And we don't stop until we're *together* again!
So, Mirka: How many hours were me and my sister apart?
I can't answer *that!* NOBODY could do that problem in their head!
I can! It's four and a half hours.
Hold on! When you took Mirka's math quiz, you couldn't even do addition!
I told you, I'm great at math!
I just don't know how to read.

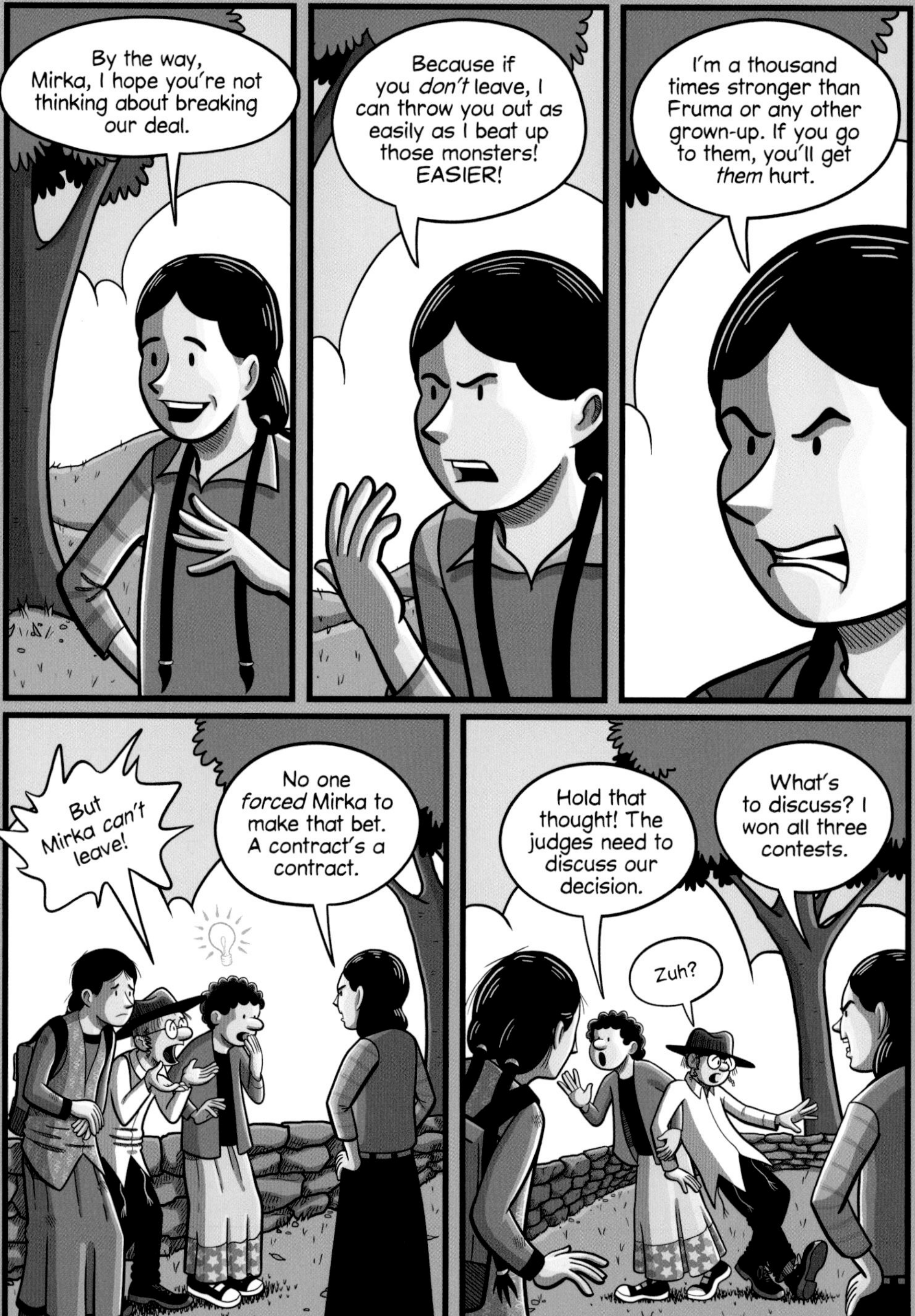
By the way, Mirka, I hope you're not thinking about breaking our deal.
Because if you *don't* leave, I can throw you out as easily as I beat up those monsters! EASIER!
I'm a thousand times stronger than Fruma or any other grown-up. If you go to them, you'll get *them* hurt.
But Mirka can't leave!
No one *forced* Mirka to make that bet. A contract's a contract.
Hold that thought! The judges need to discuss our decision.
What's to discuss? I won all three contests.
Zuh?

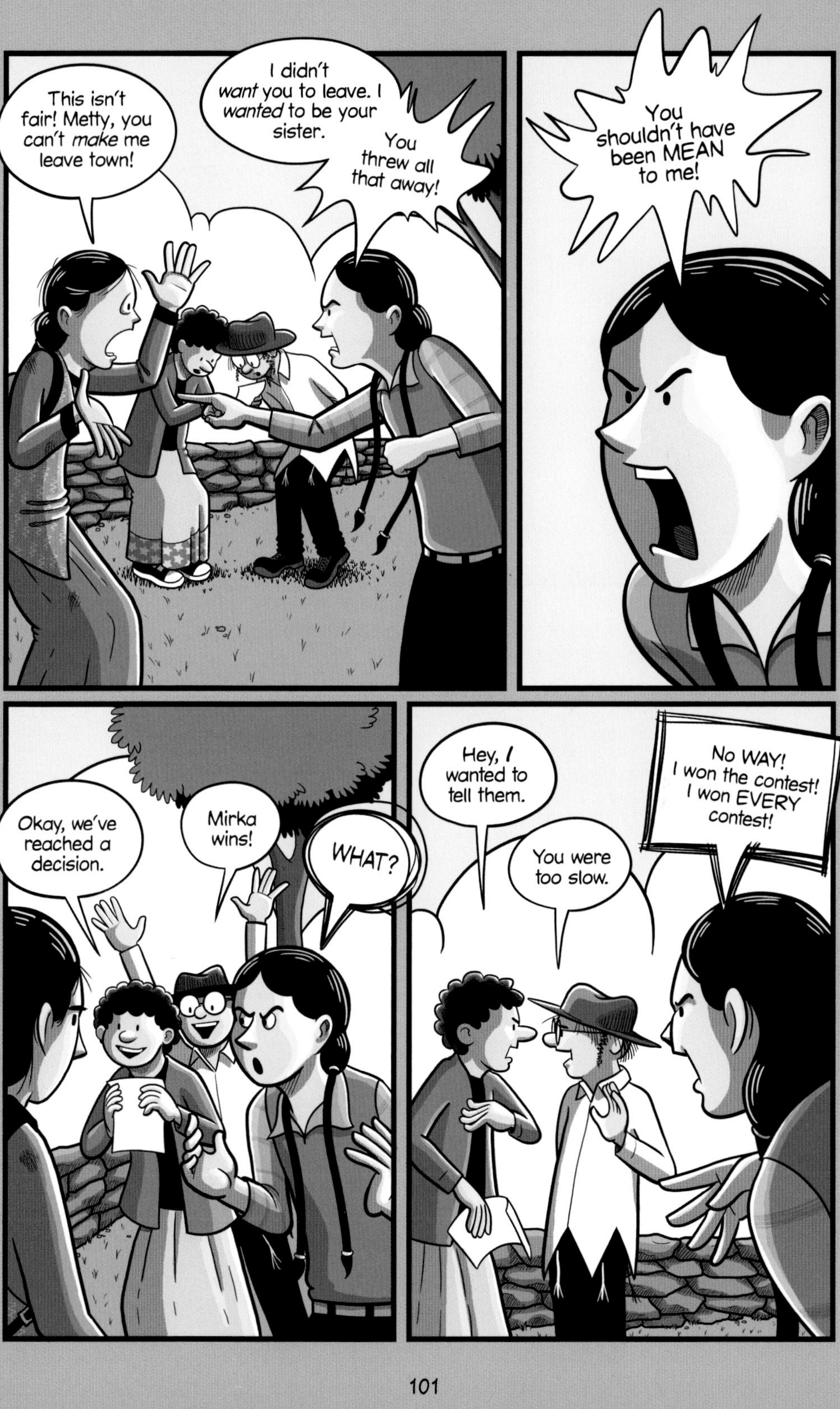
This isn't fair! Metty, you can't *make* me leave town!
I didn't *want* you to leave. I *wanted* to be your sister.
You threw all that away!
You shouldn't have been MEAN to me!
Okay, we've reached a decision.
Mirka wins!
WHAT?
Hey, *I* wanted to tell them.
You were too slow.
No WAY! I won the contest! I won EVERY contest!

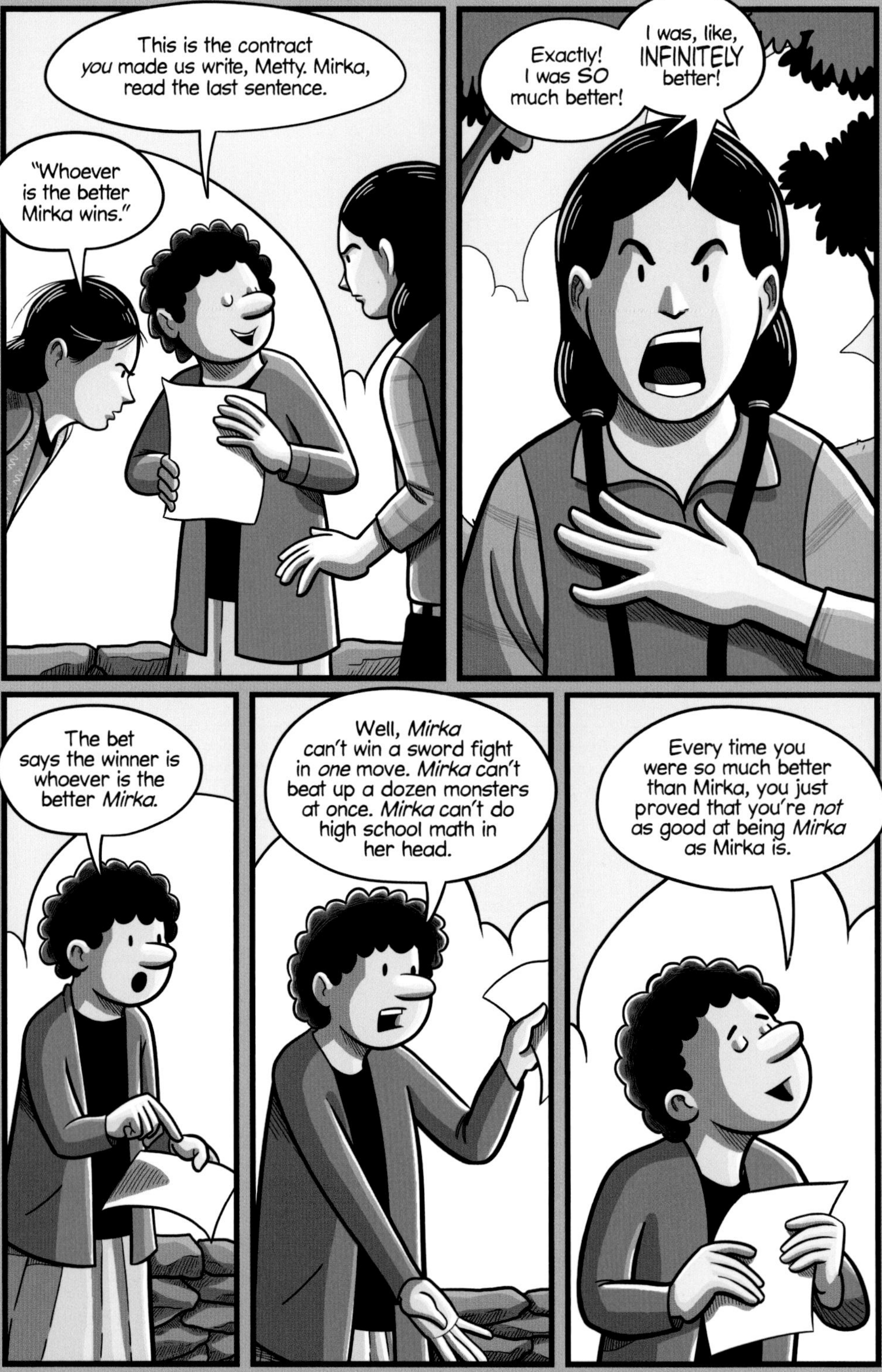
This is the contract *you* made us write, Metty. Mirka, read the last sentence.
"Whoever is the better Mirka wins."
Exactly! I was SO much better!
I was, like, INFINITELY better!
The bet says the winner is whoever is the better *Mirka.*
Well, *Mirka* can't win a sword fight in *one* move. *Mirka* can't beat up a dozen monsters at once. *Mirka* can't do high school math in her head.
Every time you were so much better than Mirka, you just proved that you're *not* as good at being *Mirka* as Mirka is.

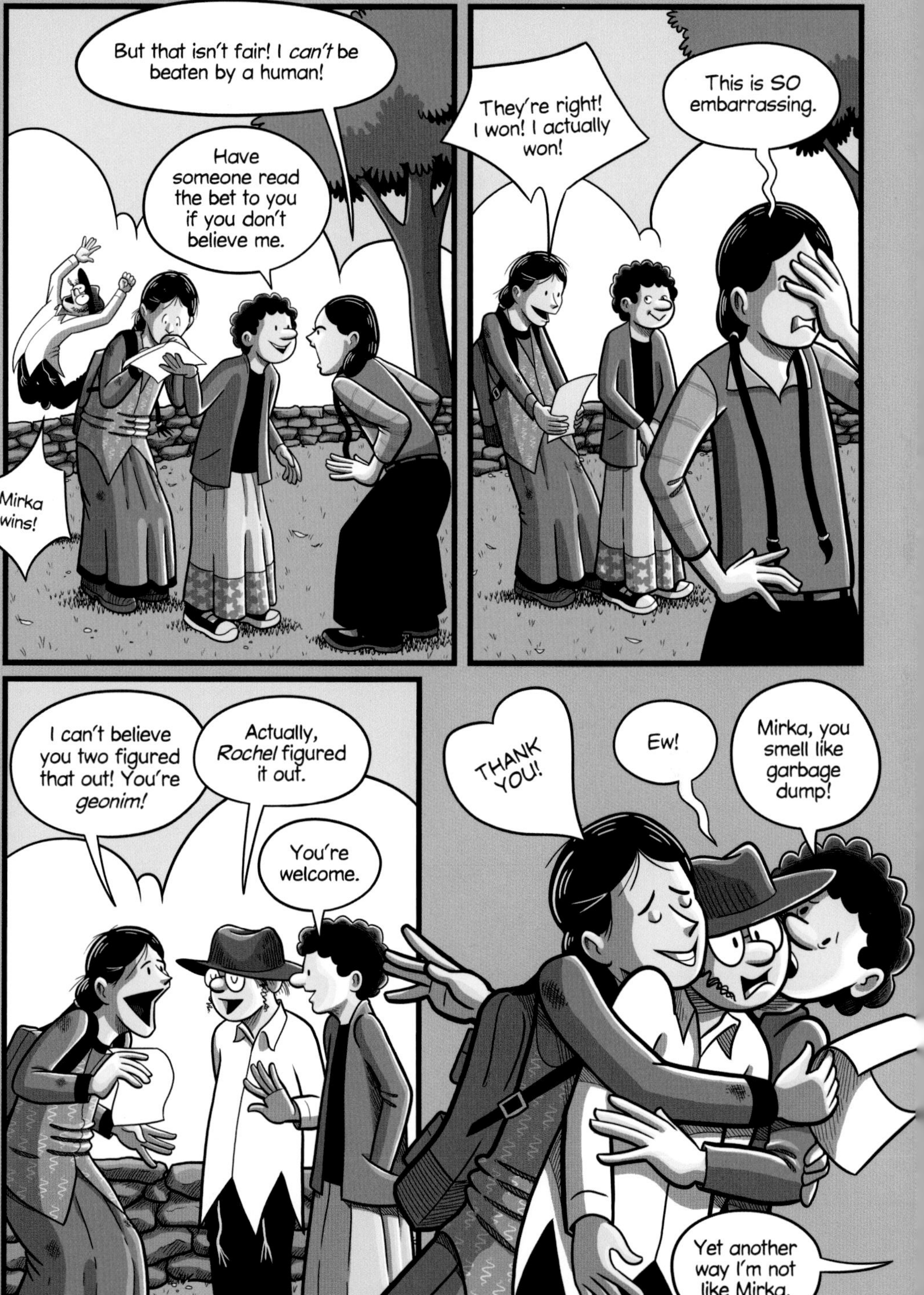
But that isn't fair! I *can't* be beaten by a human!
Have someone read the bet to you if you don't believe me.
Mirka wins!
They're right! I won! I actually won!
This is SO embarrassing.
I can't believe you two figured that out! You're *geonim!*
Actually, *Rochel* figured it out.
You're welcome.
THANK YOU!
Ew!
Mirka, you smell like garbage dump!
Yet another way I'm not like Mirka.

Geonim: Geniuses

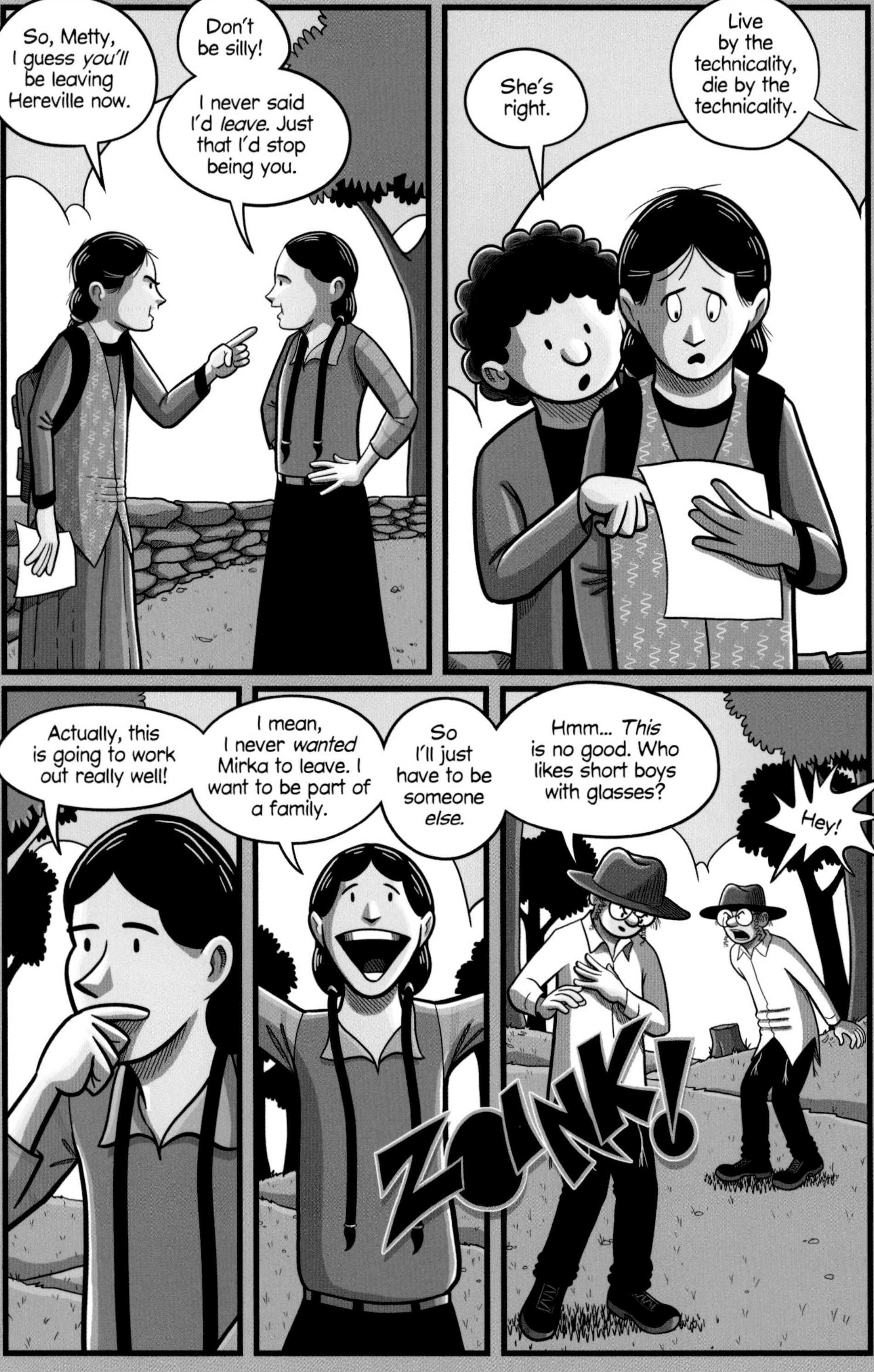

So, Metty, I guess *you'll* be leaving Hereville now.
Don't be silly!
I never said I'd *leave*. Just that I'd stop being you.
She's right.
Live by the technicality, die by the technicality.
Actually, this is going to work out really well!
I mean, I never *wanted* Mirka to leave. I want to be part of a family.
So I'll just have to be someone *else*.
Hmm... *This* is no good. Who likes short boys with glasses?
Hey!
ZOINK!

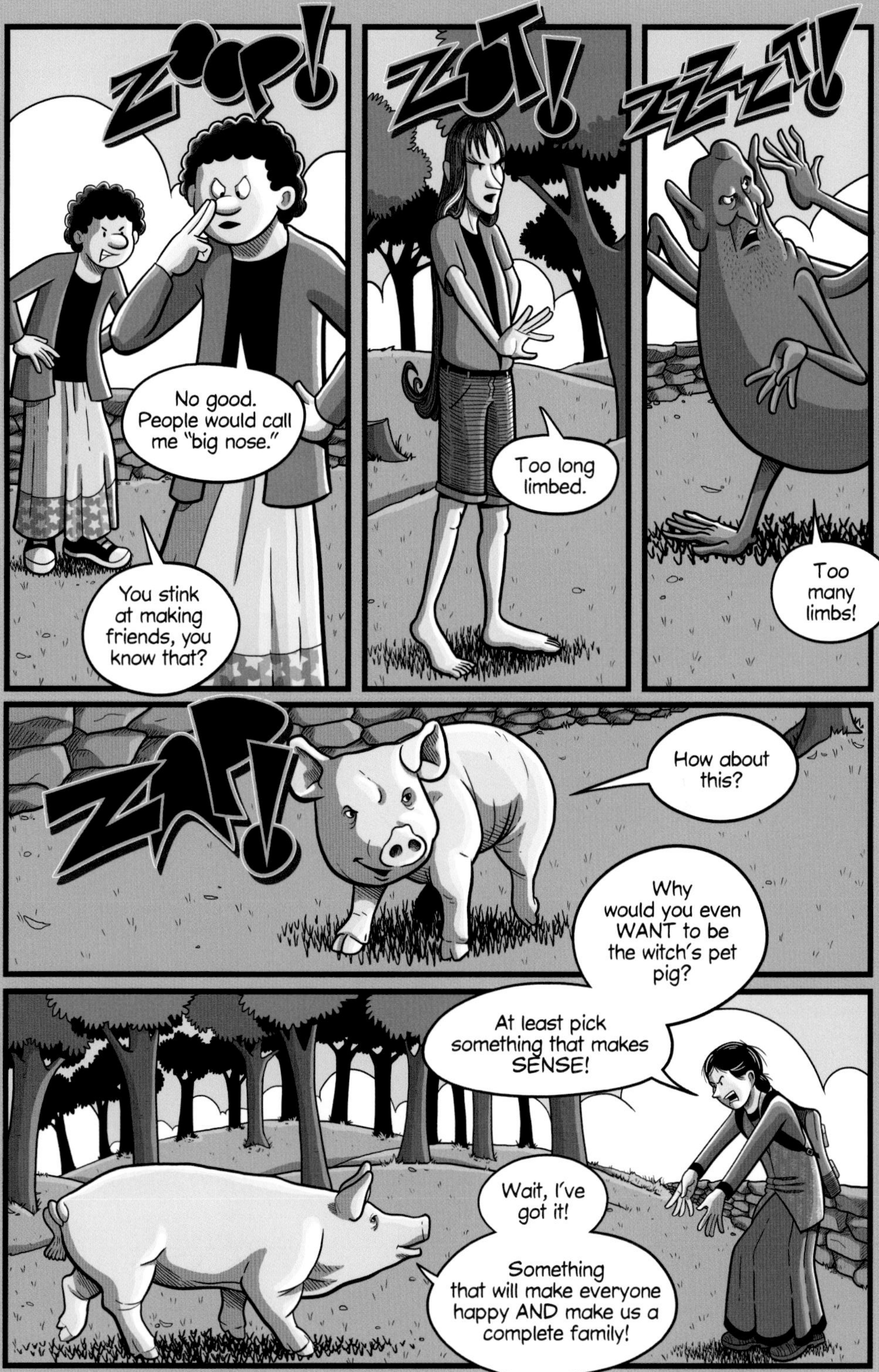
ZOOP!
No good. People would call me "big nose."
You stink at making friends, you know that?
ZOT!
Too long limbed.
ZZZZT!
Too many limbs!
ZAP!
How about this?
Why would you even WANT to be the witch's pet pig?
At least pick something that makes SENSE!
Wait, I've got it!
Something that will make everyone happy AND make us a complete family!

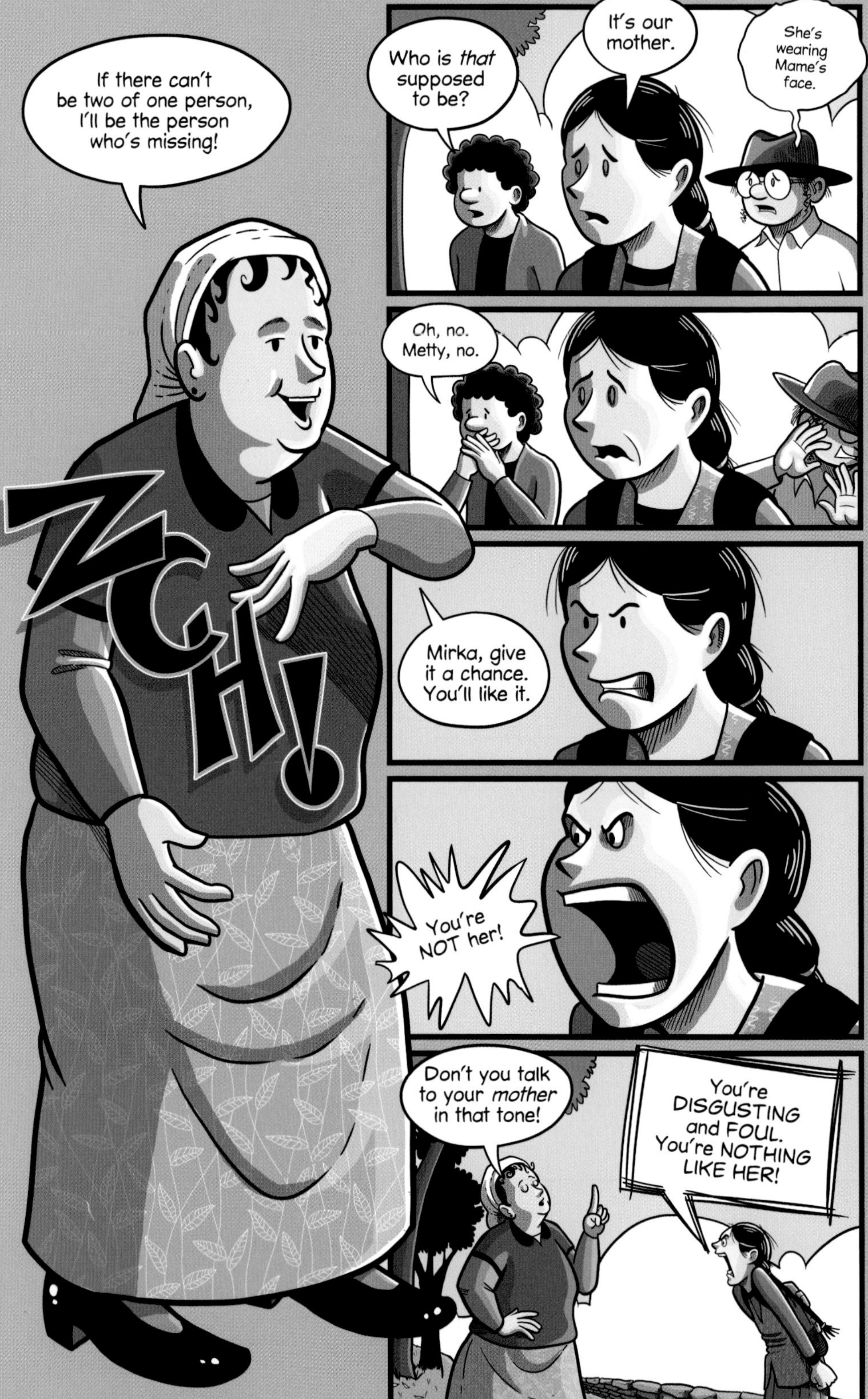

If there can't be two of one person, I'll be the person who's missing!
ZGH!
Who is *that* supposed to be?
It's our mother.
She's wearing Mame's face.
Oh, no. Metty, no.
Mirka, give it a chance. You'll like it.
You're NOT her!
Don't you talk to your *mother* in that tone!
You're DISGUSTING and FOUL. You're NOTHING LIKE HER!

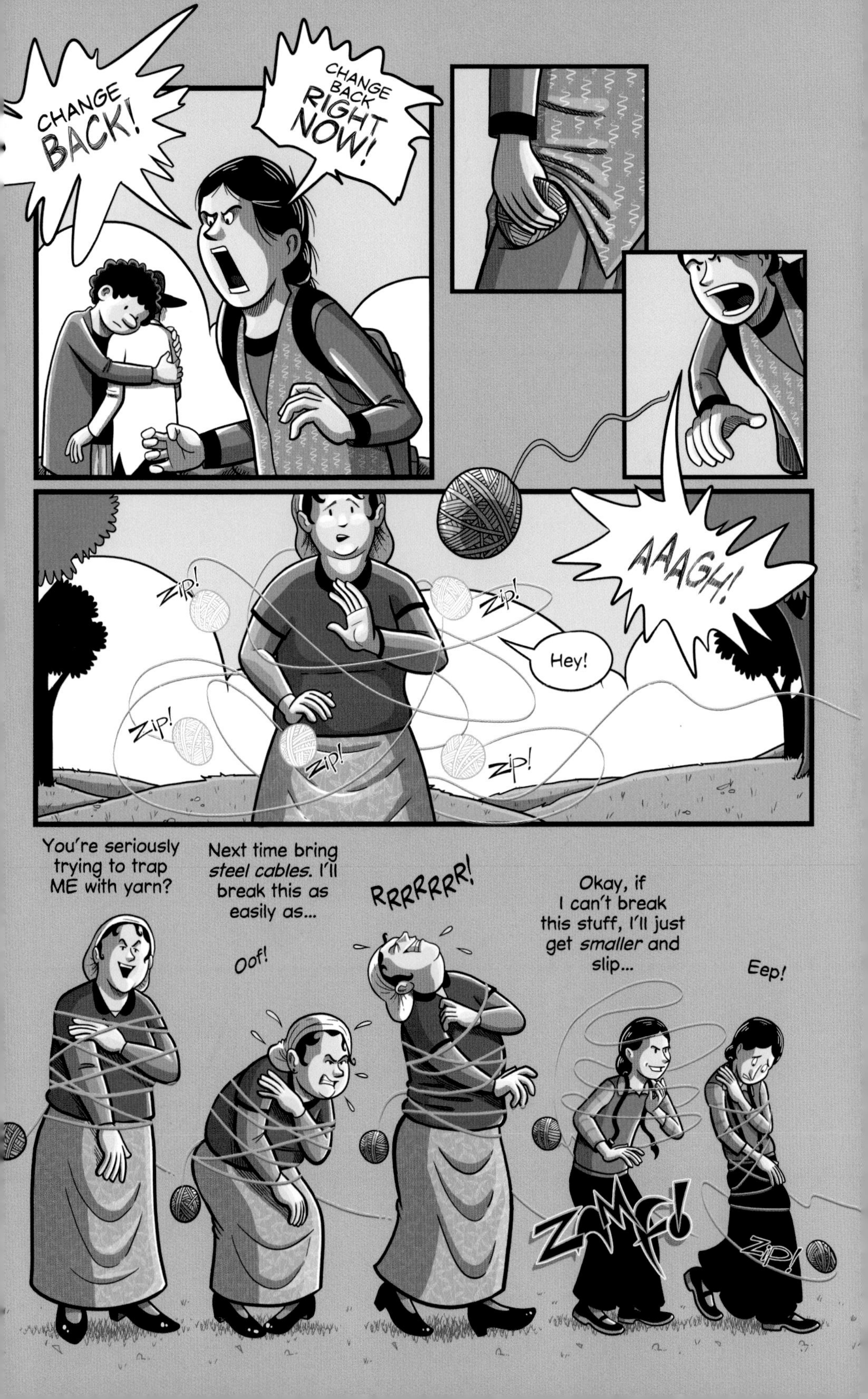
CHANGE BACK!
CHANGE BACK RIGHT NOW!
AAAGH!
ZIP!
ZIP!
Hey!
ZIP!
ZIP!
ZIP!
You're seriously trying to trap ME with yarn?
Next time bring *steel cables.* I'll break this as easily as...
Oof!
RRRRRRR!
Okay, if I can't break this stuff, I'll just get *smaller* and slip...
ZMF!
Eep!
ZIP!

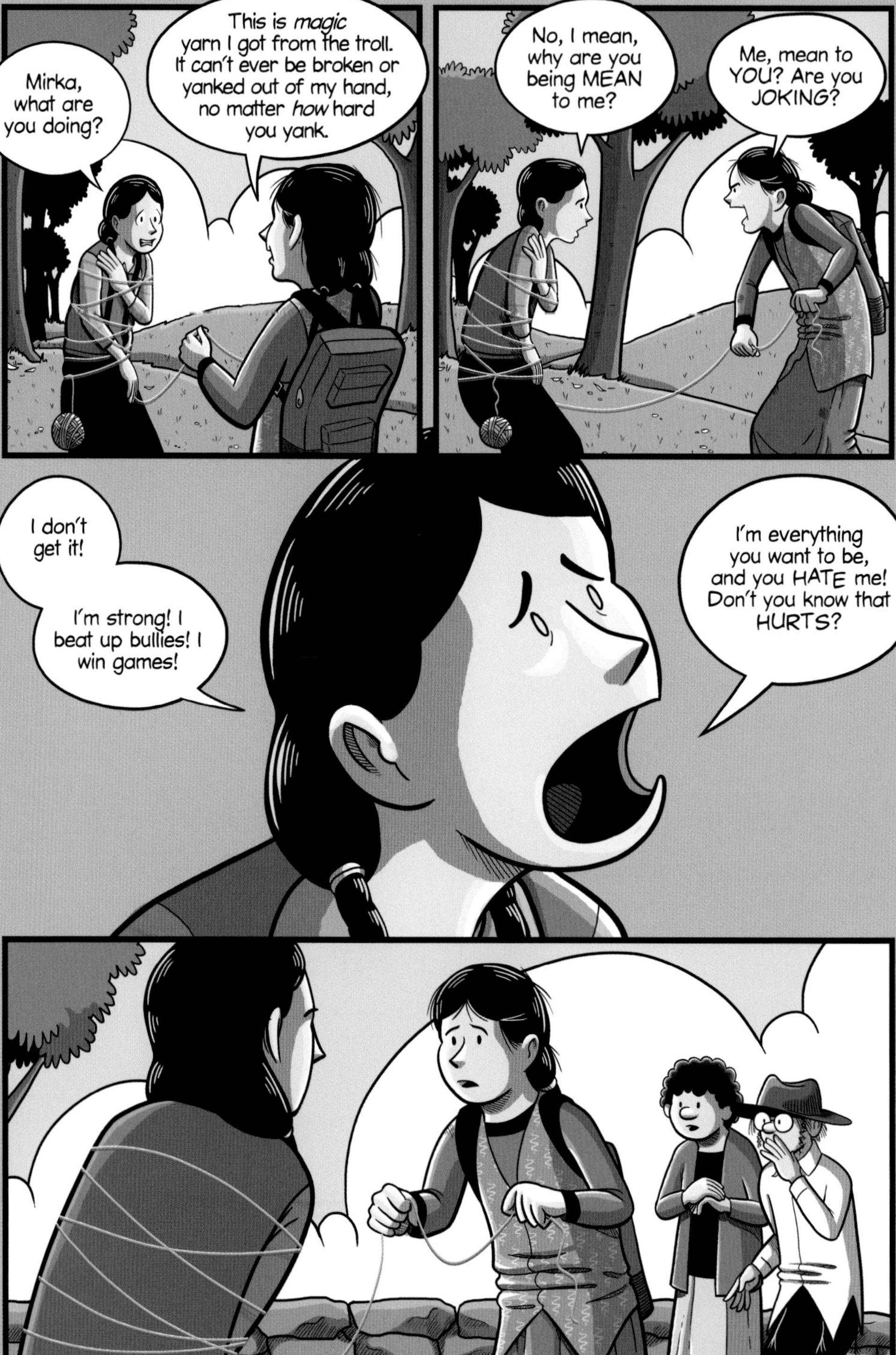
Mirka, what are you doing?
This is *magic* yarn I got from the troll. It can't ever be broken or yanked out of my hand, no matter *how* hard you yank.
No, I mean, why are you being MEAN to me?
Me, mean to YOU? Are you JOKING?
I don't get it!
I'm strong! I beat up bullies! I win games!
I'm everything you want to be, and you HATE me! Don't you know that HURTS?

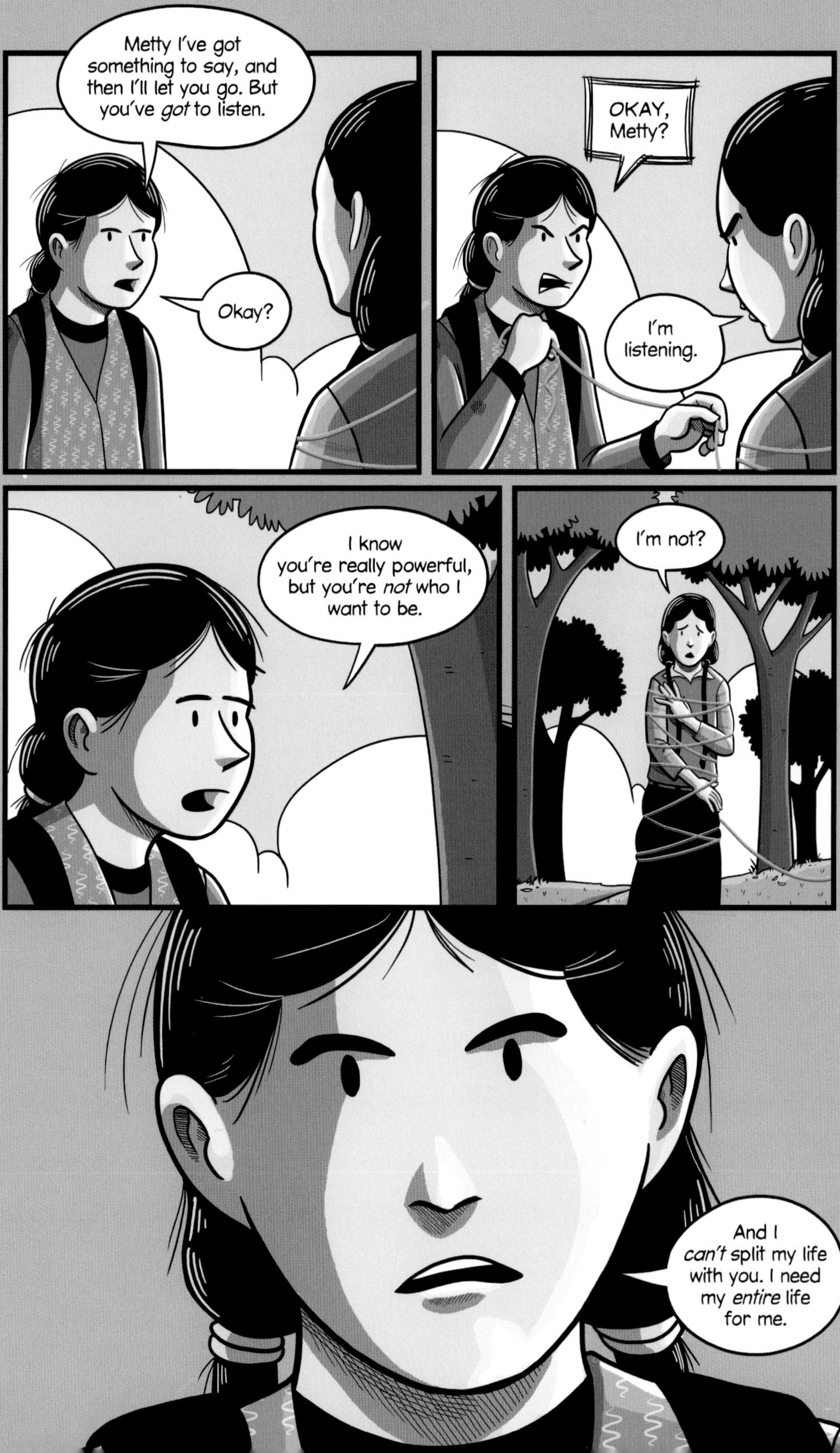
Metty I've got something to say, and then I'll let you go. But you've *got* to listen.
Okay?
OKAY, Metty?
I'm listening.
I know you're really powerful, but you're *not* who I want to be.
I'm not?
And I *can't* split my life with you. I need my *entire* life for me.

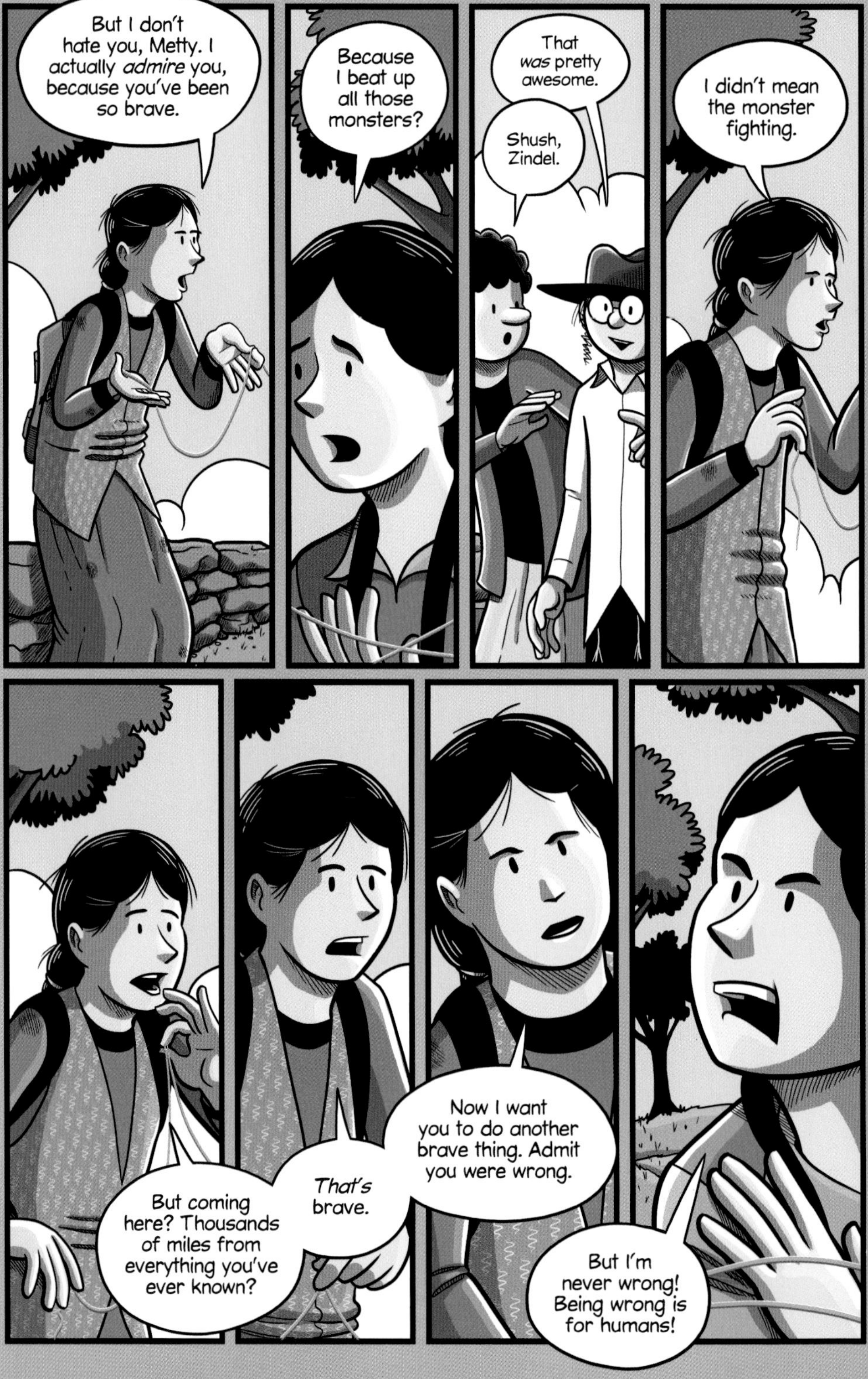
But I don't hate you, Metty. I actually *admire* you, because you've been so brave.
Because I beat up all those monsters?
That *was* pretty awesome.
Shush, Zindel.
I didn't mean the monster fighting.
But coming here? Thousands of miles from everything you've ever known?
That's brave.
Now I want you to do another brave thing. Admit you were wrong.
But I'm never wrong! Being wrong is for humans!

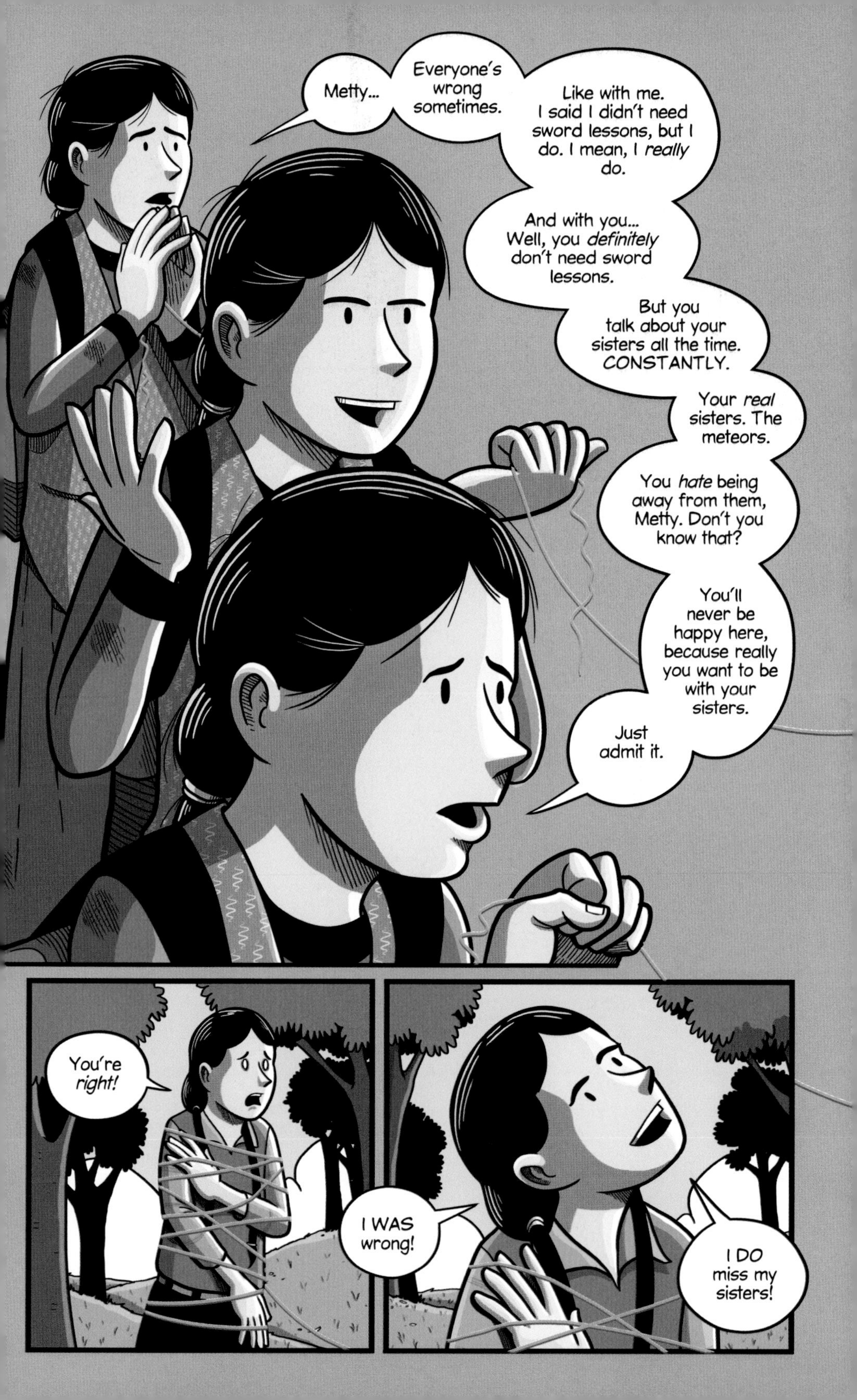
Metty...
Everyone's wrong sometimes.
Like with me. I said I didn't need sword lessons, but I do. I mean, I *really* do.
And with you... Well, you *definitely* don't need sword lessons.
But you talk about your sisters all the time. CONSTANTLY.
Your *real* sisters. The meteors.
You *hate* being away from them, Metty. Don't you know that?
You'll never be happy here, because really you want to be with your sisters.
Just admit it.
You're *right!*
I WAS wrong!
I DO miss my sisters!

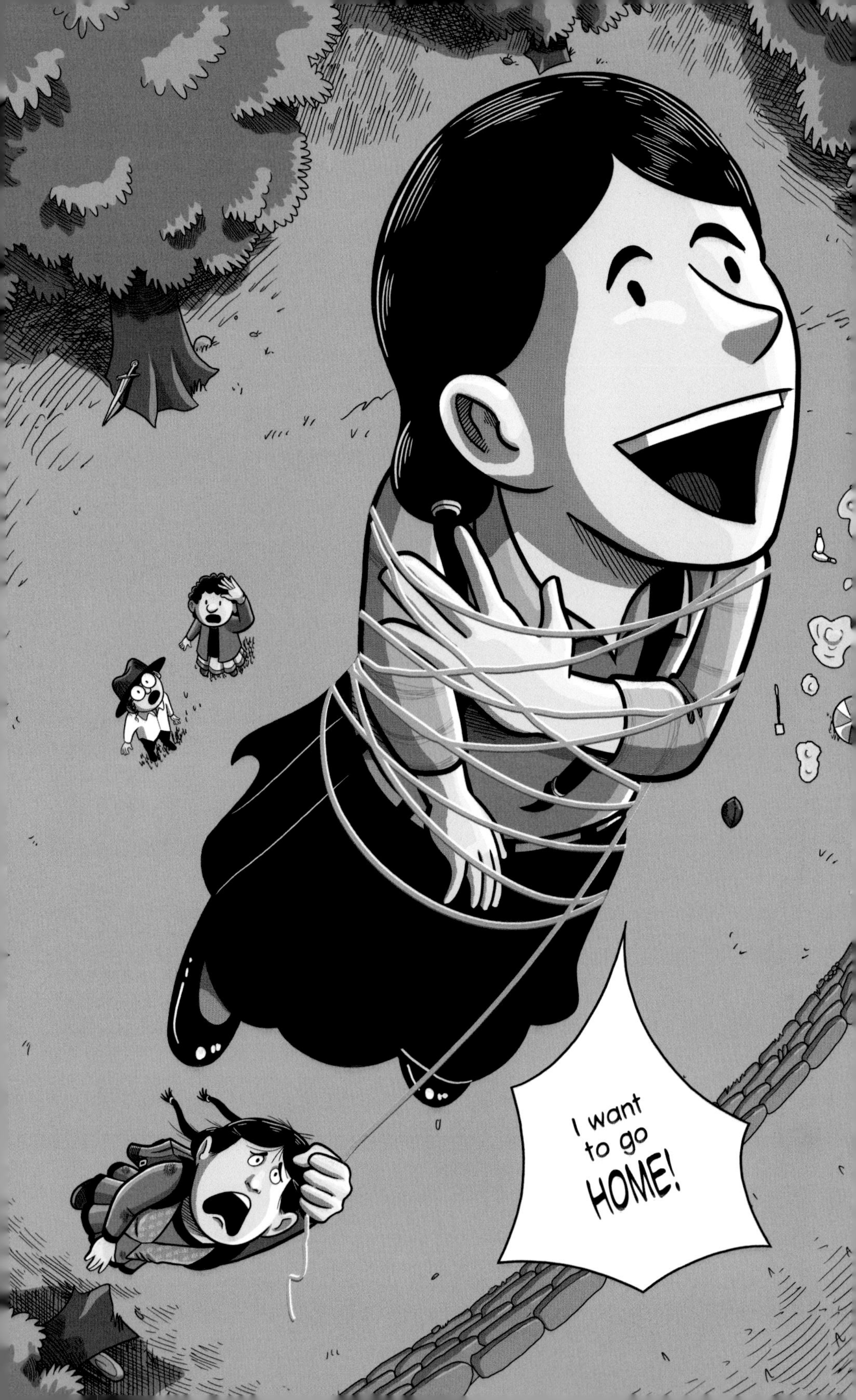
I want to go HOME!

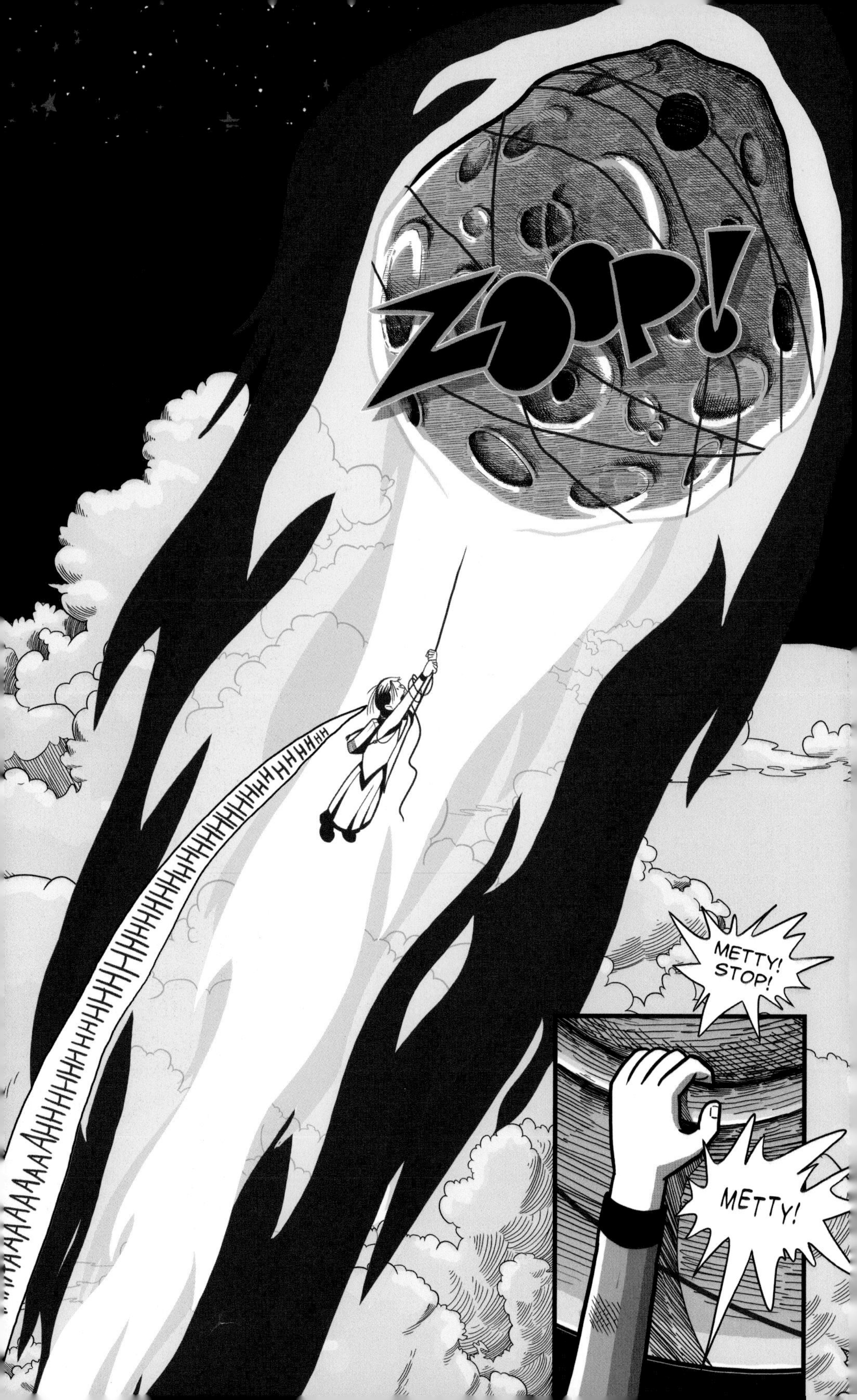
ZOOP!
AAAAAAAAAAAHHHHHHHHHHHHHHHHHHHHHHHHHHHHHHHHHHHHHHHH
METTY! STOP!
METTY!

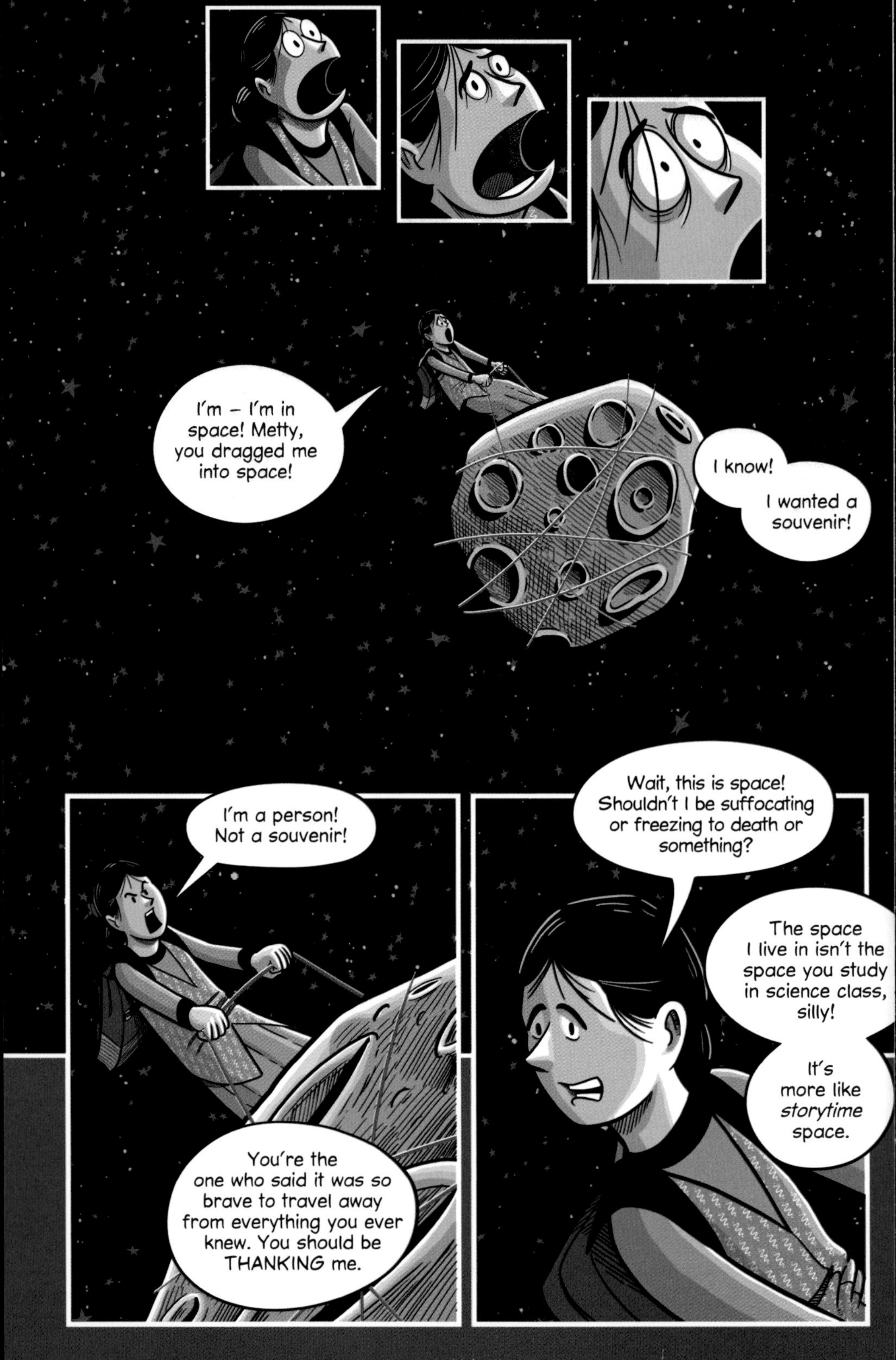
I'm – I'm in space! Metty, you dragged me into space!
I know!
I wanted a souvenir!
I'm a person! Not a souvenir!
You're the one who said it was so brave to travel away from everything you ever knew. You should be THANKING me.
Wait, this is space! Shouldn't I be suffocating or freezing to death or something?
The space I live in isn't the space you study in science class, silly!
It's more like *storytime* space.

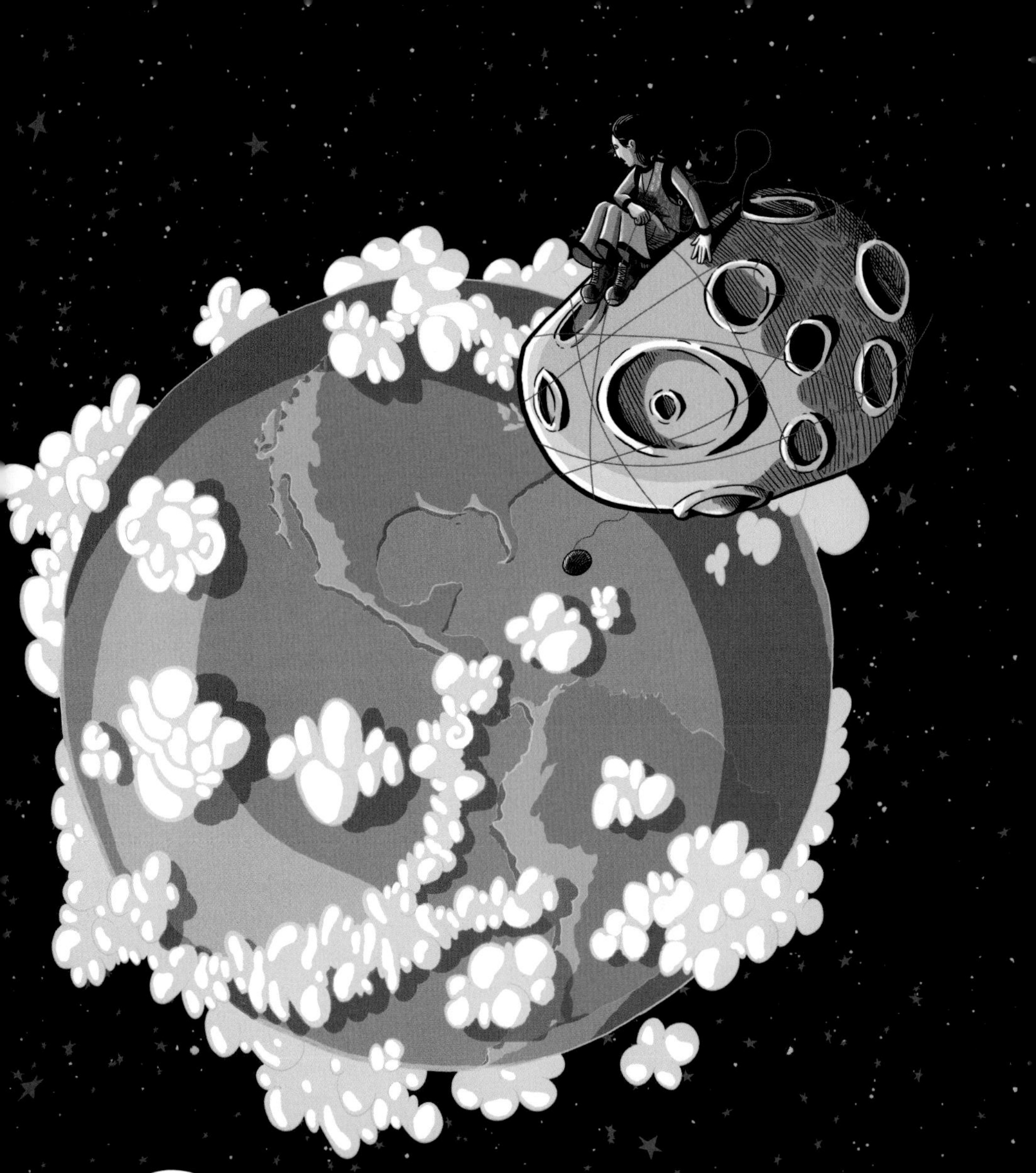

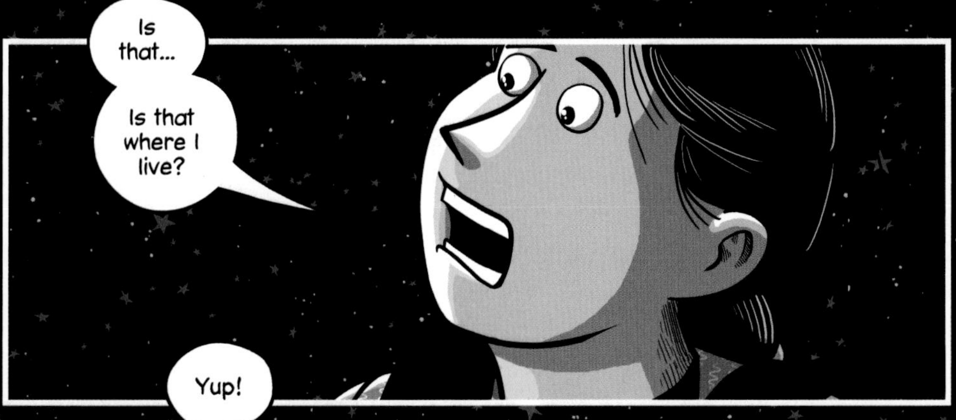
Is that...
Is that where I live?
Yup!

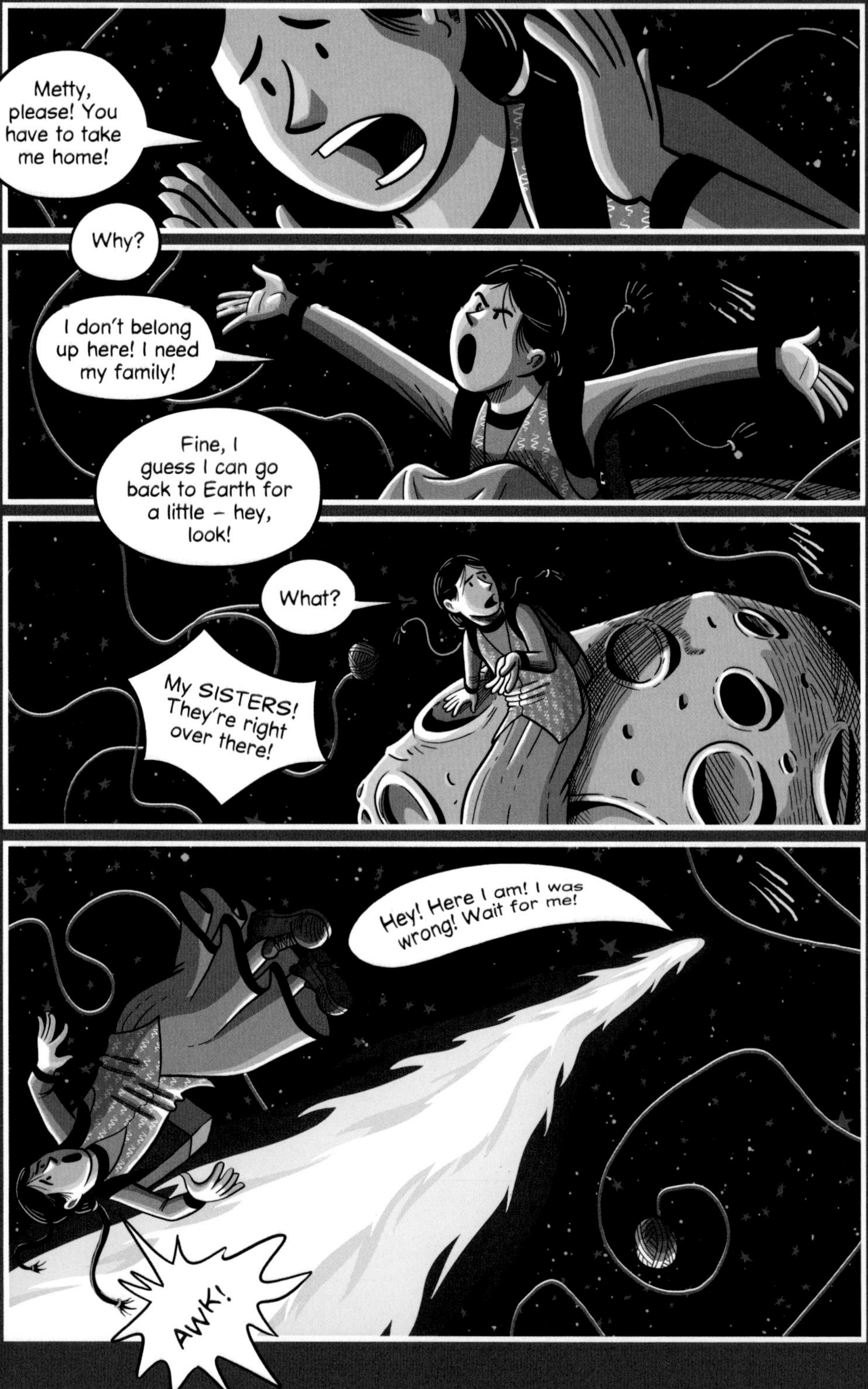
Metty, please! You have to take me home!
Why?
I don't belong up here! I need my family!
Fine, I guess I can go back to Earth for a little – hey, look!
What?
My SISTERS! They're right over there!
Hey! Here I am! I was wrong! Wait for me!
AWK!

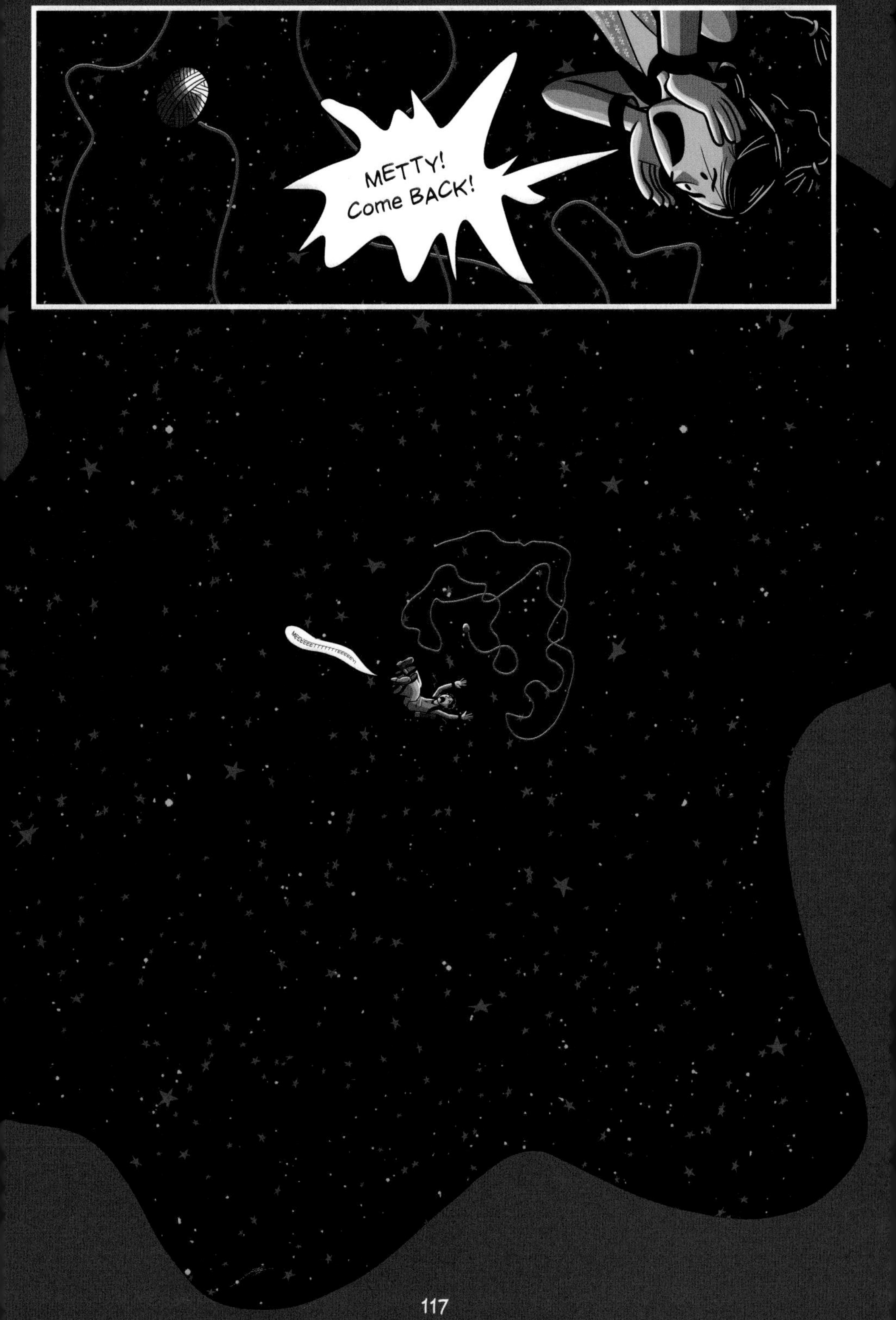
METTY! Come BACK!

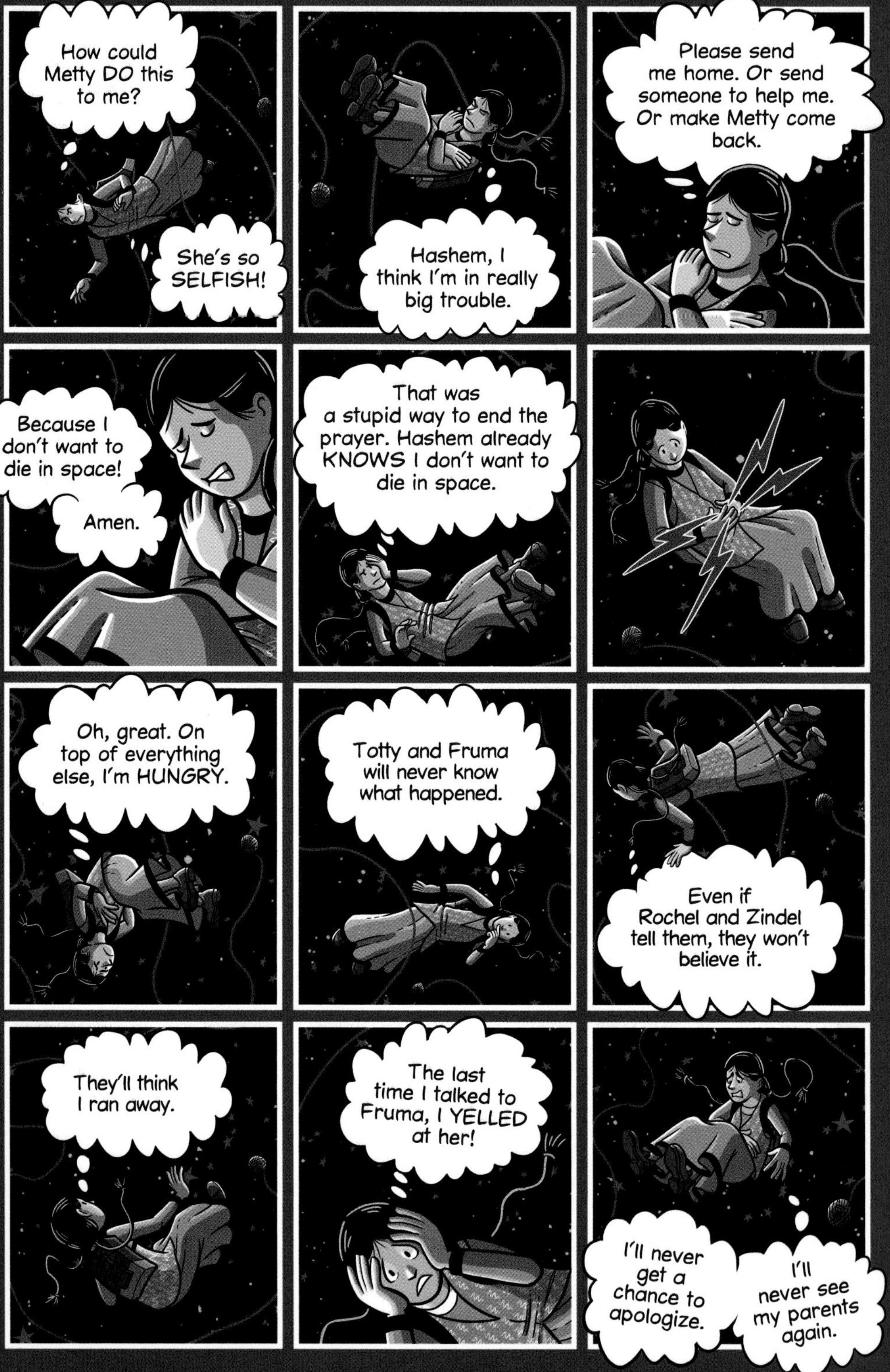
How could Metty DO this to me?
She's so SELFISH!
Hashem, I think I'm in really big trouble.
Please send me home. Or send someone to help me. Or make Metty come back.
Because I don't want to die in space!
Amen.
That was a stupid way to end the prayer. Hashem already KNOWS I don't want to die in space.
Oh, great. On top of everything else, I'm HUNGRY.
Totty and Fruma will never know what happened.
Even if Rochel and Zindel tell them, they won't believe it.
They'll think I ran away.
The last time I talked to Fruma, I YELLED at her!
I'll never get a chance to apologize.
I'll never see my parents again.

Totty: Poppa

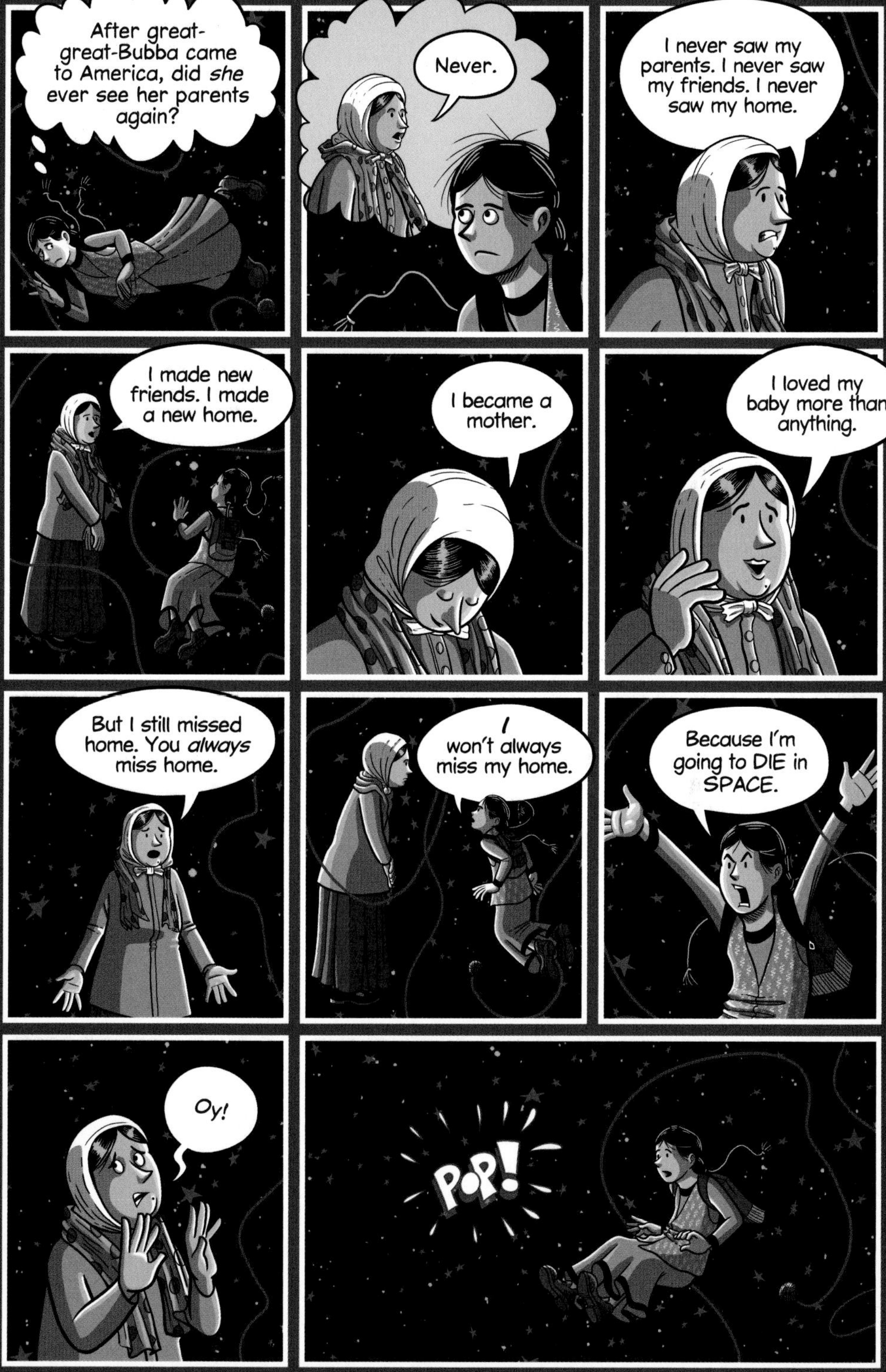

After great-great-Bubba came to America, did *she* ever see her parents again?
Never.
I never saw my parents. I never saw my friends. I never saw my home.
I made new friends. I made a new home.
I became a mother.
I loved my baby more than anything.
But I still missed home. You *always* miss home.
I won't always miss my home.
Because I'm going to DIE in SPACE.
Oy!
POP!

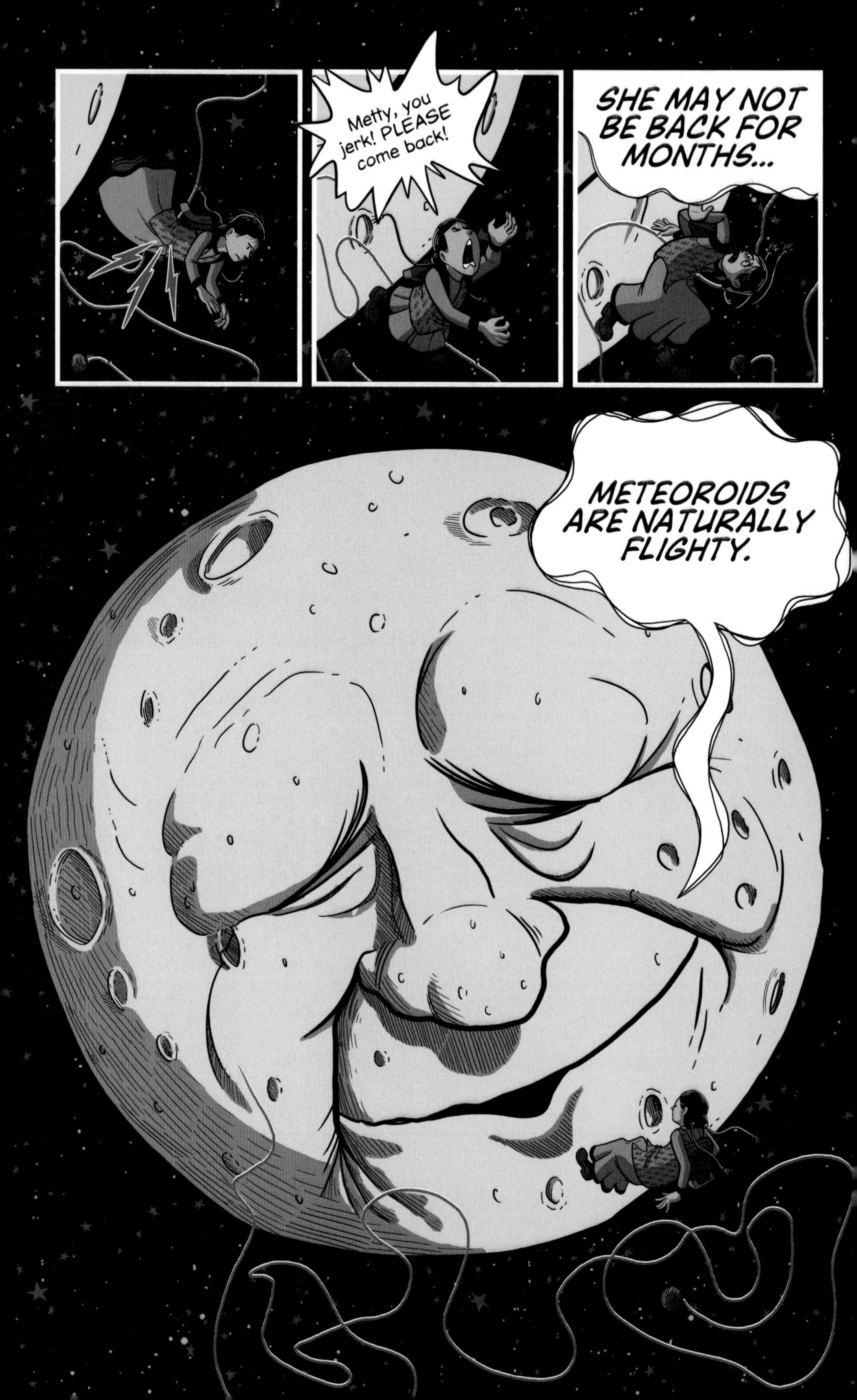
Metty, you jerk! PLEASE come back!
SHE MAY NOT BE BACK FOR MONTHS...
METEOROIDS ARE NATURALLY FLIGHTY.

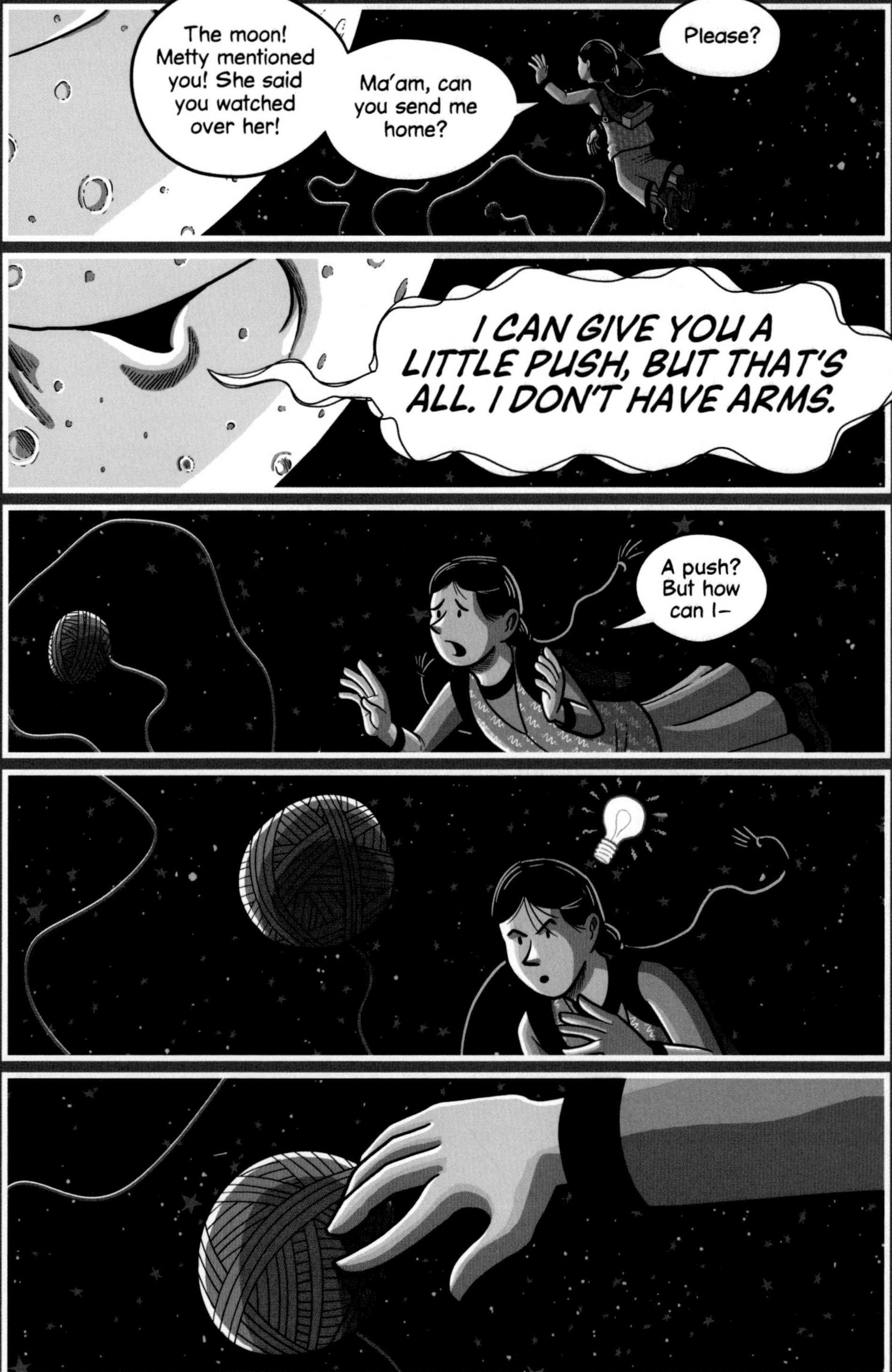
The moon! Metty mentioned you! She said you watched over her!
Ma'am, can you send me home?
Please?
I CAN GIVE YOU A LITTLE PUSH, BUT THAT'S ALL. I DON'T HAVE ARMS.
A push? But how can I–

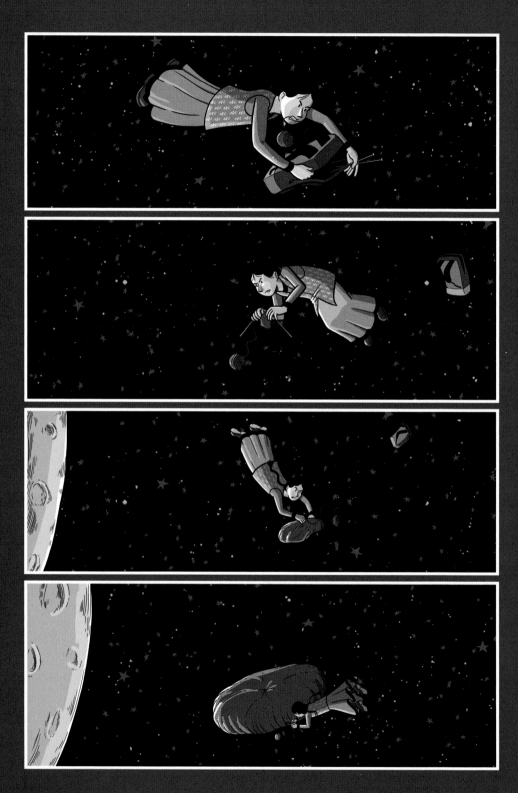

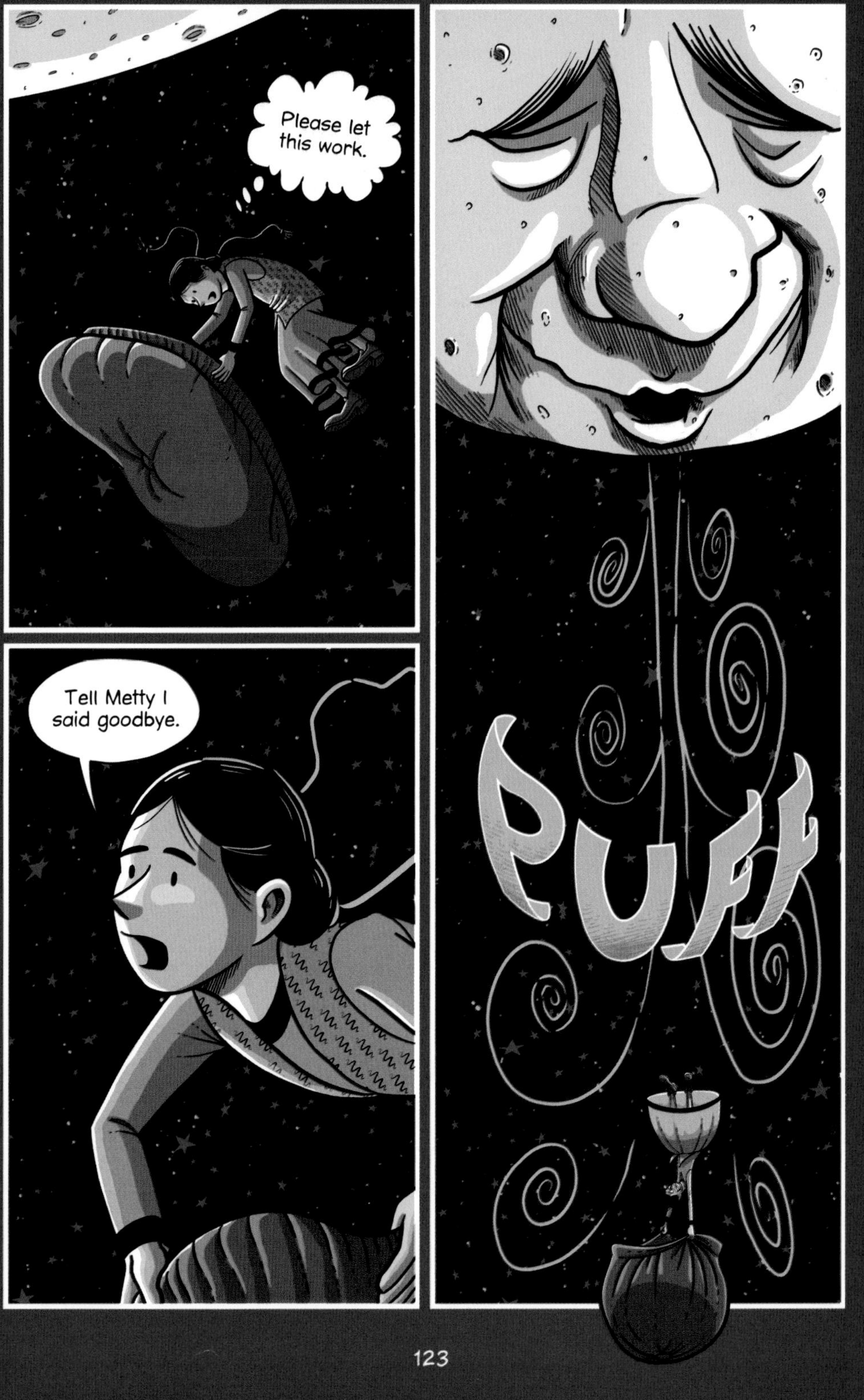
Please let this work.
Tell Metty I said goodbye.
PUFF

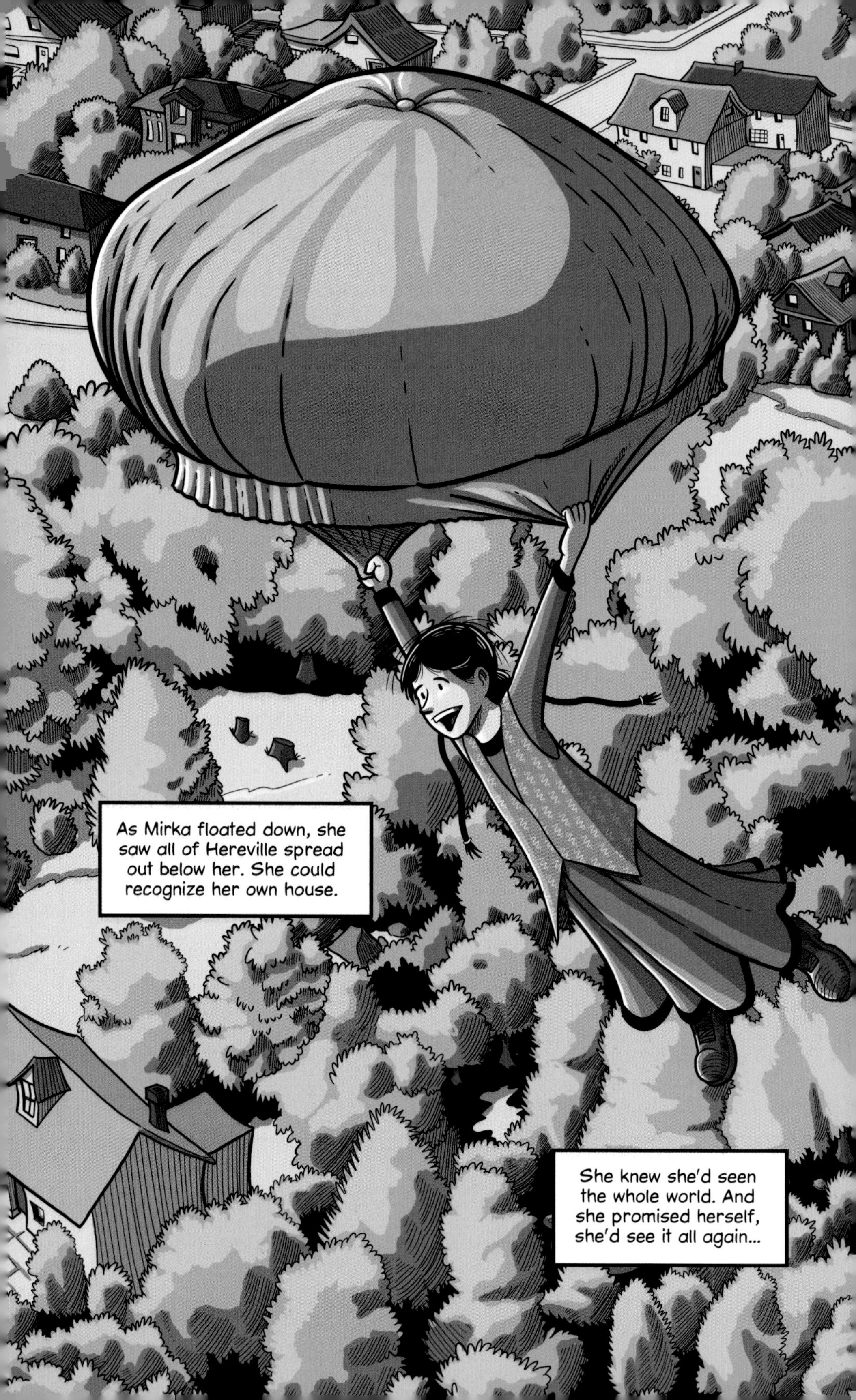
As Mirka floated down, she saw all of Hereville spread out below her. She could recognize her own house.
She knew she'd seen the whole world. And she promised herself, she'd see it all again...

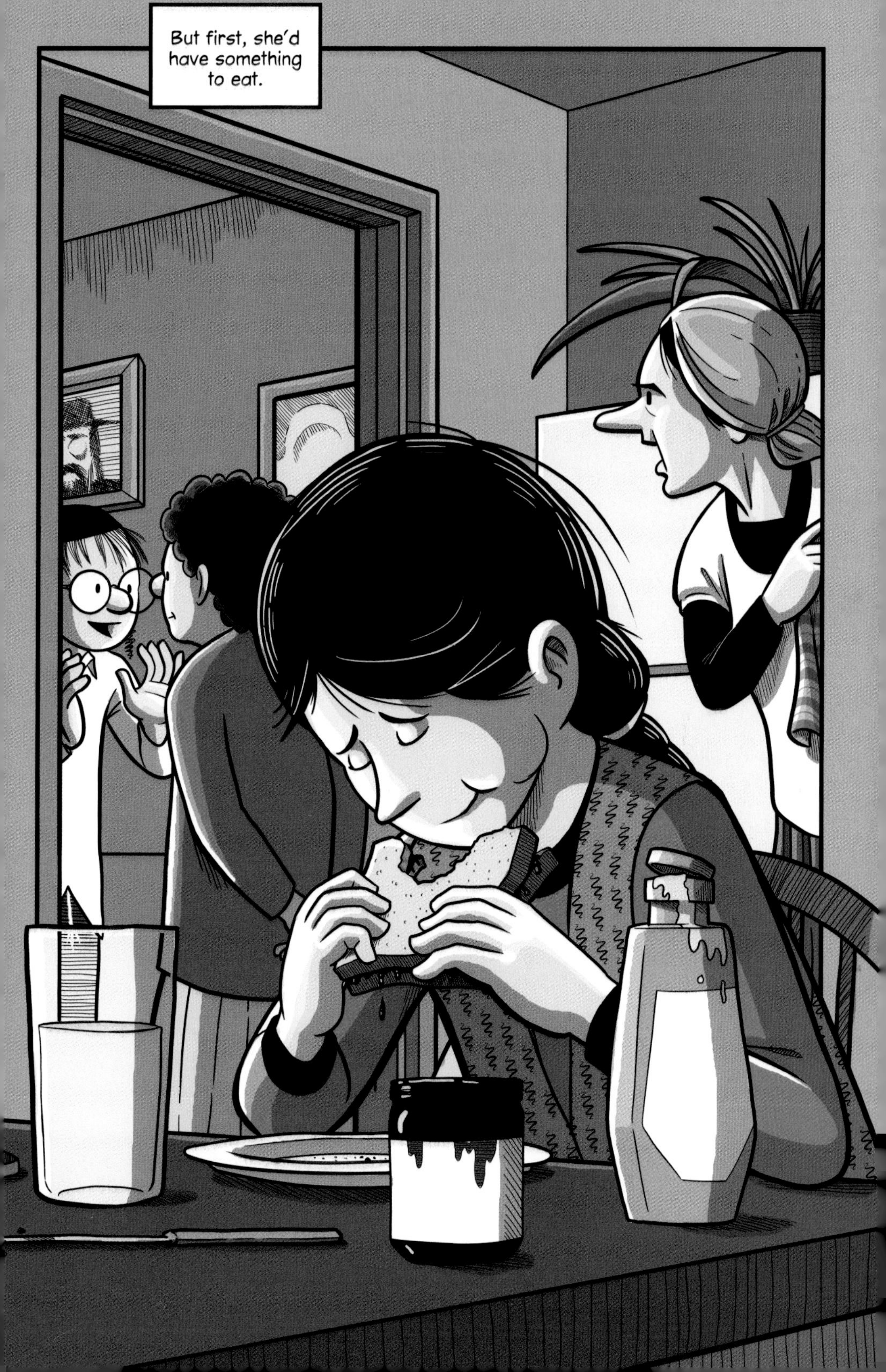
But first, she'd have something to eat.

Dedicated to the memory of my father,
Larry Deutsch, a force of nature
who loved kids and Judaism
— B. D.

ACKNOWLEDGMENTS

A *sheynem dank* (thank you very much) to Jake Richmond for smart colors and advice; Rachel Swirsky, writing guru and best friend; Tina Kim, for thirty-six pages of lovely backgrounds; my indefatigable agent, Judith Hansen; Sheila Keenan, Chad W. Beckerman, Charles Kochman, and the entire Abrams crew; the members of the Portland Comics Workgroup; my housemates; Matthew Bogart, Erin Cashier, Toby Deutsch, Noah Greenfield, Jenn Manley Lee, Kip Manley, and Richard Jeffrey Newman; and the many others who helped Mirka find her way home.

ABOUT THE AUTHOR

Barry Deutsch won the 2010 Sydney Taylor Award and was nominated for Eisner, Harvey, Ignatz, and Nebula awards that year. In 2008, he was nominated for Comic-Con's Russ Manning Award for Promising Newcomer. He lives in Portland, Oregon.

PUBLISHER'S NOTE

Library of Congress Control Number: 2012947050

ISBN 978-1-4197-0398-0

Text and illustrations copyright © 2012 Barry Deutsch

Book and cover design by Barry Deutsch and Chad W. Beckerman

Printed and bound in the U.S.A.
10 9 8 7 6 5 4 3 2 1

THE ART OF BOOKS SINCE 1949

115 West 18th Street
New York, NY 10011
www.abramsbooks.com